LOW CHICAGO

The Wild Cards Universe

LOW
CHICAGO

Edited by
George R.R. Martin

Assisted by
Melinda M. Snodgrass

Written by

Saladin Ahmed

Paul Cornell | *Marko Kloos*

John Jos. Miller | *Mary Anne Mohanraj*

Kevin Andrew Murphy | *Christopher Rowe*

Melinda M. Snodgrass

HARPER
Voyager

Harper*Voyager*
An imprint of HarperCollins*Publishers* Ltd
1 London Bridge Street
London SE1 9GF

www.harpercollins.co.uk

A paperback original HarperCollins*Publishers* 2018
1

A catalogue record for this book is available from the British Library

ISBN: 978-0-00-828358-2 (HB)
ISBN: 978-0-00-828520-3 (TPB)

This novel is entirely a work of fiction.
The names, characters and incidents portrayed in it are
the work of the author's imagination. Any resemblance to
actual persons, living or dead, events or localities is
entirely coincidental.

Printed and bound in the UK by CPI Group (UK) Ltd, Croydon CR0 4YY

MIX
Paper from
responsible sources
FSC
www.fsc.org
FSC™ C007454

This book is produced from independently certified FSC™ paper to ensure
responsible forest management.

For more information visit: www.harpercollins.co.uk/green

To Lezli Robyn

Copyright Acknowledgments

Low Chicago

a variant of seven-card stud poker

wherein the high hand splits the pot

with the low spade in the hole

A Long Night at the Palmer House

by John Jos. Miller

Part 1

IT HAD BEEN ONE hundred and forty-two years since John Nighthawk had been inside the Palmer House, and then it had been the earlier incarnation of the luxurious Chicago hotel, known simply as the Palmer.

Nighthawk's age was not apparent in his appearance. He was a smallish black man in a dark pin-striped suit with a discreet kidskin glove on his left hand. He looked to be in his thirties. He sighed as he gazed at the entrance to the hotel. *Perhaps,* he thought, *it's finally time to lay old ghosts.* He hurried across the street, dodging early morning traffic with the ease of the longtime urbanite, and entered the hotel's lobby.

Inside he paused momentarily, suddenly almost overwhelmed as one of his visions washed over him. They were part of the powers he'd gained on that first Wild Card Day in 1946 and usually came as warnings of great danger lurking in the near future. This one was more incoherent than usual, chaotic scenes of fire and ice, of great beasts and shifting landscapes, of quick flashes of the past he'd once seen and an even vaster past he'd never imagined.

He stood for a moment catching his breath, then went on to the elevator bank and up to the seventh floor, wondering what was in store for him this time around.

♣

The door to room 777 opened at Nighthawk's light knock, and he found himself looking down into the large, expressive eyes of a man even shorter and slighter than himself, no more than five four and maybe a hundred and ten pounds. The crown of his head was totally bald and there were baggy wrinkles under his soulful eyes. He looked as if he were in his fifties.

It took Nighthawk a moment to place his face. He was the spitting image of the actor Donald Meek. Nighthawk had loved him in *Stagecoach,* the original version with John Wayne. He'd seen it at the Theatre back in 1939 when it'd first come out.

"You must be John Nighthawk." The man's voice was high and flighty, fussy sounding.

"I am."

"Come in, come in, and meet the client."

Nighthawk entered the suite's siting room. It was luxuriously appointed, as one would expect in the Palmer House, with period furniture that was a little too heavy and ornate for Nighthawk's taste. Death himself stood in the doorway between the sitting room and one of the two bedrooms.

Death was tall, well over six feet, and cadaverously lean. He wore a black suit of old-fashioned cut and fabric. Rubies the size of walnuts gleamed in his silver cuff links. His face and head were skeletal, fleshless, mere yellowish skin stretched tightly over bone. His teeth, white and perfect, were exposed by a lipless grin.

"Perhaps you know Mr. Charles Dutton?" the man who looked like Donald Meek said. "The client."

"We've never met," Nighthawk said, "but of course I've heard much about you, sir."

Dutton inclined his head. "And I of you, sir. I would like to engage you to help Mr. Meek take care of me for the next few days."

Dutton's voice was as cadaverous as Nighthawk expected it would be.

"You're here for the game." Nighthawk was so sure that he made it a statement rather than a question.

Dutton's rictus of a smile may have widened a millimeter. "Quite so. You know of the game, Mr. Nighthawk?"

He did. "Poker. Dealer's choice. Seven players. Hosted by Giovanni Galante, a high-ranking member of Chicago's most prominent crime family. A million-dollar cash buy-in. Each player is allowed two attendants."

"Some bring whores," Dutton said dismissively.

"Some bring bodyguards," Meek added.

Dutton's eyes were dark and unreadable in the skin and bone of his face. "It begins tonight in a suite on an upper floor of the Palmer House and continues until one player has acquired all of the chips. I intend to be that player."

Nighthawk nodded. He frowned at Meek. The man was not physically impressive. It was hard to imagine him guarding anyone. But of course he was not the real Donald Meek. The actor had been dead for decades. But there was a certain shadowy ace from New York City who called himself Mr. Nobody who could change his appearance at will and often liked to mimic film stars from the past. And Charles Dutton had been associated with Mr. Nobody, as he recalled.

"And your ace is?" Nighthawk asked Meek.

Meek giggled. "I make problems . . . disappear."

"Okay." If Nobody wanted to keep things close to his vest, that was all right with Nighthawk.

Dutton nodded to Meek. "Mr. Nighthawk will make a satisfactory addition to our little team."

"Oh my, yes," Meek said. "I told you he was the man for the job, Mr. Dutton."

"Galante is hosting," Dutton said, "but the names of the other players are supposedly secret until game time. I know that I have the ultimate poker face . . . but it might be helpful if we knew ahead of time who else will be attending."

"And," Meek added, "if we knew if they were bringing hookers or guns. Or both."

"You being a local man, with contacts . . ." Dutton added.

"I'll get right on it," Nighthawk said.

"An inestimable choice," Dutton said to Meek. Death sounded pleased.

The game was set for a suite on the Palmer House's penultimate floor. Most of the regular furniture had been removed from the sitting room, though a couple of small sofas and overstuffed chairs were scattered around for the attendants, bodyguards, and other onlookers. A bar stood before one wall with rows of liquor bottles behind it. Doors to three bedrooms opened off the sitting room and a bathroom was located in the short hallway that led from the entrance to the sitting room.

A large purpose-built poker table covered with green felt filled the center of the room, with a lavish chandelier hanging over it. Seven comfortable leather chairs for the players were spaced around the table, with a number of other chairs a few feet back for the players' attendants. Most of those chairs were already occupied when Nighthawk, Meek, and Dutton entered the room.

Nighthawk knew all of the players already present and several of their attendants. He would have recognized most of them even if he hadn't spent the morning and afternoon hitting up his sources for information.

Foremost was their host, Giovanni Galante, presumptive heir to the Galante crime family. He was a familiar figure around Chicago. Mid-twenties, handsome in a sleazy way, he wore expensive, tasteless suits and potent cologne that failed to hide the smell of hard liquor that accompanied him everywhere he went. He was already at it, drinking whiskey out of a cut-glass tumbler, straight with only a couple of ice cubes.

One of Galante's companions sat in a chair close to the table . . . though "sat" was an inadequate word to describe the way she held herself. "Posed" was perhaps more accurate, in a tight white designer gown that plunged low down the front and was cut high up her left hip, leaving an expanse of shapely thigh exposed. The ruby earrings and necklace were no more spectacular than her lush red hair. Her skin was flawless cream, her eyes a brilliant blue. An onlooker would be forgiven for assuming she was just arm candy, but Nighthawk knew better. Her name was Cynder and she was an ace with a potent flame-wielding ability. She worked full-time for the Galante family as a bodyguard and enforcer.

There could be no doubt about the nature of the man who stood stolidly behind Galante's chair, hands clasped, eyes alive with suspicion. Nighthawk had never crossed paths with him before, but he knew of him. His name was Khan. Compared to Nighthawk, he was a relative newcomer to the Chicago scene, making his bones in the last decade or so as a freelance bodyguard. At six three and three hundred pounds, his physical prowess was evident, but the wild card virus had given him more than muscles. Half of his body was an anthropomorphic version of a Bengal tiger. His left side, including his face, was covered in black-striped orange and white fur, and he had fangs, a green feline eye, and cat whiskers. His left hand and foot were thicker and bigger than normal and had, now retracted, razor-sharp claws on all digits. To match the tiger fur on the left side of his face, Khan had grown a dark beard on the right and braided little bells into it, his own little cat joke. He mimicked the natural eyeliner of his tiger eye with cosmetics around his human eye.

As Nighthawk entered the room, followed closely by Meek, Khan's gaze swept over them both. He seemed puzzled by Meek, but when his eyes met Nighthawk's they widened a little. He nodded at Nighthawk. Nighthawk nodded back.

He and Meek stepped aside and Dutton, who liked to make a dramatic entrance, followed them into the room. Silence fell as everyone turned to look.

Dutton wore a black tuxedo of old-fashioned cut, complete with a top hat and opera cape. He was a symphony of black and white, except for the rubies that burned red at his wrists and the red rose pinned to his jacket. A black mask completely covered his face.

Galante called out affably, "Ah, you must be Charles Dutton, our guest from New York! Come in, come in! Grab a seat. Here—take this one—" He gestured to the empty chair next to the man seated to his left. "You know Jack, right?"

"Yes." Dutton's voice couldn't have been colder. He moved around the table, to another empty chair.

Galante shrugged. "Or, hell, take that one. It don't matter. Does it, Jack?"

"No," Golden Boy said. He was a handsome, apparently young man, blond, an athletic six two, maybe a hundred and ninety pounds. He looked incredibly healthy. He was Jack Braun, the infamous strongman of the Four Aces, the first group of public aces. He'd gained his powers the same day that Nighthawk had, on that first Wild Card Day back in 1946, but later he had testified against his friends before HUAC. That had earned him the nickname of the Judas Ace. Nighthawk figured that Dutton, who also dated back to that era, was not one to forgive and forget. Braun, still apparently ageless, had been out of the public view for many decades now. A mediocre acting career followed by a rather more successful run in California real estate had earned him millions.

One of his two companions was sitting on his lap, the other hanging over his chair, her arms entwined around his neck. They were twins, statuesque, voluptuous, with long, braided silver-blond hair and vivid blue eyes. They wore identical very tight, very short skirts that clung to their curves like Saran Wrap on a serving bowl.

The face of the one sitting on his lap took on an expression of concern. "What's the matter, Honey Boy?"

"Nothing," Braun murmured, "nothing at all, Hildy."

"I'm Dagmar."

"Whatever."

Dutton turned his masked features to the man sitting next to the empty chair. "Do you mind, sir?" he asked politely.

"No, not all," he replied. "Sit down. I'm Will Monroe."

Nighthawk pulled the chair out for Dutton, since Meek was carrying the briefcase that held a million dollars in thousand-dollar bills. Dutton nodded to Monroe and his companions.

Monroe was blond, mid-fifties, clearly tall though now sitting down, with an epicanthal fold to his eyes. He was slim and he wore his expensive though casual clothes quite well. His watch was a high-end Rolex, which made it expensive indeed, and he wore a gold-and-diamond ring on his left hand. The bastard son of Marilyn Monroe, he had made his own mark on Hollywood as a very successful movie producer.

Two innocuous-looking young people accompanied him. One was Gary "Pug" Peterman, Monroe's personal assistant and yes-man. A former child star, Pug had gotten his nickname from either his upturned nose, his soulful brown eyes, or his overall demeanor of a puppy who'd just been paddled for piddling on the rug. Nighthawk knew little of his acting career. He hadn't liked the first of his movies, so he'd never seen another.

Monroe's second attendant was a young woman with black hair. Her short-sleeved blouse revealed Asian ideograms tattooed on both her forearms, as well as a variety of hearts and skulls. Nighthawk thought they ruined her rather bright demeanor. His sources told him that she was Abigail Baker, an aspiring young British actress.

Nighthawk studied Monroe for a moment. He disliked predators of all types and he wondered if Monroe fit the typical Hollywood stereotype. Monroe felt the pressure of his glance and looked up at him. That almost made Nighthawk miss the bit of byplay where Meek winked at Baker and the actress looked at him quizzically. Will Monroe looked as if he were going to say something, but then the door to the suite opened and more newcomers barged in.

In the lead was a stocky, plug-like man in his fifties, who seemed as if he'd once been slim but had gained weight over the years. His shock of coarse dark hair had streaks of gray in it and was cut in Buster Brown bangs that covered his forehead almost to his eyebrows. He strutted confidently into the room, accompanied by the usual two attendants.

It was easy to pick out the bodyguard. He was tall, grizzled, and his dark hair was a bit gray, though he was maybe only pushing forty. His hands were stretched and warped out of all human proportion. They looked like slabs of meat the size of car batteries and were definitely more suited to smashing things than fine manipulation. His name was Ali Husseini, an ex-con with a rep for violence. Nighthawk knew that he'd found Allah during his last term in prison. He was better known by his ace name of Meathooks; the report on him said that metal hooks protruded from his body when he became angry. The other newcomer was just a kid, struggling with a valise that Nighthawk guessed contained the buy-in. He hardly looked to be in his teens, if that. He was nerdish, short, a little chubby.

The one with the Buster Brown haircut strolled confidently up to the table, smiling when he caught sight of Jack Braun. "Hey! Golden Boy!" He plopped down into the open seat next to him, beaming. "We met back at a card show in Peoria, what was it, '06, '08?"

"Um—" Braun was clearly bewildered.

"Charlie Flowers!" Flowers didn't seem to mind Braun's faulty memory. "Signing autographs? Remember?"

"Oh, ah, sure." Braun nodded.

Flowers leered at Dagmar. "Aren't you going to introduce me to the talent?"

Braun glanced away, looking at Giovanni Galante. "Our host— Mr. Galante—"

"Oh, sure." Flowers half stood up, reaching out. Dagmar squirmed more tightly against Braun as Flowers's arm more than brushed her breasts. "Pleased to meet you."

Flowers had meaty hands. He wore diamond rings on both pinkies as well as a huge, multi-jeweled gold ring on each ring finger. Nighthawk shook his head, half in disbelief, half in admiration, for the size of Flowers's balls. It took immense—something—to wear your World Series rings in public after being banned from professional baseball for gambling on games.

Galante took his hand with an insincere smile. "Likewise."

Flowers held on, his arm still firmly pressed against Dagmar's breasts. He gestured backwards with his chin. "That's my bodyguard, Meathooks. I know we're all friends here, but, why take chances, amirite? Oh, and that's my nephew Timmy. He's an ace, too, so watch out. . . ." Flowers leaned forward conspiratorially, bringing his face almost as close to Dagmar's breasts as his arm.

"Charlie," Braun said in a voice with a hint of warning in it.

"What?" He turned, bringing his nose perilously close to lodging in Dagmar's cleavage.

"Back off."

Flowers turned back, grinned at Galante, released his hand. "Hey, no harm done." He turned the grin onto Dagmar. "Sorry to wrinkle your dress, sweetie. Hey, Timmy. Show the folks what you can do." Flowers sat back in his seat with a smile on his face.

"Sure, Uncle Charlie."

Timmy went around the table to the wall with a set of three windows opening up to the street below. It was night already, and dark outside. He climbed up on one of the sofas that was set against the wall, fumbling for the window latch, but couldn't reach it. The kid looked back at his watching uncle almost helplessly until one of the attendants rose to his feet to help.

Nighthawk didn't know the player, exactly, though he recognized him. Once, he'd almost had to kill him, to save the world from his Black Queen, which was raging out of control.

His name was John Fortune. He'd been a teenager when they'd first crossed paths. Now, twelve years later, he was a mature man of almost thirty, a man who'd once been prominent as leader of the Committee, the ace arm of the United Nations, but had dropped from public view. He'd been in the war to save the joker community of Egypt, and the experience had hardened him, Nighthawk saw, turning him from the inexperienced young boy Nighthawk had once known to someone who'd witnessed the horrors of battle.

One of his attendants was an immense man, larger than even Khan or Meathooks, bald as an egg, and fat. "Let me help, little boy," he said in a breathy, weirdly accented voice.

Nighthawk frowned, focusing on him for the first time. He was the spitting image of Tor Johnson, the professional wrestler turned actor—if you wanted to be kind about his thespian abilities. Nighthawk recalled memories of the adventure he'd shared with Fortune all those years ago. Fortune's companion at the time had been Mr. Nobody, who had a habit of taking on the appearance of old-time movie stars—like Tor Johnson. Or, Donald Meek.

But if Mr. Nobody was with John Fortune as Tor Johnson, then, who . . .

Nighthawk glanced at Meek, who was standing by his side. The little man returned Nighthawk's gaze with bland innocence.

Tor Johnson or Mr. Nobody or whoever he was turned the latch on the window and pulled up the lower pane. The sound of the street many stories below wafted into room, as did a warm nighttime breeze. "Is that what you wanted, little boy?" the big bodyguard wheezed, and Timmy, looking out into the night, nodded.

Everyone waited expectantly, and a moment later a pigeon flew into the room. It circled Tor Johnson as if he were an atoll in the ocean and the bird was seeking refuge after a long flight, and then landed on the round crown of Johnson's bald head, cooing contentedly.

Dagmar—or was it Hildy?—broke into a giggle. "It looks like it's hatching an egg," she said, as Johnson almost went cross-eyed trying to gaze up at the bird.

The bird flapped away after a moment and sought out Fortune's second bodyguard, landing on her shoulder. She—the bodyguard— craned her neck and looked uncertainly at it.

"Kiss the pretty lady," Timmy said.

Nighthawk was a little worried about this one. All he was able to discover about the young Asian woman with the long braided hair was her name, Kavitha Kandiah. Nighthawk had been observing her as she'd been moving about the room, getting a drink for Fortune, placing a dish of candies by Johnson's elbow on the table. She moved with a fluid grace that spelled martial artist or dancer. As an unknown factor, Nighthawk thought, she'd bear watching. The problem was, so would almost everyone in the room.

The pigeon reached forward to peck at her cheek, and she leaned backwards in her seat.

"We call him Birdbrain," Flowers chortled. "Because he can control the minds of birds—one at a time, that is."

As a longtime baseball fan, Nighthawk had already detested Charlie Flowers. Now, interacting with him personally for the first time, he really loathed him.

The bird flew up from Kandiah's shoulder, circled the table, and landed in front of Galante, where it proceeded to spread its wings and do sort of a bobbing and hopping dance in front of Galante's pile of chips.

Galante had a look of intense dislike on his face. "Disgusting thing," he said. "Rat with wings."

Next to Nighthawk, Meek made a gesture with his right hand. A spectrum of light, like a rainbow, arced from his palm, striking the bird in mid-hop. The pigeon vanished.

Nighthawk looked at Meek with new interest in his eyes, as did everyone else in the room.

"I told you," Meek said to him. "I make problems disappear." He glanced at Timmy, who was looking at him with somewhat like horror. "Don't worry, kid, he's okay. I just sent him to a better place."

Teleportation? Nighthawk thought. Interesting. An extremely potent power, and useful. There was more to Meek, he decided, than appearances would allow.

"All right," Flowers said briskly, unconcerned by his nephew's downcast expression. "Let's get to business. Or sport, eh?" He elbowed Dagmar in the ribs, rubbing his meaty hands together briskly.

"Yeah." Galante took his gaze from Meek and ostentatiously consulted the expensive Rolex on his wrist. "Well, we're expecting one more player. He seems to be running late. It's past nine. Let's give him a couple more minutes—"

Even as Galante spoke there was a shimmering in the air, felt more by the brain than seen by the eye. Suddenly three newcomers stood in the room.

The woman in the center was the tallest. She was almost six feet and wore a robe of shining fabric that for some reason Nighthawk found difficult to focus his eyes on. Her skin was pale, her long black hair fell like a rippling cloak to her waist, but her silver eyes were her most arresting feature. Nighthawk felt that it might be unwise to look into them too deeply or for too long.

She embraced two others, one in the crook of each arm. The other woman was almost as tall as her, leggy, blond, with smoky-blue eyes and a bored expression on her exquisite face. She wore a black sheath dress that revealed the creamy skin of her upper breasts and displayed a lot of silky thigh. Around her long, graceful neck was a diamond choker with a single large sapphire shining like the tear of an angel.

Nighthawk was relieved—somewhat. The woman in the diamond choker was Margot Bellerose, internationally famous French actress. *Nothing to worry about there.* The ace who'd delivered her was another matter. Lilith. Teleporter and assassin. Mistress of the knife. The case that held the buy-in cash was slung around one of her shoulders.

As to the player himself—

"Siraj, Hashemite Prince of the Royal House of Jordan and President of the Caliphate of Greater Arabia," Lilith announced in a voice that managed to be haughty and languid at the same time.

Siraj bowed a precise millimeter in the general direction of the poker table and put out his hand. Bellerose took it with an air of pouty boredom and they approached the table together. Siraj was short, handsome, and dark, if more than a little plump. He was reputed to have a sharp mind and an almost bottomless bank account.

Prince Siraj took the last empty seat at the table and snapped a finger to one of the two barmaids, who hustled up another chair. Bellerose slipped into it with the air of a queen about to expire from ennui, playing with her choker as she glanced disinterestedly around the table.

"Let's get this show on the road!" Flowers suggested.

"Agreed," Galante said with a degree of oily unctuousness, "but first, the house rules. They are few, but important. Number one, gentlemen. The buy-in."

Khan strolled around the table, collecting the various bags, valises, and briefcases offered by the players or their seconds.

"The cash will be counted," Galante said, "just for propriety's sake, and be put in the suite's safe for safekeeping. Your chips are already in place before you. Rule number two. The game is over when one player holds all of those chips. Rule number three. The play is table stakes, dealer's choice, no limit. Is that all agreeable?"

Murmurs went around the table.

"Good. Play will be continuous, but if someone wants to take a break for a snack, or, whatever, heh-heh, there are private rooms in the suite to eh, freshen up in."

Flowers, eyeing one of the barmaids, a lissome joker model with bunny ears and a cute fluffy tail, asked, "All part of the service?"

"All part of the service," Galante agreed.

"Great."

"Finally, no telepathy." Galante's voice turned low with more than a hint of danger. "We have ways of detecting it and identifying whoever may be using it. The offender will lose their stake." He paused a moment. "And probably more." He looked around the table, his gaze resting momentarily on each player. "Understood?"

He got six answers in the affirmative. The last player he looked at was Dutton, and his eyes lingered.

"I know the world we live in, but this is a friendly game." Galante's smile was almost sincere. "Masks are not allowed at the table, Mr. Dutton, because of the unfair advantage that they give."

Dutton may have smiled under his mask. At least, it moved a little bit on his face. "Far be it for me to take unfair advantage, Mr. Galante," he said in his sepulchre voice.

He removed the mask and let it drop on the table before him. There were several audible gasps. Even Galante blanched a little. Flowers murmured, "Eew." Bellerose, seemingly entranced, whispered, "*Magnifique*." Golden Boy looked on, unmoved.

"Shall we play?" Dutton asked, what might have been a smile twitching across his face.

Galante grinned in reply and broke open a pack of cards sitting near him on the table.

"Of course," he said. "As host, I deal the first hand. The game starts, as always, with a hand of Low Chicago. Afterwards, winner deals and chooses the play. Ante up, gentlemen."

Everyone took one of the red chips from the pile before him and tossed five thousand dollars into the pot.

◆

There was, Nighthawk thought as the game began, an authentic rush of excitement in the air. He'd been involved in a few marathon poker games in his life, nothing approaching stakes like these, of course, and he knew that they had a rhythm, a kind of ebb and flow, depending largely on the personalities of those involved. And the seven players here, he realized, had about as wide a range of personalities as could be found. It didn't take too long to sort them out.

Galante was a bold, impulsive player. He also wore his emotions openly on his face. He took chances—it was gambling, after all—but more often than not he succeeded when he did. He also drank steadily, but he seemed to hold his liquor well.

Jack Braun, to his left, was the most distracted player at the table. One and sometimes both of the twins were hanging on to him. He had a fair poker face—a reviewer had once said that as an actor his facial expressions ran the gamut from A to B—but was careless with the way he held his cards and in the way he played. He didn't drink as much as Galante, but then he didn't hold his drink as well, either.

Charlie Flowers was the most intense player at the table. He gripped his cards tightly, he stared around at everyone as the bets were made like he was trying to read their minds. Unfortunately, he was a bad reader.

Siraj's play was as smooth and deft as his manners. He was probably, in Nighthawk's judgment, one of the two best players at the table.

Dutton, with his ultimate poker face, was the other. He too was suave and mannered, but he had the advantage of looking like Death.

Will Monroe was affable and full of chitchat. Nighthawk couldn't tell if he was just a little scatterbrained, or was cunningly trying to distract the other players as he explained, sometimes in excruciating detail, the fine points of the game to his attendant, Abigail, who didn't seem all that interested. Nighthawk kept wondering why she was there. She seemed more bored than anyone else present, except possibly for Timmy, who soon lost interest in the proceedings, but thankfully didn't call in any more birds to play with.

John Fortune was all business, as if this were work for him, not fun. He concentrated on the game, though as it started he acknowledged Nighthawk with a nod. Which Nighthawk returned. He wondered if his presence was conjuring bad memories for Fortune, since the last time he'd seen him he was being held by the Midnight Angel and sobbing over his father's death. It hadn't been a pleasant time for anyone.

Flowers got off to a bad start, Siraj to a fast one. Within the first hour Siraj had won three hands in a row, taking a lot of chips from Flowers.

"Motherfucking—" Flowers began after Siraj had called his bluff and raked in a big pot.

Prince Siraj looked at him, quirking an eyebrow. "What did you say?"

Flowers gestured impatiently. "Hey, nothing personal. Wasn't talking to you, directly."

"There are ladies present," Siraj said in his smooth English accent.

"Ladies," Flowers snorted. "If by ladies you mean whor—"

"I mean ladies." Siraj cut him off again, this time with iron in his tone. "And if you want to take a brief break and discuss this matter personally, I will be more than happy to indulge you."

"Hey, Prince, it was just locker room talk—"

"We are not currently in a locker room, Mr. Flowers," Siraj said, "and when you were you didn't know how to behave decently. Your actions were beneath contempt."

Next to him, Bellerose tittered.

Flowers flushed red for a moment. He turned and looked at Julie Cotton, the joker bar attendant, who was standing nearby, just having brought Galante another tumbler of whiskey, straight up. "Hey, girlie," he said. "Bring me a bourbon." He paused. "Does that tail come off with the costume, honey?"

Bellerose tittered again.

"No, sir," Cotton said with as much dignity as she could muster.

"Enough," Galante said impatiently. "Deal the cards. We're playing poker here, right?"

♥

By two A.M. Nighthawk was starting to think that all the bodyguards were a bit unnecessary. The game progressed with intensity, but without untoward incidents. Even though the fortunes of all players were shifting, no one was yet showing signs of worry.

Whether Dutton's supreme poker face helped him or not, he and Prince Siraj were the big winners. They had piles of chips stacked before them, representing about half the total table. John Fortune was playing with stoic skill, but so far the cards weren't favoring him. He was essentially even after the first five hours of play. Jack Braun was drunk as a lord and losing steadily, but he seemed unconcerned and was paying more attention to Hildy and Dagmar than the cards. He'd left the table with them twice, taking them to one of the private rooms for two half-hour breaks, and returning each time if not more sober at least with a happy look on his face. He and Galante, who was drunk as a pissed-off mafioso, and Will Monroe, who was steadily sipping scotch and ginger ale, had about two million in chips among them. Charlie Flowers was moaning over his pile, which was about half as high as when they'd started.

The various bodyguards all mostly remained in a state of taciturn alertness. None of them had partaken of alcoholic beverages, although the one who looked like Tor Johnson had consumed an ungodly amount of bar snacks ranging from chips and salsa to caviar-spread crackers to a dozen doughnuts of various types and fillings. Others had eaten more sparsely of the spread, which was dispensed efficiently and prettily by the bunny-eared joker and the dark-haired, dark-eyed girl, who'd also been kept busy serving single malt to Braun, bourbon to Flowers, whiskey to Galante, and other beverages to the rest of the players.

Abigail was the most attentive of the onlookers. She sat in a chair a little behind Will Monroe, following every turn of the cards. Pug the ex–child star was asleep on the far right sofa that lined the suite's outside wall. Flowers's nephew with the contemptuous nickname of Birdbrain was soundly asleep on the middle sofa. One of Fortune's bodyguards, the dancer or martial artist, occupied the third one, but she at least was alert . . . though it seemed to Nighthawk that she was watching him and Meek more closely than the game. Nighthawk never looked at her directly, but he could feel her eyes upon him and Meek and he wondered why they were the center of her attention.

"*Shit!*" Flowers exclaimed crudely and loudly, throwing his cards down in disgust as John Fortune raked in the current pot. "I need something to change my luck!" He stood and grabbed the arm of the dark-haired bar attendant named Irina. She'd just passed by his seat after delivering another whiskey to Galante. "Come on, baby, let's see what you can deliver besides drinks." He pulled her into one of the bedrooms and closed the door after them.

Fortune piled his chips, tossed in a red for the ante. "Seven-card stud," he announced.

He liked, Nighthawk had noticed, the more straightforward games, without wild cards or split pots.

By five o'clock Golden Boy was busted. All his chips were gone, as was one of the twins, who'd disappeared with Bellerose into one of the private rooms, unnoticed by everyone but Nighthawk. At least, no one had the poor taste to remark upon their absence. Braun himself was still seated at the table, but was asleep, head down upon it. Dagmar (or was it Hildy?) was curled up on the chair behind Braun, also asleep, but a lot cuter than Jack, who, much to Galante's disgust, was snoring.

"Somebody wake that stiff up. He's drooling on my card table," Galante said. "And order me a steak sandwich."

His redheaded bodyguard named Cyn stood, stretched like a cat, and went to Braun's side. She was a pleasure to watch as she pulled Golden Boy Braun upright and settled him back in his chair, then continued on her way to call room service. "Ah, Mom," Braun moaned. "It ain't time to milk the cows yet. Lemme sleep s'more."

There were general guffaws and titters around the table.

"C'mon," Flowers said, "we gonna play cards or milk the cows? I got a lot of money to win back."

"Good luck with that," Will Monroe observed dryly. He tossed in a red chip to ante for the next hand. "You got enough to cover that?"

Flowers had maybe a dozen blues and a slightly higher stack of whites, the two lowest denominations at a thousand and five hundred dollars each, respectively.

"You worry about your own pile, movie boy," Flowers said gruffly, but Nighthawk thought that the ex–baseball player had to know that Monroe was right. He was one, maybe two losing hands away from being busted.

At this point Dutton was the big winner, Fortune and Siraj were roughly tied with the second largest piles of chips. Monroe and Galante were both down.

"I'll give you a chance to last another couple hands," Galante, who had won the previous pot, said generously as he started to deal. "Five-card stud."

Galante dealt the first card facedown around the table, then the second, faceup. The exposed cards ranged from John Fortune's deuce to a queen for Prince Siraj. Siraj checked and the bet went around the table to Galante, who had a ten showing.

"Bet a thousand," he said, and everyone added a blue chip to the pot.

The third up card was dealt and Flowers got an ace, but Monroe received a second eight.

"A thousand on each," the producer said. All called but Galante, who folded.

Flowers smiled when Galante dealt him a second ace in the fourth round. He had the high hand showing, though Fortune was dealt a second deuce to join the ballplayer and Monroe with pairs. "About time," Flowers said, not bothering to conceal a smile. He tossed four whites into the pot for another raise of two thousand dollars.

Prince Siraj folded without a word or expression. Dutton folded with a smile that could only be described as sinister.

"I'll keep you honest," Monroe said to Flowers with a straight face, tossing in two blues.

Fortune silently added two of his own to the pot.

Galante dealt the last round to the three who were still in the game. Monroe got a nine, Flowers a queen, and Fortune a three.

Flowers looked from Monroe, who was expressionless, to Fortune, who had a small smile on his face. Flowers had one blue and ten white chips left.

"Check," he said.

Fortune's smile grew wider. He added six thousand dollars to the pot.

Flowers stared at him. Fortune looked back levelly. Seconds ticked away.

"Shit," Galante said, "you might as well go all in in case he's bluffing. You'll be gone the next hand, anyway."

Seconds more passed like hours crawling by. Nighthawk could see sweat beading Flowers's forehead. His hands twitched once, reaching for his final chips, and then froze as the door to the hotel suite opened. He looked back over his shoulder, but it was only a waiter delivering Galante's sandwich on a covered silver tray. He also carried a small folding table.

"Goddamn it," Flowers swore.

The waiter, an elderly man in hotel livery, came to the table.

"Who ordered the steak sandwich?" he asked.

Cyn, who had resumed her seat, nodded at Galante. "Over here."

"Bring me a whiskey on the rocks," Galante said with a glance at Irina. He returned his attention to the game as the waiter deftly set the folding table down, after Cyn scootched her chair over to make room.

Irina approached with the drink as Flowers pushed his remaining chips into the pot with an agonized gesture. Fortune looked at Monroe, who shook his head.

"Your move," he said.

Still smiling, Fortune turned over his hole card, revealing a third deuce.

"*Goddamn it!*" Flowers stood up suddenly, pushing his chair back and bumping into Irina, who staggered. The drink that she was delivering to Galante slid from her tray into his lap.

For one brief moment time seemed frozen and Nighthawk could smell the danger that suddenly speared the air. He started to rise. Irina, a stricken look on her face, started to bend over, reaching out with the cloth napkin that had been draped over her forearm. "I'm sor—"

Galante swiveled in his chair. "You clumsy bitch!" He slapped her in the face hard enough to knock her to the floor.

There was another moment of silence, broken by a wordless shout of rage from the waiter, who swung the tray bearing the steak sandwich and accompanying fries at Galante, catching him on the side of the head and knocking him and his chair onto the floor.

And suddenly all hell broke loose.

Khan rose from his seat with a feline roar and reached for the waiter, but the old man was changing. In the blink of an eye his body mass seemed to double, shredding the uniform that he wore. All the added mass was solid muscle. The waiter backhanded Cyn and she slammed into the wall and rebounded, stunned. Khan reached across Galante's fallen chair and he and the waiter grappled. They stood locked together for a moment, clearly matched in strength.

Dutton, Nighthawk thought. He grabbed his client, hoisted him over the bar, and dropped him behind it onto the floor, turning back in time to see Khan and the waiter smash onto the table and roll over it, scattering chips and cards. John Fortune dove away. Tor Johnson stood, uncertain. Flowers drew a pistol he'd had in a shoulder holster. Lilith drew a blade and moved to Siraj, but Meathooks, next to her, lashed out, catching her in the side with the metallic hooks that'd sprung from his hands. Lilith staggered backwards, her gown suddenly torn and very bloody.

It was all happening so fast that Nighthawk could do nothing but stand his ground. Besides, his duty was to Dutton and his job was to stay between him and whatever danger might come his way. So far, all of the action was across the table.

Meathooks stumbled against Flowers as he avoided the sweep of Lilith's blade. Charlie Flowers was shouting and spraying shots. One struck Prince Siraj as he rose from his chair. Khan and the waiter were hammering at each other, as a dazed Cyn pushed to her knees and unleashed a gout of flame that ripped the chandelier from the ceiling and set off the smoke alarm. Part of the heavy glass-and-metal fixture landed on Siraj. Fortune shouted, "Help him," but before either of his bodyguards could move, Khan and the waiter, still locked together, lurched off the table and bumped into Cyn. Her flames licked across the room. Nighthawk felt the heat of it wash over him, but he was only at its very edge. Part of it flicked across Meek, who cried out in pain, raised both hands, and filled the suite with rainbow light.

The rainbows seemed to wrinkle the very air. Whoever they touched simply disappeared. Only Charles Dutton, on the floor behind the bar, and Nighthawk, at Meek's side, remained. All that remained of the other players, companions, and servers were a few untidy heaps of clothing and jewelry that marked where they'd been standing, sitting, or sleeping.

The window drapes were aflame. Nighthawk, quelling the questions screeching in his brain, arose and put out the fire before the sprinklers came on, using a soda water bottle from the stocked bar. As he was spraying down the draperies the two women emerged from the bedroom, where they'd been occupied.

"Siraj?" Margot Bellerose cried. "What happened? What happened?" Her voice rose in panic. "Where is everyone?"

Nighthawk turned to Meek, who was slapping at the burning sleeve of his jacket. *Teleportation,* he thought. "Where did you send them?" Nighthawk demanded.

But Meek shook his head. "Not where. When."

Down the Rabbit Hole

by Kevin Andrew Murphy

NICK WILLIAMS HAD NEVER been to Chicago before, let alone its Gold Coast district. The Playboy Mansion was Beaux Arts, built to impress, four stories of classical French brick and exposed limestone with a steep slate roof and attic windows flanked with Grecian urns. The chauffeur who'd met him at the airport carried his suitcase up the walkway. Nick carried the Argus's case himself. He paused for a moment to read the brass plaque set over the main door: *Si Non Oscillas, Noli Tintinnare*. Nick grinned, his high school Latin coming in handy for more than the mottos of movie studios: *If You Don't Swing, Don't Ring*.

The February weather was much cooler than Los Angeles, and he wished he'd brought a heavier coat. But it was warmer inside, especially in the parlor off the black-and-white marble foyer. Hef awaited in an ornate Victorian wingback chair upholstered in rose velvet, flanked not by classical urns but by classic beauties. Two young women, a blonde and a brunette, lounged on matching divans to each side, attired in diaphanous gowns like the Muses of old . . . or perhaps a more sybaritic interpretation of Old King Cole's attendants, since the blonde was pouring Hef a snifter of cognac from the requisite decanter of an unlocked tantalus while the brunette reclined near a Delft tobacco jar and a matching porcelain box. The pipe was in Hef's hand, and he was dressed in a rich black velvet smoking jacket and slippers, all the better to enjoy the roaring fire in the parlor's fireplace. The porthole television in the burl-wood cabinet opposite glowed like a fortune-teller's crystal ball. The all-seeing eye within winked and vanished, the CBS logo replaced by the Olympic rings, then the dizzying melody of Strauss's "Acceleration Waltz" started up, a Dutch beauty entering the Squaw Valley ice arena.

"Ah, Mr. Williams," Hef said, rising as the chauffeur took Nick's camera bag, "or may I call you Nick?"

Nick removed his suit jacket, which the chauffeur also took. "Nick's fine." He doffed the new gray fedora he'd bought for the trip. He regretted letting it go, feeling like the soft felt was almost a part of him now. But the chauffeur was implacable.

Hef clenched his pipe in his teeth so he could shake hands. "Welcome to the Playboy family." He glanced up at Nick, who had a good six inches on him. "You'll do just fine. Swimmer, I understand?" Hef glanced to the television, where the skater twirled through her revolutions. "The agent said you'd hoped to compete in Melbourne, but dropped out."

"I pulled something in college," Nick confessed, failing to mention that it was an ace.

Hef swirled his cognac contemplatively. "Any chance you'll represent us this summer in Rome?"

"Doubtful." The Olympics tested for the wild card, and while Nick's ace didn't help him in the three hundred meter, it would still disqualify him. And tip his hand that he was also Will-o'-Wisp, the Hollywood Phantom, mystery ace of the movie lots, and Hedda Hopper's horror.

"Can you lie?" Hef grinned. "I know you've done some acting, and it will stir up intcrest on *Playboy's Penthouse*."

"I can lie," Nick admitted truthfully.

Hef glanced to the chauffeur. "Percy, take those to Mr. Williams's room." Hef swirled his snifter. "Care for cognac? Sherry? Port?"

"I don't drink," Nick confessed, not mentioning that alcohol made it harder to control his ace, "but I do smoke."

"Constance?" Hef glanced to the brunette.

She pulled open the drawer of the tobacco jar's table, revealing it to be a humidor stocked with a wide assortment of cigars. She also lifted the lid of a porcelain box disclosing French Gauloises. Nick took one and allowed Constance to give him a light.

It was good, and Nick took a puff while Hef gestured to the furnishings. "These used to be in the Everleigh Club's Rose Room." He took a puff of his own pipe. "Ada just passed away and we were able to acquire her whole collection."

"Everleigh Club?" Nick cocked his head and took a drag on the cigarette.

"Chicago's carriage trade brothel. Exceedingly exclusive, but gone half a century next year." Hef took another puff on his pipe. "Of course, the Playboy Mansion's my home, and our new Playboy Club will be a gentleman's club, but it doesn't hurt to have some of the gas lamp finery." He took a sip of cognac, then handed the snifter to the blonde. "Thanks, Gwen." Hef gestured to the foyer and the grand staircase leading up. "May I give you the tour?"

"Please."

Plush carpeting secured with brass runners led the way to the next floor, which was nothing if not more opulent. "Got the place last year. Built for Dr. Isham and his wife, Katherine, in 1899," Hef explained. "Supposedly Teddy Roosevelt visited. Let me show you the ballroom. We host our most swinging parties there." He ushered Nick back up the grand staircase, Constance and Gwen fluttering after them like salt and pepper moths.

If the second floor was opulent, the ballroom was beyond compare, the *ne plus ultra* in fin de siècle luxury, with tall Doric columns carved in rich mahogany instead of marble, matching paneling, a cavernous coffered ceiling with gilded rosettes and painted beams, a limestone fireplace large enough to walk into flanked with the sculpted visages of guardian lions, and, in the center of the sweeping parquet floor, a piano covered with a fortune in gold leaf, glittering like the hoard from *Das Rheingold*.

"Ada's treasure." Hef looked slyly to Nick. "We had to have it. Do you play?"

"Not one of my talents, I'm afraid," Nick admitted. "Where is everyone?"

"Oh, they're around the mansion. Lots of bedrooms. Even rumors of some hidden passageways. Still discovering all the secrets." Hef gave a wink as Constance and Gwen fluttered right and left around the dance floor in preordained orbits until coming to rest at the piano bench, starting a girlish duet of "Tea for Two."

Nick let his host escort him across the floor until Hef paused him midway, instructing, "Kick off your shoes. Just had it polished and it's nice to get the full effect."

It was a bit odd, but Nick was not going to disappoint his host, and there was a certain childlike fun to sliding across the smooth wood in your socks.

Nick's ace was electrical, the wild card having saved him from electrocution by turning him into a human electrical capacitor. It mostly gave him the power to toss ball lightning, but along with that came an attunement to the electromagnetic spectrum. Nick sensed something: not electricity, but interference, a good bit of metal somewhere in the floor below them. He didn't have time to make sense of it, his host beckoning for him to join him at the piano.

Nick took a last puff of his cigarette, then stubbed out the butt on the plum blossoms of the cloisonné ashtray atop the Chinese smoking stand by the piano's head. "Stand there," Hef instructed, indicating a small Oriental accent rug by the crook of the piano a few steps back, "you get the best sound."

Constance and Gwen fluttered their lashes coquettishly, sharing some private joke as they continued their duet, but Nick did as he was told, stepping onto the accent rug. Constance winked, reaching up to turn the sheet music, but instead pulled a gilded lever.

The floor fell out from under Nick, but not the rug, and he felt himself falling down a chute into darkness. He panicked, remembering stories of Chicago's infamous Murder Castle. He lit up with a nimbus of electricity, but it almost as quickly grounded itself on the copper sides of the chute he was sliding down, the accent rug acting like the burlap sack at a carnival slide to speed his descent. Nick concentrated, letting his electric glow come only to his eyes, illuminating the chute but not grounding on it while his ace sensed something below him, not metal, not earth, but . . . water.

A bell rang and not just in Nick's head as he came to the end of the chute and another trapdoor sprang open, spitting him out into light and brilliance.

It was instinct, Nick had felt this before, leaping from the plunge into the high-dive pool at the University of Southern California. Muscles tensed, hands placed together, not in prayer, but to part the water as he entered, steeling himself, pulling his ace taut so none of his internal reservoir would ground out.

The water was warm and the pool was deep. Nick swam down instinctively, then up and over, surfacing at a distance to the strains of more piano music, this time from a black baby grand, and the sprightly chatter and laughter of a pool party.

Women in bathing suits and a few men swam about or lounged poolside, the whole basement chamber decorated with African masks, dracaena, and birds of paradise till it resembled a mermaid's grotto.

The bell sounded again and the ceiling chute fell open, Hef coming down feetfirst, sans robe, slippers, and pipe, now wearing only swim trunks.

He plunged into the pool, then came up laughing, swimming over to Nick. "Welcome to the Playboy Family. Thought a swimmer wouldn't be too shocked with our initiation prank."

Nick smiled, teeth gritted with the realization of how close he'd come to electrocuting everyone. "Not shocked, no."

"You should have seen him dive!" exclaimed one of a bevy of bathing beauties floating like nereids nearby. "Didn't even make a splash! Like an eel!"

Electric eel, Nick thought but did not correct her.

Hef laughed and the bell rang again, the trapdoor opening as Constance and Gwen entered the pool together, their diaphanous gowns shed like moth wings, now clad only in daring bikinis, black and white. They swam over, Gwen reaching out to him, smiling. "Let's get you out of these wet things. . . ."

Nick didn't resist, Gwen releasing him from his wet tie and unbuttoning his equally soaked shirt, Constance diving down like a pearl diver and taking off his pants. Hands strayed and lingered, flirtatious and beyond. Nick stopped Constance before she pulled his boxers free, but didn't stop her entirely. *If you don't swing, don't ring. . . .*

Constance put the play in Playmate, splashing back, laughing, having teased him then stolen his socks. Hef swam over as the pair of nymphettes left the pool with their booty. "Let me show you around."

It was like Neptune introducing his court, except the mermaids were Playmates and the assorted castaway sailors and dolphin riders had been replaced by photographers, editors, and layout directors of the *Playboy* staff. Nick could hardly keep track of them all. The only one of especial note seemed to be Victor Lownes, *Playboy*'s promotions director, who was swimming about with a young actress named Ilse. "So, Hef, what do you think about Ilse's kitten idea?"

"Still like my original plan, but so long as we get Zelda Wynn Valdes to design the final costume, I don't much care."

"Then let me get someone else's opinion." Lownes glanced to Nick. "We've been batting around outfits for our new place. Hef wants satin corsets, like the gals at the old Everleigh Club."

"Got some great examples of those now," Hef pointed out. "Ada's photo albums are in the library. You need to look at them."

Lownes nodded while paddling. "Yeah, but Ilse had a swell idea: *Playboy*'s mascot is the tomcat, so she thought we could have the girls dress up as sexy kittens."

"Pussycats," Ilse purred with a pronounced and erotic Eastern European accent.

"Maybe a little too on the nose." Hef turned to Nick, explaining, "When we were first going to launch, we wanted to be *Stag Party* with a swinging stag for our mascot. But then *Stag* magazine sued so we swapped to *Playboy* and went with the tomcat."

"So what do you think?" Lownes pressed.

"Not sure, but I like the idea of Valdes." Nick knew Hollywood politics and when to be a yes-man. "She did Josephine Baker's costumes, right?"

"Some of them," Hef agreed. "Not sure if she did the 'banana dance' one, but that's the iconic look we want." He turned to Lownes and Ilse. "Make a mock-up and I'll decide."

"My mother sews," Ilse told Lownes, who said, "Done."

It seemed poolside business was as much a thing in Chicago as it was in Hollywood.

They swam on, chatting, mingling, and schmoozing, giving Nick a chance to meet the staff and get a sense of the magazine's organization. Then, bobbing atop a Jacuzzi that bubbled like a witch's cauldron or at least a tide pool attached to a thermal vent, sat a familiar face . . . familiar from newspapers and television. Hef grinned. "May I introduce our next president, John F. Kennedy?"

"Just senator for now," Kennedy said in his Boston Brahmin accent, raising his shoulders out of the pool, revealing an old scar, "but call me Jack. Who's this?"

"Our new photographer," Hef told Kennedy, "Nick Williams. Out from Hollywood."

"Excellent dive you did there," the senator complimented. "Probably be even better with swimwear."

"Everything's better with swimwear," remarked a pert Playmate perched on the edge of the bubbling hot tub in a white satin one-piece. It matched her fluffy baby-fine platinum hair, which Nick suddenly realized had huge rabbit ears sticking up out of it. Not the antennae from a television set, but actual White Rabbit–style white rabbit ears, albeit scaled up and sized for an adult woman. *Or a joker.* A matching fluffy white tail poked out of the rear of her bathing suit as she sat there dabbling her still human toes in the water. "Go ahead and stare." She laughed. "Everyone does. It's natural."

"Let me introduce Julie Cotton," Hef said, "one of our aspiring Playmates."

"I'm guessing you're Nick, the new photographer." When Julie grinned her ears stood up straighter. "Hef said you were a swimmer." She looked to Hef. "Can I have him for my photo shoot?"

"If you like," Hef said, then laughed. "You just got me to agree to give you a test shoot, didn't you? Clever bunny."

Julie's nose wrinkled as the pride transmitted to her ears, making them stand up higher. "Hey, a girl does what she can."

Kennedy laughed along with her. "That you do."

She touched her toes with their painted pink nails to his shoulders flirtatiously. "So do you," Julie said, laughing, "for all of us. You're a war hero. 'Ask not what your country can do for you, ask what you can do for your country.' "

It sounded like a quote from something, Nick thought, and evidently Kennedy thought so, too. "Nice line," he remarked. "Mind if I borrow it?"

"It's yours." She laughed lightly. "You're my favorite president."

He laughed in turn. "Not president yet. Not even nominee. Have Stuart Symington to contend with, and Lyndon Johnson, and refreshing as this party is, I need to talk with Mayor Daley tonight, or else *my* party may go with Adlai Stevenson again. But thank you for your vote."

She gave him a wistful look, as if there were something important she wanted to tell him, but only said, "I did my fourth-grade report on you."

Kennedy glanced back over his shoulder at the bunny girl. "You're from Massachusetts? Not many girls would do a report on a lowly representative."

"My family moved around," she confessed in an unplaceable midwestern accent, "especially after my card turned." She smiled ruefully. "You've helped us jokers a lot."

"Not as much as I've wanted to."

"Every little bit counts, and you're going to do more." She bit her lower lip, revealing slightly, but cutely, buck teeth. Or bunny teeth. Nick couldn't tell if it was a joker trait or the way her teeth were naturally.

Nick considered. Julie acted awfully confident for a joker, even more confident than your average ace, and he should know. Maybe she'd drawn a prophetic ace, too?

"Do you think he can beat Nixon?" Nick asked.

Julie gave a pained look. "Yeah, but . . ." Her left ear flopped over enchantingly as she bit her lip again, looking at Jack Kennedy with profound adoration and hero worship.

"Thanks." Kennedy smiled, basking in her attention. "Still need to keep up the fight, though. Nixon might still be president."

"Yeah, but he's a crook," Julie swore. "It'll come out. He won't be president long. Trust me." Her rabbit ears positively vibrated.

Nick couldn't be sure whether Julie was speaking prophecy or the quiet or not-so-quiet rage all wild cards felt for Nixon after the House Un-American Activities Committee hearings. What had happened to Black Eagle, the Envoy, and poor Brain Trust was unforgivable, especially after they were betrayed by Jack Braun, the Golden Rat. As a joker, Julie could speak her rage publicly. As an ace up the sleeve, Nick needed to keep his feelings hidden, including his shame and ambivalence.

He'd been rooting for Nixon when the Four Aces trial had been going on, an idiot high school kid in conservative Orange County, his head filled with equal parts swimming and girls—which left plenty of room for hatred of Reds and the twisted victims of an alien virus, except for Golden Boy, whom Nixon praised. But after Nick's own card turned, he'd gotten a jolt, not just of electricity but of reality. He'd had to reexamine HUAC and himself, not liking what he saw.

Will-o'-Wisp, the Hollywood Phantom, was as much an attempt to assuage his guilt as anything else. Not that idiot high school nat Nick had done much to help Nixon break the Four Aces. But a whole lot of people doing not much added up to a lot so it came to the same thing.

Even so, there were things you couldn't say when you were up the sleeve unless you wanted to attract attention. "Are you sure?" Nick asked. "I know Nixon's conservative, but I think he's an honest patriot."

"He's a crook," Julie stressed. "Trust me."

Hef chuckled. "Knew you were Californian, but hadn't pegged you for a Nixon man."

"My family's from Whittier," Nick admitted with a bashful grin. "Went to the same high school as Dick."

"Hard to compete with a hometown hero," Jack said with a laugh, "but I'll try."

Nick turned his self-deprecating grin to the senator. He'd already decided a while ago Kennedy would get his vote if he got the nomination, but he was not about to tell anyone. Not even Jack Kennedy as it turned out. "I'm willing to listen."

Nick did. He was not enough of a policy wonk to follow everything, but Kennedy's stance on civil rights was quite clear, for jokers, aces, Reds, blacks—everyone.

Hef patted Nick on the back. "Convinced now?" He then said to Kennedy, "Remember that same speech, with the same intensity. We'll have you deliver it tomorrow on *Playboy's Penthouse* when we introduce Nick. And I'll try to get Mayor Daley there for a second chat."

"Do I get introduced too?" Julie asked hopefully, her ears flopping slightly as she cocked her head.

"We'll see, but I want to see your test shoot first. Talk about it with Nick."

"Talk about what?" asked a tall blond middle-aged man walking up along the deck. He looked about Nick's own height, around six four, and even had the same epicanthal fold next to his eye like Nick had inherited from his mom. "Who's Nick?"

Nick looked closer, realizing the man looked and sounded like his uncle Fritz, if slightly older and in better shape.

"This is Nick," Hef said, "our new photographer. Nick Williams, meet Will Monroe, Julie's . . . agent."

Nick shook Will's hand as he stepped down into the hot tub. "Nice to meet you."

"Likewise." Will's smile was genuine, but cursory. He gave Nick an intent look, but then distracted by the inexorable draw of celebrity, turned to Senator Kennedy.

"John Kennedy." The senator introduced himself with a politician's handshake. "But you can call me Jack. Monroe, huh? Not perchance a descendant of President Monroe?"

"Not so far as I know"—Will Monroe chuckled, sitting down in the hot tub—"but I might have a president somewhere in my family tree. . . ."

"Any relation to Marilyn Monroe?" Nick asked. He'd never met her himself, but they'd been on the same set when he'd gotten a bit part for the swimming ensemble in *Gentlemen Prefer Blondes*.

Will gave him a sly look. "Not yet," he said with a chuckle.

"Everyone wants to meet my first centerfold," Hef pointed out, adding to the merriment. "Hell, I still want to meet her. I just bought pictures a calendar company took before she made it big." He glanced then to Kennedy. "But speaking of meeting people, think you've soaked your shoulder enough to mingle a bit before seeing Daley?"

"Happy to." Jack Kennedy climbed over the lip of the Jacuzzi and back into the main pool.

Nick could take a signal: Hef had left him to talk with Julie the joker and get ideas for her shoot. This was a test for him as well as her. Fortunately for Nick, he'd gotten over the idea of jokers a while ago, having barely missed becoming one himself.

Will Monroe asked Nick, "Join me?" He gave a glance to Julie as well. "You too."

"Okay," she conceded, her coral-painted lips forming a perfect moue, "but don't laugh if I end up looking and smelling like a wet rabbit."

Nick did a swimmer's push-up, hauling himself out of the pool and swinging his legs around into the hot tub just as Julie slipped in. He glanced to Will. "From SoCal too?"

"Yep. Hollywood. Grew up in the movie business. Mom was an actress."

"Anyone I've heard of?"

Will Monroe paused, giving a smile of equal parts humor and sadness. "Possibly."

Nick judged Will Monroe's age and did the math. "Didn't make it into talkies?"

"Oh, she had some success there." Will smiled. "Lost her, well, a few years ago, but it feels like a lifetime away."

"What about your dad?"

"Never met him." Will looked sad. "Or at least not that I knew." He sighed. "Big scandal, of course. But my mom was a bigger star, so she just went on. Papers had a field day, everyone speculating. All I know is that it was someone important, someone powerful: politician, movie mogul, maybe someone in the mob. Mom never told anyone, not even me." He grimaced. "Every time I asked her, she got angry, then cried. But I think the truth was, she was scared and trying to protect me."

Nick couldn't really understand Will's pain. He had a close relationship with his father—or at least close enough, he'd never told Dad
he'd drawn an ace—but mentioning the fact would be cruel. So he
just said, "I'm sorry." After a long moment, broken only by the bubbles
of the tub and the bright chatter in the background, he asked, "Any
other possibilities? Other leads?"

"Not really." Will shook his head. "After a while, I learned not to
ask. It hurt Mom, and I knew she wasn't going to give me an answer,
so I just went on with my life." He sighed again. "The only other
chance is something I didn't really pay attention to. When I was busy
making *The Final Ace,* my first major picture, there was this fake psychic who said she knew who my father was and would tell. And she
did. Dumped an old beat-up man's hat on her head, said she was
channeling his spirit—like bad community theater with no costume
budget. I was so used to people making up wild guesses and bullshit
that I completely blew it off until my mother threw lawyers at the
psychic to make her shut up." Will looked up over at Nick, tears in
his eyes. "That's when I knew the psychic had said something right.
I'd never seen my mom so scared, not just for herself, but for me.
She made me promise never to look into what that psychic said."

"Even a stopped watch is right twice a day," Nick pointed out. "I
know fake mediums were a big thing in the twenties, but the more
convincing ones dug up dirt on their targets first. Could be this
medium was a better investigator than she was a psychic."

"Funny you should mention that." Will gave a dark chuckle. "The
psychic said her phantom had been a private investigator too, some
minor gumshoe and background actor who'd stumbled into something bad with my mom and paid the ultimate price."

Nick felt geese walk over his grave, a horrible horripilation all the
weirder for being in a hot tub. But broken watches were often right
because coincidence was always a possibility. "Well, at least in the
twenties they didn't have real psychics. Not like now."

Will chuckled a bit too long. "No, not like now."

The conversation had taken an odder and more uncomfortable
angle than Nick had expected, so he switched the subject. "So, what
do you think about Hef guessing the Golden Globe nominations on

last week's *Penthouse* and scooping the scandal sheets? Louella Parson's livid, and Hedda Hopper's speculating that Hef's a secret ace."

Will laughed uproariously. "That crazy old bat. Actually, Hef's picks were my picks. We had a gentleman's bet, so he asked me to prove it. So I told him who would be nominated."

Nick was taken aback. "So you're the ace?"

Will shook his head. "No, just a guy from Tinseltown who knows the score."

Nick whistled. "Knowing the score like that, you should be composing for the cinema."

Will shrugged. "They're both savvy women, but Louella has her ego and alliances while Hedda has a whole arsenal of axes to grind and puts those at a higher priority. Whereas I just have a professional interest in the business and not much in the way of alliances."

"Except Hef."

"We go back a long way."

"Father figure?"

"You could say that." Will chuckled again.

"So what is your professional interest in the business? Just agent?"

"For the present," Will said, sharing another chuckle with Julie at some private joke, "but I've made some pictures myself. Not acting, mind you—producing and directing. *The Final Ace* with Arnold Schwarzenegger. *Hindenburg* with Leonardo DiCaprio."

"Sounds like Rudolph Valentino." Nick laughed. "Stage names?"

"No, their actual names."

"Never heard of them. Sorry."

"Not a problem. Didn't expect you to." Will Monroe shrugged. "They'll be famous in Hollywood one day. So will I."

"You already are to me," Julie Cotton told him. Her rabbit ears were, as warned, beginning to look bedraggled, like a wet bunny.

She was being kind and flirtatious, but Nick had been around Hollywood enough that he knew how the casting couch worked. Yet even so, he asked, "So what's the story with you two? How'd you get together?"

"Oh, you know, the usual," she said, glancing to Will. "I was working as a waitress, hoping to be discovered, then fate just threw us together. . . ."

"She brought me a martini," Will reminisced. "Next thing we knew, we were naked together in a hotel room."

"A swanky hotel room," Julie bragged. "The Palmer House."

"We realized we shared a future."

"Then Will suggested we visit his friend Hef and here we are." Julie looked about herself to the Playboy grotto and waggled her ears, a party trick making them point to their surroundings as expressively as a model's hands.

Nick shrugged. It all sounded relatively innocent or at least unremarkable. Julie was hardly the first young woman to hook up with an older man, and when you were a joker, your options were even more limited.

Even so, there was something that was itching him. Julie seemed unusually self-confident even for a modern woman, let alone a joker, and the brashness of most jokers of Nick's acquaintance was a mask over self-loathing. Nick knew that trick too well himself. Will displayed a similar confidence, and a lot more than you'd expect for a middle-aged producer who didn't much make it out of the silent era and was now playing host to a young protégée. Then again, as astute as Will was with the pictures biz, it wasn't a bad move to go in as the power behind the throne to a new player on the media world stage.

"You think Hef's going to move out to Hollywood?" Nick asked.

"You can bet money on it," Will told him.

The banter continued, pleasant but innocuous, and after setting a time for the photo shoot tomorrow, they moved on, as did Nick, chatting with Playmates, both past and aspiring, and generally getting a sense of the place. Constance and Gwen showed him the way to his room so he could freshen up before dinner, then left him to his own devices and bemusement.

The bedroom was small as things went in the mansion and nowhere near as palatial as the ballroom or Hef's bedroom, which the girls deliberately led him through. Nor was it bedecked in Gay Nineties grandeur. It had plain paneling and few frills, looking to be originally intended as maid's quarters, but had been expertly painted in black and turquoise, the latest colors, with matching carpeting, geometric sunbursts, and sleek modern furnishings. Nick's camera bag sat on a desk, his suitcase had been placed at the foot of the bed, and his jacket and hat awaited on a valet stand along with his freshly laundered and pressed pants, shirt, and tie. His shoes were likewise by the bed, his socks inside, clean and dry.

Somewhat stubbornly, Nick put the same outfit on, went to dinner, and noted seat arrangements. Hef sat at the head of the table like a convivial king, Senator Kennedy at his right hand, in the place of honor. Apparently the dinner with Mayor Daley had been canceled or postponed. An aspiring Playmate whom Nick had been only briefly introduced to—Sally something-or-other—sat to his right. Kennedy ignored her, focusing his attention on Julie Cotton sitting opposite, Julie alternately doting on his words or making him laugh with her at some witty repartee. Will Monroe sat between her and Hef, the left-hand place of a king's secret adviser, his attention focused on Kennedy, his expression a mixture of hope and sadness when his immediate dinner companions weren't looking at him, but masking it quickly with Hollywood poise when anyone gave him their attention.

Nick tried to understand what was going on with Will, but then realized that, though the man looked old enough to be Nick's father, and *did* resemble a slimmer version of his uncle, in place of Uncle Fritz's jocular charm, Will Monroe's resting expression was that of a lost little boy, looking alternately to Kennedy and Hef as if there were something he desperately wished to ask them or tell them but couldn't find the right words.

Nick was seated much farther down the table with a group of photographers and editors interspersed with Playmates and hopefuls. Their banter was a mixture of ribbing and jealousy; it was well known that Nick was the pretty boy brought out from Hollywood more for his looks in front of the camera than his talent behind it. It made for some unexpected camaraderie with the Playmates, some of whom had aspirations of their own beyond modeling, including Gwen and Constance, who sat flanking Nick like they had Hef earlier in the day.

One of the editors laughed and remarked, "So, you got the hot seat. Joker Julie talked Hef into having you shoot her."

"Kill da wabbit," Constance sang under her breath with barely disguised jealousy to the tune of "Ride of the Valkyries."

A layout director with a heavy beard grinned and paused cutting his steak—the food at the mansion was top-notch—to tell Nick, "Hef's a man of his word. He was calling Julie Cottontail his 'clever bunny.'"

"Dumb bunny is more like it," Gwen stated, a little too loudly, cutting viciously into her steak. When all the men looked at her, she said, "Don't you gentlemen know? All the girls do."

"Know what?" asked the editor.

"Julie just *asked* Dr. Zimmerman for the pill. Just like that. Like it was the most ordinary thing in the world."

"The pill?" Nick echoed. "You mean birth control pills? Those aren't fully legal yet, are they?"

"*No*," Constance said, rolling her eyes, "not unless you have severe menstrual cramps."

"Surprising the number of women who now have severe menstrual cramps," Gwen remarked. "The pill might get legalized later this year, *if* we're lucky."

"Yes, but then Julie just bounces in going, 'Where can I get the pill? I lost my prescription, because my old doctor is being a baby now, so I need a new one.'"

"Doc Zimmerman was *not* being a baby for refusing her," Gwen stressed. "He's got a wife and a baby boy to look after. He could have lost his license."

Constance nodded in violent agreement. "He has to play along with Congress's charade. They're the real babies here."

"Yeah, but Julie's no prize either. Crazy bunny is more like it," Gwen added. "Julie claims she's been on birth control *for years* when Enovid has only been available for two."

"Clinical trials for a couple years before that, if you were lucky enough to get picked," Constance chimed in, "not that they'd pick a teenager, let alone a joker." She shrugged and took a dainty bite of steak. "Julie got the pill anyway, but only because Hef called in a favor and had us give her a talk first." Constance shrugged. "Might as well call her lucky bunny."

"Oh?" Nick asked.

"Yeah," Gwen agreed in hushed tones with a glance up to the head of the table, "she could have ended up in jail. Around Christmas, Hef got a call from the Palmer House. These crazy swingers had set up in his favorite suite and were charging everything to his tab. Guy claimed he was a friend of Hef's from Hollywood and had the passwords from Hef's little black book. Hef didn't know a thing about it and hasn't even *been* to Hollywood yet. But he went down to have a chat, and the next thing we know, he's paid the Palmer House, brought them back to the mansion, and they've been here ever since."

Constance stabbed a potato with her fork. "I think he just admires their chutzpah."

Nick had to admit that he did, too, though he was fairly certain there was more to Will Monroe and Julie Cotton's story than just chutzpah.

Nick awoke to a presence at the foot of his bed. Actually two.

He was used to tuning out the electrical energy in other human beings, but only when awake. Asleep, it made him jumpy, and soon after drawing his ace, he'd even shocked people who tried to wake him up, but never so badly he hadn't been able to blame it on static electricity.

A locked door solved most of that risk, and getting in the habit of sleeping in the nude explained the need for a locked door. Fortunately, mentioning this peculiarity at the Playboy Mansion was greeted with cries of "Who doesn't?"

He opened his eyes the barest crack, seeing only darkness except for a dim bit of illumination from the narrow window. No one was standing at the foot of his bed, but his bed was placed against the wall, and the presences he sensed were just on the other side of that wall. And each bore double Ds—not breasts, but batteries.

Somewhere there had to be an ace or deuce who could sense breasts, but Nick was not him. But batteries were easy, their size and charge, and whether or not the circuit was connected. These were paired D-cells in a configuration Nick immediately recognized as indicative of flashlights switched off. And the height they were held at suggested the bearers were female, breast size unknown, but given what he'd seen at the Playboy Mansion thus far, probably at least a B-cup, likely a C or above.

And by the glimmer of moonlight coming in the window, once Nick's eyes adjusted to the dimness, he could see a tiny strip of paneling was missing, and behind the missing strip he could see the glitter of a pair of eyes belonging to the owner of one of the pairs of batteries and the presumed flashlight.

Nick tamped down the instinct to fluoresce with an aura of light and energy. It had happened a few times and was the worst defense for an ace trying to keep his card up the sleeve, and the only thing that had saved him before was that no one had seen his face. But Hef and half of the Playboy staff knew who was sleeping in the former maid's bedroom, and then they'd not just get the show they'd been hoping for, the former swim champion sleeping alone in the buff, but also get to see an ace blowing his cover.

Using a parlor trick to draw some of the energy out of the batteries and light up the flashlights was also not a good idea, nor was ionizing enough energy to light up the light bulbs in the room without touching the light switches. But touching the lights as a nat would . . .

Nick reached out and pulled the chain of the bedside lamp.

The light crackled to life as the slot in the paneling slammed shut. Nick felt the pairs of double D batteries retreat along with the associated human energy fields.

Being able to control electricity did not mean being able to control light, and Nick was blinded by the sudden glare. But once his eyes adjusted, he got up and went and looked at the paneling. The panels were smooth and polished, but he could just make out the crack in one, set in to look like a bit of piecework used to remove a knothole. Nick's ace, however, could sense the metal behind, the interference consistent with an iron bolt and a hinge.

Two more hinges were detectable as well as a latch. Feeling around on a nearby section of panel revealed a knothole not large enough to warrant removal, but the center functioned as a button. The panel at the foot of his bed swung out.

Nick had already been dropped down one secret chute—thankfully into a swimming pool and not a vat of acid—and now he'd been spied on through a peephole from a secret passage.

The chance that the architect of Chicago's Murder Castle had designed only one such building was not a chance that Nick was willing to bet his life on. So while it would usually be the height of foolishness for a former swimmer to wander nude into a dark cobwebbed passage, most former swimmers weren't aces who could conjure ball lightning charges that could hang in the air with the same illumination as Chinese lanterns. Plus his will-o'-wisps moved as he willed. And Nick could sense other people, especially if they carried flashlights.

Whoever had spied upon him was definitely shorter since they hadn't broken the cobwebs at his head height. He used his hands for that, not wanting to set the mansion on fire, and explored down the passage, will-o'-wisps bobbing before and after.

A few yards down, he found the bolt-and-hinge arrangement of another Judas peephole. Nick recalled his will-o'-wisps, letting the energy ground back into his reservoir, dousing their light, then popped the peephole and gazed out into the bedroom of two Playmates. A night-light provided soft and erotic illumination of one lying on her back in a languid pose, breasts exposed and glorious. Nick wished he'd brought the Argus and some Kodak 120. The second Playmate was not in a flattering pose, sprawled face-first into the pillow, arm dangling over the side of the bed, having apparently lost a wrestling match with the comforter.

Nick shut the peephole and proceeded on, keeping his ace alert for the presence of batteries, especially moving ones. There were a disconcerting number of flashlight D-cells throughout the mansion, all switched off at the moment, stored at heights you'd expect for dresser drawers, until Nick sensed one move and then have the circuit connected, turning on.

He vanished his will-o'-wisps back into himself, dousing the light, ready to race blind down the passage, realizing that perhaps he hadn't thought this plan through completely. The flashlight batteries moved forward and back, again and again, as if their holder were searching for something. Nick held his breath, hearing only the pounding of his heart and then a low oscillating whine reverberating through the walls.

The batteries continued to move and the whirring hum was joined by the sound of a woman moaning. Moaning in pleasure. . . .

Nick brought a glow to his eyes long enough to find the peephole, then spied in, seeing a Playmate atop her bed, naked in the moonlight, demonstrating that flashlight batteries could be used in other handheld tools, in this case a vibrator, as she came closer to finding what she was looking for, that something being her G-spot.

"*Oooooo!*" the Playmate moaned, having found it.

Nick found his erect penis sticking into cobwebs. He wiped them free then shut the peephole. The Playboy Mansion was showing itself to be less Murder Castle and more Voyeurs Paradise. But there was still more to explore.

A secret stairwell led up and down. Nick chose upstairs, finding a peephole into the library: currently unoccupied but with a light left on. A collection of photo albums lay on the coffee table, one open to boudoir photos of beauties half a century past.

Nick proceeded on, spying through another peephole into the ballroom, empty at the moment. Then he sensed the presence of two sets of flashlight batteries on the move, not in pleasure, but coming up the stairs at the end of the passage. Nick grabbed the knob on the panel in front of him and turned. It wouldn't budge and the flashlights were nearing the top of the stairs. He pulled his will-o'-wisps into himself, plunging the secret corridor into darkness.

The darkness did not last long, beams of light illuminating the end of the hall. Nick fumbled desperately then found the catch, releasing it. The panel beside him slid aside, a hidden pocket door, but rolled slowly. Nick squeezed through the gap the moment he could, turning his shoulders sideways.

The ballroom was illuminated by moonlight through the grand

windows. Nick ran to the piano, pulling on the gilded bar to the right of the music stand. He heard a click from the trapdoor, then ran to stand atop it. For a second time, he fell down the secret chute, this time on purpose. But this time also without the rug or pants. The cobwebs he was covered in offered scant protection as he discovered the slide was not so smooth when you slid down it naked.

He dove on instinct.

The pool was not deserted, but everyone there was drunk, no one questioning his use of the slide or his apparent decision that clothing was optional at this hour.

Nick took one of the mansion's guest robes from the poolside cabinet then went back to his room, half expecting someone to be waiting for him.

No one was. After a long while staring at the secret panel, Nick pulled the chain on the bedside table lamp and went back to sleep.

The next day, Nick went out of the mansion for a walk until he found a convenient phone booth and dialed a number. A woman's voice answered: "Hedda Hopper's office. Who may I say is calling?"

"Nick Williams," Nick answered.

"Nicholas darling," Hedda replied. "So, what did my favorite gumshoe find out for mother?"

Nick started with the petty gossip: the Playboy Club's theme was still undecided, but a toss-up between a revamped Everleigh Club corset models and sex kittens.

"How quaint. I'll tell Lollipop. Let's see how she spins that." Hedda laughed nastily. "But on to my question. Is Hef an ace?"

"No," said Nick.

"Does he employ one?"

"Probably not, but . . ." Nick related the bare details about Will Monroe and his Golden Globe picks.

"Well, far be it from me to say I'm *happy* with being beaten at my own game," Hedda remarked, "but I'm at least pleased that it isn't some cheating ace. Will Monroe, you say? Name's not ringing any bells. Likely assumed. I've never heard of those pictures or those actors either. DiCaprio and Schwarzenegger? A wop and a kraut? And one of the films is *Hindenburg*? Smells like German cinema. You said 'Monroe' is blond? How tall?"

"About my height. Couldn't tell precisely. We were both sitting down."

"Still not tall enough," Hedda's tinny voice snapped over the phone, speculating out loud. "Murnau was a freak back when they weren't common, just one inch shy of seven feet. *And* he was queer as a three-dollar bill. But there are rumors of him having a love child with some actress. Still . . . Just how old is this 'Will Monroe'?"

"I'd guess mid-fifties, maybe a little less."

"Likely too old then, unless Murnau fathered him at ten. But thirteen/fourteen? Murnau/Monroe? If *I* were Murnau's love child looking for an alias, *that* is what I would go for. And who knows? Very tall boy, very small woman? It's really not outside of possibility, especially if it's what put Murnau off girls to begin with. . . ." The phone held silence except for the static, then Hedda pronounced, "I'll dig on this end, you dig on that. See how far down the rabbit hole you can get."

"Okay," Nick said, "but speaking of rabbits . . ."

He told her about Julie. Hedda was not pleased. "Well," she said, "it would compromise you as my spy to have you take unflattering pictures of her, so do your best. But on to my most pressing question. Why is Hefner so certain that Kennedy will win the presidency?"

Nick wondered how to phrase it without tipping his own voting preferences. "Hef's as liberal as they come, and Kennedy was visiting the mansion. . . ."

"Kennedy?" Hedda nearly shrieked. "Talk about burying the lede! Tell me everything."

Nick did.

"Flirting with a joker prostitute in a hot tub?" Hedda fumed. "What I wouldn't give for pictures of that!" After a moment of sinister static, Hedda added, "Fortunately I know a photographer. . . ."

Once the call concluded, Nick reached frantically for his cigarette case. He felt dirty after that conversation, and even dirtier after he realized he'd used his last match in the book, then on reflex mimed lighting one and shielding it in his hands to light a cigarette. In reality, he conjured a tiny will-o'-wisp in the palm of his hand.

He took a slow draw till the cherry caught, then pulled the electric charge back into himself and flicked his hand sharply to toss the nonexistent match into the gutter before it could burn his finger. Nick took a drag on his cigarette, checking those in view for any reactions. But no one evidenced any, not the smart young couple out walking a pair of pugs, not the boy on the bicycle wearing a crowned beanie.

Nick exhaled a cloud of smoke. There was not much remarkable about a tall man in a fedora and an overly thin coat walking down the sidewalk with a cigarette. Will-o'-Wisp, or at least reports of him, was left safely back in Hollywood. At least for the moment.

After collecting the Argus's case from his room, Nick found his way to the library. He glanced to the coffee table with the photo albums and, from the angle of the open one, guessed which bookshelf held the peephole and presumably the secret door.

Julie Cotton was already there, apparently oblivious to the secret passage. Today she wore nothing but lingerie, a white satin singlet with bustier, customized like yesterday's swimsuit with a spot for her fluffy tail to stick through, sticking up in the air as she bent over a random assortment of garments stacked on a red velvet sofa. "What do you think?" she asked, straightening up and gesturing to the collection.

Nick thought she'd have given a great show to any voyeur using the vintage peephole but only said, "I think you won't have a chance to wear all those. The point of *Playboy* is to see women with their clothes off, not on."

She smiled. "I thought you read it for the articles."

"That too." Nick grinned. "But the pictures bear repeat viewing."

"True," she admitted, "but we girls get interviews too. If you could ask me one question, what would it be?"

"How did your card turn?" Nick answered honestly.

"Exactly. Most guys will beat around the bush a bit, but that's what everyone wants to know. And, you know, if there are any other surprises down there. . . ." She reached up to the top of her bustier, putting her hands atop her large and very natural-looking breasts. "Want a peep?"

Nick nodded.

With a stripper's training, she teased the edge of one side of the bustier down, then the other, exposing two pink and perfect aureoles before finally letting him see her full breasts. They were magnificent, smooth and firm with pale white skin and the faintest tracery of blue veins, without any visible stretch marks. She slid the costume down, exposing her slim middle, perfect navel, and finally, the surprise.

The surprise was something Nick both halfway expected and, he realized on some level, hoped for. The hair of her feminine triangle, while matching her natural platinum blond, also matched the soft down of an angora rabbit, just like the fluffy fur on her ears and tail.

She let the costume fall to her feet, stepping out of it, then turned around so he could see only her pert derriere and the fluffy white cottontail she twitched flirtatiously as she peered at him over her shoulder.

"Julie . . . Cottontail?"

"Yep." She cocked her head and her ears flopped coquettishly. "If you think the kids teased me with that before my card turned, you should have heard them after." She turned, falling back on the sofa, and laughed as her breasts bounced with the springs. "I was seven and mad for bunnies. Had some as pets, had the slippers, had them sewn on my clothes, Bugs Bunny pajamas, the works. Even rabbit wallpaper and bunny cutouts my mom glued on my lampshade. Plus all the books. *The Velveteen Rabbit,* of course, and the March Hare and the White Rabbit from *Alice,* and *Peter Rabbit* and *Benjamin Bunny* from Beatrix Potter. But my favorite was *Rabbit Hill,* this old kids' book that won the Newbery Medal." She looked troubled then, but then most wild cards did when discussing the trauma of their card turning.

Nick also put together her age now with what she'd said. "You were one of the first," he realized. "You changed back in '46 when the blimps blew."

She gave him a wide-eyed look like a frightened bunny. "Yeah, on Wild Card Day. In '46." She looked away. "All I knew is that I had an awful fever like the kid in *The Velveteen Rabbit,* then I dreamed about . . . *Rabbit Hill* . . . and I woke up like this." She looked up at him and her ears twitched. "What about with you?"

"What?" Nick asked. "What about what with me?"

"What was it like when you turned your card?"

"I'm not a wild card," Nick denied on reflex. "I'm a nat."

"You sure?" Julie asked, her ears perking up a bit straighter. "You asked me the way us cards ask each other, like you already knew what it's like." She tilted her head the other way. "Don't worry. If you're up the sleeve, it's okay."

Hef was right. Clever bunny indeed. But all Nick said was, "Sorry, really, I'm just a nat." He then added, since it was true and gave him cover, "I'm just from Hollywood. Lots of jokers end up there for B movies. Makes easy costuming for monsters."

"That's exploitative," Julie remarked disapprovingly, sitting there naked beside a pile of costumes.

"It's a job," Nick pointed out.

Julie gave a wry grin. "Speaking of which, since I'm already nude, wanna do my centerfold?"

"Centerfold?"

"Hey, aim high. Worst Hef can do is say no." She grinned wider, fishing around in the pile of props until she came up with a circlet of braided wheat. "What better Miss March than the March Hare?"

With that, she placed it on her head, reaching up and pulling it down over both ears. On any other model, it would have looked like a head wreath for a harvest queen or a classical accessory for a Gilded Age tableau of the Greco-Roman goddesses, the wheat sheaf crown of Demeter/Ceres. But on Julie Cotton, tilted rakishly askew like the halo of a hungover angel, it made her resemble Tenniel's illustration of the Mad Hatter's chum from the Mad Tea Party.

"Got a teacup?" Nick asked.

"Oh yes." Julie produced one from her pile of rummaged props. "And I've got something even better. . . ." With that she hopped over to the bookshelf, doing a mad little dance en route with terpsichorean grace before pulling down a volume.

She flipped it open, revealing a copy of *Alice's Adventures in Wonderland* with hand-tinted illustrations. The page she'd chanced on bore the illustration of Alice and the Cheshire Cat.

A scrap of paper fluttered out, landing on the floor in between them. Nick reached down and picked it up. The penmanship was round and feminine, European in style, with two words: *possible costume.*

Nick showed Julie. "Lownes wants the Playboy Club girls to be dressed up as sexy kittens."

"The Pussycat Dolls." Julie rolled her eyes, then raised her teacup and the book, thumbing forward a couple pages to show the illustration for the Mad Tea Party. "Rather than fake kittens, wouldn't it be better if the first *Playboy* mascot were an actual bunny girl?"

She was audacious, he gave her that. *Playboy* had yet to even feature a black girl. "You need to sell that to Hef, not me," was all Nick told her as he took the first photo.

Julie was easy to work with, eager and almost ridiculously photogenic. She donned a gentleman's waistcoat and pocket watch to give the impression of the White Rabbit, assuming the White Rabbit was a young woman with large breasts. "I'm late! I'm late!" she cried, holding a running pose with a ballerina's poise, purposefully pointing her ears back to give the impression that she was racing like the wind.

Nick used half a roll of film for that, getting her from multiple angles.

Julie cycled through her pile of props: A carrot and a shotgun made for Bugs Bunny. An Edwardian red woolen wrap and a series of three poses made for Peter Rabbit's sisters, Flopsy, Mopsy, and, of course, Cottontail. The Velveteen Rabbit was less obvious, but a beautiful nude reclining on divan with an assortment of vintage children's toys was still a sexy pose.

"So what's *Rabbit Hill* about?" Nick asked, changing film, remembering back to childhood. He'd never read the book, but he'd thought it was relatively new, not a reprint of a forgotten classic. He recalled a cover with a rabbit hopping gaily over a hill. There'd been a new copy on the shelf at his school library, but the book had looked too cutesy to bother with, so it hadn't crossed his recollection till she'd mentioned it now.

"Um, rabbits. On a hill."

"I sort of expected that." Nick thought back. "The rabbit on the cover was naked, right? Bouncing in the air but standing up?"

"Ooh, that's a good idea!" Julie exclaimed. "Let's do that!"

With that she leapt onto the sofa and began bouncing, not so much like a child on a bed as a naked woman on a trampoline. Nick began to take photos, Julie's glorious breasts bouncing for all to see, "all" in this case meaning him and the camera.

And maybe someone using the peephole. Nick felt a presence there, the electrical energy the hazy outline of a living being but with the telltale nuggets of a flashlight.

He wasn't a professional dancer, unless you counted a bit part in the men's water ballet in *Gentlemen Prefer Blondes,* but a swimmer and actor could still do sudden leaps. Nick did, angling the Argus to get a wild action shot of Julie while in the background snapping the spying eyes. The peephole snapped shut and the flashlight batteries completed their circuit as they retreated, the hazy human energy along with them. Nick continued shooting Julie until the film roll was exhausted and so was she.

He was a bit, too, and also curious if the spy in the secret passage would come back. "Want to take a break?" he asked. "Look at the albums from the Everleigh Club?"

Julie smiled. "Hef said something about those. They're here?"

"I think so." Nick picked a spot on the love seat with the best angle on the closed peephole, which now looked like nothing more than a strip of carved laurels.

Julie, still nude, picked up the open album and brought it back to the love seat so they could both look at the pictures.

The Everleigh Club girls modeled bustiers and corsets, some sporting headbands with oversize poppy rosettes to each side, the fashion of the era. White ink, neatly penned onto the album's black paper, gave the names of the girls and the various special occasions. This album, dated 1902, featured a visit from the smiling, bearded, and mustached Prince Henry of Prussia. Ada and Minna Everleigh, the club's eponymous proprietresses and madams, posed with the prince, a bevy of girls about them.

Julie giggled as she paged through the rest of the album, but Nick was distracted by the dual tasks of trying to monitor the peephole and the very close presence of a beautiful naked woman snuggled into the love seat beside him.

"Let's look at another!" Julie closed that album and picked the next at random: 1908. Highlights included a tableau with the girls costumed as Eskimos, a pair of selkie maids in sealskin coats, and a polar bear played by a large woman clothed only in a polar bearskin rug, all fawning over Admiral Peary, the famed polar explorer. A page on, another nude woman played mama bear, but this time with a brown or at least sepia-tone bearskin rug, hunted by none other than Teddy Roosevelt. Beside TR, playing his guide and gun bearer while looking directly at the camera and grinning ear to ear, stood a young man with pale skin, dark hair, and dark soulful eyes, and an amusingly upturned pug nose.

"It's Pug!" Julie exclaimed, pointing to TR's pug-nosed guide.

Nick read the caption: *Our intrepid guide, Gary Peterman, leads President Roosevelt to the lair of Ursula, the She-Bear!*

"Who's 'Pug'?" Nick asked.

"Um, a child actor," Julie answered. "He's a friend of Will's."

"Here he is again." Nick pointed to the next page, where Teddy Roosevelt posed formally if cheerfully with Ada Everleigh while Minna was escorted by Gary Peterman, again with the goofily charming grin, giving both thumbs up to the camera like the world's cheeriest Roman emperor.

"Child actor?" Nick questioned. "I assume you mean on stage, right? Because this guy's at least twenty and these photos are from 1908."

Julie bit her lip and looked at Nick anxiously. "Um, yeah. On stage.

Pug's career didn't make it into talkies. I mean silents. But he was hoping to start it up again."

"Again? Is he still around? He must be in his seventies."

"Um, I hope so. Will will want to find him. And he needs to see these. Sorry." She got up, clutching the photo album to her ample chest as if it were the most precious thing in the world, and ran out of the room like the White Rabbit late for a croquet date with the Queen of Hearts. Naked croquet.

Nick felt the presence at the peephole again and took a picture of the eyes that appeared the moment it was opened. The peephole shut as quickly and the flashlight batteries retreated. Nick suspected Gwen and Constance. But eyes were distinctive and there were a lot of Playmate photos. What was more intriguing was Julie and Will. For as much as they maintained a playful affability, Julie was possibly Will's daughter. They acted like they had a shared history, but not necessarily a sexual one.

But more to the point, Will had mentioned that he was a bastard, his mother an actress, his father presumably a rich and powerful man, but one who could be undone by scandal. Will Monroe, perhaps not the illegitimate son of F. W. Murnau, but the bastard son of Ada or Minna Everleigh and one of their prominent guests? Prince Henry of Prussia would certainly explain Will's Germanic look, as would the Dutch origins of the Roosevelt dynasty. And Gary "Pug" Peterman, the former child actor, then apparently Ada and Minna's trusted majordomo? Who better to act as surrogate father to the famous madams' unacknowledged son and nephew?

This also explained Will's interaction with Kennedy and for that matter Hefner. Teddy Roosevelt was long dead, Prince Henry likewise, but the senator was the closest Monroe might come to actually meeting his father, or at least a man like him. And Hefner was the closest thing Chicago had to a carriage trade brothel keeper like the Everleigh sisters.

Then there was the Everleigh sisters' fortune. If Monroe was the unacknowledged bastard son of one, but could find proof in the albums Hefner had purchased from Ada's estate, then he might have a good chance of suing for at least that half of his inheritance, maybe even extracting acknowledgment or at least hush money from the Roosevelts or whatever was left of the Prussian royal family.

So many possibilities. Nick didn't know if he'd guessed the right one, but he meant to follow the rabbit hole down.

That night, the taping of *Playboy's Penthouse* went much as planned: Nick was introduced as the new Hollywood photographer, then served as a foil for Kennedy to give his speech. Then Julie bounced in, introduced as nothing more elevated than a "prospective Playmate," but that in itself was a civil rights statement, as was Kennedy's conversation with her, pledging his support to the joker community.

Nick was rotated out for this, relegated to the sidelines of the penthouse cocktail party that was really just a soundstage at WBKB. Mayor Daley entered. Will Monroe stood beside Nick as they watched Julie hop to fetch drinks for Kennedy and Daley, Hef smiling, ever the genial host. Nick got out his cigarette case and wordlessly offered one to Will.

"Shorry, don't shmoke," Will told him, slurring his words. He'd been moved to the sidelines to keep up the *Playboy* image of social drinking, not wanton inebriation. "Y'shouldn't either. Things'll kill you."

"These are filtered. Companies say they're safe now."

"They're lying," Will stated flatly. "It'll come out. Trust me."

He was curiously insistent about this, like a prophet. But Nick had heard fire-and-brimstone health warnings before, mostly recycled temperance rants like Carrie Nation going on about President Grant and his lips rotting off. "Well, Prohibition didn't turn out too well either." He nodded to Will Monroe's scotch.

"I've got reasons to drink." Will raised his glass. "Trust me on that too."

"And I've got reasons for not drinking." With that, Nick put his cigarette case away and lit his cigarette with one of the numerous matchbooks that littered the set. He then whispered sotto voce, "So, Kennedy reminds you of your father?"

"What?"

Some of the best clues were dropped by drunk people, so Nick pressed on. "Put two and two together. You think your father was someone powerful, maybe a politician. Julie ran off with the album with the photos of Teddy Roosevelt. You're the right age. I'm guessing either TR or Prince Henry of Prussia, with an outside chance of F. W. Murnau."

"Always loved his work, but that would be a trick." Will Monroe guffawed and took a swig of scotch. "Murnau was gay. . . ."

"Or maybe Admiral Peary?"

"No, try again."

"Gary Peterman?" Nick prodded and saw Will Monroe's eyes go wide. "I was thinking he was a surrogate father, but maybe he's your actual father? Julie said Pug was a child actor, and you mentioned the psychic said your father was an actor. . . ."

"Pug and I had a father-son relationship, but it's not what you think." Will Monroe's eyes narrowed as he nursed his scotch, then he shrugged. "Maybe you're my father. Who knows?"

"I wasn't around in 1908 to have an affair with the Everleigh sisters."

"The Everleigh sisters?" Will chuckled. "No, my mom's an actress. A famous one. But I'm not going to tell you who. But my father?" Will smiled, his expression equal parts bemusement and admiration as he looked Nick up and down. "You even look like me, or at least like I used to. Still swim laps, try to keep in shape. But no one stays young forever. . . ."

"Except the Golden Rat," Nick put in. "Guy's in his thirties, but still looks like he's in high school."

"Just you wait." Will Monroe chuckled and took another swig of scotch, adding, "Jack swore he wasn't my dad, and I finally believed him, but he looks like me too. Or did. Or will."

Nick took a long drag on his cigarette and raised an eyebrow at the drunk man. "So Jack Braun is not only strong and invulnerable, but he can travel in time?"

"Maybe not now, but he will." Will downed his glass. "I wonder where he is now."

"In Hollywood somewhere boning a starlet."

"No, I meant my old poker buddy." Will Monroe staggered, putting his arm around Nick for support. "Jack'sh the one who told me about the Palmer House game." He paused. "If I tell Jack now to not go to the poker game, then . . ."

Nick didn't know what Will was talking about, but he did know that a drunk was passing out on him. Nick dropped his cigarette as Will dropped his glass. It shattered on the floor of the set, scotch and glass shards flying everywhere, as he grabbed the older man around the middle and eased him to the floor.

"Your name's Nick Williams." Will grabbed Nick's hand and squeezed it, looking at him plaintively. "William's my first name. But my mother always called me Will. . . ."

The alcohol on Will's breath was almost overpowering and the fumes from the spilled scotch even more so. Nick felt a shock going through him from the contact high and it was all he could do to keep his internal battery in check.

"Are you him?" Will begged, clutching his hand. "Are you my father? Will you be?"

"I'm sorry," Nick said honestly. "I can't be." He gritted his teeth with the effort to keep from lighting him up like a Christmas tree and shocking Will to death, but he forced the bleeding electricity away into an invisible ionic charge.

Floodlights overloaded, light bulbs exploded, cameramen began swearing, then with a crack and a pop and a cascade of sparks, the studio was plunged into darkness.

"What the hell!?" came Hef's voice. "We're on air!"

"Not anymore!" someone called back. "Blew a circuit breaker!"

Nick knelt by Will, cradling him like a baby, the only illumination the cherry of the dropped cigarette then the flare as it caught the spreading pool of scotch. The drunk man's face crumpled up like a wet paper bag in the hellish glow. "My father . . ." He sobbed a child's sob. "My father . . . I never knew my father. . . ."

Nick laid a hand of solace on the drunk's forehead, brushing back his hair from his eyes. "I'm sorry," Nick apologized, "I don't know who he is."

Back at the mansion, Hef had a couple Playmates who were also trained nurses. They were given the job of hydrating Will and getting him to bed. Hef took another couple Playmates to bed himself, and while there were Playmates ready and willing to join Nick, he begged off, preferring to turn in early for the night.

Of course, he'd also seen Julie Cotton still fawning over Kennedy, and part of a private investigator's job was taking pictures of men having affairs. Hedda had wanted pictures of Kennedy and Julie in a hot tub, but Nick thought he could find even hotter water than that.

This time, however, he brought a flashlight and wore clothes to explore the Playboy Mansion's secret passages, including his hat.

The mansion had more than one set of passages. The main ones, until him, had not been explored by anyone tall, judging by the breaks in the cobwebs. The secondary corridors had not been explored in years, if that, opening in secret off of already secret passageways.

Of course, most explorers weren't able to sense the electromagnetic interference caused by a spiderweb-covered bolt. Nick could and in short order found his way down a cobweb-draped corridor that led to the room where Jack Kennedy was staying.

The peephole bolt was rusted shut, but electricity removed rust. Nick looked out into dimness, able to make out the silhouettes of a four-poster bed and the two people in it, one atop the other, the one on top sporting a round tail and distinctive long ears.

"Did you hear that?" asked Julie Cotton.

"Mmm, hear what?" asked Jack Kennedy in his Boston Brahmin drawl.

"That sound."

"Just someone slamming a door somewhere."

Julie's ears twitched in silhouette. "No, it was closer than that." They swiveled toward Nick.

Nick started to swing the peephole shut but there was a faint creak so he stopped. Julie's ears stood straight up. Hoping her eyesight was only human, Nick covered the slot of the peephole with the soft gray felt of his hat brim. It muffled sound as well, but when he finally thought it safe to steal a glance, Julie's silhouette was again facing forward.

"—only thing creaking here is the bed," Jack insisted, thrusting up into her, making the springs creak with his exertions.

"I don't think so." Julie's ears twitched. "These ears are for more than just petting, you know."

"Then it's a rat." Another thrust. "This place is old."

Nick did feel a bit like Judas, but he wasn't one of Kennedy's disciples, the man was just a politician, and what's more, a married man, having an affair when he had not just a wife but kids. If Nick was a rat, he certainly wasn't the only one.

"Okay," Julie said, "but promise me one thing. Don't ever go to Texas."

"Can't promise you that." Jack laughed. "You're a crazy bunny." A grunt. "I like you, Julie." Grunt. "But it's a big state." Grunt. "Gonna have to stump."

"I don't care if you stump! Just don't go there after you're elected."

"Might wanna run for a second term. . . ."

"I want you to too," Julie cried, beginning to sob, "but you won't. Trust me, you won't. Just promise me you won't go to Dallas."

"Dallas is a big city."

"Then just promise me you won't go to Dealey Plaza," Julie sobbed. "Don't go anywhere near that damned school book depository. . . ."

"Okay," he moaned, "on one condition. . . ."

"What?"

"You quit teasing me with the crazy talk and we just have wild bunny sex!"

"*Deal!*"

With that, Julie began bouncing as gaily as the rabbit on the cover of *Rabbit Hill,* except instead of a hill, she was atop Senator John Fitzgerald Kennedy.

This was the money shot, but the room was too dark, and it would give away the game to use a flash. But unlike most photographers, Nick had an ace. He bled off electricity into the air like a Tesla coil, the ionic charge making the light bulbs light up on their own.

Light up they did, enough to get three clear shots until the bulbs in the chandelier went up like flashbulbs, overloading one after another.

"What the hell!" cried Jack.

"What on earth!" cried Julie.

Nick cried nothing, only used the distraction to slam and bolt the peephole.

The bulb in his flashlight had blown, too, but he had will-o'-wisps to light the way.

Two days later, Nick deposited a stack of photos on Hef's desk. A second smaller stack of photos and their negatives were hidden under the lining of the Argus's case.

Two other photos and negative frames, one with a blurry photo on the model but a good focus on the background, another just a shot of a bookcase, had been left out. Nick had compared the eyes in the library peephole with the eyes of the Playmates and matched them with Constance and Gwen, as expected.

Hef picked up the photos, flipping through them without comment, then began to lay them in groups atop the desk. "White Rabbit, March Hare, Peter Rabbit's hot sisters . . . What's this?"

"The Velveteen Rabbit," Nick answered.

Hef nodded and came to the last set of photos, flipping through them. He paused at one. "Great action shot. Got *centerfold* written all over it."

"Centerfold?"

"Yep," Hef said, "had a gentleman's bet with Will. He won. Asked me to make Julie centerfold. Was thinking of doing it anyway, but later. But these photos? I'm moving her up to Miss March. *And* we've got the new theme for the club. That harpy Parsons somehow got word we were doing kittens, so we're going to switch it up and unveil bunnies instead." Hef gazed at the centerfold, Nick's shot of Julie bouncing gaily in the air, then laid it on the desk. He then opened a drawer and pulled out a book, setting it beside the photograph with a grim chuckle. "Knew I'd seen this pose before."

A shiny Newbery Medal sticker adorned the cover of *Rabbit Hill*, a bunny bouncing beside it in the same pose, a hill with a little red house in the background below. "My daughter Christie's seven," Hef mentioned. "I asked Julie what sort of book a seven-year-old girl would like. She suggested this."

Nick reached out and flipped it open, noting the title page and the words below: *The Viking Press—New York 1944.* "Two years before Wild Card Day. . . ."

"Must have made quite an impression." Hef tapped the nude. "So will this."

"Yeah."

"We're going to need a clothed shot for the cover, but that doesn't have to wait until Valdes swaps the kitten costumes into bunnies. Julie already has her own ears and tail."

"Should I be the one to tell her?"

Hef mused. "Sure. Go ahead. You've earned it."

Nick knocked on the door of Will and Julie's suite. Julie opened it.

"Congratulations, Miss March," Nick greeted her.

Her face lit up while her ears stood up straight. "Are you kidding me?"

"No, it's almost as much a promotion for me as it is for you. I've gone from the pretty boy chosen for his looks to the guy who can actually shoot centerfolds." Nick grinned. "May I come in?"

"Of course."

Nick stepped inside. The suite was decked out in Oriental splendor, more elegance from Ada's collection. Will was there, too, on a chinoiserie sofa, getting an early start on the scotch. "Sorry about the other night," the older man apologized. "I babble when I'm drunk."

"No need. I think you were telling the truth, some of it anyway. You're trying to find your father.

"And you told some of the truth too." Nick looked to Julie. "I may not be a wild card, but one thing I do know about wild cards is they seldom lie about what happened when their card turned, not the little details. You said your favorite book when you were seven was *Rabbit Hill,* that it was an old book. But if you were seven on Wild Card Day, that book was only two years old, and it's not even an old book now." Nick paused, then continued before Julie could dissemble, "But it will be for you, in the future where you're from."

Julie's jaw dropped, exposing her bunny teeth.

"You're not just a joker, you're a joker-ace." Nick pointed at her. "You're the White Rabbit. You've got some power to murder the time, make it six o'clock and always teatime or fall down the rabbit hole into the past, taking others with you. But your power's not perfect and you overshot, taking Will here, who wanted to find his father, to sometime a little before he's born. But he won't say who his mother is, because then his parents might never meet and he'd never be conceived. Am I right?"

Julie said nothing, but Will took a slug of scotch. "Not quite, but close," he admitted, and took another swallow. "Very close."

Nick nodded. "The only thing I'm not sussing is Pug. Is he your son and you lost him when you fell down the rabbit hole to meet his granddad or is something else going on?"

"Something else." Will took another drink. "Abigail's former boyfriend sent him back to the Everleigh Club."

"Who's Abigail and who's her boyfriend?"

"Abigail's a young actress—British, talented, was hoping to put her in a vehicle with Pug. Abby's also an ace. She can read other aces' powers, even copy them. We call her the Understudy." Will regarded his scotch, then set it down and looked straight at Nick. "Her former boyfriend was one of the other players' bodyguards, introduced as 'Mr. Meek' but I'm sure that's an alias. He was a dead ringer for Donald Meek."

"Lots of aliases going around right now, 'Will Monroe,'" Nick pointed out. "You think you're the son of some president, but it's not Monroe, and it's not Roosevelt. Who is it really? Kennedy? Nixon?"

"God I hope not." Will reached for the scotch. He took a good swallow. "Lot of suspects. But Jack Braun wouldn't have any reason to not acknowledge me. Same thing with Hef. Hef ended up being my mentor, and Jack's been my poker buddy the past few years. Beyond that, I really don't know."

Nick took out his cigarette case. "You weren't kidding about the cigarettes, were you?"

"No," said Will, "it all comes out." Julie nodded in agreement.

Nick glanced to her. "So what's the deal with Dealey Plaza?"

She looked shocked. "How did you . . ."

"I talked with Kennedy," Nick lied quickly. "He said you were adamant that he not go anywhere near Dealey Plaza in Texas. Why? What happens there?"

Julie's ears wilted like wax tulips in the sun. "He dies. Assassinated. By Oswald."

"We're not talking about the magic rabbit Walt Disney sold to King Features, right?"

"No, Lee Harvey Oswald."

"Harvey's the invisible rabbit from that Jimmy Stewart movie."

"*I am not making this up!*" Julie ranted, her ears standing back up. "Yes, it's a dumb name, but he kills Jack Kennedy!" Her ears began to turn pink and quiver with rage. "But anyway, it doesn't matter, I've already changed history. I had sex with Jack Kennedy."

Will considered her over his drink. "You plan for him to fall in love with you and leave Jackie and the kids?"

"Pretty much," Julie admitted. "Sucks for Jackie, but I figure she'd rather be a divorcée than a widow. At least that way her kids have a living dad. And I'm not jealous—I can share. Plus I've got my ace in the hole. It's not much of an ace, and I always considered it more of a joker, but I'm using it. Already have."

"What's that?" Nick asked.

"Along with a rabbit's sex drive, the wild card gave me a rabbit's fertility." Julie grinned, showing her rabbit teeth. "You won't believe the number of birth control pills I had to go through till I found one that worked. And they won't make it for another fifty years." Julie picked up a carrot from a snack tray and nibbled it like Bugs Bunny. "And Kennedy's a Catholic, and with me pregnant now, that means the baby will arrive in November, just in time for the election. What do you think Jack's chances will be then?"

Nick stared at her. Kennedy having a love child with a joker Playmate? Hedda's photos were now just icing on Nixon's inauguration cake. "Wait, I thought you hated Nixon."

"I do," Julie swore. "Asshole's responsible for getting my grandpa killed in Vietnam. You won't believe how bad that screwed up my family. But Nixon's president in '69 anyway, so why not move up the timetable? Either Oswald ices him in '63, or Tricky Dick gets caught for Watergate a few years later. Win-win either way."

"Watergate?" Nick echoed, beyond perplexed.

"I'd recommend you watch *All the President's Men*," Will remarked, topping off a new glass of scotch, "but that's not going to be made until 1976. If ever." He took a sip, considering. "Going to royally screw up Hoffman's and Newman's careers. Are we ever going to get the Butch Cassidy Film Festival?"

"You really are a movie mogul in the future," Nick realized, looking at Will. "That's why you know all this."

"That and a film history major," Will admitted. "Who knew it would come in so useful?"

"I studied joker rights." Julie cocked her ears. "*Playboy* didn't have a joker centerfold until a letter-writing campaign in 2003. Then they overcompensated and recruited a bunch of cat girl jokers for The Pussycat Dolls. But I thought, now that I'm here in 1960, why not do it early when it might do some good?"

Nick nodded. "Looks like you thought of everything." He glanced at both of them. "Anything you'd like me to do?"

Julie bit her lip. "If anything happens to us, promise me you'll keep Kennedy away from Dealey Plaza on November 22, 1963."

"That's when he dies?"

"Yeah," she said sadly, her ears wilting, "he does."

"Then I promise," Nick swore.

The Playboy Club opened, appropriately, on Leap Day, February 29. The chic, the influential, and the press were lined up outside. Hedda Hopper, being all three, arrived in style, her latest millinery confection bewilderingly beribboned and festooned with swags of lemon-yellow silk and twists of cream-colored lace, its resemblance to a lemon meringue pie accentuated by rhinestone-encrusted lemon-wedge hat pins.

Hollywood's harpy queen arrived early, with Hef himself squiring her in, bringing her by Nick's table. "And let me introduce Nick Williams, our newest photographer, out from your town."

"He's even more handsome than Louella said. Lollipop scooped me about you hiring him." Hedda gave Hef the world's most insincere smile. "But I'll try to not hold that against him."

"Nick here even photographed our new centerfold, tomorrow's Miss March," Hef bragged.

"Well then," Hedda said, still smiling, "you won't mind if I join this handsome young man to get my own scoop?"

"Of course," said Hef, "but Nick's sworn to secrecy."

"Humor me?"

Hef took this offer as a chance to extricate himself from the Terror of Tinseltown and go greet less venomous guests. "Of course." He gave Nick a glance of mixed gratitude and warning.

Once Hef had left, Hedda snugged into the booth beside Nick, shedding her shawl and, in the same motion, reaching into the pocket of Nick's jacket where there was an awaiting packet of photographs and negatives. She slipped this into her pocketbook, covering the motion as an excuse to take out a compact and check her lipstick. "There," she pronounced, clicking the clasp shut, "I should probably take a powder room break in a bit, see if there's anything *shocking*."

Nick smiled, wondering how Hedda would feel if she knew those photographs, regardless of whether they caused Kennedy to withdraw from the campaign due to blackmail or scandal, would eventually lead to her hero Nixon's death or disgrace. Then Nick frowned, wondering how he would feel himself. Once Nixon won, if all other things remained unchanged, would there still be an assassin awaiting him in Texas in November 1963? Would there be a slightly different date or site? And if Nick foiled Nixon's assassination, would it make him complicit in Nixon's later crimes, including the death of Julie's grandfather? Or would that war even happen if the Watergate scandal, whatever it was, occurred a decade early?

Nick didn't know what to do, but his decision could wait. November 1963 was almost four years away. A lot could happen in that time. The point might be moot. Nick hoped so.

He looked across the room to where Will Monroe sat, still looking, in quiet moments, like a lost little boy, aside from the glass of scotch. Nick wished there was something he could do to bring him comfort, to help him find his father.

But after Will was born? Well, then there'd be ample time to find out whoever his father was, and his mother, too.

Of course, Nick considered, Will had said the psychic had channeled his father's spirit, and with this being in the future, the psychic could be an ace instead of a charlatan. But that future was also a long time away. And it might be changed.

After seating the fourth estate, the second was ushered in, the foremost being Senator Kennedy and his beautiful wife, Jacqueline. Hef seated Jack and Jackie with Will Monroe, whose demeanor immediately changed to one of genial surface charm, the mask of Hollywood.

Hef took the stage and the microphone. "Gentlemen, ladies, our beloved guests and fellow swingers, welcome to the Playboy Club. I know there's been some speculation as to our secret theme, the surprises for our March issue, and I thank you for waiting for Leap Day. But now, without further ado, I'd like to reveal the reason why. Cy, would you like to begin?"

Cy Coleman, the pianist, started into the *Playboy's Penthouse* theme song, but quickly segued into a jazzy variation on "The Bunny

Hop" as the curtain went up and the Playboy Playmates were revealed in their new costumes, the Playboy Bunnies, wearing silk bustiers in jewel tones with matching satin ears on their headbands. They were all huddled together in a knot, leaning forward, fluffy cottontails facing out like a bunch of bunnies. But then they rose, turned, and parted, revealing that they all bore trays on straps, like cigarette girls.

All save Julie Cotton, who rose up from where she'd been hidden, revealing herself as wearing the same satin bustier designed by Zelda Wynn Valdes, but with her own ears and tail.

Gasps erupted from the audience, none louder than Hedda Hopper's. Nick took a certain pleasure in that.

"Let me introduce Miss March, Julie Cotton!" Hef announced with a showman's flourish.

All the other Bunnies promenaded down into the club with their trays, but instead of being filled with candies and cigarettes, they bore the March issue of *Playboy*.

Hedda accepted hers, and opened it to the centerfold. Men about the club were doing the same. "Well, Nicholas darling, it appears you may have a future in photography," Hedda sniffed after a long look, "but I would suggest you look for more worthy subject matter." She folded the magazine back up, turning across the way to view Julie Cotton cozying up to the Kennedys. Julie leaned over and whispered something in Jack's ear. His expression went from happy to shocked, but just as quickly covered as Julie turned to chat with Jackie, who smiled back graciously, seemingly oblivious to the news Julie had whispered to Jack.

Hedda, however, was a better judge of human expression, and Nick watched her hard old eyes as they noted every nuance. Her lips pressed to a hard line. "You must excuse me, Nicholas." She clutched her purse with an iron grip. "I have a sudden urge to powder my nose."

She patted him on the shoulder and winked, then sashayed off to the ladies' room. Nick watched Hef continue to work the crowd while Julie chatted with Jack and Jackie, secretly plotting the future course of her life and theirs.

Will Monroe's eyes locked with Nick's, looking like he desperately wished to tell him something, but couldn't find where to begin, or how.

Nick gazed back. He felt the same.

A Long Night at
the Palmer House

Part 2

CHARLES DUTTON SHAKILY GOT to his feet and moved over to the window, shunting the drapes aside. He stared out into the sky, which was still dark with the last legs of the night.

"What's happening out there?" he asked rhetorically. Neither he nor Nighthawk nor any of the others who drifted toward the window could make any sense of the noises, flashing lights, and dark shapes they saw moving erratically on the street until a sudden burst of sheet lightning illuminated the scene for a moment. Even then, they were distracted by the accompanying rolling rumble of thunder that seemed as if it would never stop.

The escort Jack Braun had brought to the game—the twin who'd sneaked into the bedroom with Bellerose and had escaped the dangers of the fight—screamed aloud, wordlessly, turned, and ran from the room. Nighthawk and Dutton stared at other speechlessly, while Margot Bellerose sank to the floor on her knees and asked in a little voice, "What happened, *mon Dieu,* someone please tell me what happened."

Meek cleared his throat and said, diffidently, "Well—"

And then the twin returned to the room, screaming even louder. "It's changing! *It's all changing!*"

Nighthawk moved to intercept her as she ran crazily around the room, her eyes wild. He grabbed her arms, shook her. She blubbered wordlessly, the incoherent sounds she was making drowned out by another roll of thunder like the clap of doom hovering over the Palmer House.

"Breathe deep!" Nighthawk ordered the girl. He held her tightly against his chest, and could feel the tremors running through her entire body. He took a shot in the dark. "Hildy?" Her head, tucked against his chest, nodded. "Calm down. Calm down and tell me what's happening in the hallway."

"I was—I was waiting for the elevator," she got out between hiccups, "and when it came—it was different. It wasn't a regular elevator. It was a steel cage with a man in a uniform in it and he looked at me so funny, so funny, I just screamed and ran—"

"Look at the buildings," Dutton said in an awestricken voice.

Nighthawk looked. They all did, except for Bellerose, who was still frozen, struck silent and motionless. Hildy looked for only a moment, gasped, and returned to the sanctuary of Nighthawk's arms, nuzzling his chest with her face like a kitten trying to bury itself against the warmth of its feline mother.

Outside, making the sounds of giant behemoths moaning in strange pain, the buildings were shifting, growing, shrinking, grinding against each other, changing in multiple ways that lasted only for seconds before they morphed again from skyscrapers to smaller, simple structures of stone or brick or even wood, or swelled into ovoids of glittering metal connected by sweeping ramps and skeletal metallic catwalks. Once they became a set of tepees along a tranquil stream, once burned-out, destroyed hulks from a blast so powerful it must have been nuclear.

The sky itself was also changing, rippling from darkest night to strange purples shot through by rays of silver and golden light. Snowstorms and rain and fog whipped by tremendous winds howling between the buildings, but nothing except spatters of water made it down to the ground below. The rest all dissipated into mist or showers of colored sparks like the grandest fireworks display ever launched into the air.

The Palmer House itself seemed mostly immune to the strange, seemingly endless transformation. The room they were in, at least, stood like a rock in a sea of chaos. *But why,* Nighthawk wondered, *and for how long?*

"Time storm," Donald Meek said in his mild voice. "We're in the eye of a time storm."

"What?" Dutton asked, turning his attention back to inside the room.

"My fault," Meek said meekly. "When Galante's bodyguard lashed out with her fire power, I was caught in the edge of it." His singed eyebrows and ruddy, though not deeply burned face and hands, attested to that. "And I returned fire." He sighed, looked from Dutton to Nighthawk. "Unfortunately, the power can be hard to control."

"So," Nighthawk said hesitantly, "they're out there somewhere—some*when*—doing things that are . . . are . . ."

"Ripping the time stream apart," Meek said resignedly. "Changing history. Continually and at cross-purposes. There's no unified 'present' anymore—only a dozen warring 'presents' overlapping, contradicting, competing with, and melting into each other." He gestured toward the window. "A time storm."

Hildy moaned softly, and Nighthawk felt her going limp. He half walked, half dragged her to a nearby chair and set her down in it. Bellerose finally wandered closer to the others. She looked out the window listlessly.

"What will happen?" Dutton asked in a low voice.

"Oh," Meek said. "I suppose that eventually the fabric of the universe will tear and the Earth will be destroyed and maybe eventually everything else with it. Or not." He shrugged. "This is all new to me too. I haven't had this power long."

"Unless—" Nighthawk prompted. "Can you find them?"

Meek frowned in concentration. "They were scattered around the room and absorbed different levels of time shift. Those close to each may have been popped into the same time. They're all in the same space." He rubbed his chin. "Some*when* in the Palmer House, if they were sent to a time when the Palmer House exists. They're all somewhere in Chicago, anyway. If they were sent to a time when Chicago existed. . . . but I *can* sense them, more or less, like blips on the radar screen of time."

"Then we can go after them—" Nighthawk began.

"I could send you after them," Meek said, "at least one of them. But what good will that do? You can't bring anyone back. You could stop one from acting, but which one is causing the most damage? Or is it a question of accumulative damage to the time stream brought on by all of them. . . ."

"These 'rays,'" Dutton said thoughtfully, "the rainbows you shot out . . . that's what caused these temporal displacements?"

"Yes," Meek said.

"Are they reflective?"

"What? The rays?"

"Yes," Dutton said. "Of course."

"I . . . don't know."

"The bedrooms have full-length mirrors in them," Margot Bellerose offered helpfully without looking at them.

"Okayyyy," Meek said. He and Nighthawk looked at each other.

"We have to do something," Nighthawk said.

Meek looked reluctant, but nodded. "I suppose we do."

Nighthawk turned to Dutton. "Lock the door. Don't let anyone in. Barricade it as best you can. There's a couple of guns lying around." He reached down for the .38 he kept snugged in an ankle holster. "Here's mine."

Dutton took it, nodding. "Let me accompany you into the bedroom."

They turned and looked at Bellerose. She was silently contemplating the landscape below them through the hotel windows. Out of the dark sky a great flying lizard swept with leathery wings, soaring toward the window. She ducked, screaming. The lizard banked away at the last moment.

Dutton nodded to the bedroom door. "We had best do this soon," he said quietly.

Bellerose was right. The room had a full-length mirror placed strategically on the wall before the bed. "In the service of full disclosure," Dutton said to Nighthawk, "there is something we should tell you."

"A surprise?" Nighthawk said with an expectant frown.

"Of a sort." Dutton gestured at Meek grandly. "Meet Croyd Crenson."

Nighthawk pursed his lips, but remained silent. *Of course,* he thought. He should have known. "The Sleeper," he observed. That explained much. He felt more than a little annoyed at himself for not suspecting, and somewhat more annoyed at them for keeping him in the dark. "I see. The Sleeper, at a card game with seven million in the wall safe."

"Hey," Croyd said, "it's not like we were planning on stealing the cash or anything. Dutton was going to win it fair and square." He laughed, shortly and insincerely. "Heh. Sorry we didn't let you in on it sooner, but we, uh, thought it best to keep that on a need-to-know basis."

"Now that the stakes have changed," Dutton intoned, "it's best you know the truth." His expression and his voice grew even more serious, if that were possible. "Of course, sooner or later Croyd will need to sleep again. And when he sleeps, he transforms."

And loses his powers. Nighthawk eyed Croyd dubiously. "How long have you been awake already?"

"Oh, only a couple of days. Don't worry, I'm used to it. I can handle it."

So you say, Nighthawk thought. "We'd better get started," he said in a neutral voice.

"I guess," Croyd said, "we'll be right back. Or maybe not. We're dealing with time here. Who the hell knows?"

"Good luck," Dutton said. "Everything's riding on you!"

"We better get real close," Croyd said, "like hugging close."

They stood before the mirror. Side by side, one arm wrapped around the other's waist.

"Ready?" Croyd asked.

Nighthawk felt a roiling in his gut. This was the strangest, most dangerous thing he'd ever done. But it was better to die trying rather than just stand by and watch the world disintegrate around them. "Yeah. Just do—"

The rainbow arced again from Croyd's palm and hit the mirror. As the spectrum of colors rebounded and washed over Nighthawk he felt like someone hit him all over his body with the hardest punch he'd ever taken. The air swooshed out of his lungs, his testicles tried to ascend back into his abdomen, and his buttocks clenched so tightly that you couldn't pull a pin out of his ass with a tractor. He thought he was struck blind and then he realized that he'd just closed his eyes. He was naked, but warm air caressed his skin, as well as Croyd's arm, which was still around his waist. The soles of his feet were planted on thick, lush carpet.

"—it."

Nighthawk looked ahead, blinking, and realized that he and Croyd were standing behind two men. One was young, immaculately well dressed in the finest of evening attire, if, Nighthawk recognized, you were going out to do the town about a hundred years ago. He wore an expensively cut black coat and white tie, and the second man was using a whisk broom to brush off some imaginary flecks of dust from his well-clad shoulders.

They were standing before a full-length mirror and the young man was admiring his reflection in it when he caught sight of Nighthawk and Croyd materializing behind him. His eyes suddenly bulged out of his pleasantly featured face and he did a credible imitation of a goldfish removed from water gasping for breath. His lips moved, but it took a moment for words to actually issue from them. When they did, they were in a striking English accent.

"I say," he said. Then, apparently unable to think of anything to add, he continued with, "I say, I say, I say." Struck with further inspiration, he added, "What? What now? What?"

He was rather tall and willowy built. The other man, who also wore formal attire, but more in the line of someone in service, a valet, probably, was even taller and more solidly built. He turned and looked at them. He had a shrewd-looking face with an imperturbable expression and a steady, intelligent gaze.

Croyd made an embarrassed sound in his throat, took his arm away from Nighthawk's waist, and stepped a foot or two to the side.

"Don't be alarmed," he said. "We're from the future."

The valet's left eyebrow lifted a quarter of an inch, as if expressing vast surprise.

They were in a luxuriously appointed hotel room. Nighthawk could recognize the general outlines of the room they'd just left, though the furnishings were completely different. Everything was expensive-looking, if heavy and ponderous. There was a large four-poster bed, an ornate wardrobe, a smaller dresser, side tables on either side of the bed with bric-a-brac all over them, and an overstuffed chair with antimacassars on the arms and back.

"Indeed, sir?" the valet asked. His gaze swept over them briefly and then focused somewhere on a distant spot between them. "And does everyone in the future go about disrobed?"

"Ah, well," Croyd replied. "That's just an effect of time travel, itself. You can't bring anything with you. Not even clothes."

The young man had turned around and was eyeing them with a puzzled expression that somehow seemed habitual. "Rummy, that," he said, then added briskly, "Well, we can't have you sporting about starkers. There must be something you can find—"

"Immediately, sir."

"Well, fine. Fine, fine, fine." The young man beamed at the unexpected arrivals. Nighthawk couldn't help but feel an instinctual liking for him.

"Well, sit down and tell me all about this 'future' business. Or"—his expressive face suddenly took on a concerned expression—"wait a mo' . . . let's get some"—he made a helpless gesture with his hands—"you know, some, uh, before you sit, you know."

Nighthawk understood, and shook his head at Croyd, who was about to plop his butt into the overstuffed chair. Croyd caught himself at the last moment and nodded.

"Oh, sure. Sure. Very generous of you—"

The young man shook his head, briskly. "Not at all. *Not* at all. I've been touring your country—just out of New York, Boston. Fascinating. Everyone's been most accommodating. Least I can do to help out you chaps. And from the future you say! Extraordinary!"

The valet had been piling up articles of clothing from both a dresser drawer and the wardrobe, and he approached Nighthawk and Croyd with an armload. The young man's face fell as he handed the items over. "Not the new checked suits!" he said. "I just got those in New York."

"I know, sir," the valet said imperturbably. "I feel they will serve these gentlemen more suitably."

Nighthawk thought he could detect something of a note of relief in his voice as he handed the suits over. Nighthawk understood. They were not exactly his style, either.

"Ah, well," the young man said, shrugging. "Needs must, I suppose."

"Yes, sir," his man said. He watched critically as Nighthawk and Croyd dressed. "I'm afraid, sirs, that the fit is not perfect. The young master is taller—"

"That's all right," Nighthawk said. "We'll make do."

"Yes, sir."

There was something in this man, Nighthawk perceived, something that bound him to the younger man who was so generous and, well, naive was probably a kind word, with cords of loyalty and protectiveness that went deep into the soul. He nodded, and the valet nodded back.

"So," the young Britisher said eagerly as they dressed, "tell me all about the future."

"Well—" Croyd began. He and Nighthawk exchanged glances. "You wouldn't believe it," Croyd finally said.

"We can't say much," Nighthawk explained, "on the chance that you can use your knowledge to change history."

The Englishman looked crestfallen. "That's a bit of a disappointment."

"But I'll tell you one thing," Croyd said.

"Yes?" the young man said eagerly.

"Don't trust Hitler. And another thing—whatever you do, don't visit New York City on September 15, 1946. It'll be very dangerous on that day."

"Well, thanks awfully for the warning."

"You bet," Croyd said. He and Nighthawk looked at each other. "Well, time to go save the world. Thanks for everything."

"Certainly. Good luck, chaps."

Croyd paused. "One last thing."

"Yes?"

"Could you loan us a twenty?"

The young man shook his head as he reached for his wallet. "I say," he said, "they'll never believe this at the Drones Club."

"So how does this temporal tracking ability of yours actually work?" Nighthawk asked Croyd as they went down the hotel corridor, heading for the elevator.

"I kind of see those displaced in time as blips on the temporal landscape," Croyd said. "Sort of like a radar screen. I can't tell who they are and it's hard to say how many are in a given location, especially since we're dealing with a relatively small number of people."

"Seems like enough to me," Nighthawk said. "And the actual place where they landed is, essentially, the same place they left?"

They stopped at the elevator bank and punched the button for the lobby.

"Well, most times anyway. I suppose. Actually, I really haven't sent too many people back in time. Just that pigeon. Oh, and an alley cat when I first woke up. It seems like a pretty useful power, but, really, how often would the necessity for using it come up?"

Great, Nighthawk thought. *Our temporal expert seems to be groping around as much as I am.* The elevator arrived and Croyd and Nighthawk got on. The car was empty except for its operator, a tall, young black man in Palmer House livery. Seeing him took Nighthawk back through a hundred and forty-some years of memory to a time when he, too, wore the Palmer House uniform, when he worked at the hotel that stood on this very spot, before the Great Chicago Fire. Memories flooded into his mind and he clamped down on them and sent them away to where he kept them, hidden, but never forgotten.

"Floor, please," the young man said.

"Lobby," Croyd said.

"So," Nighthawk said as the door closed, "whoever we're after—"

Croyd looked at him and nodded. "Would have ended up—"

Nighthawk shook his head, his eyes shifting to the elevator operator who stood in front of him. "Say," he said, "any strange things happen in the hotel, lately?"

"Mister," the operator said without turning around, "strange stuff is always happening around here. You'd be surprised."

Actually, Nighthawk thought, he wouldn't. "Like what?" he asked.

"Well—" He thought for a moment. "Couple of weeks ago this crazy white man broke into a room, somehow, naked as a jaybird. He—"

The operator glanced back over his shoulder, catching Croyd's eye. "Sorry, sir," he said. "I didn't mean—"

"No, no," Croyd said. "This is fascinating. Do you know what he looked like?"

"Well, he was kind of, uh, stocky, I guess you could say." He paused for a moment. "And he had a funny haircut for a grown man. You know, like that Buster Brown in the comic strip."

Croyd and Nighthawk looked at each other.

"Charlie Flowers," they said simultaneously.

A bell dinged as the elevator stopped.

"Your floor, sirs," the young man said.

The air on the Chicago street was cool and crisp with the tang of early autumn. It was as crowded a street as any Nighthawk had walked down during the twenty-first century and perhaps even noisier. But he'd forgotten the old smell of the city. It all came back to him in a sudden rush when they left the Palmer House lobby.

"What's that smell?" Croyd asked, wrinkling his nose.

Nighthawk waved at the street. "Horse manure."

Horse-drawn carts and carriages were still battling the automobile for supremacy on the streets of Chicago. It was a losing fight, but there were enough of the old-fashioned conveyances that the distinctive sweet tang of horseshit still lingered on the air. They stepped into the flow of the foot traffic and let it carry them down the street until they came upon a café that had a few tables set out on the sidewalk as well as inside.

"I could use a bite to eat," Croyd said.

Nighthawk was hungry as well. Such mundane concerns as food and drink had been forgotten in the excitement of the game and subsequent events, but now they came back to the time travelers. They took a seat at one of the small sidewalk tables and a white-aproned waiter appeared almost instantaneously. They ordered ham sandwiches and beer and were surprised and happy at the size of the slabs of rye bread, the thick cuts of ham, the whole dill pickles on the side, and the mugs of beer. A pot of spicy German mustard accompanied the sandwiches, which both slathered generously on the bread.

As they tore into the thick, juicy sandwiches, a newsboy came by hawking the afternoon edition of the *Tribune*. He was a runty little kid, maybe ten or twelve, looking like he stepped out of a Norman Rockwell illustration, or, Nighthawk realized, his memories.

"Hey, kid," Croyd called. "Give me a paper." He reached into his pocket for the bill that their British benefactor had given them back in the room in the Palmer House.

The kid's eyes grew big as Croyd held it out. "Jeez, mister, I can't change a twenty."

"How much is the newspaper?" Croyd asked.

"Two cents."

Croyd laughed. "Two cents? Even when I was a kid . . ." He looked at Nighthawk in surprise. "It was three cents," he said, wonder in his voice. "Have I forgotten so much?"

"You'd probably be surprised," Nighthawk said with a gentle smile.

Croyd called the waiter over. "Give the kid a nickel," he said, "and add it to our bill."

The waiter complied.

"Keep the change, kid," Croyd said.

"Thanks, mister!"

From where he sat, Nighthawk could read the banner headlines: IRISH HOME RULE NEAR! The front page was crowded with columns of text. "Don't keep me in suspense. What's the date?"

"Oh, October 8, 1919. Say—" Croyd looked up, frowning in concentration. "I got us pretty close. Flowers has been here a month, tops. Not too much time to get up to a lot of mischief. Now all we have to do is find him. He's around here somewhere. But where, exactly? How many people lived in Chicago in 1919?"

"Two and a half million."

"Really?" Croyd looked at him.

"I do know Chicago," Nighthawk said, looking up and down the bustling street. The memories were flooding back upon him like a wave that threatened to drag him under with its powerful pull. "Wait a minute . . . 1919? October?"

Croyd looked at him. "Yeah. What?"

Nighthawk set his sandwich back down on the plate, chewing thoughtfully. "At least we missed the riots," he said.

"Riots?"

"Chicago's worst race riots—ever." Nighthawk's voice became pensive, his gaze turned inward. "The summer of 1919 was known as Red Summer because of the racial tension that spread across the entire country. There were riots in many cities. My people were coming up from the South in massive numbers. Here in Chicago the tensions boiled over when a thrown rock killed a young black man at a beach in late July. By the time the National Guard had been called in to quell the violence, almost forty people were dead, a few more blacks than whites, but most of the property damage occurred in the Black Belt on the South Side, at the hands of organized 'athletic clubs.'" Nighthawk frowned at Croyd. "Mostly Irish, mostly fairly recent immigrants themselves, competing for the jobs with the blacks coming up from the South."

"What are you, a history buff or something?" Croyd asked.

"Or something," Nighthawk said quietly. "It was pretty terrible. But, look, what else happened here in Chicago in 1919?"

Croyd, thumbing through the paper, looked up. "What?"

"The Black Sox scandal! The year the White Sox threw the World Series to the Cincinnati Reds."

Croyd's eyes widened. "Flowers would be drawn to that like a fly to shit. But is the Series still going on? Wait a minute." He flipped the pages more quickly. "Here it is." He looked up at Nighthawk. "Game seven is at Comiskey Park this afternoon."

Nighthawk frowned in concentration. "Give me a minute. . . . Yes, that's right. The White Sox win today, four to one."

"Wait," Croyd said, "the White Sox *won* game seven? I thought they threw the Series—"

"This was one of the years when the World Series was a best of nine." Nighthawk signaled to their waiter. "Pay him," he told Croyd, when the boy came over.

"Wait," Croyd said again. "They played a *nine-game* World Series? You knew that?"

Nighthawk smiled. "I'm a baseball fan."

"Where are we going?"

"I know a man—"

"You *know* a man?"

"I'll explain later," Nighthawk said as the waiter came back with their change. They had a little less than nineteen dollars left.

"You'd better. Just where are we headed?"

"You know that Black Belt I mentioned?" Croyd nodded. "We're going to a part of it called Bronzeville."

The geography of Chicago hadn't changed all that much in a century, and the details of it came back to Nighthawk quickly. The Palmer House was located fairly near the northern edge of the Black Belt, which ran about thirty blocks, from Thirty-first to Fifty-fifth Street along State Street, but, as indicated by its name, was only a few blocks wide. The heart of Bronzeville, Chicago's Black Metropolis, was around Forty-seventh Street.

They took the el, and got off at a pleasant neighborhood that consisted of rambling single-family homes interspersed with business centers lived in and run by blacks. It looked fairly prosperous, except for some spots of destruction they passed where buildings once stood but had obviously recently been burned to the ground. Rubble still remained in many of these spots like broken teeth in an otherwise healthy smile.

"Results of the riots?" Croyd asked.

Nighthawk nodded grimly. "Yes. Like I said, Irish 'athletic clubs' paid the hood a visit. And since most of the cops were Irish themselves, they weren't too interested in restraining their friends. It took five thousand National Guardsmen to enforce the peace."

"Doesn't sound pleasant," Croyd said.

"It wasn't," Nighthawk muttered. Before Croyd could question him further, he said, "Here we are," and turned up the steps of a pawnshop that was in a row of businesses—grocer, barbershop, drugstore, and other small stores.

Inside it was well lit, airy, and spick-and-span clean, with shelves stocked with every kind of item you might be looking for, from clothes to tools to furniture. Near the front, behind a glass counter that was divided by display cases containing guns—small arms, mainly—and jewelry, stood an immense black man. He was fashionably and expensively dressed, with diamond rings on both pinkies and a diamond stickpin in his tie that was the size of a walnut.

"Hello, Ice," Nighthawk said.

The man looked at him, frowning.

"You know my father," Nighthawk said.

"John Nighthawk," the man said, his face lighting in a broad smile. "You favor him, most precisely."

Croyd opened his mouth and Nighthawk stepped on his foot.

"I'm happy to say that I do," Nighthawk said. "He's a good-looking man."

"Yes, indeed," the Iceman said.

"This is my friend, Mr. Crenson," Nighthawk said, indicating Croyd, who smiled and nodded.

"Any friend of John Nighthawk's son is a friend of mine," Ice said. "Welcome to Bronzeville."

"Thanks," Croyd said. "It looks like a swell place."

Ice nodded. "What can I do for you—" He paused.

"John. After my father."

"—John?"

"Mr. Crenson and I just got into town and we'd like to attend the game this afternoon—"

Ice smiled broadly. "So you came to see Ice?"

"We know it's a hard ticket. We're willing to pay—"

Ice made a dismissive gesture. "I got what you need, boy, but the money of John Nighthawk's son is no good here." He reached into his waistcoat pocket and came out with a sheaf of tickets. "Good thing you got here now, though. I was just going to send my boys out to see what we could get for them. All prime seats. Here, take two."

Nighthawk knew better than to argue. "Thanks, Ice."

As he handed over the tickets, the pawnbroker said, "Since you're just back in town—a warning. I hope you don't have any business going on the game."

"Business?" Nighthawk asked. "You mean a bet? No. Is it rigged?"

"Sure as hell is. It's not well-known, but Ice knows all. He hears everything. You can't fart in my town without me knowing. That eastern trash comes to our town with their dirty money and bribes our boys to throw it!" There was real anger in Ice's voice and eyes. "Thank God *our* boys aren't part of that filthy deal."

"Our boys?" Nighthawk asked.

"You know—Smokey Joe and the Thunderbolt. They wouldn't take dirty money. They wouldn't let Chicago down."

"No," Nighthawk said thoughtfully.

"Anyway . . ." Ice brightened some. "Smokey Joe Williams is pitching today, and he'll show them. Tomorrow, though . . ." He shook his head. "The white boy is going, the other Williams, Lefty. Bet on Cincinnati if you want to, but I wouldn't dirty my money."

"Nor would I," Nighthawk said.

"Damn right. Well . . ." Ice smiled as they turned to go. "You remember me to your daddy. And tell him to come by sometime soon. He always brings the best when he comes to visit."

"I will," Nighthawk said as they left the shop.

Croyd looked at him. "What the hell?"

Nighthawk sighed. "I suppose I should explain." He paused. The street was quiet, with a few people passing them as they went about their daily business. "I'm . . . older than I look."

"Hey, man, I don't judge," Croyd said. "After all, I'm like, Jesus, seventy-seven myself. Or about that."

"Yeah, well, I'm older than that." There was a faraway look in his eyes.

Croyd looked impressed. "No shit?"

"No shit. I've been around a long time. And though I've done some traveling, worked for a while in lots of places, Chicago has been my home ever since I came here after the war."

"What war was that?" Croyd asked.

Nighthawk looked at him. "The Civil War."

Croyd's jaw dropped. "Hey, I'm not trying to pry or anything. We all have our little secrets, our little foibles. It's not like you're a vampire or something and drink blood to stay alive for so long." He paused a moment before adding, "Right? Because, if you were, that would be disgusting."

"No," Nighthawk said. "I don't drink blood."

"Great. That's cool." They started down the street again, heading for the el. "You know, I was a kid when the virus hit, back in '46. I never finished school." He shook his head. "Always regretted that I never learned algebra, but then it hasn't really come up much in my life. I always loved history, though."

"I've lived through a lot of it," Nighthawk said.

"You ever meet General Ulysses Grant?"

Nighthawk shook his head. "No. But I knew Teddy Roosevelt pretty well."

"Tell me about it," Croyd said.

"Well, there was this time when we were ordered to take this hill . . . you think Cuba is something now, you should have been there in the 1890s. . . ."

Comiskey Park, known as the Baseball Palace of the World, was jammed to the rafters, and then some. Even though it was one of the largest baseball stadiums of its time, every seat was taken and even the aisles were crammed with standing-room-only patrons. Ice's word was good—the tickets he'd given to Nighthawk and Croyd were excellent, box seats located on the field level, just behind the White Sox dugout. Nighthawk was impressed. He'd been to many games at Comiskey Park, before it fell to the wrecking ball in 1991 . . .

not only White Sox games, but also those of the Negro National League before, and even after, Jackie Robinson broke the major league color barrier. But he'd never seen it so crowded.

While unusual but not unique for this time, Comiskey Park wasn't racially segregated, so no one even batted an eye when Nighthawk and Croyd took their seats, right on the aisle about six rows above the dugout. Nighthawk didn't notice any other black fans in his immediate neighborhood, though that was more of an economic rather than a social commentary on the times. These were expensive seats, $5.50 each, as printed on the tickets. Though the stands were already crowded, the field itself was empty. The players had yet to appear for infield practice or even warm-up games of catch.

A vendor passed by hawking scorecards, and Nighthawk called him over. He gave the kid a nickel for the pamphlet. Nighthawk looked at the cover musingly as the kid moved on with his wares. Croyd glanced at him. "Who's that on the cover?" he asked.

"Oh, the owner, of course, Charles Comiskey. A notorious skinflint whose miserly ways in large part caused the . . ." He paused, looked around, and lowered his voice. "You know, the thing that Ice told us about."

"Right. Got ya."

Nighthawk glanced up. The players were just starting to take the field in ones and twos, strolling about and stretching desultorily. He looked back down at the program, thumbing through it. "You know how much this nickel program would be worth back in—back home?"

"How much?" Croyd asked, interested.

"I'm not really sure, but probably thous—" He stopped. "Oh my God!"

"What?" Croyd asked.

Nighthawk stood up, staring out onto the field with a shocked expression on his face. He was silent for several moments, despite Croyd's repeated, "What?" and he finally sank back into his seat.

"What is it?" Croyd asked. "You look like you've seen a ghost."

"On the field," he croaked. "Black men."

"Yeah, so . . . oh. Right."

"Jackie didn't break the twentieth-century color barrier until 1946," Nighthawk said in a choked whisper, "in the minors. Forty-seven in the majors."

He thumbed through the program until he came to a team photo. It was grainy black and white, but he pointed out the three men who were quite obviously black. The names under the photo read Joe Williams, Oscar Charleston, and Spottswood Poles.

He wasn't familiar with Poles, but knew the other two quite well. He'd seen them play, followed their exploits in the black newspapers of the day. And Ice had named them, though what he'd said was so foreign to Nighthawk that he hadn't really processed it. Smokey Joe Williams, six feet four, a towering figure on the mound who'd come out of the dusty diamonds of west Texas, half black and half Indian. He'd pitched well into his forties, and was said to throw harder than the Big Train, Walter Johnson. Said so even by Johnson himself, whom he'd faced frequently in exhibition games when black players faced major leaguers back in their day. And Oscar Charleston, a compact but strongly built outfielder, who was called the Hoosier Thunderbolt because of his combination of power and speed.

He looked out over the field. There he was. Charleston was playing catch with Shoeless Joe Jackson himself and chatting with a smaller, more slimly built black man who had to be Spottswood Poles, tossing the ball with a player whom Nighthawk didn't recognize.

As he watched a tall black man came strolling up the sidelines accompanied by another player in catching gear. He started to warm up. It was Smokey Joe Williams himself.

"Are you all right?" Croyd asked in a low voice.

Nighthawk suddenly realized that tears were running down his cheeks.

"I'm fine," Nighthawk said. "I'm just fine." He turned to Croyd and smiled. "I'm really going to enjoy this game."

And he did.

It was the fourth inning and the White Sox were leading the Cincinnati Reds 2–0. Spot Poles, who turned out to be a speedy outfielder and lead-off man, had walked in the first inning and then scored when Charleston, who was hitting fourth, right after Joe Jackson, tripled to deepest center. Charleston then homered in his second at bat. No other Sox player had done much at the plate, but no one else had to. Williams was on his game, and was throwing heat. He had a perfect game going through four innings and had struck out seven of the twelve Reds who'd come to the plate, including their own black players, the veteran shortstop John Henry Lloyd and Cuban-born outfielder Cristóbal Torriente. No one was touching Williams and maybe no one on the White Sox dared to boot a play purposely.

Not only was the game itself entertaining, but in the bottom of the first, a couple of latecomers went down the aisle, right past Croyd and Nighthawk, to the front row of boxes. A man and woman, both expensively, even extravagantly, dressed in the fashions of the day. Croyd noticed them first as they passed by. He poked Nighthawk in the ribs, and started to rise, but Nighthawk laid a cautionary hand on his arm as he watched Charlie Flowers and Dagmar take their seats.

"Keep an eye on them," he whispered. "And let's enjoy the game."

It was a crisply played match, over in little more than two hours. In the eighth inning Shoeless Joe Jackson made an incredible running catch, preserving Williams's perfect game. Williams waited on the mound to shake his hand as they headed for the dugout.

Croyd shook his head. "Is Jackson really trying to throw the game?" he asked in a low voice.

"Some say that he was in on the fix, but didn't play like it, double-crossing the gamblers." Nighthawk shrugged. "Who knows? Maybe he couldn't help himself from catching the ball. Maybe he couldn't let his teammates down in a game like this."

It was the only bit of help Williams needed to retain his perfect game. He struck out the side in the ninth inning, and the 2–0 score held up. As Williams was mobbed by his teammates for pitching the greatest game in World Series history, Charlie Flowers stormed up the aisle, a scowl plastered on his face, dragging Dagmar by the hand behind him.

Nighthawk and Croyd looked away, watching out of the corners of their eyes until they passed.

"Let's go," Nighthawk said. They followed at a discreet distance up the concrete stairs.

They stayed behind the couple, sheltered by the crowd rushing out onto the streets to celebrate the victory. Nighthawk's face was grim. He'd just witnessed one of the most incredibly historic sights of his life, and now they had to wipe it all away to mend the time line and preserve their present. It wasn't a small thing, this breaking of the baseball color line decades before Jackie Robinson. It had tremendous implications, social, political, and economic, for his people, not to mention that it righted a great wrong that had kept deserving men from performing at the highest levels of their chosen profession. Nighthawk had no idea what possibly could have triggered the historic change and, even though it was positive, he and Croyd had to wipe it away. To erase it. To bring back an injustice that would harm the social fabric of the entire nation. He had to blink back tears, this time tears of frustration and rage. But he would remember. He would remember the two hours or so of perfection, just a second or less in eternity, but something of beauty and grace that was an accomplishment for the ages.

They followed Flowers and Dagmar to the line of horse-drawn carriages waiting outside the park. The two time travelers climbed into the seat of an enclosed coach, Flowers shouting an address to the driver. Before he could pull away from the curb, Nighthawk and Croyd leaped into the coach themselves, taking the seat opposite.

"Fancy meeting you here," Croyd said, smiling.

Flowers stared at them blankly for a moment, until recognition appeared in his eyes. "You're—" he began, stopped, began again. "You're those guys from the poker game. What the hell?"

"We've come after you," Nighthawk said, "to return you to our time."

Flowers stared at him. "What?" He shook his head. "Fuck. No. I *like* it here. I know important people. I *am* important people!"

"You help fix the World Series, Charlie?" Nighthawk asked coldly.

"What if I—I mean, what the hell you talking about?"

"Come on, Charlie, it's in all the history books." Nighthawk paused. "Although I don't recall reading your name in any of them."

"Well, you will." Flowers flushed. "It was half-assed until I signed on—"

Croyd shook his head. "You've got to go back, Charlie. You both have to go back. Our present is being torn apart. History is getting all messed up. . . ."

"Who cares?" Flowers snarled. His face was dark with rage and suddenly he was holding a pistol in his hand. He still had an athlete's reflexes. "I don't give a goddamn. I was never very good at history. Let those lousy bastards take care of themselves. They fucked me over when they had their chance, well, fuck them, twice as hard—"

Dagmar, sitting next to him on the seat, had quietly taken a cosh out of her bag. She smacked Charlie hard, on the side of the head. His eyeballs rolled up and he sagged limply on the seat as Nighthawk and Croyd looked on.

She turned to them. "Oh, take me home. Take me home, *please!*" She started to cry. "I *hate it here*. It's so hot and dirty. There's no television, the movies have no sound! And the food is terrible. *Nothing* is gluten-free, they don't even have sushi. Oh, please, please—"

Croyd gestured briefly. Nighthawk could see the rainbow ripples pass between him and his targets, and then Dagmar and Flowers were gone, leaving piles of clothes and a pistol behind them.

"Jesus," Nighthawk said, "that's it? They back in our present?"

Croyd nodded in satisfaction. "Yep. That's it. Standing on Michigan Avenue in 2017 naked as jaybirds. Or jailbirds, in Charlie's case. Let the son-of-a-bitch explain *that*."

"All right then," Nighthawk said. "Let's go find a mirror."

"No place like the Palmer House," Croyd said.

The desk clerk at the Palmer House didn't bat an eyelash when Nighthawk and Croyd booked a room for the night, sans suitcases. Nighthawk, acting a part as Croyd's valet, informed him that their luggage would be delivered later that evening.

It made sense for them to return to the Palmer House. A hotel room provided the requisite privacy to make the jump, not to mention the necessary mirror. It also served as a ready source of clothing and other necessities for the newly arrived travelers. And both Nighthawk and Croyd were hungry. The hot dogs they'd had at the stadium had been a decent snack, but what they really needed was a good meal, which was just a phone call to room service away.

They ordered steaks, several sides, a couple of desserts each—most of them for Croyd—and a large pot of coffee. Black. Croyd was used to remaining awake for extended periods of time. That wasn't Nighthawk's normal lifestyle, but for now at least he was willing to match Croyd's string of sleeplessness. It might turn into a problem as their quest continued, Nighthawk realized, but for now he could deal with it. He was feeling tired, though, and at some point in the near future knew that he would have to energize himself with a jolt of life essence. Again, that was something to worry about perhaps during the course of their next jump.

After their repast, Croyd sat at the table, staring into the bottom of his coffee cup.

"Well, no time like the present," Nighthawk said.

"Yeah," Croyd said. "Very funny."

They went up to the room and stood together in front of the full-length mirror on the wall next to the bed. "Wait a minute." Nighthawk reached into his pants pocket and pulled out all the money he had. "Give me your cash. We might as well leave it on the nightstand to pay our bill. It can't do us any more good."

Croyd's meek-featured face crinkled in disappointment. "Much as I hate to part with money, you're right." He pulled out his cash and sighed. "Now look into the mirror."

The Motherfucking Apotheosis of Todd Motherfucking Taszycki

By Christopher Rowe

T FEATHERED THE JOYSTICK to the right. He felt the tower crane's cabling respond as he split his attention between the video feed on his control panel and the real-world view of the three-and-a-half-yard bucket hundreds of feet below. The bucket, carrying fourteen thousand pounds of wet concrete, shifted a few feet and came to a rest precisely on the mark his rigger had spray-painted on the ground in the middle of the busy construction site.

"That where you want it, boss?" TT asked.

"X marks the spot, TT," the rigger replied, his voice crackling in TT's earpiece.

"Fucking A," said TT.

The site foreman broke in, then. "Remember to watch your language on the radio today, TT," he said. "When the investors get here they want to get wired up when we give them their hardhats. They'll be listening."

TT rolled his eyes. He knew exactly who the "investors" on this project were and he doubted a bunch of motherfucking mob types were going to care much about whatever colorful words might float down from the crane's operating cabin while they toured the site. Still, if he could rein it in around Ma and that piss-drunk son-of-a-bitch Father Dobrzycki then he could watch his tongue around a bunch of suited-up assholes who were probably packing guns.

Just then he saw a pair of SUVs pull into the fenced parking lot.

TT was only twenty-six and had excellent vision, and had been up in the cabin long enough to learn to recognize things from above that most people normally never even *saw* from above. So he could tell easy that these were a pair of black, late-model Suburbans, windows tinted way darker than the legal limit. Not that he needed to actually see them to guess those details. Fucking mob guys all drove the same cars.

He checked the job list the foreman had handed him that morning at seven. Next up was unloading some truckloads of girders, but TT didn't see any eighteen-wheelers in the delivery yard yet—probably stuck in traffic, the poor assholes—so he figured he'd be sitting tight for a little bit. He reached into his lunch pail and took out his little pair of field glasses and the bird-watching log his younger brother Sonny had given him for Christmas. Last year, TT had been into Chicago's architecture. This year it was birds. There was a lot of time to look at shit from the crane, and you couldn't beat the view.

"Holy shit, take a look at this guy," came a voice over the radio. "They ain't going to find a lid that'll fit *him*."

That was Joey Campsos down in the welding shop. TT waited for Joey to get dinged on his language, but looking down, he saw that the foreman was busy shaking hands with some suits standing by the gate. One of the suits looked . . . odd.

TT trained his field glasses on the little gathering and saw what was fucked up about the guy Joey had seen. He was an ace or a joker or something. Big guy, all bulked out, which wasn't that weird. What was weird was that the motherfucker was half *tiger*. Not split top and bottom like the old goat-legged joker actor who advertised prescription drugs to keep your cock hard on TV. Like, down the middle. Like his left half was some big muscly mook like mob guys always kept around and his right half was a motherfucking *tiger*.

TT opened up his bird-watching log to the blank pages in the back and wrote MOTHERFUCKING TIGER MAN in careful block letters.

He did not, however, get to add any new birds to the book over the next half hour. The downtown Chicago high-rise taking shape around him was used as perching space by a lot of birds, but none he hadn't seen already. After a while, TT got bored looking at starlings and pigeons and decided to watch the mob guys and their tiger man bodyguard tour the site.

Huh, TT thought, *one of them's just a fucking kid.*

The lone member of the tour group taking their time checking out the site who was *not* wearing a slick gray business suit was a black-haired kid, maybe sixteen. He was wearing a white tracksuit. Through the binoculars, TT could make out the gold chains the kid was wearing, which probably meant they were some pretty fucking big gold chains. The guys in business suits—all wearing hardhats now except for tiger man—deferred to the kid.

Must be some high-up mob fucker's son getting his feet wet on an easy project, thought TT. He was losing interest, though—the tiger man wasn't actually *doing* anything—when the foreman came over the radio.

"Hey TT, the iron is inbound and our guests want to see the crane operate. When the beams are unchained move a bundle of them up to sixteen, okay?"

The sixteenth floor was currently the highest floor of what would eventually be a forty-story office building. TT watched two trucks slowly make their way into the unloading yard and began to manipulate the controls of the crane. He wasn't exactly nervous about being watched by the mob guys, but he was extra careful in lowering the hook for the truck drivers and the yard hands to attach to a bundle of girders.

Once the load was secure, TT began the delicate process of maneuvering it over the site and up to the sixteenth floor, where a crew was waiting to guide it in. The video feed on the jib was less useful to him during the move than it was during loading and unloading, so he was looking out and down at the carefully balanced load when he saw one of the truck drivers crouch on the bed of his trailer and *jump* from the unloading yard, arcing up and over the welding shop and the architect's trailer, to land among the mob guys.

"What the fuck?"

The mikes of the radio system were voice-activated, so TT

guessed he would have been in trouble with the foreman for offending the delicate sensibilities of the investors, but the investors were busy pulling out handguns and unloading on the truck driver. The truck driver who, TT could see, was landing some serious blows on the suits, sending a couple of them flying halfway across the site as he watched. One suit wasn't shooting, though, he was hustling the kid in the tracksuit back toward the parking lot.

"Fuck, the beams!" TT remembered. He stopped the load in its swing up and over, slightly overcorrecting and feeling the sway in the crane mast as the tons of steel came to a halt. But he shouldn't feel *that* much of a sway.

The radio was useless now, voices overlapping and cutting one another off as guys from all over the site yelled at the foreman to get down while the mob guys yelled and cursed. At least one of the mooks who'd gone flying was still alive and conscious; he was screaming. There was no way anybody would hear TT ask for somebody to get eyes on the tower to see what was causing it to vibrate.

"Shit, shit, shit," said TT as alarms sounded. The load suspended from the jib was shifting, which was bad enough. But he was getting icons flashed across the panel that indicated the whole crane was losing stability.

He cycled through the camera feeds until he found one looking straight down from beneath his control booth, and was astonished by what he saw. The jumping truck driver was now climbing the mast, reaching up for a crossbar and launching himself up fifteen or twenty feet at a time to catch the next. And right below, closing fast, came the tiger man.

"It's a hit. It's a fucking mob hit," said TT. "With motherfucking aces, oh shit."

The tiger man didn't launch himself up in jumps like the truck driver, the truck driver, who, TT could now see, was an old man. Like a hundred years old or something, but with arms and legs and a neck as big around as TT's torso. No, the tiger man just climbed, but he climbed fucking *fast*.

What the hell are they doing coming up here? TT wondered, but then, finally, a voice broke through the chaotic chatter on the radio. It was the foreman, screaming, "TT! Move the beams! Move the fucking beams!"

TT looked out at the boom. The girders were tilting badly and would soon slip free of the cable loops holding them. And if they fell, they would fall . . .

Right into the fucking parking lot! Right onto those fucking Suburbans! That's what the old man is doing, he's trying to crush that mob kid!

The old man was no longer climbing, though. He'd made his way to the slowing unit just aft of TT's cabin and was now running along the jib like he was just running down the street, headed for the hoist unit with its drum and gearbox. Tiger man was right behind him, reaching out, then yes, catching the old man before he could do whatever he was planning to do to the cable.

Tear it right in fucking two, I guess.

Then the two aces were trading blows, hitting each other so hard that TT could feel the vibrations traveling through the crane's superstructure. The old man staggered back, blood flowing down one side of his face from where the tiger man's claws had opened up a trio of ugly gashes, and the tiger man closed in.

But the fall was a feint. When the tiger man kicked out, trying to send the old man off the crane, the old man caught his tiger leg and lifted the mobster high. He swung the tiger man down hard against the jib's metal lattice, looking like a steel driver swinging a hammer down on a spike, except the hammer was a twisting, spitting, clawing ace. An ace who slumped, dead or unconscious, once he struck the crane.

The old man turned his back on his foe and walked over to the hoist unit. Then, proving TT's prediction true, he reached out and rested one hand on the main cable array. He squeezed his fingers together, and the strands parted. Below, the load fell.

"Oh, fuck. No!"

Then, in the operating cabin of a Liebherr tower crane situated in a construction site near Chicago's Loop, something happened that had happened thousands of times before across the world over the previous sixty years. Something that had been studied and speculated upon by the finest minds of more than one planet.

Inside Todd Taszycki, a change occurred on, at least, the chromosomal level. Some of those fine minds had theorized that the change occurred even more fundamentally than that, at the level of gluons and gauge basins, right down at the very bottom of matter, where the world becomes impossible to both understand and predict at the same time.

Inside Todd Taszycki, a card turned.

Outside, the girders surrendered to gravity and plummeted toward the parking lot below. TT saw people scattering.

He reached out.

And a superstructure of tightly spaced glowing neon-yellow I-beams came into existence below the falling steel, catching the girders in a net that bent, but did not break. TT felt the weight of the fallen load in his mind and instinctively added more support to the structure he had created.

Sweat dripped into his eyes and he reached up and pulled off his hardhat, absent-mindedly pulling the squawking earpiece out as he did so. He risked a glance out along the crane and saw that the old man and the tiger man were both gone.

Below, the Suburbans went peeling out of the lot, heedless of traffic.

The glowing yellow structure stabilized, and TT realized it was because he was getting used to the feel of it in his mind. He could sense the matter and the energy of it, he could *direct* the matter and energy of it.

"Well, fuck me," said TT.

TT had a cousin, Sylvia, who was a meteorologist at a TV station up in Green Bay, and a nephew, Tobias, who edited a trucking magazine. So technically speaking, he'd been around reporters before. Sylvia and Toby, though, weren't assholes.

"Todd! Todd! Is this the first time you've used your powers to save someone's life?"

"Mr. Tad . . . Tatsicko! Can you do anything else besides create magic girders? Can you fly? Can you shoot rays out of your eyes?"

"Will you be keeping your job as a crane operator, Todd?"

"Are you married? Have a special someone?"

"What does your family think about your ace power?"

Oh Christ, that last one got his attention. With the way Ma kept three televisions going all the time, not to mention her police scanner, not to mention his sister Margaret the firefighter probably having heard all about this from the emergency crews who had showed up after everything had already settled down, there was no fucking way his mother and his siblings wouldn't have heard about his "ace debut" already.

TT didn't have a clue how to answer any of the questions, didn't know which one to try to answer first, didn't know which one of the many cameras he was supposed to be looking at. Luckily, Local #221 had proved again what his pops had always said when he first brought TT into the construction business: "Don't look at dues as a cut out of your check. Look at 'em as an investment."

In this case, his investment had paid for the services of a union lawyer, a guy named Kassam who maybe wasn't as slick as the lawyers on Ma's programs but at least he knew how to talk to the media.

"It's Mr. Taszycki," said Kassam, and he spelled it out, spelled it right and everything. "And he doesn't have anything to say at this time, other than that he's glad that nobody was hurt in the incident."

The "incident," yeah, TT guessed that's what it fucking was. Tiger man fighting off a super-strong old guy trying to pull off a mob hit by pulling down his crane. None of the reporters had asked about any of that, though, which was kind of fucking odd, now that TT thought about it.

"Hey," he asked the lawyer, "what about those motherfuckers in the Suburbans?"

Unfortunately, a couple of the reporters heard him ask and they started in with the yelling bullshit again. But the lawyer and the shop steward hustled TT away from the scrum and into the architect's trailer while the foreman and a couple of the guys kept the reporters from following them.

"We don't want to get into any details of what caused the accident, TT," said the steward, who was, really, kind of a weaselly fucker TT had never gotten along with. "The main investor is pissed off that his son came so close to buying it and he's not a man who likes publicity."

"But it was a fucking mob hit," said TT. "We didn't have anything to do with it. We should call the fucking cops or something, shouldn't we?"

"It would be the Feds if we were going to call anybody," said the lawyer. "But we're not going to make any such calls. Though I'm sure you'll be contacted by them soon enough. Not the organized crime guys, though. SCARE or somebody like that. They're always interested in new aces."

"I don't want anything to do with any of that," said TT. "I don't know what happened out there. I should, I don't know, go to the fucking doctor or something."

"What I advise you to do," said the lawyer, "is seek legal counsel as soon as possible. I can make some recommendations. The reporters will file their stories and forget about you, hopefully, so long as you keep your head down and don't start fighting crime or something stupid like that. But even if the government doesn't come sniffing around, somebody will. Be careful, TT."

And that was pretty much that for TT's debut as a superpowered construction worker. Catching the falling I-beams then lowering them to the ground had been easy compared to all the bullshit that followed talking to the union and the construction company and the lawyers and the reporters. But at the end of the day, TT found himself in the mobile locker room with the rest of the crew, like usual.

The trailer was big enough for twelve showers and a bank of lockers, and the crew was big enough that it was always crowded in there come five o'clock. But today, TT noticed, he didn't have to elbow his way to his locker and wait in line for the shower. The other guys kind of made way for him in a way that wasn't comfortable at all.

Finally, he said, "C'mon, what the fuck is this? You assholes going to treat me different now? I didn't ask to get the virus and if any of you motherfuckers had been paying attention in sixth-grade science you'd know it ain't catching. At least I didn't grow three more cocks or something."

Bell, one of the riveters, said, "That'd give you a total of three, then," and the other guys all laughed and then it was more or less back to normal until TT pulled his phone down from the little shelf at the top of his locker and saw that he had a hundred and nine missed calls and forty voice mails. Most of them from Ma.

TT lived in a room above his mother's garage, and it would take him about an hour to get home, where she'd be fixing supper for him and for whichever of his sisters and brothers would be coming over tonight. On a Friday night, there would be more of them than usual. Hell, on a Friday night when one of the siblings had been on the local news all afternoon for being a fucking ace *all* of them might show up. Ma would have to put the extra leaf in the dining room table.

That piss-drunk son-of-a-bitch Father Dobrzycki would probably wander over from the Polonia Hall, too. Better stop for extra wine, then.

He was always one of the first guys to arrive on the site in the morning, which meant his truck was parked at the far end of the row. Parking was tight enough that there was a rule that you took the farthest space available when you arrived. TT had the same *We Build Chicago* bumper sticker that most of the other trucks and cars did on his F-250, and his wasn't even the only F-250. So TT figured it was either just a coincidence or because his vehicle was the most secluded from the street that the old man had crawled into the plastic-lined bed of his truck.

TT thought he was just some homeless dude at first sight, but then the old man rolled over and those three gaping wounds were still bleeding on his face from where the tiger man had clawed him. The old man looked different, though. His arms and legs weren't so heavily muscled. In fact, his coveralls hung off him like they were a couple of sizes too big. He'd actually fucking *shrunk* since his fight up on the crane.

Somebody yelled at him to have a good weekend and to try and stay out of the papers and TT threw up a hand, waving in response. The old man looked out at him from his hiding space, held up a finger in front of his lips asking TT to keep quiet.

This was a fucked-up situation.

TT walked over to the driver's-side door of the pickup and stepped up on the footrail where he could lean in and open the toolbox behind the cab. He looked around, but nobody was close.

"What's up, *dziadek*?" he asked.

The old man gave him a ghastly grin. TT could see some of his teeth through his torn open cheek.

"I have no *wnuki* that I know of," he said. "But I have been called grandfather before. Recently, in fact. Or, rather, ten years from now."

Oh yeah, this was making more fucking sense all the time.

"I'm going to get you to the ER, old man. And you should try not to talk. It makes you bleed more and it ain't too fucking pretty, neither."

"No," said the old man. "No hospitals. No police. No authorities. I will heal in time, Hardhat."

TT supposed that wasn't that weird a thing to call him, given that he was, in fact, carrying a hardhat. Still, he said, "Name's Todd Taszycki. TT unless you're my mother or my priest."

"I know your name," said the old man. "I know all about you."

And then he passed out.

TT figured his big sister Lynette, an ER nurse, would probably be at the house and he was right. Her old blue Saturn was parked on the street among a half dozen other cars belonging to various of his siblings. Because he still lived at home, TT rated off-street parking and pulled into the driveway, parking in front of the detached garage and interrupting the basketball game his brothers Caleb and Sonny were playing.

"Let's see it, TT," said Sonny, not even saying hello. "Build something."

Sonny was the youngest of the family, nineteen but living in the dorms at Northwestern. Caleb, who managed a grocery store, was the oldest. He said, "Leave him alone, kid, he's had a rough day."

"Fucking right I have," said TT. "Not as rough as my passenger here, though. Caleb, give me a hand getting him into the house. Sonny, run and get Lynette."

Then it was a gang of Taszyckis hustling to get the unconscious old man spread out on the picnic table in Ma's sunroom and Lynette yelling at them to keep clear or else go get something for her or else give her a hand.

"He has to have lost a lot of blood," she told TT. "But I don't even know if I should sew him up. Look, you can see the wounds closing on their own. I never had to treat an ace before."

"Why'd you bring him here?" Charlotte asked. She was heavily pregnant and had always been a worrier.

"What the fuck was I supposed to do with him?" TT asked.

"Todd!" Ma said. "Don't talk to your sister that way. Or in front of company. Or ever."

TT blushed and ducked his head. "Right, right. Sorry, Ma. Sorry, Charlotte."

The old man stirred then, and by this point the wounds really had closed all the way. He came to lying flat on his back surrounded by almost a dozen people, all leaning in and looking at him.

He blinked once, then said, *"Gdzie ja jestem?"*

"'Where am I?' Is that what he said?" asked Sonny. Sonny was fewer years away from Polish Scouts language lessons than the rest of them.

Ma patted the old man's hand and said, "A safe place. You're in a safe place."

Which was all well and good, and old Polish home week was a fine thing and all, but TT couldn't stop thinking about how the old man had flung the tiger man around and tried to kill the mob kid and his minders. In a way, it was good to have something to think about besides the glowing yellow girders.

Not that Ma was going to let him forget about that anytime soon.

"So," she said, turning on him. "So I see on television that you are an ace now? When were you going to tell us?"

"I would have told you if I fu—I would have told you if I knew, Ma," TT insisted. "But this was the first time anything like this has ever happened."

"I thought wild cards turned when you were a kid," said Caleb, and TT saw Lynette starting to answer him, but the old man startled them all by sitting up and it was he who answered.

"I was in my forties when the devil marked me," he said.

Ma and Charlotte crossed themselves, and then everybody else looked kind of embarrassed and followed suit.

Lynette said, "When the virus first hit New York it affected people of all ages. Caleb's right that it mostly expresses at puberty now, but there are plenty of exceptions."

TT was glad that the guys at work couldn't hear anything suggesting that he'd just now hit puberty.

Ma was staring at the old man closely. She said, "How old are you now?"

The old man shrugged. "Very old. Very old."

"You're Hardhat!" Sonny said, practically shouting. "You're the ace that fought the Lizard King and that other guy back in the sixties! You were in that movie about Destiny! Only the guy they had playing you didn't look much like you. And he sure as hell wasn't Polish."

The old man shrugged again. "It was in 1970."

The look on Sonny's face told them all that the kid didn't think that made much difference, but TT was struggling to remember the details of the fight from the Oliver Stone movie about the Lizard King. All he remembered was a guy wearing a hardhat getting his ass kicked by Kurt Russell, which wasn't particularly helpful, as Kurt Russell was always kicking guys' asses.

"So you're all mobbed up now?" TT asked. "Working as a hit man in your golden years?"

"No," said the old man. "No, it is not like that. I am . . . I am working to save people. Girls."

"There was a daughter," said Ma, nodding. "There was a story in *Life* about you after you disappeared." Ma and her articles. How did she remember this stuff? "They interviewed Dr. Tachyon. He said you lost track of your family after World War Two and you were trying to find them. That you'd spent all those years since the war trying to find them."

"But I never did, even after the alien's virus marked me. I tried for a while longer, learning many dark things about my new country. So when I realized that I would never find my wife and daughter, I decided to use the devil's gift to save other wives and daughters."

TT thought about what he knew about the Chicago mob, the rumors he'd heard his whole life, and his lip curled. "You mean the girls that wind up working for the Families," he said. "The ones they kidnap or whatever."

"They are not all kidnapped, sadly," said the old man. "Some of them choose the life of their own free will, though how a teenaged girl can make such a choice for herself is beyond me. They all learn, though. Even the ones who choose the life come to regret that decision. As for the others, the ones who did not choose, they come to despair even more quickly."

"But the guy you tried to kill today"—and TT heard Ma gasp at that—"he was just a kid. Sixteen or seventeen at the most."

"He is fifteen," said the old man. "His name is Giovanni Galante and he will turn sixteen in three days. And on that day, he will kill for the first time."

TT said, "Mob guys got some kind of fucked-up ritual where you *kill* somebody when you turn sixteen?" Ma didn't even shush him.

"No, no," said the old man. "A girl will be at the celebration. A gift from his father. She will do something to anger him and he will stab her to death with the knife he uses to cut his steak."

TT looked around at his gathered siblings and at his mother. None of them said anything. In fact, they were all looking at him like *he* was the one who should fucking say something.

Finally, he asked, "Um, and how exactly do you know that, old-timer?"

In response, the old man turned to Ma. "Madame, with your permission, I believe it would be best if I spoke to young Todd alone."

And surprising everyone, Ma nodded. "You look like you're feeling much better, Mr. . . . Grabowski, wasn't it? It does sound like you've got some things to say that may better be said in private. Unless you want me to send for Father? When was the last time you made confession?"

The old man, Grabowski, looked up at the ceiling the way people do when they're trying to remember something. "That is difficult to say, madame. It was either a long time ago or will happen a long time from now."

TT was catching a brain wave from the old man that indicated he wasn't exactly grounded in the here and now, which didn't make him much look forward to a one-on-one conversation. But Ma seemed to think it was a good idea, so he led Grabowski outside and into the workshop on the first floor of the two-car garage.

One side of the garage was given over to a workbench and room to work on projects. A small car draped in a tarp was parked on the other side. It was the candy-red 1973 Polski Fiat 126p Pops had imported before TT was born, and he and his siblings had made a long slow family project of restoring it. Right now they were waiting on some period headlamps from an Austrian dealer Sonny had found on the Internet.

"Okay, Mr. Grabowski," TT said. "You haven't said a whole lot since I found you in my truck, but almost everything you *have* said has been fucking crazy. What's the story?"

The old man nodded and leaned wearily against the workbench. "It is a long story. And a strange one," he said.

"I don't have to be back to work until Monday morning," TT said.

It was a pretty fucked-up story.

"I was a scholar," said Wojtek Grabowski. "But then the Germans came so I fought them. And then the Russians came, and I fought them, too."

"Yeah, I thought the Russians and the Germans fought against each other in that war," said TT.

"Yes," said Grabowski. "And everyone fought the Poles. It has always been this way."

TT wasn't exactly sure about that, as it seemed a little paranoid, but then again Pops always had bitched about the Russians a lot.

"I guess the timing with the virus didn't work out for you to be able to get all bulked up and throw tanks around and shit, though," said TT. He knew that wild cards hadn't started turning until after World War II.

"No, no," said the old man. "That was many years later, in California. Long after I had left Europe. Just before I went back."

TT turned and opened the little fridge sitting next to one of the garage's red tool chests. He pulled out a bottle of Luksusowa vodka then looked around for anything that would do for glasses.

Grabowski chuckled and took the bottle from him, opened it, and turned it up, taking a long swallow. He sighed deeply and said, "This is the real stuff, eh? Not rye or grain. Potatoes!" He laughed and handed the bottle back over.

TT gave an appraising look to its mouth, then said, "Fuck it, I've already got the worst thing I could catch off you, anyway, right?" He took a slightly less generous slug than the old man had, then asked, "So how'd you wind up in California? How'd you wind up in the States at all?"

"I came here for the only reason a man like me ever has to leave behind one's nation, one's home, culture, all of it."

"Chasing a dream?"

Grabowski held his hand out for the bottle. "Chasing a woman," he said, and grinned.

TT rolled his eyes. Old guys. What are you going to do?

"Okay," said the younger man. "Did you catch her?"

Then, to TT's shock, Grabowski put one hand to his haggard face and let out a sob. "No. No, I never found her. Oh, Anna. Oh, God, oh, my Anna!"

TT felt just about as fucking uncomfortable as he ever had. He started to pat the old man on the shoulder, but shit, maybe he should hug him or something. Finally, he just said, "Maybe have another slug of that vodka?"

Grabowski did, then took a deep breath. "We were married by a priest who helped hide us in the woods. She was another of the fighters, younger than me by three years, but wiser by far. I do not know why she loved me. It was a great mystery."

TT shrugged. "Maybe you were just the best-looking guy in the woods."

Grabowski half smiled at that. "When she got pregnant, I moved heaven and earth to get her out of the country. There was a British agent who we worked with sometimes, and he smuggled Anna out. She was already showing, but I swore I would do all I could to join her in America before our child was born. This was after the Russians had taken over our country."

He held the bottle out for TT to take, and TT sipped a bit. "That must have been pretty fucking hard on you two," he said.

"Yes," said Grabowski. "Yes, pretty fucking hard." The expletive was unexpected coming from the old man, but it didn't sound wrong at all. "It was '46 before I made it to America. I was on a transport packed with people from all over Europe and North Africa, anchored off Governors Island. This was September. *That* September."

"When the virus hit New York," said TT.

"We could hear the screams from across the water. They kept us aboard for three more weeks. Some thought we had been forgotten or that we were to be turned back. Some even jumped the rails and tried to swim for it. I do not know if any of those made it to shore. All I know is that eventually they processed us, and I found myself in the city with very little English, no friends, no money. It was . . . *bewildering.*"

"I fucking bet," said TT. "Were you supposed to meet . . . um . . . Anna, in New York someplace?"

"Yes, but she was not there. No one I spoke to had any information. I asked at the churches and at the consulates. I went to the Polish neighborhoods and asked at the groceries and the laundries. I asked everyone. I asked everyone I met for the next twenty-five years."

TT studied the scuff marks on his steel-toed boots.

"I do not know whether I gave up before the devil marked me or after," Grabowski continued. "But it was around then. I . . . became what I have become . . . and had the fight your brother spoke of with those children in San Francisco. And then the alien doctor came, as your mother said. He used his contacts with the American government to help me look for Anna for a little while, but I could tell that he thought it was hopeless. We did not find her.

"But I *did* find someone. I found a girl who *looked* like my Anna, who I imagined might have been my own daughter, walking the streets in Oakland. She was a Polish girl, newly come to America, who had fallen in with very bad men. Very bad men who forced her to do very bad things."

"She was a hooker or something? How bad are we talking?" asked TT.

"Yes, a prostitute. They forced that life upon her. She was afraid of me, especially after I . . . I . . . removed the threat of the very bad men. But she told me how she had come to be on the streets. She told me there were others like her. Many others. And I decided something. I decided that since I could not find my wife and child, since I could not save them, I would save others. The wives and children of other men who did not have the strength the curse had given me."

"You're saying you started fucking up pimps in California?"

Grabowski took the bottle back. "Not the pimps, no. And not in California. Even after so long in America, I did not have the knowledge I needed to make a real difference. I did not know how criminal syndicates worked in America, I did not know the official laws of the government or the unofficial laws of the street. But I told you that before the war I was a scholar. I had been studying to be a lawyer. In Poland, you see, where many of these girls were coming from, I knew better how things worked, even though much had changed under the Communists. So I went back."

"To Poland? What, after the fight with Lizard King? Is that why I've never heard of you? You some kind of secret Iron Curtain super-guy?"

"No, no. Not the way you mean. Secret, yes, but secret especially from the governments there. The Polish government, *all* of the client states of the Russians, had very strict policies about the wild card. There were very few aces or jokers there, and those who made themselves known disappeared in the state apparatus immediately. I was, what is the word? *Clandestine*."

"Like I said, secret Iron Curtain super-guy. Fighting crime and communism! Here's to you!" TT raised the bottle in a mock toast.

"I did not fight communism," said Grabowski. "And the people I worked against were often not criminals, or at least they were not treated as such. Americans believe that when the Party lost control of Russia and the other countries that mobsters suddenly appeared and took control of everything. That is ridiculous. It is the same people! The men smuggling girls to the West then were soldiers and bureaucrats. When the states collapsed, they simply shrugged off their uniforms in favor of slick suits. That is why it is impossible today to tell the difference between a member of the secret police and a mobster there, because they are one and the same."

"So how long did you do that? Bust up slavery rings behind the Iron Curtain, I mean?"

"Long time. A very long time, even after the Curtain fell. I was in Poland, Czechoslovakia, the Russian states, for . . . over forty-five years. I returned to America in 2015."

TT pointedly looked at the calendar hanging on the pegboard wall next to Grabowski. "See where it says July 2007 there, boss?"

Grabowski got a faraway look in his eye. "In July 2007, where was I, where was I? Ah! I have it. Kiev. I remember because the man I killed there was an ace who worked for the Ukrainian government. An ugly business, and far more public than most of my activities."

TT decided to let it go, or at least to set it aside for the moment. "So, eventually, whenever, you came back to the States. Why?"

"Because I learned a name. The name of the man who was responsible for much of the human trafficking between the old bloc and America. A name that came with a reputation as black as any I had ever heard."

"You're about to tell me who this was, and it's going to turn out to be that fucking mob kid, isn't it?"

"His name is Giovanni Galante. And after almost two years I finally learned where and when he would be. A particular time and date, a particular place. A poker game at the Palmer House."

"See," said TT, deciding not to let it lie there this time. "This is where you kind of lose me. This being the summer of 2007 and all."

"Yes, so it says in the newspapers. I do not know how I came to be here—to be *now*. At the card game, where I went to kill Galante, I fought with the same ace you saw me fight this morning, except that he was older. There were gunshots, gouts of flame, wild card powers of all kinds. Then the room was empty and I was alone there, naked. I took clothes from another room and soon learned that I had been thrown into the past. This was almost a month gone, now."

"And you've spent that time figuring out how to finish your hit on the Galante kid."

Grabowski nodded his head. "He will become a monster. I told you, he is only days away from killing the first of many young women he will murder by the time he is your age."

"I don't know how you expect me to believe any of that," said TT.

"You must believe me. From what I know about you, young man, you will also want to *help* me."

"Help kill a teenager? No fucking way. And what do you know about me, anyway? You said something like that before you passed out back at the site."

"You are the new Hardhat. You are Todd Taszycki, from the television program. They played it even in Poland and Russia. You are the famous Polish-American construction worker from Chicago who can create and manipulate girders of yellow energy."

TT shrugged. "You could get all that from just seeing me this morning, old man. Don't mean you're from the future."

Grabowski looked at TT for a long moment, long enough that TT got antsy. The old man was looking at him like he felt *sorry* for him.

"Listen to me," Grabowski said. "I know things that are going to happen to you. You will be famous. You will travel with other aces to fight in Egypt. And you will die."

"That supposed to be some kind of prophecy?"

"It is a *memory*!" Grabowski roared, leaping across the garage far more quickly than his appearance allowed for and grabbing TT by the shoulders. "Whether you believe me or not, I remember it! You go on the television to play games with other so-called heroes, but then you become a hero for real. You go to fight at the Nile River, and there, you will die!"

TT shook himself free of the old man's grip. "Die saving innocent people, right?"

Grabowski eyed him up and down. "Yes. Hundreds of them."

Sonny stuck his head in the door. "Ma says you guys should come eat."

TT waved. "Tell her we'll be there in just a minute."

Sonny looked for a second like he was going to stick around, but then he caught the mood in the garage and ducked out.

"Look," said TT, "I'm not going to let you kill some fucking sixteen-year-old kid. It doesn't matter if you're some kind of fucking time traveler or not. And I'm sure as fuck not going to help you."

Grabowski said, "We can discuss Galante later. I am beginning to think my purpose in being here has little to do with him and everything to do with you."

"What about me?"

"Perhaps I am here to save you."

TT nodded at the door. "Nah, I don't need saving. Big-time fucking hero, remember? That's me."

Ma had commandeered every one of TT's siblings present to throw together an authentic Polish dinner in honor, she said, of Grabowski coming to teach TT to be a hero, though where she had gotten that idea TT couldn't say.

So the family and their unexpected guest sat down to pierogis with white mushrooms and cabbage, tripe soup, roasted lamb with stewed beetroots, and a big pudding for dessert. All washed down with cold bottles of Żywiec beer. TT hadn't had that much Polish fare in one sitting in a long time, since Ma kept trim by eating mainly vegetarian dishes, but he sensed he shouldn't mention that.

After dinner, Sonny booted up his laptop and started reading highlights aloud from articles about the wild card virus, about aces and jokers and the impact of a turned card on family life. Because a card had turned in the Taszycki family, and TT's siblings were curious to a one about it.

Charlotte held her hands over her abdomen. "Should I be worried about the baby?"

TT hadn't even thought about that. Fuck, come to think about it he did remember something about how the virus spread among family members, but—

"Nah," said Sonny, reading off his screen. "The odds of it showing up in a nephew or niece aren't any higher than among the general population. Todd was a latent, that's all, and the stress of seeing those girders fall triggered his card."

TT had described the near disaster to his family, kind of glossing over the parts where their new pal Grabowski was trying to *kill a fucking kid* and fighting a tiger man, though the shape he'd been in when TT had pulled him out of the truck had kind of clued them in that there was more to the story than what he was telling. TT didn't know yet what he was going to do yet about Grabowski's declared intentions.

There was also all this time-travel bullshit to think about. TT didn't suppose it was any more impossible than aliens and flying women, or, for that matter, tiger men and projecting glowing yellow I-beams. It didn't feel like the truth, exactly, but neither did he have old Grabowski pegged as a liar, and TT put a lot of store in his instincts. Not having a solid instinct on the situation was, in fact, kind of fucking upsetting, if TT was being honest with himself.

The siblings who lived farthest from home left earliest, drifting off one at a time until there were just Sonny, who was spending the weekend at home from his summer classes to get some laundry done, and TT, who of course lived there full-time. Ma had made it clear at dinner that Grabowski would be taking TT's room over the garage and TT would be bunking it on the other twin bed in Sonny's room, which struck TT as just a tiny bit of bullshit, but then he guessed that for all her talk about welcome to our home and here's a big Polish dinner maybe she didn't want the old ace actually sleeping under her roof.

Ma turned in about eleven, and Sonny disappeared down to the den in the basement to play video games or surf the internet or something. TT walked Grabowski out to the garage, the two of them drinking the last bottles of Żywiec.

"You are lucky to have such a family. They are lucky to have you," said the old man.

TT nodded. Yeah, family was a big deal, but he didn't feel like talking about it with this guy who was at least a would-be murderer and, for all TT knew, was already a murderer in fact. Time-traveling murderer with super-strength. So instead of replying to what Grabowski had actually said, he said, "We're going to have to have another talk in the morning."

Grabowski said, "Yes. A good long talk."

TT wandered down to the den, where Sonny was blowing up aliens or saving princesses or whatever the fuck it was he was doing with all the button mashing and jittering around on the couch.

"Hey," he said. "Hey, shut that shit down. I need you to look something up for me."

"Hang on," said Sonny.

"C'mon, Sonny, push pause or whatever, I need a favor."

The images on the screen froze and Sonny was looking up at him. "A *favor*? Since when do you ask me for favors?"

"Since right fucking now and don't make a big fucking deal of it, okay? I need you to punch up on your computer there and see if there's been any news about a fight between aces in . . . oh fuck, where did he say? Kiev! Look up ace fights in Kiev."

Sonny gave him a mystified look, but pulled his laptop off the coffee table and set to typing. In just a few minutes, he said, "Huh."

"Huh what?"

"How did you hear about this? Yeah, see, there was a fight in a warehouse at the Kiev airport that sent a bunch of people to the hospital. A guy with some kind of magnetic powers or something fought a super-strong . . . old man. Hey! Is that *our* old man? No, wait, of course not, couldn't be."

"Why not?" demanded TT. "Why couldn't it be our old man?"

Sonny pointed at the screen. "Because this just happened about twelve hours ago."

Oh yeah, thought TT. *One good fucking long talk is what we're going to have.*

But in the morning, he was gone, and goddamn if the son-of-a-bitch hadn't taken TT's truck.

"I still don't see why I can't drive. It's my car," said Sonny.

"Shut up," said TT. "I'm concentrating. Anyway, it was me fucking taught you to drive."

"Are you saying you didn't do a good job?"

TT turned Sonny's battered little Toyota into the parking lot of the Italian restaurant they'd been directed to and said again, "Shut up."

The union lawyer had been happy to take TT's call until he figured out that TT wasn't calling to talk about using his ace power to advance the cause of labor or whatever bullshit he was apparently imagining. But if he'd gotten kind of distant when TT had interrupted that line of thought, he'd gotten absolutely hostile when TT told him why he was actually calling. TT wanted to know where the Galante crime family hung out, and the lawyer was offended that TT thought he would know.

Of course, it turned out that he *did* know because he was a fucking lawyer for a construction union in Chicago, but that didn't stop him from being kind of pissy about the whole thing.

"Hey, TT," said Sonny. "There's your truck!"

"Oh, shit, that means he beat us here," said TT, pulling into a spot next to a shiny black Suburban and setting the parking brake.

"You don't have to do that, you know," said Sonny. "It's not like we're on a hill or anything."

"Shut the fuck up. Always set your parking brake, it's for fucking safety."

Sonny ignored that. "Are we going in? Or are you just going to use your spare keys and take the truck?"

"*You* are going home," said TT. "I'll be along in a little bit. I have to find Grabowski."

"Found him," said Sonny.

"What?"

Sonny pointed up to the roof of the single-story restaurant. Sure enough, there was the old man, back turned to them, stalking across to the opposite side. He looked different now, like he had when TT had first spotted him yesterday morning, all bulked up and as broad as he was tall.

"What's wrong with him?" Sonny asked. "He looks like he's dosed up with steroids or something. Is that his ace power?"

TT shrugged, getting out of the car. "I guess. Look, get out of here, okay? I'm going to go up there and talk to him."

Sonny nodded, awkwardly sliding from the passenger's seat over the parking brake and gearshift to take the wheel. TT walked into the alley between the restaurant and what looked to be an empty insurance office next door, hoping to find whatever ladder or fire escape Grabowski had used to get up top.

He didn't find anything, and then he remembered the jumps he'd seen the old man making yesterday. *How the fuck am I supposed to get up there?*

Well, the old man had obviously used *his* ace power to get to the roof.

TT hadn't tried to do anything with the glowing girders since the incident at the job site yesterday, despite Sonny's harassing him all morning while they ate the breakfast burritos Ma whipped up and then made the trek out to this suburban shopping district. But he could *feel* the power inside him all the time.

Working on instinct, TT constructed a glowing yellow staircase of girders in the alley. He idly wondered if he could make any other shapes besides the I-beams, but decided not to worry about it right then. He clambered up the structure and stepped onto the tarred roof.

Grabowski was on the opposite side, looking down over the edge.

"Hey!" TT shouted, trying for that goofy-ass tone of voice where you're trying to be quiet and to yell at the same time. "Wojtek! Hey!"

There was no response, so TT started across the roof. Trying again, he said, "Hey! Hardhat!"

At that, the old man turned.

TT stopped. Grabowski looked *mad*. Real mad. And mean. His T-shirt—oh for fuck's sake it was one of TT's T-shirts from his softball league and now look at it—was stretched out so far that the seams had split, showing the old man's boulder-like muscles.

Hairy bastard, TT thought unhelpfully, holding up both hands in a peace gesture.

The old man clearly wasn't interested in peace, though. He snorted like a bull, then charged like one, head bent low.

"What the fuck?" TT barely stepped aside in time, and even at that Grabowski's outspread left hand grazed him, barely fucking *grazed* him, and it was enough to send TT spinning. And it *hurt*.

"Hey, calm the fuck down!" TT shouted, but Grabowski was turning and charging again.

Only to come up dead against a wall of closely set glowing girders extending up from the roof like fence posts. TT heard the distinct sound of something hard and heavy striking steel, and he felt one of the girders come dangerously close to buckling. As soon as he was expending willpower to shore it up, Grabowski swung his other fist, landing a second blow on another of the girders. This one *did* buckle, falling toward TT, of fucking course, and so TT let it wink out of existence.

Another one disappeared, too, not because TT willed it but because Grabowski just plucked it up and threw it across the alley to the next rooftop, where it landed heavily against an air-conditioning unit. For all that TT could make them float in air and appear in different configurations, apparently the girders were as heavy as the real thing.

Which gave TT an idea.

In his softball league—TT captained a team for Saints Stanislaus and Stanislaus Church—TT had a pretty good batting average. And since he thought he was getting the hang of this girder generation and manipulation thing pretty well, he decided to take a swing at Grabowski.

Letting all the girders he had going dissipate into nothing, TT turned sideways to the old man, brought his hands up and back next to his right ear, and concentrated. A girder appeared, its I-shaped profile eighteen inches across, made up of glowing plates a couple of inches thick. TT guessed his creations defaulted to specs, which meant that since the girder was twenty feet long, despite the fact that it felt practically weightless in his hands, it weighed just a little more than half a ton.

He pivoted his hips, extended his arms, swung through.

Grabowski had been rushing TT, arms spread wide, and the beam struck him right at the waist.

"Holy shit," TT said, letting the beam fade and watching Hardhat fly through the air. The old man arced up and completely over the insurance office, disappearing as he plunged over the far end of the next building along, maybe a hundred yards away.

Hoping he hadn't killed the old man, TT hustled to the edge of the roof. He was just about to solve the problem of how to get across the alley with a girder when the access hatch to the restaurant flew open and a couple of suited dudes in sunglasses came climbing out, guns in their hands.

"What's all this fucking noise?" one of them asked. "How the hell did you get up here?"

TT held his hands up and looked around. With Grabowski out of sight and none of his girders in existence, there was no visual evidence of the fight they'd just had. Except for the crushed AC unit on the next roof, which the mob guys didn't appear to notice, the only thing out of the ordinary was TT himself.

"I'm, uh, I'm here to check the roof," TT improvised. "The property management company sent me."

The guy who'd spoken nodded at his partner, who walked over to TT and looked up and down the alley. "No ladder," he reported.

The first guy hadn't pointed his gun away from TT yet. He said,

"I'm going to ask you again, pal. What was all that racket? And how did you get up here?"

"What the fuck is that?" asked the second one, pointing with his gun into the sky above TT's head.

It was the last thing he would say for a while, because what he'd seen was Grabowski cannonballing up and over the insurance office to land right on top of the poor son-of-a-bitch. The old man tucked and rolled, coming up hard by the first guy, who opened up with his pistol at point-blank range, to no apparent effect.

Grabowski slapped the mook's pistol away hard enough that the guy went spinning, then followed through from the other direction with his left hand, catching the guy upside the head hard enough to lift him off the ground. Both of the mob guys were down for the count, and TT was starting to feel severely underprepared for continuing a fight with Wojtek Grabowski.

Another shot rang out. More mob guys were sticking their heads out of the trapdoor. TT hit the deck. Grabowski might number bulletproof among his ace powers but so far as TT knew, the girders were his whole fucking shtick.

"Get Khan up here!" one of the new mobsters shouted, then yelped as a thousand pounds of glowing steel materialized right above him, forcing him and his friends down into the building. TT laid another girder right beside the first, sealing the exit.

Then he decided maybe old Hardhat wasn't bulletproof after all, because Grabowski was on his knees next to one of the unconscious gunmen. As TT watched, the old man appeared to wither, or shrink, his heavily muscled arms and legs diminishing down to a size that matched his head and waist. He didn't look too fucking hot, but at least he didn't look so pissed off anymore, either.

"TT," he said, "I am sorry. I was preparing to tear through the roof when you appeared. I did not know it was you."

"Yeah, well—" TT cut off. One of the girders had just shifted by a couple of inches and it sure as shit wasn't him that had caused that. "Fuck, we've got to go. They've got somebody in there who can lift a thousand pounds."

Grabowski nodded. "Khan. The tiger. Can you hold him off? It will take me a few moments to recover."

TT laid another couple of girders atop the first pair, but didn't feel any more attempts to shift them.

"Um, there's nothing stopping that guy from just walking out the front door and jumping up here and kicking our asses, is there?"

The high-pitched honk of a foreign-car horn sounded from down in the alley. TT looked down. "Goddamnit, Sonny!"

The youngest Taszycki was leaning out the window of his Toyota, gesturing wildly. He caught sight of TT and shouted, "Hey, there's a ton of guys coming out the front doors! Come on!"

Grabowski was beside him, still looking kind of beat up and tired, no help there.

"Did they have slides on the playgrounds back in the old country?" TT asked.

Grabowski looked mystified until the I-beam appeared angling down to Sonny's car. TT picked the old man up like a groom carrying a bride and plopped his ass down on the girder. They were moving pretty fast when they got to the bottom, but it beat jumping, TT figured.

He opened the back door of Sonny's car and threw the old man in, then tumbled in after him. Sonny didn't even wait for him to close the door before he threw the Toyota into gear and peeled out.

As they cleared the mouth of the alley, a half dozen guys in suits went scrambling out of the way. Sonny slid onto the highway and ramped up the speed. TT looked out the back window but didn't see any signs that they were being followed.

Then he said, "Fuck, we left my truck."

Ma was a tall woman, and Wojtek Grabowski was a short man. These facts, combined with the way that Grabowski was slumping in a chair at the table in the kitchen while Ma read him the riot act, made TT think of all the times he'd seen one or the other of his siblings in that exact same position while they were growing up. Hell, he'd been in that position more than a time or two himself.

"Sonny is nineteen years old!" Ma said. "Nineteen! And now he's probably on some kind of Mafia hit list!"

That probably wasn't true, TT thought, and not exactly fucking fair to the old man. "Ma, I told Sonny to leave when we got to the restaurant."

She turned on him, finger raised, and said, "You, I'll get to in a minute."

Fucking great.

Luckily, Caleb and his husband, Steve-o, walked in just then, Steve-o twirling TT's keys around his finger. He tossed them over. "They were in the ignition," he said.

TT shot Grabowski a look and the old man spread his hands in apology, clearly glad of the distraction.

"No trouble, though?" TT asked them.

Caleb shook his head. "We didn't see a soul. There were a couple of cars in the parking lot of the restaurant but nobody hassled us or anything. We just drove up, Steve-o got into your truck, and then we came here."

"And you weren't followed?"

The two of them exchanged a look, then Caleb said, "Todd, I work at a grocery store. Steve-o is a dermatologist's PA. How would we know if we'd been followed?"

Which was fair enough, but still kind of fucking unfortunate. TT wished one of his siblings were a PI or something. Hopefully there wouldn't be any trouble, because as far as he knew, none of his brothers or sisters so much as owned a gun. Maybe he should call his cousin Babs. Her husband was always mouthing off about having been in Special Forces even though when you pressed him for details he claimed he couldn't talk about it.

"Madame," Grabowski said, "it was never my intention to put any of your sons in danger." His look took in all of them, and TT could tell Ma was about to explain that Steve-o was in fact her son-*in-law*, which she loved to do at any opportunity, but TT decided having that particular conversation with a hundred-year-old Polish Catholic who thought his wild card power was the touch of the devil might be something best left for another day. They had more pressing fucking problems.

"Yeah, speaking of your intentions, what was your plan once you tore a hole in the roof of that joint? Just jump in and start tearing guys apart with your bare hands?"

For what it was worth, Grabowski at least looked embarrassed. "I was hoping that Galante would be there."

"Oh for fu—you mean you don't even know if the kid you mean to kill was out there? Sounds to me like you just got in the mood to crack some skulls and went off script a little bit." TT was getting worked up. "And it turned out that tiger man was there, and I bet you didn't know that either, did you?"

Sonny chimed in, "What kind of tiger man? Like a joker or something?"

TT let out a frustrated sigh, looked over at his mother, and said, "Ma?"

She got it. "Okay, boys, let's let the aces have their talk. We can go out onto the sun porch and have some tea and Steve-o can remind Sonny about why he should wash his face every night."

"Ma!" Sonny said, but he was leaving with the rest of them.

When they were gone, Grabowski said, "You have a good family. It is hard to believe you left them to go on television."

"Yeah, well, that does sound like something I wouldn't do, especially on account of the fact that I've not fucking done it," said TT.

"Yet. You have not done it yet."

TT had been thinking about the whole time-travel angle. "Look, you think you're from the future or some crazy shit like that, right? But if you're here now, telling me this stuff, haven't you already changed the past? How do you know that the Galante kid will even still have a birthday party? His people have got to be kind of concerned about security at this point, them having been attacked by a crazy old man two days in a row now."

Grabowski shrugged uncomfortably. "I cannot take that risk. If I can save that girl, I must."

Which kind of turned the problem around on its head a little bit and now TT was the one who was uncomfortable. "I don't want any girl to die, either. I don't want *anybody* to get killed."

Grabowski looked at him. "That is why you went to Egypt, then? Because of all the refugees being killed by the soldiers?"

TT rolled his eyes. "I went to Massachusetts for Caleb's wedding. That's the farthest I've ever fucking been from this house, okay? There's no TV show! There's no refugees for me to rescue!"

"Not yet," Grabowski said again.

"Oh, for fuck's sake, let's just set that shit aside for now, all right? If you honest to God believe that some kidnapped girl is going to be, what did you say, given as a fucking gift to that little Mafia puke on his birthday then I'm with you on saving her. So long as we can do it without anybody getting killed. Which is why I think we should call the cops."

Grabowski shook his head. "And tell them what? That an old man with no identification papers believes he may know where a kidnapped girl is? No, I have gone to the authorities before and there are always more questions about me than about those I am trying to save. Besides, the Galantes, the Chicago police . . ."

Yeah, TT knew what that was about. The cops might not be all bought off like in the bad old days but there was bound to be someone in the department somewhere who would get wind of any investigation and tip off the guys in the suits. And who knew what they'd do to the girl if that happened?

"So what do you know about this girl anyway? Where's she at now? Can we just cross our fingers that tiger man isn't guarding her and go kick some Mafia ass and rescue her?"

"No, no," said Grabowski. "I am sorry, but I don't have those kind of details. I didn't learn of the girl's death until years after it happened when I began investigating Galante, putting together a dossier on him. The murder is a legend among Chicago criminals ten years from now. The boy cannot control his temper."

TT gave the old man a sour look. "Yeah, that's kind of fucking going around."

"I am sorry. You are right. When the anger comes upon me, I have difficulty controlling my actions."

"Well, we're going to have to work on that for this plan to work."

"What plan?"

"The plan we come up with where you and me go save the day, asshole."

"You know, I'm pretty sure my pops was on the crew that built this place," TT said. "I remember him telling me once about building some clubhouse for a club that would never let him join."

"Italians," said Grabowski, sitting beside TT in the cab of the pickup truck, "do not like Poles."

TT said, "Yeah, maybe in your time. I think Pops was talking more about how rich people don't like hanging out with construction workers at their la-di-da fucking country clubs."

There was actually some construction going on at the suburban club right now, looked maybe like a new locker room for the tennis courts, which was a lucky break. TT had eased his truck into the far end of the parking lot, where there was a trailer, some portable toilets, and a little fenced-off materials yard set up. There was nobody working the site on a Sunday afternoon, naturally, but TT figured none of the guests arriving up at the club's main building would give them a second glance. In fact, just to complete the picture . . .

"Here," he said, handing over a hardhat to Grabowski and plopping one down on his own head, "camouflage."

Grabowski had turned out to have a good eye for spotting which of the people milling around outside the clubhouse were actually security guards, which amounted to about eight guys, and which of the guests were probably armed as well, which accounted for pretty much everyone fucking else. TT had started to ask who the hell went to a kid's birthday party carrying but then he figured the answer was probably just "mobsters."

The plan wasn't complicated. The birthday party for the budding sociopath was already well under way, but if Grabowski's story was to be believed—and since TT was sitting there he supposed that he believed at least parts of it—the big surprise gift happened late in the festivities. They were making her jump out of a cake, the sick fucks.

"Ah, this is unfortunate," Grabowski said. He was watching the clubhouse through TT's birding binoculars.

"I'm guessing that you're not talking about the general situation," said TT.

Grabowski handed over the field glasses and pointed off to one side of the clubhouse, where a breezeway led out to a patio and an enormous swimming pool. There was a guy sitting all by himself in one of the lounge chairs there, turned side on to the parking lot so his silhouette could just be made out beyond a big potted fern.

TT trained the glasses on the guy, wondering what he was supposed to be looking at, when the guy kind of turned a little to lean over and pick up a drink that was sitting on the flagstones. It was the tiger man.

"Wonder where he gets those outfits," TT said. "Not at fucking Sears, that's for sure."

Grabowski looked at him incredulously. "There are tailors for the Mafia. There are tailors for aces."

TT shrugged. "I get everything off the rack. Anyway, we knew he'd probably be here, and now we know where he's at exactly, and he doesn't know we're here at all. So this doesn't really change anything, does it?"

Grabowski said, "I suppose it does not." He opened the door and stepped out of the cab. TT followed suit. The plan was for them to skirt around to the kitchens and wait for whoever was bringing the girl to show up. If everything went perfectly, maybe they could grab her and get gone without anybody being the wiser. TT had a theory about how fucking perfectly things were likely to go, but he didn't bother the old man with it.

The old man paused by the bed of the pickup, looking over at TT's toolbox. "Do you, perhaps, have a pipe wrench in there?"

TT did.

◆

According to Grabowski's story, he was at one and one with the tiger man. He'd gotten the better of him on TT's crane on Friday, two days ago, so that was one win. But apparently the tiger man had handed the old man's ass to him at the poker game at the Palmer House ten years in the future, so that was one loss.

"Maybe he takes judo lessons or some shit like that between now and then," TT whispered.

The two of them were crouched by the kitchen's exterior doors. People in white cook's jackets and striped pants were moving in and out to a pair of catering vans in a constant stream, making it impossible for them to get any closer.

"Anyway," said TT. "He hasn't done it yet, and you busted him up pretty good the other day, so you're probably still better than him at this point on your individual personal time lines, if that makes any sense." TT realized that that did not, in fact, make any sense, and also that he was talking way too much, which he supposed meant he was nervous.

Grabowski said, "Once, in Poland, during the war, I fought with a man like you. One who talked before the fighting began."

TT figured he knew where this was going, but said anyway, "Good-looking son-of-a-bitch, I bet."

"Not at the end," said Grabowski.

One of those fucking black Suburbans rounded the end of the building and parked beside the catering vans. TT felt Grabowski tense beside him.

The driver got out and whistled over the woman running the kitchen crew, who looked none too pleased at the interruption. But after a brief exchange, she called all the workers together and told them to take what was apparently an unscheduled break, and further, to take it somewhere else. The waiters and cooks and runners all shuffled off, lighting up cigarettes, talking to one another.

When it was just the woman and the driver, two more guys got out of the Suburban and circled to the rear door of the vehicle.

Now that there were a lot fewer people hustling and bustling and shouting, TT could hear what was being said.

"The cake's inside. I still can't believe I agreed to this," the woman said.

"And I can't believe we're having this conversation," the driver said. "Mr. Galante is paying you quite well for providing this evening's meal. Mr. Galante has always paid you quite well. Don't get squeamish on me now, Doris, or it'll be you in the cake next time."

The woman humphed. "I'm too old to be scared by your threats, Frank. Especially since I know I'm *way* too old for any of the Galantes' tastes. Bring her on in." With that, she turned heel and walked into the kitchens.

"You heard the chef," said the driver. "Chop chop."

The two in back opened the cargo doors of the Suburban, leaned in, and pulled out a struggling blond girl, bound and gagged. She squirmed so much that the guy holding her feet lost his grip and she managed to kick him hard in the groin while he was struggling to grab hold of her.

"Bitch!" the guy said between wheezes, and drew back one hand. TT tensed, ready to go right then, but the driver caught the guy by the wrist.

"What are you, fucking stupid? You want to mark up little Gio's birthday present? That wouldn't be too bright, I don't think." Then he turned and punched the girl in the stomach, doubling her over. "Where it doesn't show, dumbass."

These fucking guys, thought TT, and wondered if Grabowski would give the word to go now. But then he saw Grabowski had, in fact, gone. Had gotten all big and ugly and gone *fast.*

The driver went down first, head caved in by the pipe wrench, and even before TT made it to the Suburban, Grabowski had taken the guy the girl had kicked by the arms and twisted his whole upper body so that it made a sickening crack.

"Hey!" TT shouted. "I told you not to fucking kill anybody!"

The third guy had gone pale and dropped the girl to the ground. He was struggling to get his gun out and TT suddenly realized that if Grabowski managed to take the guy out before he fired they might actually get out of here without too much trouble.

The guy got his gun out and fired.

"Fuck," said TT. He rushed over and scooped the girl up the same way he'd scooped up Grabowski on the rooftop the day before. Her eyes were wide with fright, staring past TT at the old man, who, TT had to admit, was pretty fucking frightening.

"Go!" said Grabowski. "Take her! I will hold them off!"

Which was technically part of the plan, though it had been the part TT had mentally labeled "if everything goes to shit." But he didn't hesitate. He threw the girl over his shoulder and booked it for the truck.

Everyone who had been milling around outside the entrance had gone inside for drinks and music or something, and even the guards weren't in evidence. He was breathing hard by the time he got the girl into the cab, and so was she, nostrils flaring, air hissing around her gag. *Oh fuck, the gag.*

TT pulled out his multi-tool and flipped open a utility blade. He made quick work of the girl's bonds and gag. Even so, she didn't say anything.

"Yeah, I'm here to, y'know, rescue you and shit."

She rolled her eyes. "So you've done it. Let's get out of here!" She had a southern accent.

TT almost nodded. Almost jumped behind the wheel and started up the engine. Almost left Wojtek Grabowski to his fate.

Then he said, "Fuck. Fuck, fuck, fuck." He looked at the girl and said, "Wait here." And he headed back for the kitchens.

What TT hoped to find was a once again relatively scrawny Grabowski and three incapacitated mob guys. What he found mystified him.

There weren't *three* incapacitated mob guys, there were, at a quick count, *twelve*. And the Suburban was on its roof.

The chef lady, TT had forgotten her name, cautiously stuck her head out the kitchen doors. Catching sight of him, she said, "Are they gone?"

TT looked at the carnage around him. "You mean 'Is he gone,' right? You're talking about a scary-looking guy with a hardhat and a pipe wrench, right?"

The woman nodded. "And the two he was fighting with. They just . . . they took out the whole security detail!"

"Slow down! What two was he fighting with? Was one of them that tiger asshole?"

"No!" she said, looking frantically over her shoulder. "It was a black guy and some old guy—I don't know, the white guy looked familiar, but I couldn't say from where. I thought the guy in the hardhat—" She stopped and looked up at TT. "Why are you wearing hardhats?"

TT had forgotten about his half-assed disguise, but just said, "What about him? What did you think?"

"I thought he was going to rip them in half the way he turned that SUV over and tore through all of Galante's guys, but then the black guy just touched him on the arm and he fell down. And then the two of them dragged him over to the SUV and kind of looked at themselves in the reflection off the windshield. Then . . . then they just . . . disappeared."

TT decided that maybe it would have been a better idea to stay with the girl at the truck. In fact, the more he thought about it, the more he thought he would hustle his ass back there right now.

He turned to go.

Luckily, the tiger man used his human fist to hit him.

This is fucking bullshit, thought TT, working his jaw back and forth and struggling up from where he'd been knocked on his ass. He considered whether to say something to the tiger man, but the guy was crouched, claws extended from his tiger hand, obviously getting ready to jump.

TT figured he knew how to handle this one. He narrowed his eyes and turned. A girder came into being beside him, and TT manipulated it. He pivoted his hips, extended his arms, swung through.

And missed.

"Strike one," rasped the tiger man. "You're out."

"That's not how the fucking game is played, asshole," said TT. He caused another girder to come into existence horizontally right above the tiger man's head, then another on top of that, and then a third and a fourth. Two tons crashed down on the guy, knocking him prone. Then, incredibly, the motherfucker propped himself up on his elbows and *actually started to fucking stand up*, but then he groaned and lay back down.

TT didn't check to see if he was alive. He took off.

The girl had, of course, stolen his fucking truck.

TT let Sonny drive.

He'd called the kid on his cell after he'd put a mile or two between him and the country club, and Sonny drove out to pick him up. When TT didn't wave him out of the driver's seat, didn't even say anything about the radio station that was playing, Sonny actually kept his mouth shut and didn't pester TT with questions.

It was a weird fucking day.

Back at the house, Ma took one look at his face and called Lynette and told her to come right over. TT told her he'd be fine, but then she was getting him settled on the couch in front of the television with his feet propped up on the glass-topped coffee table, which was usually no fucking way allowed, and bringing him painkillers and an ice pack.

The only thing she asked was, "Is he gone?"

TT nodded.

"That's probably a good thing, right?"

TT thought about that. He was still thinking about it when a commercial came on, all loud trumpets and shooting stars and shit.

"Oh! I meant to tell you about this!" Ma said. "They've been playing it all morning. They're going to have tryouts at Soldier Field for that new show!"

American Hero, it said on the screen. Then, *Do You Have What It Takes?*

"Huh," said TT. He wondered, briefly, if there was anything in the news about refugees in Egypt. He remembered what the old man had said about him dying. Mainly, he remembered what he had said about TT saving hundreds of lives.

And down at the bottom of him, down at the fundamental part of himself, a card turned.

"You should go on that show!" said Ma.

"You know what?" TT said. "I should. I really fucking should."

A Long Night at
the Palmer House

Part 3

TIME HOPPING WASN'T ANY easier the second time around. In fact, Nighthawk felt a lot more queasy and almost vomited as they arrived.

"Remind me not to do this again on a full stomach," he groaned to Croyd. He staggered away and sat down heavily on the bed by the mirror.

The room appeared to be untenanted, and was furnished much less lavishly than it had been back in 1919. The furniture was sleeker and modern in design, and there was a digital clock on a nightstand, its red numerals glowing. The carpet and wall colors were light, more in tune with modern tastes. The curtains were open, revealing a nighttime sky.

Croyd seemed marginally less affected by the time shifting. Rummaging through a waste bin, he found a discarded newspaper. "Two thousand seven," he announced to Nighthawk. He opened the wardrobe and smiled. "We're in luck," he began, then caught himself. "Oh, no," he said, rapidly thumbing through the clothes he'd pulled from the drawer.

"What's the matter?"

Croyd looked at Nighthawk. "These are women's clothes."

Fortunately, neither Nighthawk nor Croyd was a large man and who-ever had checked into that room of the Palmer House favored pant-suits. Croyd found a wallet in a small handbag that had been left in the nightstand with eighteen dollars in it. He showed it disgustedly to Nighthawk, who was squeezing into a satin number that had an accompanying blouse of the same material.

"That should be enough," Nighthawk said. "I know where to find more."

The shoes proved problematic, but Nighthawk managed to stuff his feet into a pair of pumps whose heels he'd snapped off and Croyd found fuzzy bathroom slippers. They didn't exactly go with the rest of the ensemble, but they couldn't be choosy.

"Let's get the hell out of here before whoever owns this shit gets back," Croyd said, and Nighthawk had to agree.

Fortunately it was late enough at night that the hotel corridors were empty. The time travelers were able to slip out of a side entrance of the hotel without attracting much attention, though the cabbie waiting outside at the head of the taxi line eyed them dubiously as they climbed into the back of his hack. "You boys need to work on your fashion sense," he observed, but Nighthawk just muttered an address in Bronzeville.

The ride was short and uncomfortably silent. The fee came to $17.50. Croyd handed him the eighteen bucks. "You need to stop be-ing judgmental," he told the cabbie, who drove away cursing at the fifty-cent tip.

Croyd looked up. "Whose place is this?"

It was a nicely kept-up single-family house sitting back from the street on a slight rise of land. The lawn around it was immaculate green, the grass just about needing mowing. Flowers bloomed in an ornamental border along the walkway that led to the front door. "Mine," Nighthawk said.

"Hang on." Croyd stopped him as he started up the walkway that led to the front porch of the wood-framed house. "What if you're home?"

"I thought of that," Nighthawk said. "But, first, this is one of let's say several places I have around town. Second, I spent most of the summer of 2007 looking for a runaway teenager in L.A. And third, if I am home this will be the perfect opportunity to tell myself not to take this job."

"It's not that bad," Croyd said, "though maybe you could tell yourself to coldcock that old waiter when he comes through the door with Galante's steak sandwich."

Nighthawk picked up the third stone from the end of the row bordering the left side of the walk. It wasn't a real stone and it contained a key. "I'd rather not meet myself on this trip," he told Croyd as they went up the rest of the walk and approached the door. He put the key in the lock. "It's just too creepy to consider. Who knows what damage we could do?"

Croyd said, "You're just afraid that you won't like yourself," as Nighthawk opened the door.

"I've lived with myself for a long time. I may know myself better than I want to, but I've come to accept things as they are. It has been a long, strange trip."

"Did you ever find that teenager in L.A.?" Croyd asked.

Nighthawk paused for a moment. "Her body," he said quietly.

The house was dark and quiet inside. He wasn't home. It had that empty feeling to it, like no one had been around for a while. There was nothing in the refrigerator except for a couple of cans of beer, and no groceries on the shelves except for some other canned stuff. It was neatly, quietly furnished, but sort of anonymous, without much in the way of a personality. It wasn't so much a place to actually live, but just a place where you kept things that you might need someday. Croyd helped himself to one of the beers, popped the can, and took it into the living room, where Nighthawk was sitting in a comfortable La-Z-Boy chair, massaging his feet.

"So where's our target?" Nighthawk asked.

Croyd took a thoughtful sip from the can. "Oh, he's around, somewhere. I can feel his presence."

"Can you be more specific?"

"It's hard," Croyd said judiciously. "Lots of people packed closely in a small, but complex area. Lots to sort through. If there was some way we could narrow our focus . . ."

"If we knew exactly who we're looking for?" Nighthawk asked.

"That would help."

"Well," Nighthawk said. "You say that the nexus of this particular break in the time line happened at the Palmer House—"

"Yeah."

"Let's see." Nighthawk went to the counter that divided the living room from the kitchen and picked up the phone book. He thumbed through it for a moment, then took down the phone from where it hung on the wall and dialed a number. After a moment he said, "Registration desk," then, after a moment, "Yes, hello, this is Garrison from the *Tribune*. That recent incident, when a naked person appeared—yes, that's right. And did any other staff member turn up who witnessed? . . . No? So, the description remains—yes, old man, freakishly muscular. . . . Uh-huh. And he never reappeared? . . . Yes, well. Probably some teleporting ace gone wrong. . . . Yes. Thank you." He hung up the phone and looked at Croyd. "The waiter."

"Yeah," Croyd said. "The crazy old mystery man. The cause of all our troubles."

"Well," Nighthawk said, "we know that he had a beef with Galante. I don't think he jumped him simply because he slapped a girl."

"That was a little extreme," Croyd agreed.

"I don't think his presence was a coincidence," Nighthawk said. "I think he came to the room to deliver more than a steak sandwich."

"You think he came after Galante?"

"It's our only viable clue."

"So, even though I shoved him into 2007 . . ."

". . . he'd still be after Galante," they both said together.

"I like the way you think." Croyd took a long swallow of beer. "So, we find Galante, we find our waiter."

"I'll make some more phone calls," Nighthawk said.

◆

Nighthawk and Croyd, now dressed in men's clothing Nighthawk had kept at the house, took a cab to within a block of the country club, then dismissed the cabbie. They'd provide their own means of transport when it came time to leave. It was dark, which at least provided some cover. They slipped around to the back of the restaurant, where Nighthawk's contacts had told them Gio Galante would be celebrating his sixteenth birthday. There were a lot of cars in the back lot, a lot of big, fancy cars and several outsized black SUVs that seemed to have overtaken limos as mobsters' preferred means of transportation.

As they were watching, one of those black SUVs pulled into the lot and parked near the rear door leading to the kitchen. A couple of thugs got out of the SUV and went around to the back door, where one dragged out a young, blond girl who was bound and gagged.

"That doesn't look good," Croyd said.

Nighthawk said, "Whatever happens, we can't interfere. You know that story Heinlein wrote about the butterfly effect? One little misstep, one slight change, could alter the whole time line. I've been thinking about it ever since our last stop—"

"It's just a story," Croyd said. "And you're wrong. Asimov wrote it, and what the hell did he know? Look—" He pointed at the girl struggling with the Mafia mooks. She'd gotten in a solid kick to the groin of one of them, but then another just doubled her over with a hard punch to her gut. "She's just a teenaged whore. What difference—oh, shit!"

Their target came out of his own place of concealment like a charging bull. It was the waiter from the hotel. You couldn't mistake his bulked-up, abnormally broad form. Only this time he was wearing a construction worker's hardhat and swinging a wrench.

Nighthawk and Croyd looked at each other. *"Hardhat!"* they exclaimed at the same time.

"What the hell?" Croyd added, in wonder.

It had to be him, the mysterious ace who'd suddenly appeared in

People's Park in 1970 and vanished thereafter . . . but why the hell he had a vendetta against Gio Galante was a mystery.

Before they could move, Hardhat crushed the skull of one of the Mafia guys with his wrench. He dropped the weapon as the guy who was holding the girl let her go. Then he simply picked him up and broke him, twisting his body like he was a rag doll. They could both hear the thug's spine snap from where they stood.

A younger man, stocky and strong-looking and also wearing a hardhat, stepped from where he'd been lurking to remonstrate with the ace. He must, Nighthawk realized, be in his eighties or nineties now, but his ace still appeared to be rather potent.

They both heard Hardhat shout, "Go!" to the younger man, who paused for a moment, then scooped up the girl from where she lay on the asphalt of the parking lot, tossed her over his shoulder, and ran down a nearby alley.

"Let's get him, now!" Nighthawk said, and he and Croyd burst from their own cover to give Croyd a close, clear shot at Hardhat. But before they could reach him, eight or nine other obvious mafiosi bolted from the kitchen's rear door and piled out into the parking lot.

"Oh, hell," Croyd complained. "Now we have these clowns to take care of too?"

Maybe not, Nighthawk thought, as they raced across the parking lot.

Hardhat charged into them. Bodies flew left and right. Guns fired. At one point the ace flipped over the SUV. It rolled over twice, scattering mafiosi, and came to rest on its roof. All the thugs managed to avoid being crushed, but that simply put most of them off-balance and made them easy targets for the rampaging hulk.

By the time Nighthawk and Croyd reached the scene most were down. Nighthawk pulled off the black kid glove he'd placed on his left hand, glided close to one, and touched him. The man flopped like a dropped sack of potatoes. Nighthawk dealt with a couple of the thugs and suddenly it was just the three of them still standing.

"Easy, big fellow," Croyd said. "We're friends—"

Hardhat, breathing heavily, charged them.

Nighthawk deftly stepped aside. The big ace unfortunately chose to focus on the wrong opponent. He was about to grab Croyd and twist him into a pretzel when Nighthawk slapped him across the back of his shoulder. He crashed to the asphalt like a ton of bricks . . . but limp bricks, nevertheless. Croyd let out a long gust of breath. "Man, that was too fucking close."

"I had it," Nighthawk said quietly.

"You didn't kill him," Croyd said. "He's still breathing."

"He'll be okay in a bit." They both looked at Hardhat critically. He was bleeding in a couple of places from bullet wounds, but none looked to be in a particularly vital spot. "I just sucked enough out of him to knock him out." He pursed his lips, looked over the fallen mafiosi. "I was a little less concerned with them—may have taken a few months off their lives."

"So that's how your ace works?" Croyd said. He shrugged. "They're likely to come to a premature end, anyway. Give me a hand with this guy."

Together, they dragged Hardhat behind the SUV he'd upended. By the time they'd stopped to rest behind the overturned vehicle, he'd turned back into a tired-looking, beaten-up old man.

"Better send him back and he can get medical attention," Nighthawk said. "I hope."

Croyd nodded, concentrated, pointed. Color flowed from his palm and Hardhat was gone. "I can't wait to learn what this was all about. In the meantime"—they both looked at the kitchen's back door, where armed thugs were just now stirring about, cautiously peeking into the parking lot—"we'd better get the hell out of here ourselves before reinforcements arrive."

"That means ending up naked in the middle of Chicago."

"Better than ending up dead," Croyd said.

They looked at their reflections in the SUV's heavily tinted window.

Nighthawk nodded. "Do it."

A Long Night at
the Palmer House

Part 4

THE AREA WASN'T MUCH different.

The country club was there. The restaurant was there. The cars in the parking lot were there, though they were much larger and there were no SUVs. Caddys, yes. Lincolns. Buicks the size of yachts, Oldsmobiles, Thunderbirds, Impalas galore.

There was one other thing. It was cold as hell. Snow was piled high around the parking lot, and in fact was coming down steadily in big fluffy flakes from the night sky. Nighthawk was already shivering. "When are we? Besides apparently in the middle of the goddamned winter."

"Nineteen sixty—I hope," Croyd said. "I didn't have much time to calibrate this jump." He looked up at the snowflakes fluttering down from the sky. "We better find some clothes, fast, before we freeze our balls off."

"Let's find an unlocked car, hot-wire it, and turn the heat on," Nighthawk said, his teeth chattering.

They went down one row without any luck. Nighthawk felt his feet almost freezing to the inch of snow that had fallen since the last time the lanes in the lot had been plowed.

"Goddamn," Croyd said. "These people are an untrusting lot of—uh-oh."

He straightened up from the land-boat they'd been bending over and looked back up the aisle.

"We're not alone, John," he said in a low voice.

Nighthawk looked over his shoulder.

"What we got here, Floyd?" a drawling voice asked.

"Looks like two buck naked car thieves, Harry," another replied.

Cops. Nighthawk squinted in the flashlight beams pointed at their eyes. More disconcerting was the fact that they were also pointing their service weapons at them.

"Care to explain why you boys are running around buck naked in a snowstorm trying to break into cars?" the one called Harry asked.

Nighthawk and Croyd looked at each other, and then back at the cops. One was small and wiry, the other was big and fat. Both were looking puzzled, but that didn't keep them from drawing a steady bead with both pistols and flashlights.

"No," Nighthawk and Croyd said simultaneously.

Croyd made a quick gesture and they were gone in a flash of rainbow light.

As they ran toward the two neat piles of clothing bunched up on the ground, Nighthawk called, "Dibs on the skinny guy's uniform."

"Damn!" Croyd said.

They were both shivering badly but managed to dress quickly despite freezing fingers and shaking hands. They put on everything, except for the cops' underwear, and both sighed contentedly when they'd bundled into their quilted winter jackets and put on their insulated winter caps and pulled down the earflaps. It was only a moment's work to use the butt of a nightstick, also left behind, to break a side window in a roomy black Cadillac, unlock it, hop in, hot-wire the engine, and slip-slide out of the parking lot, Nighthawk driving.

"Where'd you send them?" he asked Croyd, who was putting the heater on full blast.

"Two hours into the future." He paused for a moment with a

satisfied smile on his face. "Maybe two days. It's hard to say. I'd like to hear how they explain being buck naked in a parking lot at night."

"It's the wild card, Jake," Nighthawk said, quoting the old line from the Polanski film *Jokertown*.

"Yeah," Croyd said. "That does explain a lot." He hugged himself for warmth for a moment or two, staring out the windshield.

"Some place to hunker down and think." Nighthawk thought for a moment. "The Palmer House is as good as any."

"I could use a hot shower and a stiff drink," Croyd said.

"Agreed," Nighthawk said as he navigated the snowy street. The Caddy—he figured it belonged to some mafioso from the Galante family, because gangsters changed their favorite haunts as often as leopards changed their spots—was a smooth ride.

The snowflakes were more drifting than pelting down, but it was cold as hell. Chicago's streets were largely empty of traffic though it was still early in the evening. The nighttime was Nighthawk's favorite time, when it was just him and the city and the people who made the night their home. Many had chosen to stay snug in their beds this winter evening and Nighthawk couldn't blame them, but they were missing the thrill of the dark, the white blanket slowly descending from the dark sky, the fullness of the moon, and the crispness of the air. It was his time to fly, and he hadn't tired of it yet, after all his years. He thought he never would.

"We're almost there," he said quietly as they approached the Palmer House. "We probably should ditch the Caddy. We're going to be conspicuous enough in these cop uniforms, without luggage. We don't need to show up on the scene driving this boat."

"Yeah," Croyd reluctantly agreed.

The snow had stopped falling as they parked a block away from the Palmer. It lay like an unbroken white sable blanket over the sidewalks and the roofs of the surrounding buildings as they hustled through the cold, their breath puffing out like clouds before them as they went up the street. A warm gust of air hit them as they entered the lobby, which was quiet but not quite deserted on this cold winter evening.

The reception clerk watched with apparent interest as they approached the counter.

"We need a room," Nighthawk said, deciding that the best approach to take would be brief and brusque.

Surprisingly, the clerk just nodded briskly. "Yes, sir. The messenger from headquarters arrived with your luggage some time ago," he added, even more surprisingly.

As Nighthawk and Croyd exchanged uncertain glances, the clerk leaned forward and said in a conspiratorial whisper, "Management only asks that you quickly change from your uniforms so as to keep the surveillance of your suspect as discreet as possible."

"Of . . . course," Croyd said.

The clerk nodded knowingly. "I'll send a boy up with your luggage right away. Registration has already been taken care of. Here's your key, and good luck."

"Thanks," Nighthawk said, automatically taking the key the clerk was holding out to him.

"What the fuck was that all about?" Croyd asked as soon as they got into the privacy of the elevator and were going up to their room.

"You've got me," Nighthawk replied. "Has someone else taken a hand in our mission?"

"Who?" Croyd shook his head in bewilderment. "Who else would know?"

Nighthawk had no answer, though seemingly whoever was interfering seemed to be doing so to help them. This notion was confirmed when the bellboy arrived with two small suitcases while Croyd was enjoying the hot shower he'd been craving. Nighthawk, meeting the boy at the door, tipped him with a buck that'd been in the cop's wallet and he handed the bags over with a cheery smile and salute.

"By the way," Nighthawk asked the boy as he turned away to go, "what's the date?"

"Date?" The bellhop looked momentarily surprised, but then Nighthawk thought that he probably had gotten crazier questions from befuddled or boozed-up hotel patrons before. "Why, it's Leap Year day. February twenty-ninth." He paused a moment, then added, just to make sure, "Nineteen sixty."

Nighthawk nodded. "I thought so," he said, and closed the door.

He took the suitcases over to the bed and laid them on it just as Croyd came from the bathroom, a towel wrapped around his skinny form. "What have we got here?" he asked.

"Let's see."

The suitcases were unlocked. Each yielded a heavy cloth winter coat, formal, modern cut—for 1960—and rather snazzy evening wear, complete with shiny black lace-up shoes and a manila envelope.

Croyd removed one of the suits from the suitcase, and held it up. The jacket was dark, with a satin collar and lapels, the shirt had ruffles down the front and at the wrists.

"Nice," Croyd approved. "Are we going to a party?"

Nighthawk had opened the manila envelope in the other suitcase and was holding a sheet of paper and a metal key. The key had a familiar-looking rabbit-head logo as part of its design.

"I guess we are," Nighthawk said in wonder. "A party being held to celebrate the opening of the Playboy Club."

Croyd's mouth made an "o" of astonishment. "Holy shit," he said. "Have I died and gone to heaven?"

This time Nighthawk drove the Caddy right up to the front door of the four-story building on Walton Street in the part of Chicago's Gold Coast called the Magnificent Mile.

The area was lit up like a beacon in the night. The street was crowded with traffic, the sidewalk with pedestrians. Nighthawk handed the keys of the Caddy over to a valet, reluctantly relinquishing the car he'd probably never see again. It had been a fine ride. The Mafia had good taste, at least in regard to cars.

Croyd and Nighthawk went to the front door together and showed their keys to the Door Bunny ensconced in the lobby beyond the front door, a beautiful, leggy young woman dressed in the iconic outfit, this one in blue satin, complete with bunny ears and tail, which reminded Nighthawk of the young joker waitress who'd been serving drinks at the poker game.

"Welcome," she said, flashing a smile and opening the inner door for them in a manner that suggested she was a houri inviting them to paradise. And in a way, maybe she was.

The large room was crowded with packed tables and almost exclusively male patrons, most youngish, all well dressed, being served drinks by a bevy of beautiful young women wearing the bunny satin bustier and ears and tail.

"Who are we looking for?" Nighthawk asked.

"I have no idea," Croyd replied, "but I'm going to like the looking."

"Hundreds are packed into this place," Nighthawk said. "Let's split up. We'll rendezvous by the piano." He nodded toward a corner of the room where a man sat providing a jazzy background soundtrack to the bedlam of conversation.

Croyd nodded. "Got it."

They separated, wending their way through the crowd.

Nighthawk soon realized that he was awash in a sea of white faces. Few gave him a second glance, though there were some disapproving looks as he passed through. He'd had long experience with such and he'd long since evolved a method for dealing with them. Ignore them when he was focused on a particular job, respond to them when they interfered with that job. Or, sometimes when he was in a bad mood. Now he was focused like a laser, looking for a familiar face. There must be some reason why they'd been sent here, specifically, and maybe if he discovered the reason he'd discover the identity—and motives—of their benefactor.

When the meeting happened, it was totally by accident. They almost collided. Will Monroe wasn't looking where he was going, and his step was uncertain. Nighthawk grabbed him by his arm and Monroe paused, looking down with irritation. "Well, what is it? What do you—" He paused, suddenly staring. "Mister . . ." He paused, again, quite evidently searching for a name. ". . . Nighthawk, isn't it? What—"

"Don't worry, Mr. Monroe," Nighthawk said earnestly. "I've come to take you home."

"Home?"

Monroe was drunk. Nighthawk could see it on his face and read it in his swaying, uncertain stance. For a moment he stared blankly. Then sudden relief flooded Will Monroe's features. "Oh, thank God. You have no idea what we've been through!"

Nighthawk looked around the opulent room. "You seem to have done okay. Come, we need to find Meek. You can tell us all about it once we get going."

Monroe looked at him as if not quite knowing what to say. "But—but what about Julie?"

"Julie?" Nighthawk frowned in concentration. "You mean—Julie Cotton? The joker girl? She's here, too?"

Monroe nodded. "In a big way. And I don't think she's going to want to leave."

As Monroe told him about Julie's affair with John F. Kennedy, Nighthawk got grimmer and grimmer. "This is some serious screwing with the time line," he said, as he pulled Monroe through the crowded room after him. "We've got to get the hell out of here. There's Mcck!" Nighthawk pointed to a corner of the large room where Croyd seemed to have cornered Hugh Hefner and was earnestly discussing something with him. At least Croyd was talking. Hefner was listening, with an increasingly distraught look on his face.

"Come on," Nighthawk ordered urgently, dragging Monroe in his wake.

"It's called cable TV," they heard Croyd saying as they approached. "I tell you, it's the coming thing. If you start now, you'll get a jump on everyone else. See, you hook up everyone's television set with a length of cable that you run underground and then connect with your own station that you then charge a monthly fee to beam directly into their homes. You'll make millions, I tell you—Oh, hi John and, hey, it's Will Monroe—"

Croyd was hyper, breathing hard and looking intense, with a hard stare in his eyes that told Nighthawk he was speeding. He must have scored some drugs from somebody at the party.

"Mr. Meek has some fabulous ideas," Hefner said, deftly extracting himself from the corner while Croyd was distracted. "Tell him to get back to me when they're practical."

"But Hef—" Croyd exclaimed. He shut his mouth abruptly when he realized he was speaking to Hefner's back. "Hey, John," he repeated brightly.

"What've you been doing?" Nighthawk asked in a low voice.

"Speed," Croyd said conversationally. "In the john—I mean the bathroom—with Lenny Bruce. You know, he's really a funny guy."

"Concentrate," Nighthawk said.

"Sure, no problem," Croyd said. "You rounded up Monroe. Let's go."

He started to gesture, but Nighthawk grabbed his hand and held it down by his side.

"Not yet," he said. He told him about Cotton.

Croyd frowned when Nighthawk finished. "Gee, that's rough. Maybe we can leave her—"

"Not a chance," Nighthawk said. "We've got to track her down—"

"There she is," Monroe said, pointing across the room.

She was moving across the crowded floor with a distressed look on her face, headed toward the women's lounge.

"Wonder why she's upset," Monroe said. "After all, some of this party is for her. She was just named as the first joker Playmate of the Month."

"Let's find out," Nighthawk said. He started across the room after her, Croyd and Monroe following in his wake.

But someone else was on Cotton's trail ahead of them. It was an older woman. She was portly and wore a grotesque hat that made her look as if she were wearing a key lime pie on her head. It took a moment, but Nighthawk remembered her as the gossip columnist who had ruined a thousand careers, the Hollywood harpy who hated Commies and queers and wild carders, not necessarily in that order. *Hedda Hopper*. She followed Julie Cotton into the women's lounge.

"John," Croyd expostulated, "it's the girls' room—"

"I know," Nighthawk said. "Come on."

He went through the door.

"Hey—" Croyd called out, but followed him, Monroe on his heels, stopped, and looked around, wonderingly. "It's nice in here."

It was. It was like the lobby of a fine hotel, with flowered wallpaper, comfortable chairs scattered about, and a deep, soft carpet. End tables held baskets of lotions, packs of Playboy cigarettes and matchboxes of Playboy matches, with copies of the latest issues of the magazine as well. Makeup mirrors lined one wall, naughty lithographs the other.

Only one person was in the room: the bunny attendant, who was looking at them wide-eyed. Nighthawk reached into his wallet, pulled out a ten-dollar bill. He took her by the elbow as he stuffed the bill down the front of her bustier.

"Give us ten minutes." He ushered her out of the lounge and then locked the door. There was a door across the lounge that led to the area that had the bathroom facilities. Nighthawk put a finger to his lips and led the way to the door. As they drew nearer they could hear the sounds of two women arguing, interspersed with weeping.

Nighthawk cracked the swinging door, so they could hear more clearly.

The dominant voice was clearly Hedda Hopper's. "The nerve of trash like you—mixing with decent folks."

They could hear Julie Cotton's weeping under Hopper's virulent words.

"I suppose I should thank you, though," Hopper said in a triumphantly vicious tone, "you've given me the weapon to bring down that pinko Kennedy."

"What do you mean?" Julie said between her sobs.

Nighthawk peeked around the cracked door. They were standing in front of a row of sinks with mirrors on the wall above them. The half-dozen bathroom stalls were in a line behind them. The room's floor was tiled in brown Saltillo, the light was harsh and strong. They seemed to be the only ones in the room.

"I mean this." Hopper reached into the purse that was hooked over her left forearm, and took out a sheaf of photos that she waved in Cotton's face.

The joker girl looked sick. "Where—how did you get those?"

"I have my ways," Hopper said. She looked at the pictures herself, fanning through them, rapidly. "Disgusting," she said, looking back at Cotton. "Every carnal activity imaginable! John Fitzgerald Kennedy, cavorting with a joker slut!" She laughed. "A married man! A Catholic!" She managed to put as much vitriol into the word "Catholic" as she had "joker." "His political career will be over when I release these shocking, shocking—"

Nighthawk entered the room, taking the glove from his left hand.

Hopper heard him come in and turned in his direction. "Negroes!" she shrieked, a look of sudden alarm on her face.

Nighthawk covered the distance between them in a moment. He snatched the hat off her head and as she opened her mouth to shriek again rammed it in hard enough to make her stagger backwards until she butted up against the sink. He snatched the pictures from her hands, handed them over his shoulder to Croyd, who had followed him into the room.

"Burn these." He stepped forward as Hopper cringed away. He grabbed her purse. She pulled back. He grasped her jaw with his left hand, jerking her head up and staring into her eyes. She looked back for a moment, like a bird mesmerized by a snake, and then sighed and slipped limply to the floor. Nighthawk felt the energy jolt through his system. Suddenly, he wasn't tired anymore. He didn't know how much life he'd drained from the bitch, and he didn't care. He let her go, but held on to her purse. Rummaging through it, he came upon a snub-nosed revolver and a fat envelope. The negatives were inside. "And these," he said.

Croyd already had a fire going in the sink. He was dropping the photos in them one at a time, pretending not to look at them as he did so. "Too bad," he muttered. "Whoever took these had a really good eye."

"It's all right, Julie," Nighthawk said gently to the girl. Will Monroe swayed drunkenly, watching with a concerned look on his face. "You're going home now."

"Home?" Julie Cotton said suddenly in a strained voice. "You mean, 2017? I'm not going. I'm staying here with Jack. He loves me. I have nothing in 2017. I'm what, a cocktail waitress? At best. Here, I have a man who loves me. I'm carrying his child. He's going to leave his wife—"

Nighthawk saw it all in his head. High-powered politician impregnates joker girl, leaves his duly wedded wife for her. They may have destroyed the photographic evidence, but if Julie's story was true . . .

"So Nixon becomes president?" Croyd said unbelievingly, voicing Nighthawk's very thought. "In *1960?* That fucker!"

"Julie," Nighthawk said earnestly, "you have to believe me. Your relationship with Kennedy will destroy our time line. It's the butterfly effect. There was a story by Robert Heinlein—"

"Asimov," insisted Croyd.

"Never mind," said Nighthawk. "One change leads to multiple others through time, until everything spirals out of control and the future, our future, is completely fucked."

"More fucked than JFK getting assassinated in Dallas?" Julie Cotton asked defiantly, rubbing the tears from her eyes, her rabbit ears standing up straight as two exclamation points. "More fucked than the Vietnam War?"

"Nixon in the White House," said Nighthawk. "You will still get the Vietnam War. But no Civil Rights Act, no Voting Rights Act."

Julie started crying again. "I love him," she said. "What about our child?"

Monroe went up to her, put his arms around her to comfort her. "Don't worry, kid," he said quietly. "I know what it's like to grow up without a father. I'll take care of you, and when the time comes, he'll know all about what his mom gave up to save the world."

She put her head against Monroe's chest and sobbed like a lost child. The producer held her close, looking over her to Nighthawk and Croyd. "Listen," Monroe said, "have you picked up Pug Peterman yet?"

"No," Nighthawk said, "he's still among the missing."

"Well, we've seen his picture in an old photo album of the Everleigh Club. Turn of the century. Chicago's most famous bordello. Have fun." He nodded at Croyd, who waved a hand. Will Monroe and the tearful Julie Cotton were gone in the rainbow glow.

"Did we do the right thing?" Croyd asked. "She would have saved JFK—"

"And made Nixon president eight years early."

"You can't know that for sure. Maybe one of the other Democrats would have beaten him. LBJ or Hubert or somebody."

"We can't take that chance," Nighthawk said. "Not a big one like that."

They both suddenly heard a pounding on the outer door.

"And we can't stand here and argue about it," Nighthawk said.

"What about her?" Croyd asked, toeing the unconscious form of Hedda Hopper.

"What about her?" Nighthawk asked. "This'll be one of the greatest locked-room mysteries ever. Let her solve it. Now let's get the hell out of here."

Croyd gestured into the mirror.

Nighthawk again felt the prickly sensation of rushing through the time stream, but this time around there was something different to the process. Though the previous jumps had never been instantaneous—and it was difficult to measure time while time traveling—they'd always seemed to Nighthawk to be quick, blink-of-the-eye things. This one was perceptibly longer.

Then suddenly it was all over and, as usual, they were naked and momentarily disoriented in a strange place. Nighthawk looked all around in the suddenly bright sunlight, and his first thought was, *Jesus, it's hot and muggy all of a sudden,* and his second thought was, *Je-susss, are those dinosaurs over there?*

A Bit of a Dinosaur

by Paul Cornell

THINK IT'S IMPORTANT TO say, immediately, that I am in no way responsible for the extinction of the dinosaurs.

I mean, yes, they went extinct, and yes, I was there, and yes, mistakes were made. But I was not privy to any aggression toward them. Indeed, it has to be said, they were pretty damn aggressive toward *me*. The dinosaurs are not the injured party here. Well, apart from . . . the extinction . . . but I'm getting away from my point.

Listen, I have just got back from the single most traumatic episode in my life, and I'd like to be able to say that no major ecological epochs were harmed during the making of it, but I just can't, okay? I don't even know why I feel guilty about this. Without me and Tim, I mean, without the events we were merely innocent bystanders at, we'd all be covered in feathers and eating rodents right now. Not that there's anything wrong with that. Some of my best friends—but anyway.

Where was I? I have no idea. I should start at the beginning.

Hello. My name is Abigail Baker. I am a serious actor. That is to say, it's not currently what I'm employed doing. In fact, right now, I'm not entirely sure if I still have a job of any kind, but it's what I . . . am. I'm an actress just like I'm young (well, twenties) and British and what the Americans call an "ace." When all this started, I was working for Will Monroe. You know, the producer? The producer who's finally, with a series of big hits, gotten away from being just "her son." I wasn't working for him in the way that I'd *like*. That is to say, as an actor. Though we had been talking about me getting an audition. Well, to be honest, I'd been the one doing most of the talking, and he'd been listening, just about, usually while texting more important actors.

I suppose this all started when he came along to see a production of *The Pirates of Penzance* in which I was in the chorus. Everyone backstage was talking about him being there to see someone low down on the billing, but I didn't imagine that was me, until I got out front, got midway through, appropriately enough, the number "How Beautifully Blue the Sky," and found myself floating up into the lighting rig.

Of course, they left me there. At least in New York, such things are not unknown in the theater, and the custom is to simply wait until the end of the performance and then send up stage crew with hooks on poles. So I had a bird's-eye view of the whole performance, while doing my best to remain professionally still and not upstage anyone down below by, for instance, shaking too much or, indeed, screaming. I was well aware that at any moment the ace whose powers I was accidentally picking up like Wi-Fi (because that, dear reader, is the nature of my own power) might pop out to the bathroom. If they did, and that bathroom was too far away from the auditorium, I would plummet, and all that would be left of me would be an intriguing theatrical anecdote. "It's how she'd have wanted to go," they'd have said. They would have been horribly wrong. I have, actually, on some previous occasions, needed to calculate how far a theater's bathrooms were from the stage, but never with quite such manic intensity.

Still, I got to the end of the performance, and the stagehands with the poles did indeed rescue me, and backstage, now allowing myself at least a slight tremble, I was introduced to Mr. Monroe, who'd inherited his mother's expressive eyebrows. It turned out he'd come to the theater that evening to see me, and had brought along as his guest an ace who could control gravity. Will had heard of my ability and had wanted to test it out. In a few weeks he would be going along to a high-stakes poker game, and knew there would be various

dubious characters in the room, and needed to find a way to know if
there was anyone present who could read either his cards or his mind,
or perhaps control his actions.

I was about to say, because I'd become aware, without the need for
any powers, that the glorious jealousy my fellow artistes in the backstage area had been emanating as they listened in on our conversation was turning to contempt, that I couldn't possibly sign up for any
job where I wasn't being hired as an actor. I knew how disliked I was
becoming for a notoriety that had nothing to do with my skills as a
thespian. I was somewhat aggrieved that Will, of all people, being in
the business himself, had failed to understand that. However, at that
point Will had quoted an hourly rate, the glorious jealousy of my
peers had instantly returned, and I'd found myself declaring that I
was indeed between jobs, and that I looked forward to exploring a
new medium.

Will briefed me thoroughly about what to expect. I was given
photos of all the participants and their retinues, so I'd be able to immediately identify whoever it was using powers. Thankfully, more
experience with using my abilities has made me aware, these days,
of a sense of direction and intensity when I'm starting to take on a
power set. So I'm actually pretty useful as a power meter. But it wasn't
the job itself that worried me when I saw the pictures. It was the identity of the bodyguard to one of the other players. "Donald Meek?" I
said, incredulously, because the name and the face rang a bell. A
wrong bell. As if you're expecting a particular bell, but . . . look, I'm
an actor, not a writer, okay? "Donald Meek," I went on, my brain racing, "was a character actor in Hollywood in the 1940s. He was in
Stagecoach, The Thin Man . . . Goes Home, I think, *The Adventures of
Tom Sawyer, Hold That Co-ed—*"

"You know your classic Hollywood," said Will, who at that moment seriously approved of me. I had mentioned on a handful of occasions that I knew all his mother's movies by heart.

"—but he'd be much older than this now, to the point where he
would surely be very dead by now, and I watched a lot of those movies
with an old boyfriend who always pointed out Donald Meek and . . .
oh, this is him. This is him looking like and taking on the alias of

Donald Meek, and he is going to be at this poker game, and you should really be aware of that." I pointed at the photo. "This is actually Croyd Crenson, the Sleeper, and he's the wild card here, because when you meet him at that game his power that evening could be anything." Will looked guardedly at me, either because I'd use the words "wild card" in polite company, which you just don't do on social media these days, but hey, I'm a fellow sufferer, I'm allowed . . . or because he'd researched me and knew all about my prior connection to Croyd.

"Is that going to be a problem for you?" he asked.

"We're friends now. We keep in touch." Meaning Croyd always replied to my emails about six months after I'd sent them, whenever he decided that actually he wasn't Mr. 1940s guy and did know how to use the internet. He was, perhaps unsurprisingly for someone with an unusually long romantic life, reasonably okay at being decent to me as an ex. For my part, I'd kept those times I'd hated him out of sight of him and anyone else. "He'll want everything to stay calm, and if bad stuff starts to happen, he'll try to look out for me."

"Good to know," said Pug. Pug was Will's PA, Gary Peterman, a former child star, whom I knew from such movies as *The Lost Boys 2: Vampaces, Sea Trek V* (the crap one where they meet God and He turns out to be an evolved joker), and *Cowquake I-VI* (he got out while they were still "good"). His face had that stretched like a balloon look that either meant plastic surgery or a bit of joker in there or both. I hadn't added that whether or not Croyd tried to look out for me or anyone else was often down to how long he'd been without sleep and what he'd done to stay awake, but by the look on Peterman's face as he researched Croyd on his tablet, those details leapt out anyway.

I dropped Croyd a line that night, and this time got an immediate reply, and we had a quick back-and-forth talking honestly about what we expected from the game, and Croyd was as straight with me as he'd always been. I was able to tell Will, the next morning, that Charles Dutton's party, at least, was coming to the game just to play cards. Croyd had been pleasingly concerned about how I might react to his presence. His group had, of course, researched the opposition, just as Will had, so he'd seen I was coming along. He warned me about how he looked these days. It seemed that "hey, I like older men" was no longer up to the task of adequately explaining our previous relationship. I took it from his tone that he was at a calm place in his sleep cycle, and all in all I was glad that we were both planning to treat each other like adults.

So on the night of the game, I really should not have been surprised that it was Croyd, in a moment of wild abandon, who turned my entire life into poo. Dinosaur poo.

But I'm getting ahead of myself. You'll have heard by now how it all went down. For me, the most significant moment, before, you know, the descent of poo, was walking into that suite at the Palmer House and immediately meeting Croyd's stare across a crowded room. You know what it's like, seeing an ex for the first time after the breakup. I'd mentally prepared for the moment, and emotionally I was a very different person from whom I'd been then. I'd been in another relationship since, for a start, with a joker whose pansexual ambivalence was initially intriguing, then turned out to come with a side order of self-hatred that I couldn't cope with. But. Moving swiftly on. Croyd was in one of his gangster suits, the sort of thing that never goes out of style, but that marks the wearer as one of those guys who is who he is. His expression, on that classic Hollywood character actor face, instantly softened into a smile, and in that moment, I actually thought it was all going to be okay. I could feel his current power tugging at my brain. It was part of my job to tell Will what it was. Croyd knew that. I didn't understand, however, exactly what I was sensing. Some sort of . . . nostalgia combined with déjà vu? It was like nothing I'd ever felt in a power before. I had the terrible feeling I was actually going to have to ask him. I wandered over, and was about to come out with the line I'd practiced, which was the kind of thing Lauren Bacall would have said in those circumstances, calculated to both reassure him and remind him of what he was missing. I actually opened my mouth to say it, but instead, a loud voice right beside me called out, "Hey, irritable bowel syndrome!"

I acknowledge a few nicknames. That is not one of them. However, I knew exactly to what it was referring. I turned to see a young boy with enormous glasses and a mop of hair pointing at me like he'd won a prize. He had, oddly, a pigeon sitting calmly on the hand that wasn't pointing. "Yeah," I said with a sigh, "that was me."

"I knew it! Your ad is always on during the late night anime on Saturdays. Is it you saying the words at the end? Like, 'may cause death'? 'Cause your British accent isn't very good."

"I agree." That was Croyd, stepping forward, smoothly charming, but oh God, there was that intense look in his eye, like the charm was only seconds away from being pushed too far. He hadn't told me what his current power was, having only said in our email exchange that he hadn't taken on anything that could affect the game in any way. My own feeling that I might well "cause death" for this young interloper was nothing compared to the genuine danger when Croyd was like this. "Now, if you'll excuse us, the lady and I—"

He was about to brush the boy off by saying we needed to talk, but the anime fan took it as a cue for introductions. "Timothy Karstens. Call me Timmy." He shook Croyd's hand, then did a little duck away from reaching for mine, not sure if that was reasonable. The pigeon looked at him questioningly, and he glanced back as if to chide it. "Charlie Flowers is, like, my uncle? My thing is games, and so he said I should get to know poker, and that there'd be lots of famous people here. Like you. I mean, you are kind of famous. Because of, you know, the irritable bowels."

"Is he bothering you?" That was Flowers, walking quickly over, interrupting my complicated emotion about how it was nice to be thought of as famous for whatever reason. "It's okay, he's not some kind of mental case. Kid, don't you know better than to shoo some bird that lands on you? Diseases and stuff."

"It's no bother," I said quickly, realizing Flowers was about to drag Tim back to his group. Because he was nervous of the boy talking to anyone. I dialed up the cute a little and let out some of my pleasure at being recognized. "He just wanted an autograph. He knows me from my television work!" Which made me seem hopefully as shallow as quite a few of those in the room seemed to be.

"Oh yeah." Flowers's face lit up. "Irritable bowel syndrome!" I managed to grin back. He looked sharply back to the kid. "Okay, when you're done, you're with us, and you stay with us." And that had an edge of force to it. What sort of uncle, I wondered, was Mr. Flowers, to invite a child to an occasion where there might be violence? A very old-fashioned and uncaring one. And one, I suspected, with an ulterior motive.

Croyd had worked that out, too. "Okay, kid," he growled, as soon as Flowers was out of earshot. "What does the bird do?"

"What are you talking about?"

"I can sense powers," I told him. "And right now I'm sensing from you . . ." It was very slight, I realized. It wasn't an ace thing. It was a deuce thing. I saw the look on the boy's face turn to one of desperation, and I started to feel very sorry for him. He looked back to the bird, and it flew off and across the room to land on top of a tall bookcase, looking down on the card table. I caught Flowers giving the boy an approving glance.

"I can control birds," said Tim.

"You can control one bird," I said.

"Charlie brought me here to see through its eyes—"

"You little—" began Croyd, thinking he knew exactly what that bird was doing up on the bookcase.

But Croyd was wrong. I put out a hand to hold him back. "But you can't do that," I said.

"And you mustn't tell him!" Tim was looking even more desperate, glancing between me and Flowers, who'd thankfully been taken aside into conversation with his buddies. "He *asked* me to do this. He knows what I do is *useful*. He doesn't want me to cheat for him, he just wants to know if anyone else is, so I figured I could just keep on telling him nobody was, and at the end of it he'd—"

"Pay you?" Croyd sighed.

"No," said Tim. "He just said I could . . . hang out with the guys."

I felt so sorry for him. Trust me, actors know what it is to be needed. I looked to Croyd. "He really can't look at the cards. So we're just going to let this slide, aren't we?" After a moment, Croyd nodded and stalked away.

Tim looked at me like I was his absolute hero. He was, what, about twelve years old? "The other kids," he said, choosing his words carefully, "they call me Birdbrain. As an insult. 'Cause I always liked birds, always knew tons of shit about 'em. I mean, stuff. Sorry. But then I found out what I could do, and like, hey, ace name!"

"Sure," I said. "You go for it."

He gave me the most vulnerable little smile. "Thanks. You have a good evening. Love the ad. Be lucky." He headed off back to the Flowers contingent. I watched him go, and found myself watching the empty, cynical look on Charlie Flowers's face, as compared to the desperate hope of that boy. There are some people in this world, dear reader, that give one the impression that they have simply never been thumped hard enough. Unfortunately, those tend to be the people who, in reality, have been thumped entirely too much.

I put Tim out of my mind and headed back to Croyd. I'd had that cool line ready, and now I was going to use it. I opened my mouth as I sauntered over, but Croyd spoke first. "So, you worked out what *I* can do?"

"Nope."

He looked charmingly surprised. "I've been trying to experiment with it, fast as I can, as much as I can. I guess it's . . . world changing. The stuff of philosophy. Never heard of anyone else being able to do it. So I got to be careful how I use it, try not to do any harm."

Which I'd like to say was typical him, but, you know, only sometimes. Even as he said it, he had that look in his eye that put a kind of gunslinger irony on "harm." He reiterated that it wasn't anything I needed to worry about. "World changing, kid. Not game changing. Not for this game, anyhow."

And of course, when all hell broke loose, that irony vanished completely and it turned out that, as usual, when it came to me, Croyd Crenson could at times be completely, arse-tighteningly, wrong.

I spent the evening sensing, then whispering to Will about, a large and varied array of powers. These days I can, given fair warning, psych myself up and hold a power at bay, just sensing its surface details, what it "wanted" to do to me, instead of immediately letting it. (Fair warning had not been given before the theater incident.) But that means keeping my guard up, which turned out to be, across several hours of poker, pretty exhausting, like holding an awkward weight with every limb I had. Still, at least I got used to the proportions and placing of said weights, with the same aces mostly in the same chairs. There were some heavy hitters in here. It was . . . interesting to be in same room as John bloody Fortune, for a start, though I couldn't sense any powers from him. Tim kept looking over at him, exactly the sort of famous person he'd come here to see. That part hadn't just been a cover story. Except then Flowers actually reached over and cuffed him, got him to pay attention, and Tim smiled back at him like that was a grand acknowledgment of his existence. Also around the table were several people whose powers I positively had to fight off. Jack Braun, the former Tarzan, projected a sort of brute strength that came with a side order of deliberately obtuse, the sort of American I really have problems with. I couldn't quite meet his eye, though he kept trying to smile aggressively at me, like he did with almost everyone around the table. The guy who said "tiger" at my power senses, the one called Khan, was someone I'd picked out as dangerous at the briefing, and in real life he was . . . well, let's just say I was aware of him in *all* sorts of ways. Tim's bird kept flying from one vantage point to another, and Flowers nodded in approval every time it did so. Hell of a tell.

Then, however, that "old waiter" walked in. I immediately started to tell Will that someone who could increase his strength had just entered. Even as I said it, I was fighting down the urge the new arrival's power was thrusting onto me, that every muscle in my body wanted to escape my clothing. (I end up suddenly naked really far too often for someone who's vowed never to do a nude scene.) In that same second, however, the tiger strength and speed of Khan also amped up for me as he leapt for the new arrival, and so did the fire powers of Cynder, as she blasted randomly skyward, and I realized I was suddenly about to sprout hooks from every part of my body as well and it's probably fortunate for me that . . . well, I overloaded, I think.

As the darkness rolled up into my eyes, I recall feeling again that signal of weird nostalgia and déjà vu, only now it had suddenly amplified. I felt whatever Croyd's power was, washing over me. I felt it as regret, the roaring up of the deepest layer of memory right into the middle of my mind. I was stunned by the recollection of seeing the sea for the first time, a paper hat on my tiny little head, an ice cream falling from my hand as—

I fell.

It wasn't like any sort of unconsciousness I'd previously experienced. My vision narrowed into a sort of tunnel with every possible shade of light stretching into absolute darkness, and my sense of self cut out. Even with my conscious self gone, I was still aware of . . . extraordinary, sudden movement, in a sort of instinctive, emotional, way.

When I came around . . . or sort of woke into my body again . . . something in me thought I was being born. It was very warm, it was wet, I was naked . . . yes, irony upon ironies, this was yet another of those occasions. These conditions persisted, and I realized I had my eyes closed, and that everything else my senses were aware of had returned to . . . well, I want to say normal, but that takes "relatively speaking" into dimensions that phrase was never meant to encompass. I opened my eyes.

I closed them again. Then, slowly, trying hard to keep calm, willing myself to see only what was real, I allowed the light in again.

I was lying, naked, as I mentioned, in a jungle. Truly enormous and very unusual leaves were above me, water dripping from them onto me. Truly enormous and very unusual insects buzzed between them. I was at the edge of the tree line, the light of a truly enormous . . . moon, without some of the features I'd normally want to see on the moon . . . illuminating me. Through the gaps in the last few trees, which had been reduced to ashes and charred, collapsed, trunks, I could see a plain beyond, on which . . . was grazing a herd of . . .

Oh. Oh my fucking stars.

"Croyd Crenson!" I bellowed as I leapt to my feet. "You complete fuckwit!"

Because here I was, looking out on a vast herd of enormous, meaty creatures, their bodies giving off steam, birds that weren't actually birds, more hairy than feathery, flocking all around them in enormous swirls, presumably catching enormous insects. Dark, stormy clouds broiled overhead. It looked to be just past sunset at who knows what millions of years ago.

In the time of the dinosaurs.

That had been Croyd's power. Frigging *time travel*. And he'd used it during a fight at a poker game.

I found that I was taking enormous breaths, out of sheer panic, and that . . . was weirdly satisfying. The air was somehow better than what I was used to. It actually smelled . . . great. I mean, full of the stench of enormous piles of dung, but hey, I grew up in the country. Under that, and the brilliant green smell of the jungle, there was something utterly invigorating. Now, I think that was probably higher oxygen levels. Which is very much a two-edged sword. Yes, you can run a bit longer. But because of the additional fire risks, you're going to have to.

I turned left and right. Shit. Shit shit shit. Time travel. One small step for woman. One giant leap for just me, bloody on my own. What should I do? What *shouldn't* I do?

I looked down at my bare feet, and hopped quickly out of the way of a rather huge millipede that was rushing toward me, and thankfully on its way without having had eating me in mind. Then I gave a little cry of fear and looked back to where my feet had landed. "No stepping on butterflies," I reminded myself, again out loud. Because there had been that story about how time travel worked, hadn't there? By that writer, was it Arthur C. Clarke? That had made it pretty damn clear that any action I took here could have big consequences down the line. I had no idea if that was the case in real life, but I wasn't going to risk it.

I felt that I was probably going to be talking to myself quite a lot in the . . . two minutes to seventy years or so of life in dinosaur land that I had left. "No, no thinking about that, either." I was British, I reminded myself. I was pretty sure that there was no way a fossil of me could reveal that I'd been blubbing, but just in case, I wasn't damn well going to. Also, a fossil of me would be irritatingly helpful to frigging anti-evolution idiots, so I should make sure to . . . get myself . . . no, perhaps later for that train of thought.

At any rate, I was not going to despair, just because I was . . .

stranded zillions of years before any human being would ever be born. Shit. Shit shit shit.

My mum always said if I went into show business something like this would happen.

I took a few careful steps toward the edge of the jungle. Some sort of blaze had indeed been through here quite recently. There were signs on the ground of older ashes, too. And I didn't like the look of the clouds above the herd of . . . whatever those were. The creatures had now started making enormous lowing noises. The cries were so divorced from the calls of any animal I'd heard that they were, actually, the worst thing I'd experienced thus far.

Until, that was, the very next moment, when I heard a voice from the nearby foliage. "Err, hi?"

I spun around and managed to grab and wrench away one of the big leaves to cover myself, basically in one startled movement. From out of the undergrowth, his hands covering his . . . whatever . . . stepped Timmy, also entirely naked. "How long have you been looking at me?" I said.

"I haven't. I mean, I saw you, and then I—"

"If this is a fig leaf—no, it can't be, can it?—if this is something that evolves into a fig, a kind of proto-fig, and you and I . . . I mean, okay, we're now the first people, but that doesn't mean—I'm saying don't get any ideas, okay?!"

He just stared uncomprehendingly at me. Perhaps understandably, yes. Because I'd really gone there before anyone in their right mind would. But perhaps you'd be so kind as to tell me what anyone in their right mind would do at any given moment of this situation?

The boy was looking, I realized, very lost and very scared.

"Sorry," I said. "You . . . scared me. God, actually, I'm really glad I'm not alone here."

"Me too."

I wanted to give him a hug. Except also really not. In movies about prehistoric times, everyone seems to quickly stitch . . . furs, no, not much in the way of fur around here, I thought. I wondered how much the temperature dropped at night. I wondered if Croyd would realize what he'd done, and, if he was still alive, be able to rescue . . . but

no, if so, that would have happened . . . immediately, wouldn't it? If
he could find us, if he'd ever found us . . . here he'd be. Immediately.
Probably. Whatever the rules for this stuff were.

Shit. Shit shit shit shit shit.

I had to get control of myself. For the sake of the kid. "Someone
will find us," I said. Even as I said it, I realized he was looking over
my shoulder, and that all the blood had drained from his face. A
warmer, even wetter, stream of air was wafting gently down onto my
shoulders, and the smell of dung had increased, suddenly, exponen-
tially. And this time it smelled distinctly meaty.

I turned slowly around and looked up into a world of feathers,
bloodshot eyes, and enormous teeth. It must have been strutting
around the edge of the jungle, sizing up the herd of animals on the
plain. It moved its head slowly, to better look at me. It must never
have smelled anything like people, I realized. It didn't actually know
whether or not we were prey.

I was about to roar at it. I swear. I was about to leap up and down
and wave my arms and try to scare it. I was not about to sprint away,
leaving it to discover whether or not it liked human flesh by means
of Timmy.

Which was when the dinosaur gave a little squeal of panic, spun
on its axis, meaning I had to jump over one hell of a tail, and sprinted
off as fast as its little ballerina legs would carry it, making panicked
warning squeals as it went.

I was fully expecting, when I turned to look back at Timmy, to
see an even bigger dinosaur behind us. But there was just Timmy.
He was panting with relief. But he also looked like someone who'd
just seized a life belt and found it was . . . I was going to say made of
gold, but that would actually be very bad news for a life belt. I realized now, as I felt once again his power, what he'd just done.

Timmy could control a single bird. Which meant, it seemed, he
could control a single birdlike dinosaur. "I did it," he said. "Shit, I
did it!"

"Language, Timothy," I said, feeling as if I had to do my best to
act in loco parentis. At least the kid now had something to hang on
to. I didn't want to deflate him by telling him that if he could do it,

so could I. As long as I stayed reasonably close. "But, wow, thanks for saving us." I enjoyed seeing his face light up. Then I looked down and realized I'd let go of the leaf.

I gathered it quickly up again, wondering about the realities of the situation once more. One particular reality was for me about two weeks away, and for that I'd need to have found local approximations for certain items. Which seemed like a pretty big ask. In the short term, there was more than enough water, but who knew if the ancestors of the fruit and veg we knew were poisonous? Still, we could between us presumably get a small dinosaur to baste itself over an open fire. If it was safe to do so, given the butterfly effect and everything. But wasn't every fruit we might eat something's ancestor, too? Wasn't the bacteria in the air? Had Arthur C. Clarke really thought this through? Sod it, I decided, I'd take a future with no tangerines, or whatever, rather than starve.

Was there anyone else nearby with us? I started to shout the names of everyone I could remember who'd been nearby at that poker game, and Tim immediately joined in. We kept that up for a while, uselessly. I realized that Tim had been about the same distance across the room as the distance he'd been from me when he'd arrived here. If the others had landed in the same time, they would surely have been just as immediately obvious. I stopped shouting. So did Tim.

Now I'd had a few moments to . . . no, I was still shaking with shock, so I wouldn't say I'd calmed down, but now I wasn't actually experiencing immediate terror . . . I realized there was a certain silence in my head. For the first time since my powers had manifested, I could feel Tim's abilities, but nothing else. There would be, I realized, an entire world of nothing else out there. I let my power reach out, feeling the relaxation of it, sheer relief after the effort of the poker game, and found, right on the edge of my range . . . what the hell was that?

I turned to look, out across the plain, past the dinosaurs. I couldn't see anything, off into the distance. But it was somewhere in that direction. I told Timmy to stay put, but he yelled in fear that he wouldn't. I explained I was only going a few feet to get behind some bushes and try to get some clothing together, and he haltingly said he'd do the same, but that we should keep talking. So we did. Well, I kept up my monologue of hopeful nonsense, talking about what the journey had been like for me, and he just said "yeah" nervously on several occasions. I tied some knots in leaf stalks, and ended up with a reasonably all-concealing . . . well, Tinker Bell costume, honestly. By the time I got back, Tim had gotten himself a single leaf success-fully tucked up round his . . . yeah.

"Okay," I said, "I don't want to get you hopeful, but—" And I explained what it was I'd felt.

He got all hopeful. "It's your friend, it must be!"

I told him it almost certainly wasn't, because I couldn't feel Croyd's time powers, and I didn't recognize in this faint signal the signature of anyone else who'd been in that room, but even so, I did share a little of that terrible hope. I didn't want to head out of the shelter of the jungle, but if there were others in the same situation, who'd for some reason landed far away, our chances of survival would vastly improve if we could find them. We headed out onto the plain, mak-ing our way around the edge of the great lumpen herd of slowly cir-cling meat. They didn't react to our presence. We were too small to worry them. A number of biped predators were stalking about the edges of the forest. I explained to Timmy the nature of my power, and he looked downcast for a moment, having lost his uniqueness, until I further explained that I could control a dinosaur only while he was around. Together we kept a watch and managed to steer away anything that took an interest in us. I got a handle on how to use his power pretty damn swiftly, because I had to.

I looked up as we walked, at that great sky that hadn't ever been looked at before by human eyes. In the gaps in the clouds, the stars were coming out. I wondered if the constellations would be familiar and felt another pang of geologic time. I was just starting to get the first hint of perspective on how small and insignificant we were. Be-fore we arrived, nothing on this world *knew*. It had all just *existed*: churning, cycling, unconscious meat. And at some point, probably soon, *we* would not know either, and we'd be swallowed up by it, per-haps literally, and the great unknowing would resume, undisturbed. It felt too big to bear. So I was doing what little mammals always did, what people always do: I was refusing to bear it. I saw a meteor. Then a bigger one, a fireball that flared for a second and made Timmy shout in new fear. Then it was gone, then a cluster more, like fireworks, then nothing. I looked to Timmy. He was choking up, trying not to sob. What at home would be just a shooting star was here a potential threat. This long silence had let him have a good long think about our situation.

I wish I knew what it was I was following. For all I knew, I'd discovered dinosaurs with ace powers. Which would be both an amazing scientific wonder and an enormous pain in the arse. Though there was no way I could think of that anyone could have got ace powers before the wild card virus had been released.

We covered the ground pretty fast, marching along. All that oxygen. The plain wasn't covered in grass as such, more a sort of rough moss and weed cover, with very light and rather sad-looking leaves, despite all the ash underfoot. That big moon gave us enough light to see as we crested a low hill and looked down and saw a farther plain beyond, in the direction from which I was sensing the powers.

In the middle of the next plain sat . . . oh my days . . .

"It's a spaceship!" yelled Timmy. Then, a second later, "Oh shit, it's a spaceship."

Because, as I was discovering myself, that's pretty much the natural reaction when one sees a spaceship in the middle of . . . well, I was about to say "an everyday setting," but . . . My first thought was that we must be looking at a Takisian ship. Takisians who'd visited Earth way, way before they were supposed to have. And not in one of those iconic, seashell-shaped ships that had been all over the books in my school library, and were a favorite tongue twister when I was little . . . so actually, even given that we were millions of years in the past, probably *not* Takisians. Which was a good thing, considering their willingness to treat the human race as guinea pigs. Still, at least this was an actual spaceship, and not a blazing pod like those that had brought to Earth that other sort of alien from my schoolbooks and childhood nightmares, the Swarm. Instead, this was a squared-off black-and-white object, with a sort of flattened dome on one corner and a tower on the other, landing gear, and huge wheels dusty from the plain. Under a sort of awning we could just about see moving figures.

I looked at Timmy. He was as nervous as I was. "Okay," I said. "We sneak closer. We try to work out if they're friendly. Somehow. I mean, maybe they're flying a . . . friendly-looking flag."

Which was when I discovered that no plan survives contact with dinosaurs.

The roar came from behind us. We spun around. Running at us, blasting out low, powerful notes that felt like they were vibrating my body and tiny mammal soul at the same time, came . . . well, I still haven't quite worked out what they were, but they were like scary enormous ostriches with sort of hand claws, and there was a whole pack of them.

Timmy and I must have had the same thought at the same instant, because suddenly the leading two ostriches spun on their running claws and leapt at the others following, but that caused only a moment's kerfuffle and feathers flying and shrieks before our two champions vanished into the pack and the rest all swung together, like a flock of psychopathic starlings, and raced at us wing tip to wing tip.

We turned and sprinted for the spaceship.

We ran like scurrying mice under that gigantic sky. We ran screaming and yelling and waving our arms to whatever was ahead. Even getting zapped by space death guns, or whatever, was better than dying messily in a two-person amateur production of *Oh Shit It's Dinosaurs*. As we got closer, the figures ahead started to react, to run about making gestures. So, these were going to be someone new. First contact. With me and Tim here the rather surprising representatives of humanity. Today was turning out to be, as my mother would say, "somewhat eventful." We were running in sheer hope, and fear of what was behind us. As someone who knows story shape, I realized suddenly in my guts that the big obvious shaggy dog story twist here was for the two of us to be immediately zapped for our naive desperation.

The screams on our heels were getting closer. Tim and I kept reflexively turning two more dinosaurs back at the others, but the others just rode over them and kept going, and there were so damn many of them.

Ahead, the figure closest to us resolved itself in my vision. I was ready for anything.

It was the guy from whom I used to buy magazines.

He had seen us, and was now running toward us, waving his arms. Behind him came several other beings of various shapes and sizes, waving various appendages. The power I'd sensed earlier lay behind them, inside the ship, and, I started to realize, it must be truly enormous for me to have felt it at that distance.

However, the closer the lead alien got, the more certain I was that here was my local news vendor. I wasn't getting a sense of any powers from any of these guys, which meant they surely must be aliens, and not victims of the wild card virus. But him being here meant exactly the opposite.

"Jube!" I shouted. "Hey, Jube!"

"You . . . *know* these guys?" panted Timmy.

I wanted to say I knew one of them considerably less well than I thought. Jube was a joker who ran the magazine stall round the corner from my apartment in New York. He looked somewhat akin to a bipedal blue walrus. He normally favored Hawaiian shirts and little hats, even in the hardest Jokertown winters. Here, he was dressed in some sort of scarlet uniform, bare-armed and -legged. I suddenly realized that actually I'd *never* got any sense of what Jube's powers were, but surely that was because I last saw him before my own abilities had matured to what they were now?

He raised a hand, and in it was . . . ah, that was actually one of those space death guns I'd been worried about, wasn't it? I didn't have time to react beyond a first jolt of fear. There was a flash. I grabbed Timmy and threw us to the ground a second before an explosion showered us with soil.

I heaved with my legs and managed to pull the screaming boy to his feet, ready to hopelessly, meaninglessly, run in a third direction again, caught between the screeches that were now almost on us and this new danger. Only then I saw something that had been revealed by the explosion. In front of us, the dust and soil that had been thrown up was hanging in the air, tiny lightning bolts zapping around it, an ozone smell and a stream of smoke indicating its disintegration. A blue glow flickered into a dome shape around the camp. Inside that dome, what I'd taken to be our newsagent-led alien attackers were gesturing urgently.

"They didn't want us to hit their forcefield," I yelled. "They're trying to help us."

As I said it, a gap opened up, right in front of us. We ran at it and leapt through just in time to land, roll over as the field slammed closed behind us, and witness . . . an enormous quantity of chicken flash-frying itself. The screams and the smell and the splattering and sizzling sounds were . . . well, pretty damn satisfying, actually.

We lay there, panting, and, led by my newsagent, the mixture of aliens stepped . . . and oozed and scrabbled . . . forward to meet us.

I got to my feet, hauled Timmy up, and raised a hand. I was panting. "Hello. We're humans. From here. I mean, actually, yes, here, but not yet. I mean, this is our world. Or it will be. But if you're planning on . . . I mean, I really should emphasize it's still *ours*—"

I was perhaps not the ideal spokesperson for the human race. Hey, the first guy on the moon surely had a speechwriter.

I stopped, realizing that my audience was at best not following my meaning, and at worst still possibly hostile, and decided simplicity was the key. I pointed at Jube. "Jube?" I said.

He pointed at me. "Jube?" he said.

I knew it! I threw my arms around him. "In a few million years," I said, "the two of us are going to bond over the editorial direction of *Entertainment Weekly*."

"*Entertainment Weekly*," he replied, carefully hugging me back.

"So are you a time traveler too? Are you *all* time travelers?" Perhaps Croyd's power hadn't been as novel as he thought. Or perhaps Jube was just incredibly long-lived? But no, of course not, he could only have become a joker, only gained any special abilities, after the wild card virus release in 1946. If he wasn't a time traveler, this didn't make any sense.

One of the other aliens stepped forward. None of this bunch were what pop culture would have recognized as stereotypically alien—either handsome and humanoid or roaring shape-shifting monsters—but this guy was like nothing I'd seen on telly or in films. He was a tiny gray biped with enormous black eyes, a slit of a mouth, and a frail, thin body compared to his big head. He wore only a sort of gray loincloth. He struck me as incredibly cute, and that cuteness was welcome in that moment. He held up a long thin device with a bulb on the end, and made a kind of shoving gesture with it.

"He seems to want something," whispered Timmy nervously. "He's kind of gesturing for us to . . . turn around."

Jube gently pushed the little gray guy back and took something from a pouch on his belt. He fiddled with the gizmo thus revealed, and turned a few dials that seemed to spring out to meet his big fingers. All the while he made small barking sounds, which suddenly became . . . "testing, testing . . ."

"Ah, that, that!" I said. "That's it! That's English! Like you were speaking before!"

"English?" he said. "What's that? Lady, I was just copying the sounds you made. I had to let it scan you, 'cause we had nothing in the ship's memory. Who the fuck are you people?"

"We're not Takisians, if that's what you're thinking."

"That's not what I was thinking, because what the fuck is a Takisian?"

His accent was exactly like Jube's even. Except the news vendor had never been this brusque. "Jube," I said, "listen, in the future—"

"Jube? What's Jube? Stop throwing this stuff at me like I should know!"

"Oh, was that maybe just your joker name? I never asked if—"

Jube looked to the gizmo again. "It could be badly tuned, I guess. I don't joke a lot, you know? Let's start again. I'm Petitioner Assistant Snorsk."

I slowly, horribly, realized that I had perhaps broken the record for going abroad and running into someone who looks just like someone from back home. But how could Jube be so like this guy, when, as a joker, he was literally unique? "Oh. *Oh.* I really am terribly sorry. I seem to have mistaken you for—"

"We're on this planet to observe two events, the bosses tell me, one of which is a space-time anomaly. And here you are. So I gotta ask: Are you it?"

I looked at Timothy, he looked uneasily back at me. "Yep," I said, "that's us." We were way beyond stepping on butterflies now. I got the feeling I was talking here not to some kind of space commander, but to an ambitious junior. And God save us from ambitious juniors. So the unexpected intervention of the little gray guy was very welcome.

"I'm terribly sorry," he said, "if I may interject?"

"You're British!" I said, delighted. Obviously.

"I'm sorry to say that is an honor the details of which thus far elude me. I am, your most humble servant, a Moho underling by the name of—" He pursed his thin lips as best he could and gave a little fluting whistle. "The translator device favored by my colleague renders our speech patterns into the closest equivalent to which you have an affinity. Thus, myself: 'British,' whatever blessed condition that may be. My colleague—"

"New Yorker," I said. "Because I thought he was an old friend of mine." And not at all because he was blunt to the point of rudeness. I realized as I said it that my own accent had leapt up several social strata, as it tends to when one runs into the aristocracy. I felt the immediate need to know exactly what sort of ranks and social positions I was dealing with here. Hearing an upper-class accent unexpectedly can do that to you. I mean, to *one*. "So you're an 'underling' and he's a 'petitioner assistant' . . ."

"Oh yes," replied Whistle, "we're terribly, terribly important. No, not at all! Bottom of the greasy poll, that's us. My species has been a member of the twenty-two for some considerable time, but his—"

"We ain't members, okay?" barked Snorsk. "The Twenty-two picked me up from where I was stranded and I ended up workin' for them." He looked to Whistle. "And should you really be carin' and sharin' so much with the space-time anomaly here?"

"The Twenty-two?" I asked, hoping to get one more answer before the others acknowledged the truth of what Snorsk was saying.

"Twenty-two species," said Whistle. "All working together, exploring, researching, and negotiating such lucrative trade agreements! And please, Snorsk, my old chum, these two are obviously such delightful people, why, we should make sure our superiors treat them as guests."

"Stop puttin' it on. You're only interested in the one thing." Snorsk indicated the rod that Whistle had been gesturing with earlier.

"Yes," I asked, nervously, "what *was* that about?"

Whistle looked at Snorsk and gave a little sniff of that tiny nose. "Perhaps later," he said, and sighed. He gestured toward the spacecraft. "Shall we?"

As we were led under the awning and toward an entry port, I watched Timothy's reactions. I'd been in New York long enough to accept people with all kinds of different body types. I was relieved to see that Timothy wasn't shying away from the tentacles and such. It was as if he were so deeply freaked out that this little bit of icing on top didn't make much difference. "There's a dinosaur in there," he whispered to me, nodding toward the ship. "It's not happy."

I could feel, picking up on his power, that he was correct, but that feeling was suddenly overawed for me by . . . it was like a shadow had fallen over my mind. As I said, human beings don't have much in the way of perspective about their place in the cosmos. Even the arrival of the virus and the alien who brought it hardly dented our sense of superiority. "Dr. Tachyon" pretty quickly took on our customs, after all, canny sod that he must have been. But now, here we were, two apes way out of our depth.

The shadow sitting gently across my mind was the immense, close presence of . . . the biggest power I'd ever felt. A power the nature of which I simply couldn't fathom. It had only just decided to notice me. I was aware that I should be picking up associations from it, getting flashes of meaning that should guide me toward being able to use it. But this was like . . . a fly looking at an airliner. They're both in the same line of business. But I realized that I was unconsciously trying to pull my power back rather than connect with it. That would be like trying to drink from the end of the fire hose.

"You look scared," Timmy said suddenly. That was obviously making him even more scared.

I stopped and took a breath, made sure I wasn't about to suddenly be overwhelmed, and the power seemed to realize, to pull back slightly itself. "What?" I said. "Sorry, I was just wondering if I'd left the oven on."

He didn't laugh. He was barely reassured.

The aliens led us into the ship, into the shadow.

The first thing I noticed was the vegetation. Some of the corridors had ferns and bushes actually growing on the walkways, so it was a bit like walking on the plain outside had been. The lighting varied wildly, depending, Whistle told me, on which species most frequented each part of the ship.

The aliens eventually brought us, by way of an overgrown path, to an entranceway that opened out into a domed hub, inside which the undergrowth ran wild. The dome was populated by . . . well, my first thought was that the ship was run by giant golden bats. Or, actually, shit, were these dinosaurs, or at least something related to birds? No, for all the claws and tufts and the ruffs and the wings, they were furry, not feathery. And there was also, perhaps fortunately, no feeling in my head that I might be able to control them. There were eight of them, swinging from what could only be described as perches, claws striking out to activate controls, viewscreens swinging to stay with their ever-changing eyelines. Along the floor and over the instruments ran . . . euw! Huge greeny-black grubs!

I knew, better than most, not to judge. I looked to Snorsk. "So are any of these guys the . . . captain?"

"Like we have a captain! These guys are the Aevre, they fly the ship." However, the power I had felt did not lie here. It was somewhere farther in. Then I gasped. It had suddenly moved. It was right behind me.

I turned around. And realized, as I did so, that I might have just given away more about my own abilities than I cared to. But I hadn't time to worry about that, because I was looking at . . . well, for a moment I thought I was looking at Father Christmas, or an elderly aunt of mine whose passing away was my first experience of death, or at . . . whatever it is you feel in cathedrals sometimes. Then the appearance of what was in front of me shifted, or I had the feeling it had always been what I was now seeing, and why on earth would I think it had ever looked different?

This was a little old lady. This was one of my acting heroes. This was . . . Margaret Rutherford, best known for her portrayal of Miss Marple. I looked between her, Snorsk, and Whistle. "Oh come on," I said. "This is a dream, right?"

"My dear girl, this is no dream," said Margaret Rutherford. "Or if it is, it is equally so for us, and we are both the dreamers and the dreamt." She had that gleam in her eye that had always been there when Miss Marple knew perfectly well who the villain was.

"Who are you? Why do you look like that?"

"I found what you would consider most comforting and wore that."

"What do you mean 'found'?" I noted she hadn't answered the first part of my question.

"I'm not looking into your mind, if that's what you mean. Certain aspects of who anyone is are visible on the surface. Dear me, I'm making you *more* uncomfortable. I've just allocated quarters for you both. Perhaps you'd like to find warmth and rest there for a while before joining me for a spot of dinner?"

I could just about believe that the concept of "a spot of dinner" was visible on the surface of my consciousness. What was troubling me most about this being of incredible power, apart from the incredible power, was her absolute lack of surprise at seeing us. I looked to Tim. He was shaking. He'd reached the limit of what even a young, adaptable mind could accept. "What are you seeing her as?" I asked.

"My . . . my mom . . ."

"Oh," said Margaret Rutherford. "Goodness, we certainly can't have that. Now I'm the same actor for both of you."

Tim relaxed a little. I thought that for his sake, though I had a lot more questions, I'd best accept that offer of a bit of stillness and quiet. "Who is she?" I whispered to Whistle and Snorsk as they led us off down a mulchy corridor.

"The ship's Trader," said Snorsk.

"That doesn't sound so important," said Timmy. He was looking around, distracted. Using his ability, I could also feel, now the enormous power being had departed, that there was a dinosaur somewhere near, and that it was troubled, scared.

Whistle chuckled. "She is the owner of the ship, our employer, the most important person within . . . well, I'm not sure where the next nearest Trader ship is, but within several hundred light-years."

"You lot wouldn't happen to be able to travel in time?"

"Oh dear no, we wouldn't be so interested in space-time anomalies such as yourself if we could."

We were taken to quarters seemingly designed at least for bipeds, with flat beds, and water running down the wall in what looked to be an artificial re-creation of a waterfall. I realized I was thirsty and tried some, and was about to tell Timmy it was okay when he stuck his head under and started gulping it down. Then he sat down on the floor with a thump and started to cry. I fell beside him, grabbed him, and we held each other for a while, the only familiar things remaining in our worlds.

After a long while, after he'd cried it out, I asked Tim about his family situation. "It's no big deal," he said, wiping away the tears on the back of his hand, not willing to look me in the eye. "It's not like I'm abused. They just . . . don't notice me much. Until Charlie did. He's been . . . great. He's really included me. Which isn't like him, 'cause he's really hard-core, and . . . I know he's kind of using me, okay? But that's okay, because I'm using him, and once those guys get to know me, they'll see I can be useful, they'll see there's a place for me. I just gotta find a reason for them to take me and my power seriously. And I just gotta get back there, because . . . because all this is so . . . I just want to go back home, you know?"

I told him I did. After a while, I encouraged him to get up. We were able to find, in the various pods and baskets of the chamber, clothes that vaguely fit us, and so we joined the Trader for dinner in what bore an uncomfortable resemblance to hospital gowns, though thankfully they had backs. She rose from a small round table in the middle of what looked like a meadow, with comforting blue skies overhead, and gestured for us to sit on tree stumps to join her. "You made it look like home," I said.

"She did not," said Timmy.

"I thought it best you share one experience, so I had to choose between two quite different aesthetics," she said. "I'm terribly sorry, Timothy. It seems I can't do anything to please you today."

"S'okay," he whispered, looking at his shoes. I wondered if he was ever going to be able to cope.

"What do we call you?" I asked.

" 'The Trader' will identify me to the crew. Unless there's another one of my people about, that will suffice. Individual names are so dull, don't you think?" I opened and closed my mouth, unable to frame a reply. She seemed to notice. "Oh my dear, you must feel so out of your depth. I do wish I could be more help. Tell me, how exactly did you get here?"

Beings of various species had started putting in front of us food that, while it looked unfamiliar, at least smelled edible. "Umm," I said. "Ah . . ." Because I was, after all, addressing a being of terrifying power who had me by the ovaries. I had never felt so small and insignificant. And I've met theatrical agents. Now I was close to her power, it didn't feel at all like that of an ace. It was utterly different in nature. Different and scary. So that was something I'd learned about my own power: that I could pick up on all sorts of things. What I was wondering was: If this deity-sized old lady was so interested in time travel, and couldn't do it herself, what would she do if she had it? I'd been worried about stepping on butterflies. Here was the biggest butterfly of all. And it could do the stepping. "Sheer accident, I suppose. I don't know much about it." I glanced at Tim, and he nodded. For him that was rather more true than it was for me.

"Oh dear," she said. "You're lying. You at least know the mechanism. A person is involved. A person dear to you." I could feel her starting to probe deeper into my thoughts.

I had to risk it. I grabbed the fire hose and sucked. Her enormous power rushed into my head. I immediately regretted doing that and desperately tried to let go, but then it was pulled away once more.

"Don't do that, dear girl," she said. "Or your head will literally explode."

"I'll do it every time you bloody well try to poke my brain. Or his. I'm sure I can ramp up quickly enough to explode my head before you find anything out. And I'm sure you now value my head more than his, because you'll have sensed how little he knows."

Timmy looked between us, aghast.

The Trader sat back, tapping her mouth with her finger. "Goodness me, you are quick on the uptake. How is it that you can interact with my natural abilities, I wonder? I know of several intelligent biped species. None of them can do that. That is a new thing that is going to happen in the universe, at whatever future point you spring from. Interesting, actually, that you're a mammal."

"Why?"

She shook her head. "If you're not about to volunteer information, neither am I. Well, this has been nice." She stood up, having not eaten anything. "Do finish your dinner." And without a moment when she seemed to have actually vanished, she was gone.

We sat there for a bit, not saying anything. I felt, and so, seemingly did Tim, that we might be still being listened to. Finally, we tried a bit of the local fruit and veg. It was fine. After an hour or so, some crew members arrived and escorted us back to our room. I wondered whether we would have been allowed to leave the ship.

That night, Timmy and I stayed awake. The Trader had definitely given the impression that our conversation would continue. I doubted her motives were entirely dubious. She seemed to run a humane ship, after all. It was her power that worried me. We were cut off from all law, all human rules. I had to learn a lot more before I could trust her. Perhaps she was giving us time to do that. But I wanted to do it in a rather proactive way.

We waited until the ship got a little quieter, which wasn't saying a lot, then pushed open the quasi-wooden door and ventured out into the corridors. I led Timmy after me. He seemed to be keeping it together. He'd mentioned to me an idea that seemed like a good first step in working out how things really were here. "Let's find that poor dinosaur," he whispered.

Of course, I could feel it, too. That sense of projected saurian misery. The closer we got to it, the more the corridors filled with those insect things, skittering back and forth. Suddenly, I heard a voice from behind us. "Oh, hello. Are you out for a stroll?"

It was Whistle, with that probe of his in hand. He gestured to it, seeming almost embarrassed. "The mating customs of my people mean I am often found tiptoeing away from nighttime entanglements.

Even our form of greeting indicates the possibility of romance. Other species and their physical differences have for us always been the greatest adventure. But surely I cannot hope that you are on the same joyful mission?"

"Nooo," I said, boggling just a little. Timmy was violently shaking his head. "We just . . . couldn't sleep."

"Well then, allow me to give you the grand tour. Have you met the Queen?"

"Do you mean—?"

"Not the Trader, dear hearts, the Queen!"

I allowed him to lead us. It turned out we were still heading toward the dinosaur I was sensing. We walked through a pair of double doors into an open area in which sat . . . well, it took all my liberal joker-friendly sentiments not to scream at what I saw. Inside the dome was a sort of giant blobby insect thing, wrapped in an embrace with . . . it took me a moment to work out what I was looking at. It was like an enormous embryo, that is to say, an embryo the size of an adult human, in a sac of nutrients, pipes feeding to the transparent, bulging walls. The creature inside was curled, unborn, mostly just an enormous brain, but with hints of tiny limbs, eyes. It was the sad dinosaur that had been calling to Tim and me. "Oh," I said, "that sort of . . . Queen. Is the dinosaur . . . part of it?"

"What are you doing to it?!" whispered Timmy, horrified.

"It's a bit of a failed experiment," said Whistle. "We grew it here. The Queen is the heart of the ship, responsible for our sensors, security systems . . ."

"Why did you attach a dinosaur to it?" I looked up at the poor thing, certain now that only Timmy and I could feel its pain. I was certain also that I wasn't entirely happy with a culture that allowed this.

"Its brain is used to augment the Queen's processing power. The Trader seems to like these dinosaurs of yours. She's a great fan of highly evolved species. We've been collecting DNA from them, presumably with the aim of breeding and trading them."

I looked to Timothy. His expression was now one of pure rage. I realized, in that moment, that to him this was one of his beloved

birds being caged and abused from . . . well, before birth. "It wants
to get out," he whispered.

"Well, ah, that's a bit above my—"

"Let it out!"

"Perhaps we could ask the Trader if—?"

"No! No more!" Tim closed his eyes. The dinosaur embryo thrashed
and started to bellow. "Come on!" he cried, and grabbed my hand.

We left Whistle behind us, flailing and desperately calling after
us. We ran through a ship in which the vegetation had begun to
thrash as if a storm were rushing through it. Every door was suddenly flying open, every alarm blaring. Tim, I realized, had used his
power over the dinosaur to throw a spanner in the works. "I had to
stop it," he yelled to me. "It isn't meant to be here! It doesn't have a
place here! It wants to die!"

The grubs were rushing everywhere. Nobody blocked our way as
we headed to, and out of, the main doors, which were standing open.
I couldn't feel the power of the Trader, I realized. Surely she could
stop us if she wanted to? "Where can we run to?!"

"Back to where we arrived! That's where they'll come to find us!
Or we can hide there! Until the aliens have to go!"

I must confess, even having seen the dinosaur/insect Queen
combo, I was conflicted as to whether or not this was the best move.
But I had no idea what kind of punishment Tim might have invited by
doing this, and figured in the moment that following him was ful-
filling my duty of care. I could always negotiate with scary Miss
Marple with Tim safely in hiding. And there was a slim chance someone might indeed come looking for us. If the aliens had sensed our
space-time anomaly, maybe others could, too.

We ran across the plain as lightning started to strike on the
horizon. In the gaps between the clouds, I realized I was now seeing many, many more shooting stars. I remembered something Snorsk
had said: that the ship had come here to observe two events. I skidded to a halt. "Tim," I shouted, "I think we should go back—!"

But he wasn't listening. He was running for dear life. He was
running for that tree line as if there he would find once again the
only home he had.

I set off after him again, yelling, as the rate of shooting stars overhead increased every second. I ran across the plain like a rodent. I ran with the sky falling. "Tim!" I yelled, as I burst through the tree line behind him, "I think it's the meteor. It's the frigging meteor that kills the dinosaurs!" Tim was nowhere to be seen. I kept calling his name, more desperate by the moment. The meteor had landed somewhere in Mexico, hadn't it? Just for once, that didn't seem that far from Chicago. Whether we'd freeze in a global winter or . . . or with all this oxygen, all it would take would be one chunk of flaming rock to land within several miles—!

I have never been more grateful to have the image of standing on a beach in a paper hat rush into my head, as it did at that moment. I spun around. Behind me had appeared Croyd, naked in that new old body of his, and a small man who'd been one of the guests at the poker game, whom I knew from my research to be John Nighthawk. "We got the right time!" said Croyd. He must have had some means to find us geographically, too, because we'd just run for the tree line; it would have taken us a while to find the place where we'd appeared.

I couldn't help it. I ran to him and stared into his triumphant smile.

Then I smacked him round the gob.

As he dragged himself to his feet, I was about to finally come out with my Lauren Bacall line, when Tim ran past me and grabbed Croyd's hands. He'd come from the underbrush. He was carrying something under his arm. "Don't be angry with her," he pleaded. "Please! We gotta get home!"

"Kid, of course we're going to—"

All sound was cut off in that moment by the brightest light I had ever seen. It was like flashlights had suddenly illuminated the southern horizon. I now realize this must have just been the light of the impact reflected off the clouds, not even the light itself. "Take us back!" I shouted. "Now!"

"I say, wait a mo!" That familiar voice had come from above. A small, silvery flying pod was descending at the edge of the jungle. In it sat Whistle. "I've been sent to persuade you to come back."

"No!" screamed Tim.

"Is the ship all right?" I called to him as he stepped from the pod. I was fighting off a very British urge to apologize.

"Oh yes, the disruption only lasted a few moments. In fact, as soon as I'm back, with or without you, we're about to take off, because as you may have noticed, the second event we came here to observe is about to—"

Another sound came from across the plain, a dull roar. We all looked in that direction. A blaze of light was rising into the sky.

Whistle stared at it in horror. "Oh, the absolute *rotters*," he said.

And in that moment I knew that, somehow, we had all been part of the Trader's plan. Or one that she'd come up with after meeting us, at any rate. If she could track one space-time event, she surely knew we were about to be rescued. She must, for some reason, want Whistle to come to the future.

I looked to Tim, and saw what he had under his arm. He was carrying a dinosaur egg.

"I had to save one," he said. And he looked at me with such a determined expression that I couldn't insist he part with it. Charlie Flowers was soon going to have a very big reason to take "Birdbrain" seriously.

"Oh—" began Croyd, and I think he was going to finish that with "—kay!" But at that moment he gestured frantically just as a wall of light and sound and heat hit us and the edge of the jungle, and something from his hands hit the silvery shell of Whistle's flight pod and I was suddenly on the déjà vu express again, and then—

I was standing in the middle of an enormous stadium, full of people. I was naked. Again. Damn it. I became aware that the shouts of the crowd had now turned into a roar of . . . well, I think it was mostly applause. I looked round. Standing with me were a twelve year-old boy clutching a huge egg and a little gray alien. They were both also naked. And, erm, well, I don't quite know how to put this, but I think Whistle might find himself to be quite popular in his new time period.

I covered myself. Ballplayers . . . Cubs players . . . came running over, either laughing or telling us off, asking if this was some stunt, but to give them due credit, those actually soon became concerned questions. Whistle was looking round, lost, without his translation device or his beloved cultural . . . probe. He let out a long, untranslated whistle.

Security people ran on. I was provided with a blanket. I asked what day it was and found out we'd been gone for less than forty-eight hours. I directed all questions to Will Monroe's office. After a while, a lawyer and some of Will's assistants arrived and were allowed to collect us. Local law enforcement had been informed, but the Cubs weren't pressing charges. Indeed, something was said about me pitching the first ball next season. So there's that.

We had maintained throughout that Whistle was a kid in a costume. Thankfully, nobody seemed to feel they had the authority to question that. As we were driven, fully dressed, out into blissful, sunlit Chicago once again, he looked as mournful as Tim and I looked relieved. A call had been put in to Charlie Flowers. I hoped, if he was also back from a time-travel experience, it might give him some more empathy with the kid. I took both their hands. "It's going to be all right."

Whistle obviously didn't understand my words. Tim just hugged the egg tighter to his chest. The experience sat in me, as yet undigested, but it was already starting to chill me, and it has ever since. There has been time, after all, for millions of years of consequences. At least nothing has changed about the present day. But what has the Trader done, in all that time, with her knowledge of the future?

When I heard he was back from his efforts to save everyone who'd been in that room, I called Croyd, and after asking about who and how and all the times he'd been to, I finally got to use that line I'd prepared. Which had gained somewhat in pertinence. "Every time I see you," I said, "I realize how much older we both got."

I also said sorry for hitting him. He just laughed. I think I can rely upon that.

I worry particularly about Jube. I haven't yet returned to New York, but when I do, what am I going to say to him? Did the tide of genetic anomalies ebb and flow enough to have made him look like he does by accident? Or is there something deeply wrong underneath all we experienced? Is there some meaning behind Jube's resemblance to Snorsk?

Because, if so, that might be jolly bad news for the human race.

A Long Night at
the Palmer House

Part 5

"THIS IS GOING TO be kind of tricky," Croyd said as he gazed at the shiny curved side of the spaceship.

"I didn't need to hear—" Nighthawk began, but his final words were spoken into the void of the time stream as Croyd sent them on their way with the usual gut-jarring results.

Again, it went on for what seemed to be far too long as they journeyed across millions of years. Actually, Nighthawk suspected, the trip took place between the beats of his heart, though it was hard to figure out the actual duration of their journey. He was getting somewhat used to the process, but the side effects of the transition were still quite disorienting.

They landed in the usual denuded state in the countryside near an open road underneath a tree that looked comforting in its familiar modernity. As did the cab sitting in the shade under it, if in the cab's case by modern you meant a model made somewhere in the middle of the twentieth century.

The cabbie was sitting behind the wheel, reading a newspaper. He was a middle-aged black man, portly, dressed in a cap and a work uniform that had the name of the car company stitched over the pocket of his shirt. He lowered the newspaper and looked out the window at Nighthawk and Croyd. "You must be the gentlemen I was sent to pick up," the cabbie said. "A white man and a black man, both naked as jaybirds." He nodded.

"Sent by who?" Croyd asked, after he and Nighthawk had exchanged glances.

"I don't ask no questions," the cabbie told them, "and I don't answer none. There's clothes for you in the back seat."

"Our unknown benefactor strikes again," Nighthawk said.

"It could be a trap," Croyd said suspiciously.

"If so," Nighthawk answered, "I want to be dressed when we have to fight our way out of it."

Croyd shrugged. "You have a point."

The clothes fit. Better yet, so did the shoes. They were all mid-century casual style.

"Can you answer this question?" Croyd asked as he pulled up his pants. "What's the date?"

"It's the twentieth of September, 1942," the cabbie said.

"Not too bad," Croyd said in a satisfied voice as the cabbie looked on in studied disinterest. "I was aiming for the temporal anomaly in 1929—so thirteen years off in over thirty million. That's a pretty small error."

"We'll just have to jump again," Nighthawk said.

"That we will." Croyd was still self-satisfied. "But there also happens to be an anomaly in 1942. We'll take care of this one, then move back to 1929 and then we'll be in striking distance of the Everleigh Club."

They looked at the cabbie, and he just shrugged. "It's all Greek to me."

Nighthawk said, "Uh-huh," and turned to Croyd. "Sounds like a plan, I guess."

"I'm supposed to give you this." The cabbie handed them a newspaper through the driver's-side window after they'd finished dressing. Nighthawk took it from him and Croyd stood, annoyingly, over his shoulder, to read the front-page headline that screamed out in banner type: NAZI SPY CAUGHT IN LOVE NEST WITH DEAD ARAB.

Below the headlines was a photo of a bewildered-looking Jack Braun wrapped in a sheet and wearing handcuffs, being led off by cops.

"Get in," the cabbie said. "I was told to take you to the Palmer House."

Nighthawk looked at Croyd, nodding. "Of course. There's no way we're going to be able to bust Braun out if he's already in police custody. He's either in the House of Corrections or the Cook County Jail, depending . . . believe me, it'd take an assault team of aces to get someone out of either place." He paused, frowning. "I wonder why they think Braun's a Nazi spy?"

Croyd shrugged. "He pops up mysteriously in a hotel room. He has a German surname. It's 1942."

"Must be more to it than that."

"We'll have to ask him when we rescue his golden ass," Croyd replied. "But why the Palmer House?"

"We have to get to him before the cops do."

"Riiiiight," Croyd said, nodding.

"Just give your names at the front desk," the cabbie told them as they stopped at the Palmer's entrance. "There's a reservation waiting for you."

Nighthawk and Croyd exchanged glances, Nighthawk shaking his head in bewilderment.

"Wish we could tip you for all you've done for us," Nighthawk said.

"Don't worry about me," the cabbie told them. "I've been well taken care of. You gentlemen take care of yourselves, now." Whistling tunelessly, he pulled away from the curb.

It was like the man said. They told the reception clerk their names, he handed over the room key that was waiting for them. As they entered the elevator Croyd nudged Nighthawk surreptitiously, gestured with his eyes toward the young black operator who'd just asked them their floor number.

Nighthawk nodded. "I heard you had some excitement here a couple of days ago."

"Yes, sir," the young man said. "Some crazy man somehow got

into a suite, shot a foreign gentleman." He looked at Nighthawk with a scandalized expression on his face. "And they were both *naked*."

"That's pretty strange," Nighthawk commented.

"Sure was," the operator said, warming to the story. "They scared the professor so much that they moved him right out of there. And you know what?" he added conspiratorially. "They wasn't the police that arrested the crazy man. It was the FBI, sure enough. Then they took the professor and his wife away somewhere else."

"The professor?" Nighthawk asked.

"Yeah. Some little Italian guy. Nice guy, though."

Nighthawk mulled that over, trying to link the date and an Italian name in his mind in the few moments they had before they reached their floor. *Chicago, 1942. An Italian professor.* It finally clicked as the elevator came to a halt and the door dinged open.

"It wasn't Dr. Fermi, was it?" he asked.

The elevator operator thought for a moment, then nodded. "Yeah, that was his name. He was always so polite—your floor, sir."

"Thanks," they both said, not to be undone by the foreign professor, as they exited the elevator.

"Well, that explains it," Nighthawk said. "Enrico Fermi."

"Wasn't he a scientist?" Croyd said as they walked down the hall. "Had something to do with the atom bomb, right?"

"Yeah," Nighthawk said, "something. He designed and supervised the construction of the first nuclear pile to have a controlled, self-sustaining reaction. You know, the one they put in the old squash court under the football field stands at the University of Chicago. The one they built as part of the Manhattan Project, starting, well, right about now."

"Holy crap," Croyd said. "So someone calling himself Jack Braun shows up naked in his hotel suite with a dead guy? No wonder they thought he was a Nazi spy."

"I'm sure Braun had a calm, rational explanation for it. He probably told them he came from the future. He was drunk as a skunk at the game, you will recall."

Croyd rolled his eyes as they stopped at the door of the very same suite where the action had taken place several days before and which their unknown benefactor had thoughtfully reserved for them. Croyd opened the door. They went in, looked around. It was very nice.

"Well," Croyd said.

Nighthawk nodded. "No sense prolonging this."

"Yeah." Croyd thought for a moment. "Let's go in from the bathroom. That'll give us a fraction of a moment of surprise before we rush in with our junk hanging out."

Nighthawk smiled at the thought of Donald Meek saying "junk."

"What?"

"Nothing," Nighthawk said. "Drop the cops, or the FBI agents, or whoever the hell has a gun first. Just remove them from the scene. That'll give us a chance to deal with Braun."

"Good plan," Croyd said. Then he shrugged. "Or, at least as good as it can be."

"You realize this all depends on your pinpoint control of the time stream," Nighthawk warned. "We're talking about arriving seconds before or after Braun. Even being minutes off might prove disastrous. I can't even think of the paradoxes that might occur if we have to go after them *again*. The notion makes my head hurt."

"No pressure," Croyd muttered. The expression on his face made Nighthawk wonder how much longer the Sleeper could go on.

A pleasant-faced, clean-cut, well-dressed young man was sitting on the toilet when Croyd and Nighthawk popped into the bathroom. He was the very picture of a young, bright-eyed FBI agent. The look on his face was something to see as the time hoppers materialized in front of the sink right next to him. He began to stand up, started to reach for the gun holstered in a shoulder rig under his left arm, then reached for his pants. His indecision proved unfortunate.

Nighthawk popped him a hard one right on the point of his jaw. His head snapped backwards and hit the wall behind the toilet, came forward again. Nighthawk crossed with a left that slammed him into the bathtub, where he went down in a heap. Nighthawk was on him instantly, but he was out like a light.

"Dibs on his pants," Nighthawk said in a low voice.

"Not again!"

"Ssshhhh," he shushed Croyd as he reached for the towel hanging in the rack by the sink. "Toss me that washcloth."

He quickly gagged and bound the FBI agent, whose identity was confirmed by the badge he carried in his hip pocket. Nighthawk relieved him first of his pants, then of his gun. He hoped he wouldn't have to use the gun, but at the very least it might come in handy as persuasion. He put on the man's pants and cinched his belt tight around his waist. He looked down at him, still unconscious in the bathtub.

"You could take his shorts," he said to Croyd in a low voice.

"Ewww, really?"

Nighthawk shrugged. "Up to you." Naked, Donald Meek looked a bit like a shaved monkey. The boxers that the unconscious agent wore wouldn't have helped much.

"Screw it," Croyd said, which did sound funny in Meek's voice. "I am what I am."

"I'll lead," Nighthawk said quietly. "If we can get the drop on them maybe you won't have to pop away any of the agents. In any case, we have to be quick."

"Okay." Croyd glanced down at the still unmoving agent. "We better get going before they send out a search party for this guy."

Nighthawk went quietly on naked feet to the bathroom door, Croyd following just as silently after him. He unlocked the door, pulled it slightly open. The bathroom was located in the same spot as it had been in the future, in the short hallway before the suite's front entrance and the sitting room. From that room came the sound of murmured conversation, the clinking of cups being set down, of silverware scraping across plates. Obviously, someone—a few people— were having tea, or a light snack.

Nighthawk looked at Croyd and mouthed the words "Where's Jack?" and Croyd shrugged helplessly. Together, they crept silently up the short hall to the unobstructed entrance to the sitting room.

As they moved, Nighthawk realized that he could detect at least three voices. One, male, speaking excellent English with a musical

Italian accent. Another, female. Her English was less certain, her accent thicker. The third was a younger man speaking flawless English with a drawl. He addressed the other two as Doctor and Signora Fermi, and Nighthawk nodded. His suspicions were confirmed. Fermi had probably recently arrived in Chicago to take over the construction of what became known as Chicago Pile One, and the rest was nuclear history.

The government was putting him up at the Palmer House before finding regular housing for him. Nice work, Nighthawk thought, if you could get it. Of course, Fermi was worth it. The man who'd left Italy because of restrictive laws they'd passed that affected his Jewish wife had helped the Americans beat the Germans to the atomic bomb. The use the bomb had been put to was debatable, Nighthawk reflected, but if the Germans had won the race everyone in his time in America would be speaking German, at least to their overlords. It was no wonder that they'd leaped to the conclusion that the strange intruders, no matter how weirdly they'd arrived on the scene, were probably German spies.

With that thought, as if on cue, came the sound of sudden thuds in the sitting room, followed immediately by the noises made by chairs scraping across the floor, china being dropped, and a woman's choked scream.

Nighthawk whirled into action, Croyd at his heels.

There was chaos in the sitting room. Jack Braun and the body of poor Siraj had materialized. Prince Siraj was lying there bleeding. Signora Fermi was sitting at a small table, her hands to her face, looking at Siraj's body and screaming. Jack had been in the process of falling backwards when the time beam had struck him, so he continued to fall backwards, stumbling into an FBI agent, who was reaching for his gun. Fermi had been conveying a pastry to his mouth. He was still sitting in his chair, not quite knowing where to stare himself.

Nighthawk and Meek added more chaos to the situation by revealing themselves, Nighthawk shouting, "Jack, take the FBI guys!"

For all his drunken state and the uncertainty of his position, Braun was a man of action with good instincts. He pushed off the one agent, the mere flick of his wrist sending him slamming back into the wall, and headed for the other. The second agent belatedly reached for his gun. The look of astonishment on his face turned to terror when his shot ricocheted off Jack's chest. Before the bullet could strike Jack his entire body began to glow with the golden sheen that contributed so heavily to his name and legend. He reached out and grabbed the agent by the shirt, lifted him effortlessly with one hand, and whirled, throwing him into the other where he lay on the floor, fumbling for his own weapon. They collided with an audible smack and both lost any interest in the proceedings. "What the fuck!" Braun roared. He stared at Nighthawk, panting more from sheer surprise than exertion.

"Hang cool," Nighthawk said, "we're here to send you home."

Jack looked around, his general attitude resembling that of the bull ready to destroy the china shop. "Where am I now?"

"Croyd!" Nighthawk yelled.

Croyd was suddenly at his side, color blooming from his hands, and Jack was gone.

Signora Fermi was reduced to a silent, gaping expression. The professor looked on with astonishment.

Nighthawk turned to him. "It's an honor to meet you, sir," he said.

Fermi's soulful eyes turned to him. With his bald head and bags under his dark eyes he looked like a larger, better-fed version of Donald Meek.

"I don't know if you've actually formulated it yet," Nighthawk told him, "but in about four years you'll have the answer to Fermi's Paradox." He winked at the doctor, and turned to Croyd. "Let's blow." Together they both went down the hall, back to the bathroom.

"Extraordinary," said Enrico Fermi.

Stripes

by Marko Kloos

ONE: PALMER

ONE MOMENT, SOME HULKED-OUT meathead was trying to pull Khan's head off his shoulders and, from the feel of it, almost succeeding. The next moment, Khan pushed back into empty air with all his might. Not even his reflexes were fast enough for him to catch his momentum, and he stumbled forward and plowed face-first into the carpet.

Teleporter, he thought at once. *The guy's strong as a freak,* and, *He can teleport? Some guys get all the good skills.*

The suite around him, which a moment ago had been noisy with the sounds of no-holds-barred tussling, had turned quiet as quickly as if someone had turned off the sound with a switch. Khan gathered himself, rolled over on his back, and jumped back to his feet, claws out and ready to cut. The suite had been plunged into darkness, too, but to his left eye, that made almost no difference at all. But there was nobody in here with him. Ten seconds ago, he had been wrestling with whoever had made an attempt on his client, that little prick Giovanni Galante, and the room had been full of people. All the high rollers, their bodyguards, the girls who were serving the drinks. And now it was completely empty. Khan had walked in wearing an expensive suit, a Colt .45 automatic in a python-skin holster, and a thousand-dollar pair of shoes, and now he looked down at himself and saw that he was naked, without a scrap of clothing on his body. No suit, no shoes, no socks. No gun. No underwear.

"What the fuck," he said out loud. "What. The. *Fuck*."

Nothing in the room looked right. Khan was a bodyguard, and when he had walked into this suite earlier tonight, he had memorized the layout before Galante had even made it to his chair at the end of the table. You had to be able to read a place and predict threat directions in his line of work. Never seat the principal near a window. Always make sure you have your back to a wall. Sit in a place where you can see the door, so you can spot trouble coming as soon as possible. Khan had mapped the suite in his head thoroughly—every piece of furniture, every corner, every bar or counter solid enough to hide behind. And the room he was standing in looked nothing like the one he had walked into with Giovanni Galante earlier.

Oh, it was the same room, no doubt. The geometry was the same—door ahead and to the left, two bedrooms on the far side, two over on his left, a bathroom by the little entrance hallway. But aside from the lack of people, the furniture was all wrong. The huge card table that had been in the middle of the room—the one he had flipped over while fighting off the ace who had attacked Galante—was no longer there. In its place stood a coffee table and a couch, and two matching armchairs on the short ends of the table. They looked red in the darkness, and there were little tassels on the bottom fringes of the chair covers. The bar at the other end of the room was gone, and there was a fireplace where there had been a liquor cabinet and a sink before.

The room smelled different, too. In fact, the whole place did. It stank like tobacco smoke, the sort of smell that permeates walls and carpets in a place where smokers live for years. It made Khan wrinkle his nose in disgust. He had never liked the smell of that shit even before his card turned. Now, with the super-acute sense of smell of his tiger half, it was almost like a physical assault on his olfactory nerve. When he thought about it, the place didn't sound right either. The Palmer House was inside the Loop, and even though it was the middle of the night, it shouldn't have been this quiet out there. This was downtown Chicago, after all.

Khan checked himself for injuries. There weren't any to speak

of—a bunch of bruises from where the ace who had attacked
Galante had pummeled him a few times, but there were no broken
bones, and he knew the bruises would stop aching and disappear in
an hour at the most. He padded over to one of the windows, which
now had heavy red brocade curtains in front of them. Then he reached
out and moved the curtains aside to get a look at the outside.

"What the fuck," he said again. It seemed to have become the
theme of the evening.

Outside, it was dark, and it was snowing. And while Khan knew
that he was looking at the corner of State and Monroe—he knew the
topography inside the Loop like the stripes on the left side of his face—
it wasn't the State and Monroe he knew. The streetlights, the power
lines, the signs on the stores, everything was off. There was snow
piled up on the edges of the sidewalks, which as unusual enough considering that Galante had been bitching about the August heat and
the shitty air-conditioning in the Palmer when they had walked in.
A car puttered along Monroe, and it looked like something straight
out of a museum. There were more cars parked by the curbs on
Monroe and State, and they all looked old, yet new at the same
time, like someone was holding a street meet of perfectly restored
vintage cars out there.

I know where I am, he thought. *The question is,* when *am I?*

There had been other aces in the suite with him and Cyn when the
fight started. Cyn, Golden Boy, Meathooks, and a few others that
Khan knew by reputation, powerful and dangerous people. The Arab
prince's companion in particular had worried Khan—not because she
looked like a huge physical threat, but because none of the guys in
the room could keep their eyes off her for longer than ten seconds.
None of the high rollers would have been careless enough to just bring
regular muscle along, not with the stakes on the table. The aces in
the room had been the most impressive concentration of fearsome
abilities he had ever seen in one place together. Shit, everyone knew
Giovanni Galante's temper.

The guy who attacked him hadn't been in the suite when the game
started, though. He had been dressed as a waiter, brought Galante

his steak, and then it had all gone full rodeo within a second or two. But Khan didn't think the false waiter was responsible for this. First the fists and claws had come out, Cyn had started tossing flames, then someone had whipped out a gun and started shooting . . . but someone else had unleashed a big can of temporal whoop-ass right in the middle of the fight. Khan didn't know if he was the only one in the suite who had been ripped from the time stream and unceremoniously dumped some*when* else, but he supposed it didn't much matter right now.

That false waiter—he knew he hadn't seen the guy before, but now his brain told him otherwise. It was like there were two sets of memories battling for dominance in his tired brain. One memory said he'd never met that freakishly strong guy swearing in Polish. Another said that he had fought him before, years ago, on a construction site somewhere on the South Side. Khan vaguely remembered fists and steel girders, and a massive headache when it was all over. And he couldn't quite figure out which memory was true. Maybe they both were.

The living room part of the suite was empty, but there were four bedrooms in the place, and all the doors were closed. Khan stepped next to each door in turn, smelling and listening, hoping the place wasn't rented out to some rich family or a bunch of foreigners on a leisure trip. But the bedrooms all smelled like nothing but laundered linen and cigarette smoke.

He opened all the doors and started going through the closets for something to wear. If he stepped out looking the way he did, he suspected that the negative attention would be much worse than usual. Whenever this was, it looked like it was well before the first Wild Card Day, and nobody out there would know shit about jokers or aces. With luck, they'd just flip out and consider him a circus freak. With a little less luck, they'd call the cops and try to pump him full of buckshot. Khan wasn't in the mood for either right now.

The closets in the bedrooms were empty. There was a walk-in coat closet by the door, but that one was empty as well except for a laundry bag on a coat hanger. Khan checked the bathroom and found two bathrobes hanging on hooks. He tried one on and promptly tore it in half along the seam in the back when he tried to slip his arms into the sleeves. He tossed the robes aside and went back to the walk-in closet. The laundry bag was a big piece of canvas that looked like a sleeping bag. He popped out his claws and tore holes into it for his head and arms. Then he slipped the whole thing on. It was tight, but it did at least make him feel like he was wearing something.

There was a mechanical clock ticking on the mantelpiece of the fireplace. It showed ten past two. Even at this hour, leaving the suite through the door and wandering the Palmer House hallways didn't seem like a good idea. Khan was good at sneaking, and he was sure that security cameras were not yet an issue whenever this was, but there was no way to make it through that huge lobby and out the door without being spotted.

He walked over to the windows on the far side of the room, which looked out over an alley and toward the next building on State. They had simple latches, and he popped them and opened both. They weren't worried about people falling out and liability lawsuits, whatever the year was right now. Khan looked to make sure nobody was out on the sidewalk right below him, and then leaned out of the window. There was a fire escape, but it was three floors below the windows of this suite. Outside, the wind blowing through the alley was bitingly cold.

Khan muttered a curse and swung his legs over the windowsill. Then he let himself drop down to the fire escape three floors below. He landed with a muffled crash and the alarming sound of creaking and popping steel as his three hundred pounds of mass landed on the grating. For a moment, he expected the welds of the steel to give way under him and kick off a pancaking collapse, but the structure merely groaned under his weight. A few minutes later, his hands and feet were numb with cold, but he was safely down in the alley.

State Street to my right, he thought. *The park is to my left. Two blocks across Wabash and Michigan Avenue. Find a place to hole up, get warm, figure out what to do next.*

He set out down the snow-covered alley, as quietly and swiftly as he could on numb feet. Two blocks to cover and safety, and maybe some warmth.

TWO: LAKESIDE

THERE WAS NO PARK yet, of course. Not the one Khan knew from his own time, the one they had just finished in the late 1990s. In what was still the present time in his own mind, you were in Millennium Park as soon as you got across Michigan Avenue. But this Michigan Avenue, in whatever year this was, didn't border a park. It was a rail yard, rows and rows of tracks, some with freight cars parked on them. It didn't look very inviting at all. But he had gotten too cold on his dash through the alleys, and his mind was still coming to terms with the fact that *this* now wasn't *his* now, so Khan leapt the fence and went into the yard to look for shelter anyway. At least he wasn't likely to run into anyone out here at two thirty in the morning.

The wind was blowing stronger out here near the lake. The rows of railcars were tempting, but Khan didn't try to open any. He would have been able to get into even the locked ones, of course, but he was tired and didn't want to be halfway to Indianapolis when he woke up. Moreover, some of the railcars had people in them. He could smell them, hear them moving around even in their sleep, and dealing with freaked-out bums was low on his short list of things he wanted to manage tonight.

There was a maintenance shed a quarter mile down the tracks, and he didn't sense anyone in it. The door was locked with a heavy padlock, which he grabbed with his tiger hand and tore off. Inside, the place smelled of grease and oil and mildew, but it was a shelter from the wind, and there were some tarps stacked in a corner he could use to cover up for the night. There was a metal advertising calendar on one of the walls that said CENTRAL CHEMICAL CO., MANUFACTURING CHEM-ISTS, and on it was a dirtied sheet of paper that said 1929–JANUARY–1929 across the top, with the days and weeks of the month in the rows underneath.

Nineteen twenty-nine, he thought with amazement.

Whatever that ace in the hotel room had unleashed, it had knocked Khan eighty-eight years into the past. He wondered what had happened to the other people in the suite when it happened. Were they here—or would they be here soon—in 1929, freezing their asses off in the streets of Chicago? He almost had to chuckle at the thought of that little shit Giovanni Galante, buck naked, without his shiny tracksuit and his gaudy hundred-thousand-dollar jewelry, or his cash or credit cards, trying to figure out what the fuck was going on. The kid was practically helpless without his cell phone and a responsible adult to watch his ass.

Khan scratched together his knowledge about 1929 while he was making himself a sleeping nest in a corner of the shack. His sister Naya had brought him all sorts of books from the library during those agonizing months after his card had turned and the wild card virus had slowly changed him into what he was now. Mostly fiction, but lots of other stuff, too. He had always liked reading about history.

Prohibition, he recalled. Speakeasies. Booze smuggling. Gang warfare. Not a lot unlike the shit that went down in the present—his present—with crack and coke and amphetamines. It was sort of his world, they just used a different commodity.

Nothing about this made any sense, and he wasn't about to try and unravel it tonight. Khan decided to sleep on it and then figure things out tomorrow. Maybe he'd be back in the suite up in the Palmer in 2017 when he woke up, with a drunk Galante sleeping off his booze coma next to a trio of high-dollar hookers. Not exactly something Khan would wish for under ordinary circumstances, but at this point it would improve the situation massively.

He wrapped himself in the musty-smelling canvas tarps and closed his eyes. Sleep came surprisingly easy, considering what a weird-ass night it had been so far.

Khan woke up with the first daylight from the ruckus of a freight train slowly rumbling across the train yard on a nearby track. A fucking *steam* train, chuffing past the shack slowly like something from an old movie. It smelled like burning coal and hot grease. He checked the wall of the shed, where the same calendar still hung: 1929–JANUARY–1929. Outside, a way off still but coming closer, were voices, undoubtedly rail yard workers showing up for the morning shift.

Looking the way he did, he figured it wasn't wise to show himself in broad daylight. He got up, gathered the canvas tarps he had found, and looked around for other useful stuff. There were grease buckets and tools, nothing he wanted to burden himself with at the moment. He found a length of rope and took that as well, and a knife he found in a drawer underneath the workbench. Then he opened the door a crack to peek outside, and took off across the rail yard toward the lake. The snowfall had picked up in the night, and the shed was out of sight in the snow squall when he was a hundred yards away.

Down by the lake, there were plenty of spots that were just unkempt slope covered in shrubs and small trees. Khan found a spot at the base of a tree that was sheltered from the wind on three sides and spent the next half hour making the ugliest tent in the world out of the tarps and the stolen rope. Then he huddled down in it and waited for nightfall.

He had been dozing lightly when he heard someone coming down the slope where he had set up camp. It was still dawn outside, but the snow had slacked off. He could smell the two guys who were headed straight for his little tent—body odor, mostly, with some booze and cigarette smell thrown in. They stopped in front of his tent and started talking quietly among themselves, probably thinking he was asleep. Then one of them bent down and grabbed one of the sides of his tent tarp.

Khan let out a low growl.

The guy who had grabbed the tarp let it go as if he had burned himself.

"What the hell, Eddie. Some fucking animal."

"Piss off, the both of you," Khan said. "Find another spot and let me sleep. I don't have anything to steal, trust me."

"If you got a dog in there, asshole, it ain't gonna help ya much," the other guy said from outside. "Why don't you come on out."

"Don't make me," Khan grumbled.

"Oh, I insist," the other guy said. Khan could smell the gun oil and the powder in the cartridges before he heard the cocking of the hammer of the gun the guy had in his hand now.

"You may wish you hadn't," Khan said, and stood up, flipping the tarp back and over his head as he did.

There were two of them—his nose hadn't lied—and they both looked a little rough, winter coats that were on the ratty side, worn-out shoes, unshaven faces. One of them was maybe five nine, and wearing a driving cap on his head. The other guy, the one holding the gun, was considerably larger, probably six one to Khan's six three. Khan grinned, knowing full well that even in the low light of dawn, they couldn't miss the three-inch canines on the left side of his mouth. Both guys stepped back quickly, and he could smell the sudden, sharp stench of fear on them.

"What the hell are you," the smaller guy said.

The bigger guy—presumably named Eddie—didn't bother trying to find an answer to that. Instead, he raised the revolver in his hand and aimed it at Khan's chest. Then he pulled the trigger. His finger made it halfway through the trigger's arc before Khan lashed out with his left hand, the tiger one, extending his claws along the short way to Eddie's wrist. Eddie's hand, now separated from the rest of him, was still holding the gun when it flew past the shorter guy and thumped down into the underbrush on the slope somewhere.

"Didn't I say you may wish you hadn't insisted?" Khan said. "Now look what you've done. Idiot."

The shorter guy didn't have a gun, that much Khan could smell. But he did have a knife, a fixed blade that looked like it had started life as a butcher's knife. To his credit, the short guy had balls. He pulled the knife from his coat pocket and thrust it at Khan's side. Khan leaned back and avoided the blade easily. With his feline reflexes, he could have lit a smoke while waiting for the blade to arrive at the spot where his chest had been just a few tenths of a second ago. Then he grabbed the smaller guy with his right hand, pulled him close, and threw him down the slope and into the underbrush, the same way

Eddie's hand and gun had gone. The small guy yelped as he crashed into the thicket and rolled down the slope in the darkness.

Eddie didn't seem to be in the mood for a fight anymore. He stood doubled over, his left hand around his right wrist, which now ended in a stump that squirted blood onto the snow rather messily. He groaned and looked up at Khan with an expression of utter disbelief.

"What the hell *are* you?" He echoed the earlier words of his shorter pal.

"I could explain, but you don't have the time," Khan said. "You need to get your ass to a hospital and get that sewn up before you bleed out."

"You're not gonna kill me." Eddie's face was contorted with pain, but Khan saw the concern, and the quick glance toward the claws still sticking out of his left hand. Khan wiped them on the laundry bag he was wearing for a tunic, then retracted them.

"I should. Probably do the world a favor before you jack someone else and try to shoot them in the gut for nothing. But I'm not going to. Now get the fuck out of here."

The big guy turned around, still half crouched and holding his bleeding wrist.

"Wait a second," Khan said. "Leave your coat. I'm freezing my ass off."

Eddie peeled himself out of his coat without complaint, probably more than happy to lose only that worn-out garment instead of his head.

"You're not worried about me ratting you out?"

Khan laughed. With the vocal cords from his feline side, it sounded like a cross between a cat purring and a motorcycle idling.

"Go ahead, if you think they'll believe you. Now drop the coat and beat it."

With the two transients knowing where he had camped out, Khan pulled his pathetic little tent up and looked for a new place to wait out the day, which was a pain in the ass. On the plus side, Eddie's coat was warm and almost fit him properly, even if it did smell like someone had dragged it through a piss-filled ashtray repeatedly. And he would have had to lie if he'd claimed that roughing up those two idiots hadn't been the first fun he'd had since right before he'd walked into that fucking Palmer House, one night ago and eighty-eight years in the future.

THREE: DOWNTOWN

AFTER THREE NIGHTS IN the underbrush by the railway yards, Khan was starting to get convinced that this was not a temporary thing. Every morning, he woke up hoping to see the familiar walls of his apartment's bedroom, or even the suite at the Palmer Galante had booked for the night. Khan had worked for many clients he didn't like personally, but Giovanni Galante was now the first one he officially hated. Not only was the guy a punk and a shitbag, he had also triggered whatever had bounced Khan back in time the better part of a century. The worst thing was that he couldn't even look the little prick up and cut him to ribbons because Galante wouldn't be born for another sixty-odd years.

If he was going to be here for good, he figured that he'd have to find a way to get around and do something constructive, because huddling in a tent by Lake Michigan in the freezing January weather was getting tedious. On the fourth night, Khan decided to make a few supply runs into downtown.

There were plenty of stores nearby, in and around the Loop, and neither of them had an alarm system worth a shit compared to 2017 standards. Khan hadn't even known they had burglar alarms all the way back in the 1920s, but a lot of the bigger stores had them installed, primitive things working with copper contacts on the door frames and windowsills. They were easy enough to bypass or destroy outright by pulling the alarm boxes off the walls, where they were usually mounted high up near the gutters.

Clothing proved to be a bit of a problem. There were lots of clothing stores and tailors, but none of them had anything on the racks for a physique like Khan's. He got lucky in a place where they sold working clothes, overalls, and heavy winter work jackets for longshoremen or rail yard workers. That made him look more like a regular person except for the fact that half his face and one hand sticking out of the sleeves of his new heavy jacket looked decidedly inhuman.

He found a temporary solution in a pharmacy down by Randolph and Lake, which had medical supplies stashed in the back: bandages, Plaster of Paris for casts, crutches, and all kinds of stuff that looked like quackery to Khan. He loaded up a bag with stuff that looked useful for what he had in mind. Two hours and a side trip for food to a corner grocery on Lake later, Khan was back in his hideout for the night. He had found another service shack at the southern end of the train yard, and that one had a proper bathroom in it. At least he had gotten knocked back to a time when indoor plumbing was already a thing.

It took a bit of time and practice, but a little while later, he had used a bunch of bandages and a plaster half mask to turn himself into a fairly convincing recovering burn victim. The plaster mask covered the tiger part of his face completely, and the bandages helped tie everything into place and cover his furry left paw. He could still rip everything off quickly, but now he could pass casual muster on the street as just some poor longshoreman who had gotten himself torched in a warehouse fire or something. People in 2017 weren't very aware of their surroundings most of the time; he suspected that things weren't all that different in 1929.

There was no cooking setup in the shack, but Khan had taken stuff from the grocery store that didn't require preparation—bread, sandwich meats, cake, candy, a bunch of other high-calorie junk. He ate all of it while sitting at the small table in the service shack and reading the newspapers he had grabbed on an impulse on the way out of the store. If the date on the masthead was right, it was Wednesday, January 30, 1929. The prices on the grocery store ads in the back of the paper were ludicrously low—Campbell's soups for ten cents a can, peanut butter for twenty-nine cents a pound, six cents for a sixteen-ounce can of pork and beans. He had hauled back a shitload of groceries from that store, and all in all, he had probably stolen five bucks' worth of food. Of course, the average weekly paycheck right now was fifty or sixty bucks, he reminded himself.

Nineteen twenty-nine, he thought with wonder, reading news-paper articles with local names he didn't know, reporting on events that had happened almost ninety years ago in Khan's head.

I won't be born for another fifty-six years, he thought. *Naya won't be born for another fifty-seven. Shit, by the time the old man is born over in Punjab, I'll be three years from collecting Social Security.*

Naya. Thinking of his little sister stung much more than the bit-ing cold outside, more than the hunger he had felt the last three days before the grocery store break-in.

I'll never see her again, he thought. *I'll be eighty-nine by the time she's born. If I make it that long.* He knew his history, and he knew that the time between now and 1987 was anything but peaceful. The Great Depression. World War II. The wild card virus. He'd have to live for another eighteen years disguised as a burn victim or some-where out in a shack in the wilderness before he could even be himself again without people trying to kill him or stick him into a circus.

I can't live in a shack and steal bread and canned pork and beans from the grocery store for eighteen years, he thought. *If I'm stuck in this, I have to make the best of it. I have to go back to doing what I know.*

He wasn't much into sports, so he had no idea what to bet on to become rich in the past. He didn't know anything about the stock market other than the fact that it would crash hard later this year and usher in the Great Depression, and he had no money or con-tacts to mess with stocks even if he did. But he did have his strong arms, the claws at the end of his left hand, and the ability to see and smell trouble coming. Khan was a bodyguard for shady people with money, and if he wasn't certain of much else right now, he knew that the city of Chicago was lousy with those in 1929.

Every place has a feel to it, especially big cities. New York felt like New York, L.A. like L.A., and you were never in doubt which one you were in even if you were to lose your eyesight. Smell, sound, weather, even the din of the bustle around you were different in every city. And Chicago still felt like Chicago, even though the sensory details were muffled and filtered somehow, like he was look-ing at everything while wearing tinted glasses and noise-altering headphones. But after walking the nighttime streets inside the Loop for a few days, even the old cars didn't seem out of place anymore, and he had gotten used to the smell of cigarettes and 1920s personal care products. There was the familiar rattle of the el cars overhead, the cold wind coming in from the lake, everything he remembered from 2017, so familiar that he could imagine himself back in his time when he closed his eyes.

The criminal scene, however—there was nobody he knew. No contacts, no family, no reputation. The Galante family wasn't even on the map yet. None of his old principals were. Khan knew about Capone, of course, and his rival Bugs Moran. But there was no easy *in* for him, nobody he could ask for an introduction or a favor. He briefly thought about getting some attention by walking into a speakeasy or two and stirring up trouble, but he dismissed the idea almost as soon as it popped into his head. He knew he could scare the shit out of the locals, but that wasn't the kind of attention he wanted, not yet anyway.

Can't work my way up the way I did after my card turned, he thought. *I need something big, something that will put me on the map instantly.*

The answer came to him somewhere on Wabash, at one in the morning. He was out for one of his nighttime walks, when few people were out in the freezing cold. A poster in one of the grocery store windows—a six-pack of soda bottles, with a frilly heart next to them and a Cupid in one corner.

VALENTINE'S DAY! Your party guests will welcome COKE—Take Home Several Cartons Today!

He felt like slapping himself on the side of the head. All those history books he read, born and raised in Chicago, and the date and year hadn't popped into his head earlier. The St. Valentine's Day Massacre—February 14, 1929. That was less than two weeks away. Khan knew it was going to be a bunch of Bugs Moran's guys getting shot to ribbons by a Capone hit squad. He knew it was going to happen. He even remembered some of the names. Hard-ass Frank Gusenberg, one of Moran's enforcers, who would briefly survive the shooting and tell the cops that "nobody shot him" even though he'd have fourteen bullet wounds in him. Fred "Killer" Burke, a nasty piece of work pulling triggers for Capone. Khan didn't remember all the players, but he knew when and where it would go down, and that was all he needed.

He didn't remember the address, but he knew the name of the warehouse—SMC Cartage. Two minutes in a phone booth were all he needed to get the address of the place, 2122 North Clark Street. The travel map of Chicago Khan had swiped a few nights earlier— God, how did people ever live before GPS and cell phones?—told him that 2122 North Clark was up in the Lincoln Park neighborhood. And blessedly, he saw that Lincoln Park, all twelve hundred acres of it, already existed in 1929. Best of all, 2122 North Clark was only a block from the park.

Khan felt more energized than he had been since that fucked-up poker game. It felt damn good to have a plan again. He didn't bother going back to the rail yard to collect his stuff. It was a bit of a hike to Lincoln Park from downtown, he could hit a shop or two along the way for more food and supplies, and he wanted to beat the sunrise.

FOUR: CLARK

THE TWO-BLOCK AREA AROUND the SMC Cartage warehouse was much smaller than the Loop. Khan scouted it every night, and by the time Valentine's Day came around, he knew every last detail about this little stretch of 1929 Chicago—every store, every alley, every streetlight—and he had even started to memorize the license plate numbers of the cars in their regular nighttime parking spots.

For a little while, Khan had been worried that the time stream may have been thrown off by his arrival, that history had started to take a different flow around him somehow. Maybe the massacre wouldn't happen. Maybe everything he thought he knew about the events to come was already wrong. But it eased his fears when he noticed that he wasn't the only one staking out the warehouse. This part of North Clark was lined with residential buildings, and one of them was almost right across the street from the warehouse. Khan had a nose for danger spots—it was his job, after all—and he knew that three or four guys were holed up in one of those apartments and kept a steady watch on the garage every day for three days running. He knew which car they drove. One night, he even ventured into the apartment building from the rooftop and stood in front of their door for a while, listening to them talking in low voices. They carried guns, all of them. Khan could smell the gun oil and the powder in the cartridges. He could have popped the door off the hinges and cut all three of them up before they could draw their guns, of course. But there would just be three dead mobsters in a rented apartment, with nobody to carry word back to the guys they were trying to kill. Khan had to let them go through with their plan until the last moment, until the triggermen had Moran's men lined up.

On the plus side, February 14, 1929, started just like Khan's old history books said it did. On the minus side, it didn't end precisely how he had planned to rewrite it.

The dawn had brought a light snowfall, and the streets were covered in dirty slush. Khan was out in the daytime for the first time in a week. A guy his size with half his face in a mask would have drawn attention no matter how much he tried to blend in, so he was crouched on the flat rooftop of the brownstone building next to the warehouse, huddled underneath a ratty and dirty piece of tarp. He roughly knew how the whole thing was going to go down, and once Capone's gunmen showed up, timing would be critical.

The sun had been up since seven, but neither Capone's nor Moran's men were early risers. It was well past eight before Khan saw the first of Moran's men arrive at the warehouse. They were all dressed much more nicely than Khan—suits, ties, long winter coats, snazzy hats. It looked like the movies hadn't lied, and that the mobsters of this day liked to be dressed in their best when out and about on business. He had to admit that these guys looked much more sharp than Giovanni Galante in his tracksuit.

I'm going up against Capone, Khan thought, and the idea put a grin on his face, cold and uncomfortable as he was on that snowy rooftop. *Al motherfucking Capone.* This was stuff right out of the history books.

A bit past midmorning, two cars puttered down the alley toward the garage. The one in the lead was a marked police car. It was followed by a shiny black sedan. Khan slipped off the tarp that had kept him covered, and stretched his arms and shoulders a little to get the blood flowing again. He extended the claws on his tiger hand and took off the oversize boot that covered his left foot so he could extend his toe-claws as well.

In the alley below, the two cars came to a halt. Khan saw movement out of the corner of his left eye and looked down the alley to see two men in suits and winter coats stop cold at the sight of the police car. Then they turned and walked back around the corner toward North Clark. Moran's men, Khan figured, or maybe even Moran himself. *They think the place is getting raided.*

The doors of the cars opened. Two cops got out of the police car. Khan knew they were Capone's triggermen, merely dressed like cops, but Moran's men had no way of knowing that, and they'd all line up for them in front of the wall without a fuss in about thirty seconds. Phase two of Capone's plan undoubtedly involved the two men in civilian clothes who stepped out of the second car. They were dressed smartly as well, long woolen winter coats and fedoras, and each of them carried a Thompson submachine gun. Khan watched with a little thrill as they took magazines out of their coat pockets and loaded their guns. *Tommy guns,* he thought. *Just like in the fucking movies.* He knew his way around guns after ten years on the job. Nobody used Thompsons anymore because they were heavy as fuck and about as ergonomic as railroad ties, but he had fired one a few times before, and they made a lot of .45-caliber holes in things very quickly.

The guys dressed as policemen took shotguns out of the back seat of their police car and opened the back door of the garage. Then they walked in while the two guys with the Thompsons waited silently, one on either side of the door. A few moments later, Khan heard shouting from the inside of the warehouse, someone shouting commands, a dog barking. The two guys with the Tommy guns waited a few beats, then followed the fake cops inside.

The roof of the SMC Cartage building was two floors below that of the brownstone, so Khan swung himself over the edge of the roof and climbed down, using his claws for traction and the vertical gutter tube on the corner of the building for a handhold. He dropped onto the garage roof as quietly as he could. Then he jumped from the edge of the garage roof to the alley, an easy twenty-foot drop. Both cars in the alley had their engines running, and the black sedan behind the police car had a driver behind the wheel who gave Khan a wide-eyed stare. Khan decided that he didn't have the time to deal with the driver. He just shot the guy a hard look and went inside through the back door.

There was a truck parked in the garage. It stood between the back doors and the main part of the warehouse, where the two fake cops had finished lining up Moran's men against the wall. They were busy disarming them, pulling weapons out of waistbands and pockets and tossing them toward the middle of the garage. There was a dog tied to the bumper of the truck, a German shepherd, and it was barking at the fake cops, who went about their business undeterred. The two smartly dressed hoodlums with the Tommy guns stood by the front of the truck, just out of sight of the men who were lined up against the wall, and with their backs turned to Khan.

This is going to be a piece of cake, Khan thought. He covered the distance swiftly and quietly. Maybe he could pull this off and save Moran's men without any shots alerting the neighborhood.

Then a car horn blared outside in the alley. The driver had found his nerve after all.

Khan was almost within arm's reach of the two suits with the submachine guns when they turned around at the sudden noise. One of them was a little faster than the other, and obviously not new to the killing business. He brought up his Tommy gun just as Khan reached him. Khan swiped at the gun with all the force he could muster, which was a lot. The ten-pound submachine gun went flying across the garage and crashed into the brick wall to Khan's right, hard enough to make the stock shatter and the drum magazine fall out. Gun, stock, and magazine clattered to the cement floor of the garage. The back of the drum magazine popped off when it hit the floor. The .45-caliber cartridges inside, propelled by the wound-up mainspring of the magazine, spewed out of the drum with a strangled-sounding *sproing*. With the gun out of the way, Khan grabbed the gunner by the coat and threw him roughly along the same trajectory the gun had taken. He hit the wall hard, bounced off with considerably less resilience than the Tommy gun, and fell to the floor.

The second Tommy gunner managed to get a burst off just as Khan grabbed the muzzle of his gun and pushed it away from him. The hot gases from the compensator at the end of the barrel burned Khan's hand, and he let out an inadvertent roar. He doubled his grip on the barrel of the Tommy gun, yanked it away from the shooter, and flung it backwards and out of sight. Then he grabbed the goon by the lapels of his coat and head-butted him. The move had the desired effect—the Tommy gunner went slack—but the plaster mask on the tiger part of Khan's face took half the hit and crumbled like an eggshell. A good chunk of it fell off and disintegrated on the cement floor.

In the garage in front of Khan, things had gotten a little more restless at his appearance. Moran's men, who had been lined up along the wall in grudgingly docile fashion, were now turning their heads to see just what the hell was going on behind them. The two fake cops, both holding their double-barreled shotguns, clearly didn't know what to make of this unplanned turn of events. Khan could smell sudden and sharp fear on both of them.

"Guns down," he half roared. "Don't do anything stupid."

When you tell someone to not do anything stupid, they'll go ahead and do something stupid nine out of ten times. One of the fake cops couldn't quite make up his mind whether to keep aiming his shotgun at Moran's men or swing it around at Khan, so he did neither, kind of waving the barrel around halfway. The other cop wasn't plagued with indecision. He brought his own shotgun up to his shoulder and aimed it right at Khan.

Khan was still holding the unconscious Tommy gunner by his coat lapels. He picked him up and threw him toward the cop with all the force he could muster, which was a lot. The unconscious guy probably weighed two hundred pounds, and when he hit the fake cop, both went to the floor hard. The shotgun in the cop's hand barked and spewed a load of buckshot into the wall above the back door.

The other fake cop had finally made up his mind about which threat to prioritize and swung his shotgun toward Khan. Now unencumbered, Khan dodged to his right and crossed the distance with a single leap just as the shotgun roared. Then Khan had the gun barrels in both hands, wrenched the shotgun from its owner, and snapped it in half. The fake cop scrambled backwards and pawed at the holster on his belt to get out his revolver. Khan swiped his tiger hand down the front of the fake cop's uniform, and his claws sliced neatly through leather harness, pistol belt, uniform fabric, and skin. The leather harness gave way, and the gun thumped to the floor, still in its leather holster. Khan made a fist with his right hand, the human one, and pounded the fake cop in the temple. He was a big guy, six one at least, but he went down like a dropped sack of cement.

If Khan had intended to keep his intervention low-key, the plan was a total failure. Two shotgun blasts, a burst from a Tommy gun, one very loud and angry tiger roar, and now lots of yelling and screaming as Moran's men finally realized that the cops weren't genuine, and that the guy roughing up the hit men was half Bengal tiger. Nobody even tried to go for the guns piled up in the middle of the garage floor. They all just started running for the back door. Outside, in the alley behind the garage, the getaway driver must have heard enough to convince him that things had very much not gone according to plan, because Khan got a brief glimpse of his face as the car drove past the back door and up the alley at what passed for full throttle in 1929. A few moments later, the garage was empty except for Khan, the four unconscious would-be killers, and a dog who was barking himself hoarse.

"Oh, for fuck's sake," Khan said.

He went over to where the dog was tied up and severed the leash with a swipe of his claws. The dog shot off toward the back door without so much as a look back.

"*You're welcome,*" Khan shouted after him.

FIVE: MORAN

MORAN'S MEN HAD SPLIT up in the alley. Most of them were running to the left, toward Dickens Avenue. Two had picked the other way and turned right to run north. One of them—Khan couldn't decide if he was the smartest or the dumbest of the bunch—had climbed into the fake cop car to make a motor-assisted getaway, but he was either not familiar with the car model or not a very skilled driver. By the time Khan reached the back door, the cop car was just barely in gear and moving. Khan caught up to it easily. He jumped onto the passenger-side running board, opened the door, and plopped himself down on the passenger seat. The driver yelped and tried to open his own door to jump out on the move, but Khan yanked him back by the collar of his shirt.

"*Whoa* there, sport. You sit tight."

"*What do you want?*" The driver sounded like he was about half a degree away from blowing his mental circuits. Khan reached over with his right hand and straightened out the steering wheel before the car continued its momentarily rudderless course and plowed into the side of the brownstone next to the garage.

"I want you to calm the fuck down. Take the wheel and drive this fucking car before you kill us both. Now look forward. Don't look at me."

"All right, all right," the driver said.

"You try to jump out again, I'll haul you back and twist your head off, do you understand me?"

"Yeah, okay. Okay. Jeez. Okay."

Khan tried to file the face of the driver in his brain's database of historical knowledge, but came up short. He knew what Capone and Moran looked like, but he hadn't known the names of most of the people at the garage, would-be killers or would-be victims.

"Keep it straight. Get out of the alley and take a right on Dickens, go toward the park. Got it?"

"Yeah, I got it."

"What's your name?"

The driver looked at him sideways and swallowed hard. Khan supposed it didn't help that the side of him the driver could see was his tiger half, not the human one.

"May," the guy said. "Johnny May. Look, I'm not even with those guys. I'm just a mechanic. I fix cars."

"Johnny May," Khan repeated. "Turn right here on Dickens."

"Yes, sir."

They took the turn, and Khan looked around for the rest of the Moran gang, but they were all out of sight already. *Fear can make a man pretty fast,* Khan thought.

"Do you have any idea how lucky you are, Johnny May? You and the other Moran boys?"

"Look, I told you I'm not really—"

"Yeah, you're just the mechanic. Those guys that lined you up right before I got there? What do you think they were going to do?"

"I don't—I don't know. The two cops came in and told us to get up against the wall. They frisked us. Took all the guns. Those other two? I didn't even see them."

"They came in after the cops," Khan said. "With loaded Tommy guns. Did they look like cops to you?"

"Aw, jeez."

"Yeah," Khan said. "Capone's guys. They were after Moran. They were going to shoot everyone in there. And they wouldn't have given a shit that you're just the mechanic, trust me."

"My dog," May said. "We gotta go back. I left the dog tied up."

"I cut him loose. Does he know where home is?"

"It's too far. I live on North May. We gotta go back for him."

"Forget it. Unless you want to talk to the cops. They're probably on their way right now. That was some noise we made back there. What's his name?"

"Huh?"

"The dog. What's his name?"

"Highball."

"Highball," Khan repeated. "Shepherd?"

"Huh? Yeah. I've had him since he was a puppy."

"He'll be fine."

They drove in silence for a little while, Khan pointing whenever he wanted Johnny May to make a turn. He noticed that May tried to avoid looking at the tiger half of Khan's face, but that he wasn't quite successful, glancing at Khan quickly whenever he thought his passenger wasn't looking.

"Where are we going, mister?" May finally asked after they had gone five or six blocks.

"You're going to go home," Khan said. "To your wife or girlfriend or mother, or whatever. After you ditch this car somewhere. It's got cop markings all over it. But first, you have to do me a favor."

"And what's that?"

"You take me to wherever Bugs Moran hangs out these days. I need to talk to him."

May blanched visibly.

"I can't do that, mister."

"Sure you can. You think I want to kill the guy? If it wasn't for me, he'd be seven guys short tonight. Do I look like I'm with Capone? Huh?"

"No, mister, you do not."

May swallowed hard and focused on the road again. Khan hoped that nobody had called in a suspicious police car leaving the scene, because he really didn't want to duke it out with the Chicago cops out in the middle of Lincoln Avenue.

"So help a guy out. Drop me off and point me in the right direction. And then you can go home. Look for your dog. Have a damn drink. Be happy that you're not bleeding out on the floor of that garage right now with a bullet in your brain."

May was badly shaken, and Khan didn't have to pry much. They turned west, then north again, until Khan was pretty sure they were back in the general area just west of Lincoln Park. The snow had started to fall again, fat flakes drifting from the sky and reducing visibility. Somewhere north of Armitage Avenue, May pulled the car over and pointed ahead.

"I don't want to drive up there in this thing, but it's the Parkway Hotel. Mister Moran's apartment is up on the fifth floor, in the place that overlooks the corner. Look, just don't tell 'em I showed you, okay?"

"Relax," Khan said. "But do remember that I have a really good memory, Johnny May who lives on North May Street and has a German shepherd named Highball. You lead me on a wild-goose chase, have me knocking on some Italian grandma's apartment door while you hightail it back to town, I'm gonna come look you up. Are we clear?"

He let out a rasping little growl for emphasis, just enough to make May squirm in his seat and lean over to get as far away from him as he physically could without opening his car door.

"Yes, we're clear, mister."

"Good. Now get out of here. Go home to your sweetheart. And start checking the paper for a new job tomorrow. Fix cars for people who don't have enemies with machine guns."

"The money's good," May said. "I got a family to feed. I got seven kids at home."

"You won't be feeding nobody when you're on a slab at the city morgue," Khan said. "Ditch the car. Go home."

It was snowing harder now, so it didn't look too odd for Khan to cover his head with the top part of his coat. He got out of the car and watched as May drove off and turned right at the next intersection. Then he started walking in the direction May had pointed him.

The Parkway Hotel building was right across the street from Lincoln Park. Khan had been sleeping a few hundred yards from Moran's apartment, almost in his line of sight, for a week without knowing it. He went back to his hideout in Lincoln Park and made himself another burn mask disguise with the supplies from the drugstore. Then he waited out nightfall, reading the newspaper and eating cold baloney sandwiches. Well after dark, he went to the Parkway Hotel and ducked into a side alley. Fire escapes were easy to reach when your vertical leap was fifteen feet on a lazy day. He climbed up to the fifth floor and let himself into the corridor through a window. The corner apartment was directly to his left, and the locks in 1929 were shit compared to the modern high-tech stuff in his time.

The apartment didn't exactly scream "gangster boss," but it was also clear that there was no little old Italian grandma living here. There was a booze cabinet, all the furniture was nice, and it took

Khan only five minutes of snooping around to find a stash of cash and three guns hidden in various locations around the apartment, out of view but ready to access in a hurry if you knew where to look. He put the guns on the kitchen counter, picked up the nicest one—a lovely blued Colt 1911, the bare-bones ancestor of the gun he had carried in 2017—and unloaded the others. The Colt had a full magazine, and Khan chambered a round and flicked the safety on. Then he went over to the liquor cabinet, which was artfully concealed behind a bookshelf, and helped himself to some whiskey. It was rotgut compared to the stuff he usually bought back home, but it was his first drink in a week, and he sure as hell needed one after the last few days. He sat down in a comfortable armchair in the corner of the living room, put the gun in his lap and the whiskey on the side table, and killed some time counting the money from the stash.

Moran and his lieutenants must have been thoroughly spooked by the shooting at their main headquarters, because they didn't show up at the apartment until just before midnight. Khan could hear and smell them long before he heard the key turning in the lock he had picked earlier. He counted four different voices and smells, and three of them were familiar to him from the warehouse tussle earlier.

The first one into the living room was one of the guys from the garage. Khan guessed he was one of Moran's enforcers, because he smelled like violence and didn't seem like the accountant type. Moran came in second—Khan recognized him from the pictures in the history books. He didn't know the third guy, but the fourth looked a lot like mook number one, so Khan guessed they were brothers. The living room was dark, and he waited until everyone was in the room before he turned on the little standing lamp next to the armchair.

"What the f—"

The brothers both went for their guns. Khan raised the cocked pistol and shook his head.

"Nuh-uh, boys. Let's not make any undue ruckus."

They hesitated, which wasn't a hard thing to do when you stared down the barrel of a .45 automatic. Moran, to his credit, seemed more concerned than outright afraid. The guy behind him gasped when he saw Khan.

"It's the *guy*, Bugs. The same guy. From the warehouse."

"Tell your boys to keep their heaters in their waistbands, Mister Moran," Khan said amicably. "I have really, really good reflexes. But I'm not here to harm you."

Moran looked at the two bodyguards, then back to Khan. He bit his lower lip and shrugged.

"Pete, Frank. You heard the gentleman."

The two brothers relaxed their stances. Khan wasn't worried about the third guy with Moran. He had kind of a bookish look to him, and he didn't radiate the same sort of attitude the two enforcers did. Khan couldn't even smell a gun on the guy despite the events earlier today.

"You came pretty close to getting your tickets punched today," Khan said. "All of you."

"You would know. You were there," Moran said. "Or so Adam says."

"He was there," one of the brothers confirmed, and the other one nodded. "Took out all four of them. He's not lying about those reflexes."

"So you're not here to kill me," Moran said. "And you're not here to kill my guys, or you could have done it back at the warehouse earlier. So why *are* you here?"

"For a job interview," Khan said. One of the brothers chuckled, and Moran joined him.

"For a job interview," Moran repeated, and looked at the guy next to him, the one he called Adam. "Can you believe this guy?"

Khan lowered the gun, but left the hammer cocked. Then he nodded at the couch and the other two armchairs that were set up around the coffee table in front of him.

"Why don't you have a seat, and we'll talk things over. But please don't try to make a run for it, any of you. I'm not here to hurt you, but if you run off to bring back trouble, I'll put two rounds into each of you before you can make the door."

Moran looked at his enforcers and nodded. Then he walked over to the armchair directly across the coffee table from Khan and sat down.

"He's got a cat face under that mask," one of the brothers said. "Looks like a damn tiger. Like some sideshow trick."

"I'd like to see that," Moran said.

Khan lifted his left hand and held it out for them to see, covered in orange and white fur as it was. He extended his claws slowly, and all four of the men in front of him flinched or gasped. Then he hooked one claw underneath the plaster of his mask and pulled it off carefully.

"I'll be damned," Moran said. "What on earth *are* you, exactly?"

"I can't really explain that in a way that would make sense to you," Khan said. "At least not yet. For now, let's say I have an *affliction*."

"An affliction," Moran repeated. "I see. Do you have a name?"

"They call me Khan."

"That's it? Just *Khan*?" Moran smiled. "I can work with that. Nice to meet you, Mr. Khan. Now, you want to tell me what went down at my warehouse this morning?"

"You should have a rough idea by now. That wasn't a police raid. The cops weren't cops. They were a hit squad. Looking for you. I don't think I need to tell you who hired them."

"I knew it," Moran snarled, and looked at Adam, who was still standing and regarding Khan warily. "That fucking low-life beast."

"Jesus, Bugs. He damn near got all of us. You, me, everyone," Adam said. Khan's brain finally supplied a last name for the guy: Adam Heyer, the gang's bookkeeper, Moran's business manager.

"I saw the cop car pull up in the alley," Moran said. "Figured it was a shakedown raid. So Ted and I turned around and went for a coffee. Warned off Henry, too. If I'd gotten up a little earlier . . ."

"If it wasn't for him, we'd be dead now," Heyer said. "Them guys were locked and loaded. They weren't there to collect. You should have seen it, Bugs. He just tossed 'em like they were nothing. Snapped one guy's shotgun right in half."

"How did you know this was going to go down?" Moran asked Khan. "You didn't just happen to stroll through the alley, did you?"

"No," Khan said. "I knew they were going to hit someone because they were staking you out, so I decided to stake them out in return."

"They were staking the place? From where?"

"They had a room in the apartment building across the street. The one with the double entrances. I didn't know who they were after," Khan lied. "So I had to wait it out and figure something out on the fly."

"I'll be damned," Moran said. "Right under our noses." He looked back at the two brothers standing on either side of Heyer. "We gotta get out of town for a bit. Let things cool down. Figure out what we're going to do about that greasy little prick."

Khan noticed that Moran had not called Capone by name so far, as if the name were distasteful to him.

Moran turned around and looked at Khan again. He let his eyes wander to Khan's clawed hand, then to the pistol on his lap.

"Mr. Khan," he said.

"Just Khan, please."

"Khan. Okay. We are going to go out to a little place in the country. I was wondering if you'd care to join us. We can discuss your proposal on the way. Whatever it is you're proposing."

"Bugs," one of the enforcer brothers said. "You sure that's a good idea? I mean, look at the guy. You want to take him out to the place? If he's with Capone, he can do whatever he wants with us out there."

"If he's with Capone, we'd all be dead by now," Moran said. "And I think that this gentleman could do whatever he wants with us anytime, anywhere."

He smiled curtly at Khan.

"You don't like Capone, do you?"

"I don't like bullies," Khan said. The answer seemed to please Moran.

"Sure," Khan said, and lowered the hammer of the gun in his lap. "I'll come along. Let's go for a drive."

"Great." Moran slapped his thigh and stood up. "Call the rest of the boys, Frank. We're going to go out for some fresh air."

SIX: INDIANA

THE GANG LEFT CHICAGO in a small convoy of three cars just before sunrise. Khan sat in the back of the first car, with Moran next to him and one of the enforcer brothers—Frank Gusenberg—in the front passenger seat. Khan had reapplied his plaster mask, and his tiger hand was gloved. He had Moran's .45 tucked away underneath his coat, but he wasn't worried about having to use it. In the tight confines of the car, his claws were quicker and better than any gun. He wasn't even encumbered by a seat belt, because there weren't any. It felt weird being in a car without basic safety features. Khan wondered what they would think if he started telling them about headrests, satellite navigation, and anti-lock brakes, or the five-hundred-horsepower Benz with the two-thousand-watt sound system he drove back in his own time. Gusenberg was nervous, the driver even more so, and both of them smoked like chimneys, flicking the glowing butts out of the windows and letting in a cold burst of winter air every time. Khan watched the windblown, snowy February landscape roll by outside as the Cadillac sedan purred its way south.

"So what do you do when you're not knocking Capone's guys around?" Moran asked.

"I'm in the personal protection business," Khan replied. "I'm a bodyguard."

"And you've been doing that for a while now?"

"Twelve years," Khan said.

"So you're pretty good at what you do."

"I'm the best at what I do."

In the front seat, Frank Gusenberg let out a little derisive snort, but Khan ignored him.

"I've never lost a principal," he said. Until a few weeks ago at the Palmer House, he thought. But as far as he was concerned, his sheet was still clean. He had only lost Giovanni Galante—physically, temporally lost him. Khan didn't know which year Galante had found himself in, but he knew that the little shit had still been alive when the event happened, and only thanks to Khan.

Chicago was smaller back in 1929, and they were in the country-side soon, crossing from Illinois into northern Indiana. The farm-lands south of Gary were the boring ass end of the world as far as Khan was concerned, and he found that they had already been the boring ass end of the world back in 1929.

"As long as that vicious little greaseball is out there, I guess I'll always have a need for bodyguards," Moran said. "And you've certainly given one hell of a job interview at the warehouse already." He pointed to the cars behind them with his thumb. "Without Adam and Johnny May and the Gusenberg boys here, I'd have to close up shop on the North Side. You did me a big favor back there. You stick with us for a bit, I'll see what I can do for you."

An hour south of Gary, they left the main roads and turned onto a series of ever-narrowing side roads, crossing train tracks, passing isolated farms, and driving through small two-stoplight towns: Kersey, Stoutsburg, Wheatfield. The snow had picked up steadily on their drive, and Khan was starting to get worried about the winter-handling qualities of 1920s tire technology.

Ten miles out of Wheatfield, they took a left onto a dirt road. A few miles farther down, the driver took a right turn onto a narrower dirt road that hadn't been cleared of snow yet, and Khan thought they'd get stuck for sure and freeze to death here in Ass Bend, Indiana. But the Cadillac puttered on, and the two other cars followed slowly in its wake.

There was a farm at the end of the dirt road, set back from the road a quarter mile. Khan saw a large barn and a grain silo, and the farmhouse was a big one, two floors and a wraparound porch. The three cars chugged up the driveway and parked by the side of the farmhouse. Khan got out of the car and stretched his limbs. It was freezing cold out here in the middle of nowhere, but the place was isolated, and they'd notice anyone coming up that quarter-mile dirt driveway well before they got to the farmhouse.

Inside, the place was warm and cozy. They all walked into the side door, which led into a big kitchen with a cast iron stove in the center of the room that was radiating heat. Moran and his guys took off their coats and hung them from hooks by the door, and Khan followed suit. A few moments later, a woman came down the stairs nearby and walked into the kitchen, and the men acknowledged her with respectful nods and murmured greetings.

"Very sorry to drop in on you on short notice, ma'am," Moran said.

"You know it's not a bother, Mister Moran," she replied. "I've got the back bedrooms ready upstairs, but some of your boys may have to bunk on the floor. I wasn't expecting all of you."

She looked at Khan, who felt a little out of place in this kitchen, dressed in longshoreman weather gear when everyone else was wearing suits.

"Who is your tall friend?"

"This is Khan," Moran said. "Just Khan. He helped us out back in the city. Khan, this is Mrs. Sobieski. She owns this farm. We stop by from time to time when we need to get out of the city for a while."

"Izabela," she said. There was just the faintest familiar Polish lilt in her voice, and Khan figured that if she hadn't come right off the boat, her parents had.

"*Dzień dobry,*" he said on a hunch. "*Jak się pani miewa?*"

"*Bardzo dobrzę, dziekuję,*" she replied, almost reflexively. Then she turned to Moran and smiled a little.

"Your friend speaks very good Polish."

"My mother is Polish," Khan said. "Her parents came from Łódź."

"Mine are from Katowice," Izabela said. She reminded him a bit of his mother, back when he was a teenager, right before his card turned. She had the same dark hair, the same understated beauty that a hard life hadn't quite managed to paint over yet.

Moran's men obviously knew the place. They made themselves right at home, pulling up chairs to the big kitchen table and getting out their cigarettes. Khan tried to map the place in his head discreetly—entries, exits, corners, approaches to the kitchen door from outside. For a bunch of guys who had almost gotten machine-gunned by their rivals the day before, Moran's guys were not nearly paranoid enough about their safety, but Khan wasn't about to change his habits. Letting your guard down could get you killed, whether it was 2017 or 1929.

Later in the afternoon, when the gang was dispersed all over the house, Khan sat at the now empty kitchen table and awkwardly sipped a cup of coffee around the plaster bandage with the right side of his mouth. Behind him, Izabela took a big pot of hot water off the wood stove and filled two tin buckets with it. He gave her a curious look.

"For the chickens," she said. "It warms them up."

She took a bucket handle in each hand and lifted the buckets. Then she walked toward the kitchen door, with the hot water in the buckets trailing wisps of steam behind her.

"Let me help you," he said, and stood up. He opened the door for her, then deftly took the buckets out of her hands as she passed him. She looked amused.

"I can take care of this," she said.

"I'm sure you can. Lead the way," he said.

They walked over to the barn, through snow that was knee-deep. Izabela opened the sliding door wide enough for them to step through, then flicked a light switch on the inside wall. There were a few cows, not even half a dozen, some goats and sheep, and maybe two dozen chickens that were huddled in an enclosed coop at the other end of the barn. Khan put the buckets down, and Izabela filled up the water pan in the coop, which had a layer of ice on top of it. The hot water dissolved the ice and steamed in the cold barn air. The chickens hopped off their roost one by one and came to get their free warm-up.

"That's not a lot of animals for a farm this size," Khan said.

"We had more," Izabela replied. "When my husband was still alive. Ten horses, thirty cows. A hundred chickens. But there's only so much I can do by myself."

"Sorry to hear about your husband."

Izabela stepped into the back of the coop and stooped down to collect eggs from the laying boxes. She put them into the pockets of her apron. To Khan, they didn't look like a lot of eggs for so many birds, and he said so.

"They slow down in the winter. When it's warm, it's one egg per day from each of them. And when they stop laying, they go in the soup."

"What do you have to do with these guys?" he asked. "Moran and his gang. You know what they do, right?"

"They are bootleggers," she said. "My husband ran a still. Two hundred gallons a month. One day, they stopped his truck while he was delivering to Mister Moran's warehouse. Capone's men. And they shot him."

"Sorry," Khan said again.

"Mister Moran helps me out. I don't run the still, but they come and stay here sometimes, and he pays me for it."

She looked at his face and reached up to touch the plaster mask. "What happened there? This doesn't look like you really need it."

Khan was intrigued by her total lack of fear. He was three times her weight and a foot taller, and they were alone in a semi-dark barn in the middle of rural Indiana, but she wasn't afraid of him at all.

"I'm hiding my face with it," he said. "Half of it, anyway."

"Why?"

"So I don't scare people."

"Let me see," she said in Polish. He sighed and pulled the mask off the left half of his face. He had expected her to scream and run for the door, but instead she put her hands in front of her mouth. Then she reached out to touch the fur fringe hanging down from his jawline.

"How did this happen?"

"A virus," he said. "A sickness. When I was fifteen."

"Did it hurt?"

"Oh, yeah. Worst pain I ever felt. It took months. When it was done with me, I looked like this."

"How long ago was that?"

Khan didn't quite know whether to answer *sixteen years ago* or *in seventy-two years*. The week was already complicated enough. So he shrugged and said, "A while ago."

He picked up the buckets and stepped around the chickens that were filling their beaks from the warm water pan.

They trudged back to the house through the snow. The farm looked nothing like his own place, or even the house he grew up in, but Khan felt a swell of homesickness when they walked back into the warm kitchen. The kind you feel not for a place, but for people. For some reason, it hadn't fully hit him until now that he'd never see Naya or his mother again, that he was stuck here for good out of his own time, among people who regarded him as a sideshow curiosity. The wild card virus wouldn't hit New York City for another seventeen years. They would be long and lonely years, and whatever fun he'd had finding himself at the tail end of the Roaring Twenties was dissipating quickly. There was no way home, because home was Naya and Mom, and they didn't exist yet.

Galante, he thought, *I hope you got bounced back to 1929 too. Or 1931, or 1935. Just as long as there's a chance I'll bump into you, and I get to strangle you with your own fucking guts.*

SEVEN: FARMVILLE

THE NEXT DAY, MORAN sent one of the guys into town for sundries and newspapers. When he came back a few hours later, he brought several different papers with him, which Moran and his lieutenants read over breakfast. Several of the papers made reference to the incident at the warehouse. The cops had arrived not too long after the gunfire, but the warehouse had been empty, with just some shell casings and two broken guns on the floor. Without suspects or victims, the cops had nothing to do, nobody to arrest or question.

"He's gonna try again," Moran said, slurping his coffee. "Son-of-a-bitch knows I'm gonna come after him for this."

He turned to one of the Gusenberg brothers.

"Remember when we went to his place a few years back? In Cicero? A thousand rounds into that inn, and the bastard walks away."

"Yeah, but there wasn't a clean set of drawers left in that place," Gusenberg said, and Moran chuckled. Then his expression turned serious again.

"He guns for us, we gun for him. One of these days he's gonna run out of luck. He can't stay holed up in that hotel forever."

Or yours is going to run out, Khan thought. He was standing across the room by the kitchen window, sipping his own coffee and look-ing out of the kitchen window. The history books said that the cops really started cracking down on Capone after the St. Valentine's Day Massacre, and that the whole thing spelled the beginning of the end for both Capone and Moran. Four more years of Prohibition, and Capone would be in prison for tax evasion before the end. That was the old history, of course, before Khan had stuck his claws into the time stream. Without the massacre at the warehouse, both Capone and Moran would ratchet up the conflict. Moran certainly seemed like the type. Khan could smell the anger radiating off the man.

Well, at least I'll have secure employment for a while, he thought.

Khan spent the day checking the farmhouse from all angles. The snow out beyond the farmyard was knee-high, but he slogged through it to circle the place. To see how you have to protect a location, you first have to think like someone who's trying to get into it. Some of Moran's men were watching him from the windows as he did so, talking among themselves as they did. He knew that they still didn't trust him fully, especially not the Gusenbergs, whose main contri-bution to Moran's organization wasn't intellectual wattage.

He helped Izabela with the water and the animal feed again, grate-ful to have something to do that let him use his muscles. Physical labor made him feel useful, like he hadn't gotten all that strength just to hurt people. The hay bales for the cows weighed eighty pounds at least, but he took one in each hand and carried them to the cattle enclosure over the gentle protestations of Izabela. Then he brought in half a cord of firewood and restocked all the wood stacks in the house, which gave him a good opportunity to see more of the interior layout.

Moran and his guys had the drinks and playing cards out after dinner. Khan was a fair poker player himself, but he didn't feel like socializing with the gang or blunting his senses with bootlegged hooch. Instead, he got some more coffee and took a chair by the kitchen door, in sight of the others but far enough away to remain out of their tobacco smoke cloud. They stayed up until well past mid-night, strategizing and talking about people Khan didn't know, and by the time they all turned in, it was blissfully silent in the kitchen again except for the popping logs in the wood stove that kept the place cozy.

When he startled awake, he had no idea how long he had been asleep by the wood stove in the still-warm kitchen. The house was quiet except for the occasional creaking of settling wood beams and the soft tick-tock from the clock on the mantelpiece in the living room next door. Moran's men were asleep in their bedrooms on the other side of the house. Izabela must have turned off the lights and covered him up, because the kitchen was dark, and there was a wool blanket loosely laid over him. The drowsy human part of Khan's brain told him to go back to sleep, but the tiger part was awake and restless. Something wasn't right. And when something set Khan's fur on edge, he knew that it was wise to listen to the tiger.

He swept the blanket aside and kicked off his shoes quietly. Then he stood up and tuned in to his senses.

There was movement on the driveway outside. It was a dark, moonless light, and there were no outside lights on either farmhouse or barn, but his tiger eye didn't need the light to see the trouble coming. Five, six, seven, eight, nine guys, all in winter coats, coming up the driveway from the dirt road, where Khan saw the two cars they had parked a quarter mile away to keep the noise down. Everyone was armed. Khan saw the distinctive drum magazines of Tommy guns, and one of the guys coming up the driveway carried an honest-to-goodness BAR, a Browning automatic rifle that could pop out twenty .30-06 shells in three or four seconds. A broadside from that thing would do even him in for good. By the time Khan had startled from his sleep, the armed group had already covered half the distance between road and farmhouse.

Khan considered shouting down the house to warn Moran's guys, but that would just end badly. They had as many guys inside as the crew outside did, but Moran's men were asleep. By the time they were awake and ready to fight, the prepared group coming up the driveway would be pouring fire into the farmhouse already. He hoped that Izabela's bedroom was toward the back of the house as well. The '06 from that BAR would pierce through wood and drywall like an ice pick through a loaf of bread.

Darkness worked in his favor much more than in theirs. Khan opened the kitchen door as quietly as he could, and then dashed across the farmyard and into the barn.

He had almost reached the door on the other side of the barn when it opened, and one of the armed visitors stuck his head in and looked around in the darkness. The chickens were in their usual nighttime stupor, but the cows shuffled around a bit, and one of the sheep made a muffled noise. The guy in the doorway made a face at the smell. *Not a country boy,* Khan thought.

There was no time, no opportunity for going light on these guys. The man in front of Khan had a Tommy gun in the crook of his arm, and if he managed to fire off a burst, the cat would be out of the bag, so to speak. So Khan leapt the rest of the distance, yanked the Tommy gun out of the guy's grip, and then slashed his throat with one forceful swipe of his claws. The guy fell forward with a gurgle, twitched a few times, and let out a last wet breath from his ruined throat. Khan picked up the submachine gun. It had a hundred-round drum in it, a heavy thing the size of a dinner plate. The bolt of the gun wasn't cocked yet, and Khan worked the charging handle quietly. Then he stepped out of the door and stealthily made his way to the corner of the barn.

The other eight hit men were almost past the barn, and only fifty yards from the front of the farmhouse. Once they were in the farmyard, they started fanning out in a semicircle. Khan raised the Tommy gun, but immediately realized that any missed rounds from this angle would hit the house instead.

Well, shit. But it's not like they are paying attention to what's behind them, he thought. Khan put the Tommy gun down into the snow beside the barn, flexed his muscles, and let the tiger take over.

Even after all these years, it was still a little frightening to Khan just how easily the fighting and killing business came to his tiger half when he put it fully in control. He moved so quickly that the world seemed to shift into slow motion. He was on the first two hit men half a second after his leap. Both of them went down hard, clothes-lined by a three-hundred-pound half tiger at the end of a thirty-foot leap. Their guns skidded into the snow. The next man down the line was missing an arm and the shotgun he was holding before he had even turned toward the new disturbance. Khan slashed him twice across the throat and chest for good measure.

Five left.

One got a shotgun blast off that clipped Khan in the side with a few buckshot pellets. It took his breath away for just a moment, and the tiger brain went into full autopilot mode. Khan yanked away the shotgun with his human hand, grabbed the hit man's head with his tiger hand—it fit easily—and wrenched it sideways. There was a sharp snap, and the hit man dropped on the spot with the lack of coordination particular to the freshly and suddenly deceased.

Four.

The first machine-gun fire of the night broke out. The farmyard was dark, and the remaining hit men didn't know what or who was ripping them to shreds from the rear, and Khan could smell their sudden fear and panic. He dodged and rolled to avoid the burst of fire from the BAR. Then he kicked out with his clawed foot and took the shooter's right leg off just below the knee. The hit man screamed as he went down. Khan yanked the heavy BAR from his grip and swung the gun around. The last three attackers were running up to the farmhouse, where a light had just come on in the kitchen, outlining the door. There was nothing but dark Indiana landscape behind the trailing hit man from Khan's angle, so he brought the gun up and squeezed off a quick burst. The guy dropped and skidded through the fresh snow face-first for a yard or two, then lay motionless. Then the last two hit men were inside the farmhouse.

Khan cursed and ripped the magazine from the gun, then tossed it aside. Then he sprinted back toward the kitchen door.

Inside, there was shouting in the living room to Khan's left, and then three gunshots in quick succession. A moment later, another shot rang out that had a ring of finality to it. But in front of him, in the middle of the kitchen, one of the hit men had Izabela in a choke hold, and the muzzle of a shotgun pressed against her chin from below. He looked at Khan with unconcealed terror in his eyes.

"I'll fucking blow her head off! I'll fucking shoot her! I'll fucking . . ."

Khan had been to the firing range several times a week for the last twelve years. The 1911 in his waistband was not very different from the one he carried back in his own time, and it functioned exactly the same. With his tiger reflexes, he could have made the shot five times, but only one was necessary here. Khan drew the .45, flicked off the safety, brought the pistol up in a two-handed grip firmly enough to make the grip panels creak, and pulled the trigger. The bullet hit the middle of the guy's forehead. Khan knew that the man was dead already before he was halfway to the floor. He would have pulled Izabela to the ground with him, but she flinched with a shout and shrugged him off, then went to her knees.

Moran's men streamed into the kitchen, all of them armed and in various states of dress. Khan flicked the safety of his gun back on and stuck the .45 into his waistband.

"Any more?" Frank Gusenberg wanted to know. He seemed out of breath, and Khan could smell he was so high wound with stress that his nerves were practically humming with tension.

"Other than this dope here? I got six more in the yard," Khan replied. "One inside the barn. You get the one in the living room?"

"Yeah," Gusenberg said. "The fuck did they come from?"

"They parked out by the road," Khan said. "Walked the rest of the way. They were halfway to the house before I heard them."

"Some fucking bodyguard you are."

"He did just fine," Moran said. He had walked into the kitchen last, a snub-nosed revolver in his hand. "If he laid out eight guys. Go check, Frank. Take Peter. And go see if they left someone with those cars."

Peter and Frank Gusenberg came back into the farmhouse ten minutes later, their coats frosted with snow.

"Like he said, Bugs. Six guys out in the yard. He ripped the arm off of one."

"You know any of them?"

"Yeah. One's Fred Burke. The one in the barn."

"Fred Burke," Moran said. "Egan's Rats. That ape." He looked at

Khan. "You did the world a favor, my friend. That was Capone's number one cleanup crew you just took out."

Moran's face contorted with anger. He snatched a coffee mug from the kitchen table and threw it against the wall, where it shattered and made a dent in the plaster.

"That bastard. That filthy swine."

"We've been using this place for years," Frank Gusenberg said, and looked at Khan. "Then this guy shows up, and the first night we're back here, they know exactly where we went. I wonder why that is."

"Somebody ratted us out," Moran said. "Or we had a tail all the way from Chicago. Who gives a shit. You think Capone would let this guy kill his best wrecking crew? Use your fucking brain, Frank."

Next to Khan, one of Moran's men—Weinshank?—had finished frisking the dead guy on the kitchen floor. He'd had that shotgun of his, a Colt pocket pistol, and a wallet with a small stack of bills in it. Weinshank took out the money, counted it, and put it in his own pocket.

"Get that piece of shit out of here before he gets his blood all over Mrs. Sobieski's floor," Moran ordered. "Get rid of the other bodies too."

"Ground's frozen, Bugs," Frank Gusenberg said. "What do you want us to do with them?"

"Put 'em in their fucking cars, drive 'em out into a field somewhere, and set them on fire," Moran snapped. "Do I have to do all the thinking around here?"

He looked at Khan.

"Go help these guys, will ya? And when you're done, we're heading back into town, first thing in the morning. You're riding with me, 'cause we got stuff to talk about."

He jammed his hands into the pockets of his trousers and looked out into the dark farmyard.

"Two hits in three fucking days. We're gonna go back downtown and show that greaseball how it's done right."

They carried the bodies back to the cars parked by the road a quarter mile away. The Gusenbergs each drove one of the cars, and Khan rode with Frank Gusenberg in the second car while four of the dead hit men were stacked up on the back seat like bloody cordwood. They drove around in the dark Indiana countryside for twenty miles until they found an old abandoned homestead. They drove the cars behind a half-collapsed barn, and the Moran boys got out gasoline cans and splashed their contents all over the vehicles. Then Frank Gusenberg lit a cigarette and ignited the trail of gasoline. It took a little while for the cars to catch, but after a few minutes, the tires and ragtops caught fire, and then the upholstery in the interiors. Khan had smelled burning bodies before. People who claimed it smelled like barbecue never had to smell a human body burn up. While they watched the cars go up in flames, the Gusenbergs and the other Moran man, a jumpy guy named Schwimmer, went through the wallets from the bodies and removed the cash before tossing them into the burning cars. Frank Gusenberg counted out the money from the two wallets he had emptied, then turned to Khan and held out a stack of bills.

"Your share," Gusenberg said.

"Keep it," Khan replied. "I don't need it."

Gusenberg shook his head and smirked at Khan.

"You did these guys, you should claim your share. One hell of a thing you did. You barely left any for us to finish."

One of the other guys, the accountant named Heyer, had followed them with one of the gang's Cadillacs, and Khan and the other three returned to the farm in the Caddy. Khan had the scent of gasoline and burning hair in his nostrils all the way back.

They rode back to Chicago not too long after sunrise. Khan rode in the back of the lead car with Moran again, who was still seething.

"You asked for a job, I'll give you a job," Moran said. "I can't keep looking over my shoulder every time I walk down the street on the North Side. Kill Capone. Take the bastard out for me. I'll pay you fifty thousand."

Khan tried to calculate how much fifty grand was in 2017 money. Moran took the silence as hesitation.

"Seventy if you get Frankie Rio too. That's his bodyguard. And if you kill Frank Nitti—a hundred thousand. I'm dead serious. A hundred thousand, cash. You'll never have to work a day in your life again."

"I'm a bodyguard, Mr. Moran," Khan said. "I'm not a contract killer. I don't do that kind of stuff."

"What are you talking about? You just killed seven of Capone's best guys like someone swattin' flies on a windowsill."

"They were coming to kill us. That's different."

"Ain't no difference there," Moran said. "Any of his guys will do us in if they get the chance."

"And if they come for us, I'll kill them too," Khan replied. "But I'm not in the business of striking first."

"Don't matter who strikes first. Only who strikes last. You get rid of my problem for me, I'll be running the whole market in Chicago. I can make you rich. Think about it."

Khan had no problem taking a life. His ledger had a lot of names on it. But every last entry on his list was someone who had swung the knife, aimed the gun, struck the blow first.

"I'll think about it," Khan said, even though he already knew that his answer wouldn't change, not for any amount of money.

Moran leaned back in his seat and rubbed his hands together.

"Oh, and you're hired," he said. "You're my chief bodyguard now. How's five hundred a week sound?"

"Five hundred a week sounds good to me," Khan said, but his mind was already somewhere else. This would have to do until he had his legs under him, but he had decided that he didn't care much for Moran. The man reminded him too much of Galante, throwing money around to make others clean up his shit for him. The Roaring Twenties had seemed so wild and romantic in his history books when he was a kid, but it turned out that the game was the same as it was in his time, and it didn't matter whether its name was bootlegging or crack hustling. It was all just little minds in expensive clothes climbing over piles of bodies to get power, dogs pissing on lampposts and snapping at each other.

EIGHT: RESET

THEY WERE BACK IN Chicago in the early afternoon. Moran didn't want to use the warehouse at 2122 North Clark just yet, in case the cops were still going through it or Capone's men were staking it out for a second attempt. Instead, they went back to the Parkway Hotel, two blocks from the warehouse and a much more public setting. Moran had Khan walk ahead and scout the lobby and the elevator, and the two Gusenberg boys were bringing up the rear, guns ready under their winter coats. But Khan smelled no trouble. He didn't doubt Capone would go after Moran again—the two seemed to have a massive anger hard-on for each other—but it wouldn't be today.

"We need to get you a place to stay," Moran said a little while later when they were sitting in his living room. Moran had a drink in his hand even though it was just two in the afternoon. "I want you close by. I've got some of my boys here in the Parkway. How do you feel about that? I'll call downstairs and have them set you up here on the fifth floor."

Khan shrugged.

"Sure. Beats a tent out in the park."

"That's where you've been living? Jeez. You can afford better now. And we need to get you to a tailor and get you something nice to wear. So you don't stick out as much."

"He's gonna stick out no matter what," one of the Gusenbergs said.

"We can fix him up with something better than that plaster. Don't worry. By the time we're done with you, ain't none of Capone's guys want to come close to you, my friend."

◆

Peter Gusenberg and Moran took him to a place downtown where a very old and slow tailor measured Khan for the better part of an hour with his tape measure. Khan had to take his overcoat and shirt off for the measurements, and he didn't miss the veiled looks of

fascination and repulsion from Gusenberg when he saw his unconcealed muscular frame, with the demarcation line between fur
and skin running exactly down the center of his body. Even though
he must have been the strangest and most unusual person the tailor had ever measured, the old man never lost a word over his appearance or anything else, limiting his utterances to directions for
Khan to lift an arm, turn halfway, let his arms hang by his side,
and so on.

By the time they got back to the Parkway, there was an apartment
ready for Khan, a three-room unit two doors over from Moran's place.
His tailored suits wouldn't be ready for another two weeks, but they
had bought him some off-the-rack clothes that were a lot nicer than
the workman's overalls and weather coat he had been wearing.

"Put your stuff away and settle in," Moran told him. "Make yourself at home. We're going out to dinner at Ralphie's in an hour. I'll
need you to keep an eye out while we're there."

"Not a problem, boss," Khan said.

They left him to square his things away. The apartment was pretty
nice, even if Khan didn't care much for 1920s decor. At least it wasn't
the seventies, he told himself. He stashed the new clothes in the bedroom closet and put on a pin-striped suit. They hadn't found a dress
shirt with a collar wide enough for him to button it and wear a tie,
but even without that accoutrement, he looked much better than he
had since he arrived in this decade. There was some money in his
pocket, a loaded .45 on his hip, and he didn't feel like a tent-dwelling
bum anymore.

One day at a time, he told himself while he checked the fit of his
suit jacket in the mirror. In seventeen years, the wild card virus would
hit New York City, and then he could be himself again. He planned to
be long out of the bodyguard business by then. Prohibition would end
in another four years, and then people like Capone and Moran
would have to go back to robbing banks or holding up racetracks
again. That gave Khan four years to pile up enough mob cash to ride
out the Great Depression and World War II, preferably in a neutral
country where the dollar went far.

They went out to dinner. Well, Moran and his accountant had

dinner, while Khan sat in a booth close by and sipped club soda, keeping an eye on the place while Moran and Heyer ate steak and asparagus tips. After dinner and drinks, one of the Gusenbergs picked them up in front of the restaurant, and Khan walked ahead and made sure the neighborhood was clear before Moran and Heyer got into the car. They drove back to the Parkway Hotel, talking business, Khan mostly ignoring them while he kept an eye on the surroundings.

Back at the hotel, Moran dismissed Khan at the door of his apartment.

"I'm going to talk some more shop with Adam. Why don't you tap out for the night. But keep your eyes and ears open. You smell any funny business, you come and tell me. Ain't nobody got any business on this side of the fifth floor except our guys."

"Will do, Mister Moran," Khan said.

"Peter says the cops are done with the warehouse. We're going back in the morning to get the trucks running again. Show that greaseball guinea he can't run us off our turf. Make sure you're ready to go by eight. I'll send Frank over to fetch you."

"I'll be ready," Khan said. "Have a good night, sir."

He went into his own apartment, locked the door and the security chain, stripped off his suit, and took a long, hot shower. Then he checked his .45, put it under the pillow, and climbed into bed while still damp from the shower. Stretching out and sleeping in a proper bed after weeks of camping out felt decadent—not quite as great as making love to a beautiful woman or eating a perfect two-hundred-dollar filet mignon, but pretty damn close.

The radio woke him up in the morning. It popped into life in the living room at low volume with a commercial for laundry soap.

He knew the radio hadn't been on when he went to sleep, and he was pretty sure they didn't have timed outlet switches back in the 1920s. Khan reached under his pillow for the .45, flicked the safety off, and quietly climbed out of bed.

He sensed his visitors even before he opened the bedroom door. They were sitting on the living room couch, side by side, looking like they were waiting for room service or the morning paper. Khan recognized them both immediately. They had been attending one of the players back at the Palmer House in 2017, the guy with the skull face—Charles Dutton. One of them was a small black man with wrinkles in the corners of his eyes. He was sitting with his hands on his lap, looking around the room with a mildly interested expression. His companion looked considerably more ragged. Khan had run across plenty of tweakers, and this guy was pumped to the gills with amphetamines. He too looked around the room, but he was fidgeting and tapping his feet on the carpet. He looked like he hadn't slept in days.

Khan pushed the door open all the way and leveled the .45 at the two visitors.

"Good morning," the black man said, unperturbed.

"So it happened to you too. Whatever that was. I was starting to think I was the only one."

"Oh, no." The black man started to pull off the glove he was wearing on his left hand. "You were not the only one. Khan, was it? You were with Mister Galante."

"Please tell me he's around too. I'd love to have a word with him in private."

"We have not, *uh*, bumped into him yet. But he's not in 1929, if that's what you mean. You're the only one who ended up in this year."

"So it happened to everyone? Whatever it was."

"I'm afraid we don't really have the time to get into the details, but my companion here, Mr. Meek, accidentally blasted everyone in that suite all over time. We have tracked down a few of you, but we still have a lot of pickups to make, and my companion is getting tired."

"He looks a little rough."

"He feels a little rough, too," Mr. Meek said. "Cut the palaver and get to the point, Nighthawk."

"The point," Nighthawk said. "The point is that you, Khan, have a choice right now. You can't stay in 1929. Your presence has mucked up the time stream. Just our being here with you is altering reality in 2017 as we speak. Are you familiar with the butterfly effect?" He exchanged a look with Mr. Meek, who frowned.

"What you did at the mob warehouse is having downstream effects you can't even begin to predict. You prevented the St. Valentine's Day Massacre."

"So I kept a few mobsters alive," Khan said. "It was just seven guys, you know. And two of them weren't even with the gang."

"The public outrage after the massacre got the Feds motivated to bring Capone down. It was the beginning of the end for him. Without that event, you've probably extended the gangland wars by five years," Nighthawk said.

"Who really gives a shit who controls the bootlegging in Chicago?" Mr. Meek growled. "Capone, Moran, whatever. You know someone's gonna rise to the occasion. Prohibition's over in four years anyhow. Let's just grab this guy and go back."

Nighthawk shook his head and held up a hand to interrupt Mr. Meek. Then he looked at Khan intently.

"Even worse—those seven Moran boys are alive when they should be dead, Khan. They will kill people who would have lived full lives without your intervention. They will have children that should not be born, that will mess up the time stream in ways nobody will be able to fix. What if one of them has a son who turns out a street thug, and that kid kills your grandfather before your mother is born?"

"You can undo what you did in the hotel suite?" Khan asked.

"My associate can," Nighthawk said. "He can bring you back to the future . . . or the version of it that exists after you've thrown a big boulder into the time stream."

"And if I say no?"

Nighthawk looked around in the hotel room.

"Then we would have . . . conflict. But you really want to remain here? In this year? A joker-ace like you? How long do you think you'll be able to fool people with disguises?"

Khan's first thought was of Naya and his mother. He had already resigned himself to the fact that he'd never see them again. How could he *not* go back home? His presence here mucked up the time line, Nighthawk had said. What if he stayed, and changed history to the point where Naya wouldn't even be born? The thought gave him nausea.

"No," he said firmly. "You can get me back, you get me the hell back. I only did what I did because I figured I'd be stuck here for good."

"I completely understand," Nighthawk said. "I can't say I wouldn't have done the same thing." He smiled, and there was a twinkle in his eyes. "And changing the outcome of the St. Valentine's Day Massacre. Who gets a chance to rewrite history like that?"

"So let's go," Khan said. "Get me back to our own time. You'll get no argument from me."

Nighthawk and Mr. Meek exchanged a glance.

"There's only one problem. You have to fix what you changed. Get the time stream back on track. So we get back to our own reality, not one we won't recognize."

"And how do you propose I do that?" Khan asked.

Nighthawk looked at his companion again and shook his head with what seemed like genuine sorrow on his face.

"The people that should have died need to take their predestined place in history. And that's against the wall of that warehouse. The public needs the outrage. The Feds need the catalyst to go after Capone."

"Oh, you have *got* to be kidding me." Khan lowered the .45 and leaned against the frame of the bedroom door. "You want me to go over there and machine-gun the whole lot?"

"They were already machine-gunned," Nighthawk said. "They died. You're just making sure they stay dead. For history's sake. That is the price you'll have to pay to go home."

"Hell of a price," Khan growled. "I'm a bodyguard. I'm not a murderer."

"I wish I had a more palatable alternative, trust me. I don't relish the idea either. But you have to decide, and you have to decide now. My companion is getting more tired by the minute, and we have more people to track down and get back in time before he goes to sleep again. We can't do it because it has to look like Capone's guys did it."

"Give me just a minute," Khan said, even though he knew that he had made the decision the second his sister's memory had popped into his head again.

"Let's just get him back right now," Mr. Meek said. "I'm fucking tired, and I have my limits. If he takes off, we'll spend too much time tracking him down again. And then we'll lose all the rest of them, if you want to talk about fucking up the time line completely."

"No," Nighthawk said firmly. "Khan will undo what he did. And we will give him an hour to get it done." He gave Mr. Meek a sharp look, and there was a tense moment of silence between them.

"Fine," Mr. Meek said. "One hour. But you best keep me busy. Because if I nod off, we are all fucked. You, me, Tiger Boy here, and all of known history."

Frank Gusenberg came to fetch Khan twenty minutes later. Nighthawk and Mr. Meek were in his bedroom, out of sight, waiting for him to return—or getting ready to hunt him down again if he didn't.

"Where's the boss?" Khan asked when they stepped outside.

"The boss likes to sleep in a little," Gusenberg said. "He'll be along after he's had his coffee. We don't need him to get the trucks ready anyway."

They walked down Dickens Avenue and took a right onto North Clark. Khan could see the front of the warehouse just a block ahead. The sidewalk edges were lined with knee-high walls of dirty snow, pushed up by the city plows.

"Hey, just so you know, I wanna say sorry for what I said back at the farm," Gusenberg said. "About you being in cahoots with Capone's guys. You're all right. No hard feelings, right?"

"No hard feelings," Khan said, feeling like the world's biggest asshole.

They walked into the front entrance of the garage. Everyone was there, milling around and smoking cigarettes—Peter and Frank Gusenberg, Heyer the bookkeeper, the other four guys who had been there first time around. In the back of the garage, Khan saw the familiar face of Johnny May, looking up from under the hood of one of the trucks.

You dumb bastard, Khan thought. *Jesus. Seven kids. Shoulda read the want ads in the paper.*

There were seven men in the garage, the .45 in his coat pocket held seven rounds, and Khan's hand-eye coordination was out of this world. He cocked the hammer of his pistol quietly and let out a sigh.

For Naya.

"Just so you know, fellas," he said to the room in general as he brought out the Colt. "This ain't personal."

A Long Night at the Palmer House

Part 6

THE ROOM WAS ORNATELY, almost stuffily decorated, with a canopied four-poster bed, an overstuffed chair with claw-legged feet, dangling tassels, silk overthrows, and pillows piled upon it, end tables crowded with bric-a-brac and trinkets of all sorts, an ornate padded stool with a brocaded fabric seat set before a mirror attached to a table that was packed with makeup and perfume bottles. There were numerous gilt-framed pictures on the velvet-papered walls, most of them more than vaguely pornographic, and an almost naked girl with only a gorgeous silk robe draped around her voluptuous body reclining languidly on the bed.

She looked up, a little startled, but recovered her composure immediately.

"Oh! I didn't hear you gentlemen come in." She smiled sensuously, with readily apparent welcome. "It's more for two at once," she purred.

Nighthawk and Croyd looked at each other.

"It worked," Croyd said.

"I never doubted you," Nighthawk replied, lying only a little. In fact, he was becoming concerned about Croyd's state of mind, as well as more than a little tired himself. They'd been awake a long time. Croyd was still under control, but some of his ideas were getting a little wild. Since they seemed close, temporally, to their latest quarry, he'd thought the best way to trace him would be to go to the physical location where Monroe told them he'd be, then travel directly there through time.

It was easy to get to the spot in 1929. Nighthawk knew where the Everleigh Club had been located—almost anyone who'd lived in Chicago during the early part of the twentieth century knew about the club—which turned out to be an abandoned building on the South Side, on a run-down section of Dearborn Street. Two buildings, actually. Twin connected brownstone mansions at 2131–2133 South Dearborn. Nighthawk recognized the location, though it was but a sad shade of its former glory.

"Do you know where we are?" he asked his companion as they stood across the street from the obviously abandoned structure, which, sadly, seemed to be waiting for the inevitable wrecking ball.

"No idea," Croyd said.

"This part of Chicago is called the Levee." He gestured at the run-down street that seemed to be sleeping under the thick blanket of snow. "From the late 1800s through the first decade of the twentieth century, it was Chicago's red-light district."

Croyd quirked an eyebrow. "I'm shocked that you would know this, John."

"Uh-huh," Nighthawk said. "And that, my friend," he continued with something of awe in his voice as he pointed to the desolate structure across the street, "was the finest brothel in Chicago. Maybe the best house of ill repute in America, if not the entire world: the Everleigh Club."

Croyd nodded, impressed. "Well, let's hope it's open when we get there."

The girl shifted slightly on the white silk coverlets, her long, curly red hair spilling like a sunrise against a pile of silk-covered pillows. She leaned forward, her robe sliding slightly more open to artfully expose the entirety of one large, firm, dark-tipped breast.

"I've rarely seen gentlemen so ready for my attentions," she said. "Where are your clothes?"

"You wouldn't believe me if I told you," Croyd said.

"Try me," she purred, shifting her long, slimly muscled legs languorously, more welcomingly.

"Back in 1929," Croyd said.

She frowned. "You're right."

"Forget that," Nighthawk said. "Actually, we're looking for someone."

She smiled. "Won't I do? I adore chocolate," she said, and then shifted her gaze to Croyd, "and vanilla. Especially at the same time." She licked her lips slowly.

"Eh—yes," Nighthawk said. He glanced at Croyd. "Who are we looking for?"

"Uh . . ." Croyd blinked, and focused. "Peterman. Pug Peterman."

"Oh, Puggsly?" she said, surprised. "Why, yes. I'm sure he's downstairs. He helps Miss Minna as a kind of greeter and arranger. In fact—he helped her plan the big party they're throwing tonight for our foreign guests." She suddenly shifted, quick and graceful as a cat, and was facing them, kneeling, with her palms flat upon the mattress. "Royalty is visiting the Everleigh tonight. A prince!"

"Is that so?" Croyd asked.

"Prince Henry!" she exclaimed. "He's German, you know."

Her avid gaze was lowered, centered upon their groin areas.

"Is that so?" was all Croyd could repeat.

"He'll be happy to see us," Nighthawk said, though he wasn't entirely sure. "He'll make it worth your while."

"Oh," she said, springing lithely off the bed, "I'll be happy to do a favor for Puggsly."

As she brushed past them, Nighthawk could feel the heat radiating off her body, could smell the floral perfume scent wafting off her hair and clean, supple skin.

Peterman was happy to see them, if not overjoyed.

"Back from the future?" he asked, then turned to the girl who'd followed him back to her room. She was watching with wide eyes. It was rather crowded with all four there. "I can tell," Peterman added, "because you're naked. It happened to me and Irina when we ended up here, too." He shook his head. "Man, we went through some tough times at first. Jenny, get some clothes for my friends here." He looked back at Nighthawk and Croyd, who were getting so familiar with being denuded that they were almost used to it. "You'd be surprised at the things that frequently get left behind in a brothel, even one as high class as this."

"Irina—the waitress?" Nighthawk asked. "If she's here too, that's another name off the list."

"So what do you guys want?" Peterman asked as the girl hustled off on her errand.

"To bring you home," Croyd said.

Peterman frowned. "But I am home, now," he said. "I like this place. I've got a great job helping Minna and Ada run this place. The pay is good, the side benefits are unbelievable, believe me. I get to meet important, interesting people—"

"We don't have much of a choice, Pug," Nighthawk said, and explained about the unraveling of the time stream.

"It's like that story by Asimov," Croyd added after Nighthawk was done. "You know, the butterfly effect."

"Heinlein," Nighthawk corrected automatically.

"Well, I don't care who wrote it," Peterman said. "I like it here. Besides, you'll never convince Irina to leave. She had nothing in 2017. Here, she's one of the most admired of the butterflies—"

"Butterflies?" Nighthawk interrupted.

"It's what the Everleigh sisters call the girls who work for them. Look," Peterman said earnestly. "You don't know what it's like here. Minna and Ada—they care for their girls. They teach them manners and diction and how to act in society. They dress them well and feed them well and guard them against harm. They're not brutal pimps. The butterflies make a hundred, some as much as four hundred dollars a week. Can you imagine that?"

"It won't last forever," Nighthawk said. "If I remember right, Chicago went through a moral crusade and the Everleigh was shut down in like 1910 or 1911."

"Well, it's only 1902, so we got a while."

Jenny returned, her arms full of clothes, which she dumped on the bed. "All I could find were these spare butler uniforms," she said.

"Come on," Peterman said. "The party in the honor of Prince Henry of Prussia is starting downstairs. Get dressed." He paused. "Unless you'd rather go naked. I'm sure there'll be lots of that going on before the night is over."

Nighthawk wasn't *that* comfortable with public nudity, yet. He grabbed a pair of pants and stepped into them as Jenny watched, giggling as he put on the rest of uniform. At least it fit and, given the racial tenor of the times, Nighthawk figured he could blend in a bit more if he was dressed as a servant. By long experience, he knew that servants were basically out of sight and out of mind of the paying folk. In the end, Nighthawk and Croyd wore outfits similar to Peterman's, though less grand. They included white cotton gloves on both hands.

Peterman checked his ornate pocket watch. "It's past one thirty. Dinner is probably over now and the show will be starting."

"Show?"

Peterman nodded. "Oh, yes, Minna and Ada have something very special in mind." He smirked proudly. "I helped."

The top floor of the Everleigh Club consisted of a number of rather small bedrooms, thirty or so, where the butterflies entertained their clients privately, or sometimes in small groups. The first floor had two entrance halls, the dining room, which was designed to mimic a luxurious Pullman porter car, and twelve parlors, each with its own theme.

Peterman led them downstairs. Jenny had to excuse herself because she had to get into her special outfit for the upcoming entertainment. Peterman took them through mahogany- and walnut-paneled hallways with sumptuous tapestries on the walls and ornate Persian carpets on the floors. Gold-framed paintings of nude women were everywhere.

He took them to the musical parlor, which had a piano covered in gold leaf. A dozen men sat behind a long table, Prince Henry of Prussia surrounded by his entourage. They were already well into the bottled champagne that'd been placed around the table in ice buckets and was constantly being restocked by servants in the Everleigh Club livery as it was drained.

"That's him," Peterman said quietly, surreptitiously indicating a tallish, middle-aged man. He was bearded and his hair lay close to his skull and was parted almost in the middle.

Croyd sniffed. "Doesn't look like much."

"He's the kaiser's younger brother. He's touring the country, basically on a goodwill mission." Peterman added proudly, "The Everleigh is the one place in Chicago that he really wanted to visit."

A trio of musicians, two violins and a cello, was seated near the gold-plated piano. They struck up a tune as Minna Everleigh, clad in a clinging silk gown, suddenly appeared in the room's entrance. She was a smallish, attractive woman in her late thirties, but what you noticed most about her was the jewelry she wore: a scintillating diamond collar, half a dozen sparkling diamond bracelets on both forearms, and gleaming gemstones on each finger. Nighthawk saw Croyd's eyes bug out at the sight of all those rocks.

"Gentlemen, for your entertainment and edification, our ladies will reenact for you a sacred Greek rite depicting the death of the god Dionysus, whom some say is our patron deity." She raised her arms dramatically. "Ladies!"

"Now just stand against the wall and look servile," Peterman said softly as a troupe of thirty courtesans dressed solely in abbreviated, tight-fitting fawnskin streamed past Minna like a flight of moths chasing an unseen moon. The costumes were so brief and formfitting that they left no doubt whatsoever that the dancers wore nothing under them. The music rose to a wild wail as they danced around the table, gyrating and leaping, where the astonished Germans sat, their hair flowing free and wild as their movements. They whirled about and the lead dancer suddenly broke from the pack. Nighthawk gripped Croyd's arm and gestured. It was Irina.

She twirled across the floor, heading toward Prince Henry, and leaped right into the astonished prince's lap, encircling her arms around his neck and squirming madly. Others followed suit, until his entire entourage was grappling with the girls.

Minna made another gesture and suddenly the lights dimmed. The girls abandoned their lap-dance partners, and sprang back onto the floor, attacking a great cloth bull stuffed with cotton that a liveried butler had dragged into the room. They tore at it with nails and teeth, ripping its fabric skin and gouging out tufts of cotton—metaphorically—flesh. Nighthawk supposed this represented the death of the Greek god. He and Croyd exchanged glances.

Minna gestured again and things got really weird. Male servants of the house brought out platters of raw sirloin steak, which the girls tore to pieces with their teeth, their faces soon streaky with blood that ran from the rare meat.

Croyd's mouth hung open. "What the fuck . . ."

Nighthawk only shook his head, but the Germans loved it. They stamped and cheered and waved bottles and glasses high.

Minna suddenly clapped her hands and the girls fled giggling from the room.

"Give my butterflies a chance to wash up and change for the rest of the evening. In the meantime"—she gestured expansively at the bottles of champagne sitting in ice—"please, drink!" She snapped her fingers and one of the servants gave her a champagne glass. "To the health of Kaiser Wilhelm the Second of Germany!"

As one, the Germans rose and knocked back glasses of champagne to the health of their kaiser. Other toasts came quickly. By the fourth or fifth the butterflies were returning to the parlor, this time dressed in evening gowns. Then the serious drinking started.

After a bit some of Henry's entourage drifted off with chosen butterflies to their private room on the second floor. The string trio continued to play and there was dancing that ranged from the spirited to the sensual, given the dancers' various moods and temperament and the amount of champagne they'd imbibed.

At one point Nighthawk felt compelled to join the others in livery in filling glasses, as the demand was endless. While on one such mission, he noticed Peterman whispering to one of the butterflies. He kept an eye on her as she approached Croyd very closely and whispered in his ear. Croyd smiled, and hand in hand they slipped away from the room. Nighthawk glanced surreptitiously at Peterman, but he was busy ordering around a couple of the other servants.

Nighthawk busied himself for a while serving the Germans and wasn't really surprised when Jenny approached him and suggested that they take a break in her private room for a while. He demurred. She pressed him, but, to her eventual disappointment, failed to convince him to leave the party.

Nighthawk bustled about, pretending to be busy. At one point he noticed Peterman and Irina in deep conversation, and finally after almost an hour Croyd rejoined the party. Not only did he seem happy, he also seemed very tipsy.

Much to Nighthawk's mixed horror and amusement, Croyd, champagne glass in hand, seated himself in a momentarily empty chair next to the prince, and engaged him in what seemed to be a serious discussion. Nighthawk approached the pair.

Croyd had not only gotten himself laid, he was also drunk as a lord. "You've got to make your brother understand," he was saying seriously to an equally inebriated and more than somewhat bewildered Henry, "that he can't start World War One, because if he starts World War One, *then* we get Hitler, and no one wants Hitler, do they?"

He was so earnest that the mystified prince just shook his head. "No, of course not."

Croyd fixed his gaze on Nighthawk. "You don't want Hitler, do you, John?"

"No, Croyd." He turned to Henry. "You'll have to forgive my friend, Your Highness. He likes to talk politics when he's in his cups."

"But what is this Hitler?" the puzzled prince asked.

Nighthawk was saved from answering that difficult question as suddenly a slipper flew past them and struck a stack of filled champagne glasses that were pyramided on the table waiting for takers. One of the glasses fell into the upright slipper.

Nighthawk looked over his shoulder. It was off one of the butterflies who'd been dancing enthusiastically around the table, high kicking in time with the music. In fact, it was Irina. She froze, staring at Nighthawk, as Croyd lurched to his feet and picked up her slipper. All eyes in the room were suddenly on him. "Well," he said gallantly, holding up the slipper. "We can't let you get your little foot wet." He held it to his lips and drank down the champagne before offering it back to Irina.

"On with the dance," someone yelled.

"Why should that fellow have all the fun?" one of the Germans asked. He grabbed a nearby courtesan, lifted her leg, and shouted, "Off with your slipper!"

Everyone cheered and reached for the nearest girl. Slippers were removed, filled with champagne, and toasts were drunk as a strange and somewhat unsanitary tradition was born.

Irina reached out hesitantly and took the slipper from Croyd. "I know you. From the poker game."

"We're here to take you back," Nighthawk said.

Her eyes suddenly grew large, almost terrified. "No, please. I don't want to go—"

Nighthawk was about to reply, but he paused for a moment, unable to explain what was happening to the time line in this mad environment. Before he could say anything, she fled, running out of the parlor.

Nighthawk pursued her. Croyd paused for a brief bob of his head toward Henry, then took off after him. They ran down a quiet corridor. All the action was happening either in the music parlor or on the second floor. The rest of the place seemed deserted.

Irina ran, but ultimately there was nowhere for her to go.

Nighthawk caught up to her as she backed into a dead end where the hall stopped in a gigantic mirror. Croyd stumbled to a halt behind him. Peterman was there, waiting. He had a pistol in his hand.

"I can't go back," Irina said. "Don't you see, I'm *nothing* there. Less than nothing. They treat me decent here."

Nighthawk shook his head. "Looks like you don't want to go, either," he said to Peterman.

"That's right," the onetime child star said. "I'm through carrying Monroe's coat. I'm sick and tired of being his yes-man. Irina and I have both made lives here—we're not going back."

"I'm sorry," Nighthawk said. "We have to repair the time line—"

"I don't give a shit about your time line," Peterman snarled. "You're not taking anyone back if you're dead."

He switched his attention to a bewildered Croyd.

"No, Pug!" Irina suddenly called out. "Don't kill him!"

She was closest to Peterman. She reached out and shoved him as he pulled the trigger. The gunshot echoed in the closed-in hallway as the bullet clipped Croyd's cheek before it buried itself between the eyes of a smiling nude woman hanging on the wall. Peterman swore and swiped at Irina, but Nighthawk was already on the move.

He tore the white cotton glove off his left hand and slashed Peterman across the cheek, almost in the exact same place where his bullet had cut Croyd. It was a stinging slap, but he also put a touch of his power into it. He felt the sweet ecstasy of Peterman's life-force surging into him, enough to wash away the weariness that'd been dragging him down. He didn't take much, just enough to make Peterman slide bonelessly to the carpeted floor.

Irina stared at him. "Did you kill him?" she asked, looking at Nighthawk with terrified eyes, sudden shocked tears running down her cheeks.

Nighthawk shook his head. "No. Just knocked him out."

Croyd, suddenly looking sober, stepped over Peterman and pointed. "Off you go, Puggsly." And the child star vanished, like he'd never been there.

Croyd draped his arm over Nighthawk's shoulder.

"I just can't stand crying women," he said, then yelled, "Duck, Irina!"

The girl had the wits to follow his order. Nighthawk tried to pull away, but Croyd held on as he bounced a beam of energy off the mirror over Irina and it struck them solidly in their chests.

"Dammit, Croyd!"

Nighthawk was angry. Naked, again, and angry.

"She was just a teenaged hooker—"

"You mean *another* teenaged hooker," Nighthawk said irritably.

"Sorry." Croyd did look contrite. "I just couldn't do it to her. I guess I have a soft spot in my heart—"

"For teenaged hookers," Nighthawk interrupted again.

"She did save my life."

Nighthawk sighed. Croyd did have a point. Although Nighthawk's own weariness had vanished, he thought charitably that Croyd was probably in worse shape. Not to mention also drunk and speeding. He shut his mouth, knowing that someone had to maintain control during the remainder of this temporal circus, and that someone was him.

"Let's see if we can find something to wipe the blood off your face," he said to Croyd.

They were still in the hallway of the Everleigh Club, but it was different now, desolate and chill, and not only in the physical sense. The life had gone out of the place. The corridor was devoid of all furnishings, the wallpaper was dirty and partially torn away. The floor was filthy and debris was strewn about.

"Looks like nobody's been here for a while," Nighthawk said.

There was no lighting. It was dark, like the inside of a deserted building.

"Hey," Croyd said. "Look at this."

He'd wandered back up the corridor toward where the music parlor had been and stooped over to pick up a neatly bundled package.

"It's clothing," he announced.

There were two bundles, actually, and they contained everything they needed from shoes to hats. Even new, neatly folded underwear.

"What the heck," Nighthawk muttered, stunned to mildness. He slipped into the briefs and put on the pants, checking the pockets. From the left front pocket he pulled out a roll of bills, several hundred dollars' worth. He held them close so he could see them better in the dimness. They were crisp and clean and from the early part of the twentieth century. In the right front pocket of the pants was a business card. It read, *Fortune Films, Props. John Fortune and William Creighton,* and gave an address out on Wells Street.

Croyd, also dressed, called out, "Hey, look—a newspaper. Dated June 5, 1913. Damn, I was off five years. I was aiming for 1908. Oh well. Guess I wasn't that badly off, shooting on the fly. And drunk."

"No," Nighthawk said thoughtfully. "That's not what's worrying me. Someone clearly knows the trail we're following."

Croyd stopped buttoning his shirt and looked at him. "Yeah. But who?"

Nighthawk shook his head. "Damned if I know."

Nighthawk and Croyd taxied to the address they'd found on the business card and discovered that Fortune Films was a large complex of buildings and standing sets located on the outskirts of Chicago. It was a buzzing beehive of activity, with people in and out of costume scurrying about purposefully. There were cowboys and Indians, Romans in armor and togas, Arabian sheiks and sultry-eyed harem girls, camels, horses, men in ordinary work clothing delivering to soundstages items large and small of nearly every description.

They stopped at the small guard station at the gateway and were waved on through by the uniformed gatekeeper after they'd identified themselves.

"Almost like we're expected," Nighthawk commented to an equally mystified Croyd.

The taxi dropped them off at the soundstage that the guard had directed them to. It was a large building, almost hangar sized with large sliding doors big enough to admit elephants or airplanes. Nighthawk and Croyd took the normal-sized door cut into one of the sliding panels. It was dark inside and they took a moment to orient themselves. Adjacent to a far wall was a brightly lit stage surrounded by a score of people watching as a scene was filmed.

As they got closer and could discern details, Nighthawk saw that they were staging some kind of Arabian Nights fantasy inside what seemed to be a harem room, complete with colorful handwoven carpets, hanging bronze lamps with open lattice designs, billowing silken wall hangings, and a bevy of barely clad courtesans who were showing a lot more skin than might be expected on a silent movie set. They were all posing around a marble fountain that was spouting water high into the air and contained rose petals floating on its surface, as well as a languid Irina Adamczyk luxuriating sultrily in the perfumed water.

"Holy cow!" Croyd remarked. Nighthawk could only agree.

Standing beside the man cranking away at the camera was John Fortune, directing the scene.

He looked a shade older than at the game, and Nighthawk realized that for him five years or so had passed. He was a mature man, not the young teenager he'd been when Nighthawk had first met him, nor the young man who'd led the Committee in the war to save the Egyptian jokers.

Right now, his attention was on the scene playing out in front of him as he directed Irina through the scenario, speaking aloud because, of course, this was after all a silent film.

"That's right, Irina, very good, looking great. You're pensive, as if thinking deeply, but at the same time yearning, wanting. Suddenly, you hear something and you look quickly to your left. Your eyes widen, you rise, slowly, from the pool. Your handmaids run to you. . . . Yes, that's right, hold them up and wrap them around her waist."

They were, Nighthawk noted, gauzy draperies that didn't quite hide the parts they covered, and left her bare from the waist up in what was an utterly frank and sensuous pose.

"Okay, Creighton, enter the scene. You've fought through hell to come to her, yes, great, great . . ." Creighton was a tall, slim man with an Arabic cast to his handsome features. "You take her in your arms and say, 'At last, I have come for you'"—and Creighton dutifully repeated his lines in a somewhat exaggerated manner—"and you kiss," Fortune continued, and they did, with a passion that was so real that it seemed it could set fire to the film stock that was recording it.

"Aaaannnddd, fade, and cut." Fortune smiled and said, "It's a wrap!" He turned and looked at Nighthawk and Croyd. "What took you so long?" he asked them.

The offices of Fortune Films were moderately sized and modestly decorated. Framed movie posters advertising scores of films hung on the walls, depicting, among other actors, Charlie Chaplin, Broncho Billy, Fatty Arbuckle, and William Creighton, "Man of a Million Faces." Film titles included *Birth of a Notion, Sherlock Holmes' Chicago Adventure, The Song of Solomon, Dracula on Lake Michigan,* and many westerns, comedies, and historicals.

"Sit down," Fortune said, indicating the three comfortable-looking chairs before his paper-littered desk. "Creighton will be joining us in a moment. Irina is"—he thought for a moment—"a little skittish when it comes to seeing you again. Considering your last encounter, I don't blame her."

Fortune smiled gently at them. For a young man, Nighthawk reflected, he had already been through more in his lifetime than any three or four men should have had to endure.

"So you were expecting us," Nighthawk said.

"Irina told us some time ago that you were around," a serious-looking, leanly built man of middle age said as he entered the office and lowered himself into the final chair before Fortune's desk. "We didn't think it'd take you that long to get around to us."

"How do you know her?" Croyd demanded.

"You might say," the newcomer said, "that I've known her, well, intimately for quite a while. I first met her at the poker game and then, later, or, I guess, you could say earlier, at the Everleigh Club. What is it, John, five years ago now?" He was addressing Fortune, not Nighthawk. Fortune nodded. "I was one of her regulars. When we got the studio running, she came to work with us and we turned her into a star."

"She told us all about you," Fortune explained. "How you came to the Everleigh Club to take her and Peterman back to 2017. How Peterman tried to stop you."

"How she probably saved my life," Croyd said.

Fortune nodded. "And you granted her hers."

"He has a soft spot for teenaged hookers," Nighthawk said.

"I think we've mystified you long enough." Fortune nodded at the newcomer. "This is my longtime bodyguard, my partner in Fortune Films, my friend. At the poker game he was Tor Johnson. Today's movie fans know him as William Creighton, the Man of a Million

Faces, the greatest makeup artist of all time. In our time he's Mr. Nobody."

"Call me Jerry," the man of as many names as faces said.

"We arrived in 1908 bewildered, naked, and penniless," Fortune continued. "It took us a while, but once we got ourselves settled, we knew what to do. It's been pretty much forgotten in our time, but Chicago was one of the early centers of the movie industry. It'd already started by the time we arrived, so it was a natural thing to get into. After all, we'd had the benefit of over a hundred of years of moviemaking knowledge. We started by churning out the same basic stuff that was being made at the time, but added subtle, sophisticated improvements. *Song of Solomon,* which we just wrapped, will burn up the screen. It sizzles, thanks to Irina and Jerry."

"We made the first twelve-reeler years ago," Mr. Nobody said, "shamelessly swiping from filmmakers from our own time, from Hitchcock to Tarantino. The audience loved it."

Nighthawk frowned. "Don't you worry that your movies will change things?"

Croyd groaned. "Oh, Christ, does this mean that we're going to have to go back *again* and stop you guys before you got started?"

Fortune shook his head. "I don't think so. Irina did say you were trying to wipe out the changes that'd broken the time stream, but Jerry and I haven't really changed anything in any way that others have imitated. They can't. We're kind of a unique operation, relying on our foreknowledge and Jerry's ace ability to shape-shift into damn near anything human or near human. Besides"—his face took on a sad expression—"like most silent movies, much of our work will be lost over the years. The film stock we have today is pretty fragile. Most of it will disintegrate within three decades or so."

"And, unlike Irina and Peterman, we're willing to return to our home time," Jerry said.

"So she's still adamant about staying?" Nighthawk asked.

"She's a movie star here," Jerry said. "She's happy and well-adjusted. Hasn't had any children, unlikely to have any. Eventually"—and here, his serious face took on a sadder cast—"her star will fade and she'll be forgotten like virtually every other silent film star, from Broncho Billy to Ben Turpin." He sighed. "I will miss her. Greatly."

"It's been fun playing movie mogul," John Fortune said. "But it's time to go home and work on some of the problems of our own time."

"You're willing to give all this up?" Nighthawk said. "You must have made a fortune."

Fortune and Jerry looked at each other. "Well," Fortune said finally, "I suppose we can trust you guys. Yeah, we have made a crap ton of money."

"And," Jerry added, "knowing that you were on our trail and that we couldn't take anything with us, we converted most of it because we didn't want to leave it all as cash in banks with the Depression looming on the horizon."

"Converted?" Nighthawk asked.

"Yep. To gold coins and high-end gemstones. Diamonds, rubies, emeralds."

"I even managed to track down three Honus Wagner T-cards. In really nice shape. It was like finding needles in a haystack, but I did it," Jerry said. "They should go for more than three million apiece back in 2017. My usual line is movie memorabilia, but maybe I'll keep one for myself. Charlie Sheen will be green with envy."

"But what did you do with it all?" Croyd asked, mystified.

Fortune nodded. "Well, we made sure it was well protected in a lead-lined coffin, paid for and registered for perpetual care, and buried it in a cemetery which we know will survive under a headstone with the name Tor Johnson over it."

"It was a big coffin," Jerry said.

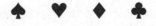

The Sister in the Streets

by Melinda M. Snodgrass

"**S**ISTER MARY-CATHERINE! SISTER MARY-CATHERINE!" The use of her full name and title and the thread of panic in the young male voice told her the problem was real and probably severe. Often the young people jamming Lincoln Park called her "penguin" or Nunzilla, or asked when she was going to sing or fly. It didn't bother her because for the most part they were so cute and earnest and starry-eyed. *"We're gonna change the world!"*

At thirty Sister Mary-Catherine had a more jaded outlook. She had nursed bodies broken by riot police in Bolivia and Guatemala, handled gunshot wounds in the Congo. Her feeling was that while the world might change people's sinful natures didn't. Her medical degree had been used mostly to heal the wounds of war and revolution, which was a sad commentary.

The young man who ran up to her was as gangly as a colt, with long matted brown hair and wide, frightened blue eyes. He wore a leather vest that exposed his hairless chest, dirty jeans, and was barefoot. A girl, her wreath of braided flowers slipping over one eye, was clinging to his arm. They were panting and sweat beaded their faces. It was a very sultry August night in Chicago, and it reminded her of her days in the Congo during that country's failed revolution.

"Bad trip?" Sister Mary-Catherine asked.

"I don't think—"

"We don't know," the girl interrupted. "She just *appeared*."

"And she's bad hurt, Sister, so we better hurry."

Grabbing her medical bag, she ran after them as they wove through the crowds. She was grateful not to be coping with the floor-length skirts that had been required when she first took her vows. The knee-length skirts were far more practical and sanitary in hospital settings.

Smells of cooking food, the sweet aroma of pot smoke, unwashed bodies, and patchouli incense floated in the air, and in the background the ominous scent of tear gas left over from the march earlier in the day and the police action that evening. A spotlight raked across the swarming crowds but this one was benign. It was Turtle floating overhead, a guardian angel making sure the protestors were safe. At the edges of the park were more lights strobing blue and red—police cars, and lines of police waiting like the monsters ancient people used to draw onto the edges of maps.

There were murmured conversations, the throb of drums, strumming guitars, and singing. Some of it good, most of it emphatically not. Mary-Catherine thought longingly of the choir at her convent or even the MC5 concert where they had Kicked Out the Jams earlier in the evening. That had been before the police moved in and tried to enforce a curfew. That attempt had been thwarted by Turtle so the crowds remained, though not without some casualties. She and Dr. Young had spent the later half of the evening dealing with bumps, bruises, and watering eyes from the tear gas. The one serious casualty—a broken arm—had been taken to Cook County Hospital by the doctor.

She could have lived cloistered when she had joined the Poor Sisters of St. Francis, but she wanted to serve God by alleviating suffering, so she had become a doctor. It also helped that the church paid for her education. Something her family could never have afforded. As to why she had been rotated back to the United States—she had a feeling it was because of worry she identified too closely with the downtrodden communities in which she had served. Little did the mother superiors know that the revolution was coming to America.

There was a knot of people gathered in a circle. Her two guides held back and Mary-Catherine pushed through. Lying on the trampled grass was an extraordinarily beautiful and horribly injured unconscious woman. She was also completely naked, but there was nothing sexy about it since her body was bathed in blood from the left breast, which was hanging by a thread, the four long slashes in her upper right leg, and the cuts across her belly. Mary-Catherine hoped the moist gleam she saw was muscle and not intestines.

There was the smell of burnt hair and part of the mane of jet-black hair had been burned away. The skin on her right shoulder was burned and blistered. Mary-Catherine dropped to her knees on the trampled grass, and yanked open her case.

"There was like this loud pop and then she was just here." The boy offering the added information had a scraggly beard that imperfectly hid his acne.

"She's gotta be a wild card," another added, muttering around the Astro Pop that hung out of his mouth like a peculiarly shaped cigar.

"Get to the perimeter. Get one of the cops to radio for an ambulance!" Mary-Catherine ordered.

"I'm not talkin' to those pigs," a young joker man in a Lizard King T-shirt muttered. The wattles that hung beneath his chin like a peculiar green-and-yellow beard waggled as he talked.

She jumped to her feet, grabbed the front of his T-shirt, and yanked him in close. The wattles stiffened in alarm. "Then she's going to *die* and it will be *your* fault! So maybe you could set aside your self-righteous bullshit for one second and help me save this woman!"

She pushed him away, and went back to her patient. The chastised boy and several others took off running. Fortunately toward the police. The bandages in her bag weren't up to the task of trauma this great. She pulled out a roll of medical tape, and glanced around the watching crowd, spotted two girls with reasonably clean T-shirts.

"Give me your shirts!" Fortunately the era of free love also seemed to go with no modesty so the girls she'd selected quickly pulled off their shirts, revealing tanned, bare breasts.

She laid the torn breast back in position, and heard a moan and a retch from the crowd. Folding the T-shirt to form a rough bandage, she taped it tightly to stop the bleeding. She then did the same to the thigh. The woman moaned, struggling toward consciousness. The last thing Sister Mary-Catherine wanted, but she had no way to sedate her. Slurred words tumbled from her lips.

"Jasper, Niobe. Home. All wrong." She appeared to have a British accent.

"What is your name?" she asked. "Can you tell me your name?"

"Lil . . ."

The boys returned from the edge of the park, pulling her attention from the woman. "They were really shitty," one boy said.

"Did they radio?" the nun demanded.

"Yeah, but the roads are blocked so they said it wouldn't be quick," the boy answered.

"They seemed *happy* about it," the joker boy added.

"Well, it was only *one* of them," his companion offered in an attempt to be fair.

"Well, I can't wait." The woman had slipped once more into unconsciousness. Mary-Catherine jumped up and ran toward the roving spotlight. Stood under it and waved her hands over her head.

"WHAT DO YOU NEED, SISTER?" Turtle's voice was amplified by the speakers.

"I have a badly hurt woman. She needs to get to the hospital. The roads are blockaded. Can you take us?"

"SURE."

Turtle followed her back to the huddle. The woman was muttering, hands flexing as if reaching for something. Sister Mary-Catherine indicated the woman.

"THIS MIGHT BE A LITTLE SCARY," Turtle warned.

She felt the grip of a giant force closing carefully around her body, and she was lifted into the air. As her sensible black shoes left the ground she had a moment of panic, but forced it back. She had endured worse moments.

"Try to keep her flat," she called up to Turtle as she hung beneath the shell.

"OKAY." The woman floated up until she hung next to Mary-Catherine. It was like she was lying on an invisible stretcher.

"WHERE DO YOU WANT TO GO?"

"Cook County."

"YOU THINK THE COPS DID THIS?" Turtle asked.

"I don't know. I don't think so. The kids said she just appeared."

"MAYBE AN ACE."

They were floating over the heads of the cops now. Helmeted heads craned back and faces were pale blurs under the spotlight and the streetlights.

"HOPE THEY DON'T DO SOMETHING STUPID WHILE I'M GONE," Turtle said, and Mary-Catherine sensed it was more of a warning to the cops than an innocent remark.

Of course she knew about the virus and wild cards, but growing up in Hudson, Wisconsin, she had never actually come in contact with a victim of the virus. During her medical training she had treated jokers; the virus did terrible things to the human form and most of those afflicted had various kinds of health problems. She met a few more jokers during her work in Africa and South America, but she had never met an ace. She glanced over at her patient. The woman herself seemed perfectly normal, though if it hadn't been for the blood and muscle tissue Sister Mary-Catherine would have suspected those breasts owed their perfection to silicone rather than genetics. The one intact breast seemed far too firm to be real.

They soon reached the hospital and Turtle gently lowered them to the pavement in front of the emergency entrance. Someone must have been watching because orderlies rushed out with a gurney and quickly got the woman inside.

"I need saline, lots of it, disinfectant, and start an antibiotic drip," she ordered as she began to unwind the makeshift bandages.

As she uttered the final word the woman's eyes snapped open, her hand shot out, and her fingers tightened on Mary-Catherine's throat. Wheezing, she tried to pull air into her lungs and she felt cartilage grinding at the vise-like grip. Her hands clawed at the woman's. She found herself staring down into strange silver eyes.

Turtle was right, and I'm about to be killed by an ace, came the errant and foolish little thought. Blood pounded in her ears, muffling the sound of people shouting in alarm.

Orderlies grabbed her shoulders. The woman cried out in pain as hands gripped the burns. Her fist flew back and hit one orderly in the face. He fell back, blood spurting from his nose. She rolled off the exam table and went to deliver a sweeping kick to the other orderly, but her torn leg couldn't support her weight and she fell. The torn breast was flopping on her chest, blood flowing across her rib cage and belly.

Mary-Catherine leaped in behind her, got an arm around her neck, and pulled her close. "You've been hurt! You're at the hospital. Let us help you and you'll be all right."

An orderly was filling a syringe with sedative. Mary-Catherine shot him a desperate *hurry* look. He darted in from the side, and injected the tranquilizer.

"Fuck you all," the woman muttered. She slumped as the sedative took effect.

Dr. Quentin Young pulled aside the curtain screening the woman. Mary-Catherine was glad it was him and not some of the older doctors. They tended to condescend to her despite her medical degree. Dr. Young never did.

What brought them together was their advocacy for the poor and downtrodden. Sister Mary-Catherine had elected to take her skills to the third world. The physician chose to work in America. He had helped found the Medical Committee for Human Rights, which had brought medical care to civil rights workers in the South, and had brought health care clinics to the Black Panthers. He had even done a rotation at the newly founded Blythe van Renssaeler Clinic in New York's Jokertown, which meant he had experience with wild cards. They had met because they had both volunteered to help the protestors who had gathered in Chicago. Sister Mary-Catherine liked and respected him.

He pushed up his heavy black-framed glasses with a forefinger and ran a nervous hand through his shock of unruly dark hair. "What have we here, Sister?" There was a touch of silver at his temples. At forty-five he was probably the oldest person involved in the ongoing protests.

"She's an ace. According to the kids she just appeared, naked, injured, and violently disoriented." She touched her throat. "She broke Miles's nose."

He pulled her hand away from her throat. "And tried to choke you?"

"Like I said, disoriented," she said as he began his exam.

"Knife cuts?" Mary-Catherine asked as he removed the makeshift bandage on her thigh.

He shook his head. "I think these are claw marks."

"Big animal."

He gave her a quick smile. "If it was an animal. Who knows in this world we inhabit. We need to get her into surgery and reattach that breast. Sew up the tear in her belly. Fortunately it didn't get past the muscle."

"She's going to have some terrible scars. Poor thing. She's so beautiful. I need to get back to the park."

"They're not going to let you through with the curfew. You may as well stay here. Assist me."

She jumped at the chance.

◆

Sister Mary-Catherine pulled down her mask. Dr. Young rotated his neck, which gave a loud crack. They watched the woman be wheeled away. "If she was as disoriented as you said it might be best if someone stays with her."

"I'll do it."

She followed the woman from recovery to a room, and checked her vitals. She then pulled over a chair, settled down next to the woman, and began to pray the rosary. The rosary had been her father's. The black onyx beads alternated between smooth and carved with a rose pattern. The click and feel of the beads between her fingers was wonderfully soothing, but the worldly was overshadowing the holy. The tension in the streets had been growing. One protestor had already been killed, a young Native American man shot by police ostensibly for drawing a knife on them. She dreaded to think what would happen once the convention actually began, which was today now that Sunday had slipped into Monday.

Several hours passed and pale gray began to show outside the window. Mary-Catherine began the morning collect. *Lord God Almighty, who hast safely brought us to the beginning of this day, defend us in the same by Thy mighty power, that this day we may fall into no sin—*

The woman gave a gasp that was almost a moan, and her eyes snapped open. Sister Mary-Catherine broke off and looked up quickly from her breviary. She watched in shock as the woman's features began to shift.

"No! No! What's happening?" the woman cried.

Mary-Catherine ran to the door and yelled for a crash cart. She then raced back to the bed, and tried to decide what to do. She reached out and gripped the woman's shoulders, only to feel the bones shifting and cracking beneath her hands. It was grotesque and terrifying. The sheet dropped as the breasts vanished, the bandage over the repaired breast sagged as the tissue vanished.

It only took a few minutes and the black-haired beauty was gone, replaced by a man. He had neatly cut dark brown hair, a somewhat beaky nose. He looked to be the same height as the woman he had replaced, but with everything rearranged. His elegant, manicured hands flew to his face, the long supple fingers exploring his features. There was also a band of white on the fourth finger of his left hand where a ring had once rested. The eyelids lifted to reveal blue eyes in place of the woman's silver orbs. Sister Mary-Catherine stood back a few prudent feet away just in case this new person proved to be as instantly hostile as the female version.

"Where? Where am I?" he asked hoarsely.

The nurses with the crash cart burst into the room and the man flinched, eyes widening in fear. She waved them back. "It's okay. You're not needed."

She turned back to her now male patient. "You're in the hospital. You were badly mauled."

He lifted the loose bandage and stared at the seeping incision around his left breast. "God damn."

"Well, at least you still have an English accent," she said somewhat acidly. "Everything else has certainly changed."

He frowned at the far wall. "I was . . . Lilith."

"Oh, that's what you were trying to say when I asked your name. Last night you only managed to get out Lil. I had hoped it was Lily, but I suppose Lilith is more appropriate given her . . . attributes."

He lifted the bandage again. "Well, one *attribute* has certainly been defaced."

"I expect some men will find that sexy," Sister Mary-Catherine replied.

His eyes raked her. "In the same way some men like naughty nuns," the man replied, and gave her a smirking smile.

It was wrong but she found herself enjoying the sparring so she shot back, "So Lilith. From the Hebrew—female demon, night hag. What's your name now? Beelzebub?"

"You're a very odd nun. And no, it's . . . it's Etienne? No, Bahir. . . . Noel? I think it's Noel." He was frowning again. She recognized that particular furrow in the forehead.

"You probably need pain medicine."

"Probably, but I'd like to clear my head. I'm trying . . ."

"What?"

"To remember. There were people screaming. Then I tried to go home, but there were strangers there too. They screamed. Then . . ." He shrugged helplessly. "I don't know where I went."

"You appeared in Lincoln Park."

"Lincoln Park. Lincoln Park." It was a musing singsong. "Oh, right, Lincoln Park. I visited the art gallery there before the . . . game . . . So I'm still in Chicago?"

"Yes, you are in Chicago."

He pushed back the sheets. "I have to get back to the Palmer." He tried to sit up and gasped in pain.

Mary-Catherine again gripped his shoulders and helped lower him back onto the mattress. "No, I'm going to get that bandage reset and then you're going to sleep. Things will probably be clearer after you rest."

♥

Once Noel was snoring Sister Mary-Catherine gave him a quick physical. She studied the stunted male genitalia, parted his thighs and palpated the rudimentary vagina. She stepped back and snapped off her gloves and noted on the chart—*Hermaphrodite. Ace. Possible psychological explanation for patient's ability to assume a female form.*

She then went off to the Palmer Hotel to see if anyone could cast some light on her enigmatic patient, only to find it behind an almost impenetrable line of police and Secret Service agents.

"I understand the vice president and Senator McCarthy are staying here," Sister Mary-Catherine said as she tried to cling to her fast vanishing patience. "But I have a disoriented patient who claims to be staying here. I'm trying to get some information to help him recover his memory."

The Secret Service agent was an implacable monolith in a black suit as he stared down at her unblinking.

She tried again. "Has anything . . . odd happened here recently?"

That caused the impassive mask to shift. "Odd? Sister, have you looked around? All these hippies and yippies and freaks invading the city."

"They are in fact U.S. citizens exercising their First Amendment right to free assembly," she shot back waspishly. "But I meant in the hotel. May I please talk with the manager?"

The agent stared at the gold cross that hung on her white blouse and finally nodded. He allowed her through the front doors. Inside there were more police, and more agents. They were trying so hard to be unobtrusive that they stuck out like alligators in a child's wading pool. She noted that everyone getting on the elevators was presenting ID to police.

The desk clerk was a young man in a neatly pressed suit. She outlined her situation. "It would have happened late last night."

"Oh yeah, Gerald, the night manager, told me about it when I came in to work. It was like two A.M. when suddenly this bleeding, naked woman just appeared in the suite. There were a couple of McCarthy staffers working late. They freaked out. She attacked them, broke one guy's arm, and then just vanished. We had to have a cleaning crew up there early this morning to get the blood out of the carpet."

"So she didn't say anything?"

"No, apparently not. Just beat the shit—um, sorry, Sister, beat the tar out of them."

"Okay, thank you."

She started back to the hospital through clots of young protestors singing and marching, lines of police, and glaring residents who seemed to be viewing both sides with disapprobation. Halfway there she decided to swing through the park to get a read on the pulse of the protestors. The relaxed atmosphere from the night before was gone. Movement leaders were in the crowds discussing a march to the International Amphitheater. Others were practicing self-defense moves. The cops at the outskirts of the park clutched their nightsticks and watched the snake dancing and karate moves with trepidation.

Mary-Catherine passed by the kids in charge of Pigasus, the enormous black-and-white pig the yippies had nominated for president. The animal was grunting and snuffling. Mary-Catherine crossed to them, and gave the hog a pat on the back.

"You are feeding him, right?" she asked.

"Yeah, he's eating leftovers," one girl said.

"He really likes those new Big Mac sandwiches," another offered.

"Okay, just take care of him, okay? You really should let the authorities take him."

"No way, man. No telling what the pigs would do to him," a boy said with absolutely no self-awareness of the irony.

Probably treat him better than they will you, she thought, but she kept that to herself.

A night without sleep and clothes she hadn't changed in two days sent her back to the convent for a nap, a wash, and a change of clothes. She tried to slip out without being spotted, but Mother Superior Perpetua was reputed to have eyes in the back of her head, and she proved it again.

The older nun had not given up the traditional habit. The long skirts whispered across the stone floor and her heels rapped as she effectively cut off Mary-Catherine's escape.

"You were not at mass yesterday, Sister."

The blue-veined and gnarled hand was held out. Sister Mary-Catherine knelt and kissed the ring. "No, Mother. There were too many injuries. Thank God nothing serious but lots so I needed to stay."

"I think you *wanted* to stay and that's something quite different." She folded her hands across the front of her scapular with its embroidered red cross. "It concerns me. I think you identify too closely with these young people. Our concerns are not of this world."

"But our duty is to heal in the world, Mother. There's a reason I'm not in a contemplative order." She knew she was being "pert" and she braced for a rebuke, but the older woman just sighed and drew a hand across her cheek. The scent of soap and incense wafted off her.

"I love you, Sister, for your passion, but I pray you will not be led too far astray as some in our church have been."

Mary-Catherine considered giving the expected response, but realized she didn't want to lie. "I'll try, Mother," was the best she could manage.

As she trotted down the steps from the convent she reflected on the Berrigan brothers, Philip and Daniel. Both priests, both activists. Also the revolt of a number of American priests against the pope's Humanae Vitae regarding contraception. Having worked in poor developing countries, Mary-Catherine secretly shared their objections. The plight of woman without the means to prevent pregnancy was not a pretty one. She had nursed and lost too many women enduring their seventh or eighth childbirth.

Back at the hospital she found Etienne, Bahir, Noel, holding the receiver of the phone in his room and staring at it in bemusement. "What's wrong? Forgotten how to dial?" she asked. She noted his color was better.

"Why do you have such ancient phones? I've seen better in the third world," he said.

"Sorry we're not up to your exacting standards."

"I need to make a long-distance call to my wife and I doubt the hospital allows for that. May I use your phone?"

"My convent won't let you make a long-distance call either, though I might be able to convince Mother Superior."

"Cell. Phone," he enunciated slowly. "Or do your vows preclude such modern conveniences?" he added spitefully.

Staring at him in confusion, Mary-Catherine hesitantly said, "I'm not sure what you mean when you say cell phone. I've used a radio transceiver in Africa, but. . . ." Her voice trailed away and she shook her head. His expression now matched hers. She changed the subject. "Wife. So you're starting to remember."

"Some. The events of last night still have large gaps."

"Well, I can fill in some. You apparently appeared in a suite in the Palmer House, knocked the crap out of some of the staffers, and vanished again leaving blood and a broken arm in your wake. You next appeared in the park and that's when I got involved. I got Turtle to bring us—"

"Turtle? What the hell is he doing in Chicago? That old fossil hasn't been seen in public for years."

"Old? Not seen?" She knew she sounded like an idiot from the man's expression and that made her mad. She glared at him. "He's here for the convention. He's protecting the protestors, and keeping your sorry self from bleeding to death last night."

Noel lurched up and grabbed her arm. His grip was painful. "Who is the president?"

"What?"

"Tell me!" His voice was a rough growl.

"Ow! Lyndon Johnson, and you're hurting me!"

He fell back against the pillows with a moan that wasn't due entirely to pain. "Oh God, oh God. It's 1968."

"Wow, you're a quick one. Also the sky is blue, and you're clearly disoriented."

"No. I'm lost. Jasper . . . Oh God—" He broke off and threw an arm across his eyes. "My name is Noel Henry Matthews, I was born December third, 1981. And I'm completely and utterly fucked."

She spent the rest of the day working and reflecting on her odd patient. She had soothed him, telling him, "What you are is delusional from trauma and blood loss. Sleep will help." She had backed it up with a shot of morphine as he had murmured about having to find a way back.

That evening she stopped in the bathroom, removed her coif and veil, and rumpled her shorn hair. She rinsed her face and stopped by the nurses' lounge for a coffee and whatever stale Danish might be available. The TV was on and tuned to the convention, cameras focused on Mayor Richard Daley's bulldog face.

"As long as I am mayor of this city, there's going to be law and order in Chicago!"

"Well, that was conciliatory," Mary-Catherine said as she chewed on an apple Danish. The filling was glutinous and fairly disgusting, but hunger overrode distaste.

One of the older nurses pursed her lips. "It's the fault of these young thugs. They should go home or back to school. Do something useful."

"Maybe they think this qualifies as doing something useful," Mary-Catherine said with such cloying sweetness that the older woman flushed.

"Well, this isn't the way."

I've been in Guatemala. Sometimes this is the only *way,* she thought as she left the room.

She wanted to get back out in the streets, go to the park, read the pulse of the city, the police, and the protestors, but found herself stopping by Noel's room. There was something fascinating about the injured man . . . woman . . . ace. To find him collapsed on the floor between the bed and the door. With the aid of an orderly she got him back into bed and checked his stitches.

"What in heaven's name were you thinking? You're lucky you didn't tear open these wounds."

"I have to go. Have to find a way back. Have to go home."

She lightly touched the pale spot on his finger. "I'll accept you were married, but it looks like you left that state."

"No. I guess nothing can travel through time other than the living person."

"Good to know marriage still exists in the future. Are there flying cars? Do people just eat food pellets?"

"You're making fun of me. You don't believe me."

"No, I don't. It's crazy."

"In a world where people possess astounding powers and you cavil at *that*?" His tone was acidic. "How can I convince you?"

"Tell me something that's going to happen."

"Humphrey will be nominated and Nixon will win."

"Nonsense. Humphrey hasn't run in a single primary. He's tainted by his association with Johnson. The party won't be stupid enough to take it away from McCarthy."

"Oh you sweet innocent."

His tone was so condescending that she wanted to hit him. Knock that smug smile off his face. She managed to keep her reaction limited to sarcastic words. "Whatever. And since it's August we won't be able to test it out for two more months."

"Has the convention started?" Noel asked.

"Yes. Daley just gaveled it into order."

"Let me think. Let me think. I read a monograph by an excruciatingly dull Canadian scholar about '68. *Battleground Chicago*." He pressed his fingertips against his closed eyelids, lips moving soundlessly. His eyes snapped open. "Tuesday night a journalist is going to be assaulted by security inside the amphitheater and your Mr. Cronkite is going to refer to them as a *bunch of thugs* and earn the ire of Mayor Daley."

"Daley's a pig, but he's not stupid. They'll beat the hell out of the kids, but they're not going to risk alienating journalists or delegates."

He gave a bleak little smile. "Time will tell." He looked toward the window, where night had fallen. Even through the walls they heard the wail of sirens. "Or perhaps my mere presence here has already shifted the time line. Will I vanish? Of course if one goes down that line of reasoning one would do nothing. Be terrified to act. Fortunately I'm not a particularly passive person."

Mary-Catherine glanced toward the floor where he had fallen. "Clearly not. Now stay in bed. We'll worry about the future once we get there."

She started for the door.

"A favor."

"What?"

"Please get me some clothes. I'd rather not leave here in a hospital gown and I did rather arrive with nothing."

"All right."

"One more thing." She turned back again. "If I'm right will you help me?"

"Yes. I'll help you." It was a promise she wasn't likely to have to keep.

"I think we've got a bunch of thugs here, if I may be permitted to say so." The stentorian tones of Walter Cronkite.

The images seemed seared on her eyes. The dark-haired young journalist being manhandled by security as he tried to interview a Georgia delegate being hustled out of the hall. The blow that sent him to the floor. His breathless report to the older, venerable newsman about how the security people had hit him in the stomach and "put him on the deck."

She was in Dr. Young's office, where he had one of the new portable color televisions on a metal stand. He blew out a gust of air and ran a hand through his tousled hair. "If this is happening inside what's going to happen to those kids? Maybe you should stay off the streets and out of the park, Sister."

"He was right," Sister Mary-Catherine whispered.

"What? Are you listening to me?"

"Yes. No. Sorry. I have to go." She snatched up the suit that Young had brought from home for their mysterious patient.

Noel was sitting up and frowning at the far wall. His eyes were clouded. Expression bleak.

"Okay, I'm inclined to believe you," she said.

"So, it happened to that reporter—"

"Dan Rather."

"Whatever." He waved her off and winced at the movement.

"So, what are you going to do?"

"Try to get home."

"And if you can't?"

"I could make a killing in the market." He gave her a teeth-baring smile that never reached his eyes. "I'd invite you to join me, but you've got that whole vow of poverty thing going."

She tossed the clothes on the bed. "I need you to remember everything you can from that monograph. I'm going to try to get you to Hayden and Davis and Dellinger. No point going to Rubin and Hoffman. They're gadflies."

"And why would I care what happens to these young fools in the streets? I've seen a lot of popular uprisings. Almost all of them are either pointless or end badly. And there is this whole butterfly effect when it comes to time travel. I'm not keen on wiping out my own future or doing something that endangers my wife and son."

"I thought you weren't a particularly passive person."

"I'm very motivated when it comes to *me*. I find altruism to be overrated."

She folded her arms across her chest and glared at him. "You want my help. This is how you get it."

"Now *that,* I understand."

"I'll remember to never appeal to your better nature," she shot back.

"Wise choice."

She had to help him out of the bed and assist him as he dressed. His face was white, lips compressed into a thin line with pain by the time they were finished. "I'll get a wheelchair, and stop by the pharmacy and grab pain meds for you."

"Let me go with you. Once I've seen a place I can easily return."

"How?"

"I can teleport. Well, that's not technically true. My other selves can teleport."

"There are more of you?"

"Just one. You haven't met him yet."

"So introduce us."

"Can't happen until morning."

"You really are just full of psychological hang-ups, aren't you?"

"And now you sound like my old handler."

A wheelchair was procured. He lowered himself gingerly into it and she pushed him briskly down the hall to an elevator. At the pharmacy she was lucky. The nurse on duty had stepped away, and Mary-Catherine grabbed several bottles of Dilaudid.

Then they were out in the sultry night. She helped Noel to his feet. The heat smothered the city, the scent of tear gas laced the air. "It's about six miles to the park. Can you—"

"No. I can't. Get us a car."

"The cops have the streets barricaded."

"So let's get a cop car."

"What?" Then the irony struck her and she chuckled. "Can you really hot-wire a car?"

"Oh, dear Sister. I have so many nefarious skills. You have no idea. But before I lead you into a life of crime are we sure this is a good move? Will these people you mentioned believe me any more than you did?"

"I'll tell them about Rather."

He shrugged and his breath caught as the burns rubbed against his shirt and coat and the stitches were pulled. He dug out a bottle and dry-swallowed a couple of Dilaudid.

Mary-Catherine tugged at her lower lip and considered. "Actually, the person we really need to convince is Humphrey. He was a progressive warrior until Johnson neutered him. He would consider the good of the country."

"Great!" Noel's tone was cheerfully manic. "How do we get close to the vice president of these United States?"

"Let's think about that."

"Let's think about that over a meal."

"You have no money."

"I can handle that."

"More nefarious skills?"

"Absolutely."

They ended up in front of a French restaurant. They had a few minutes before closing. Noel drew his thumb across the bills in the wallet.

"Where did you get that? I didn't see you—"

"I should hope not. Bloody terrible magician if you had. I took it off some gentleman near one of the hotels. At least the suit did not mislead. A tidy sum."

"You picked him because of his suit?"

"Yes, it was Savile Row. Always stick with the classics." She should have been shocked. Instead she chuckled.

An obsequious maître d' bowed them into the restaurant. The borrowed suit wasn't all that fine, and the fit was less than perfect, but there was something in the Brit's demeanor that demanded respect. Mary-Catherine stole a sideways glance at the beaky profile. Not handsome but . . . there was something. She reined in her errant and galloping thoughts, offered a quick prayer though she wasn't entirely certain what kind of protection she was seeking. Guidance on how to make a difference.

They were seated, menus offered with a flourish, and the maître d' retreated. It was a very fancy restaurant. There were no English translations of the French words. Mary-Catherine's eyes flickered across the pages. The prices made her blanch.

"You need a translation."

"I picked up a little French in the Congo. I'll manage."

A waiter arrived and fluent French flowed between the server and her enigmatic companion. *"Très bien, monsieur."* The waiter departed. A few moments later he returned with a glass of whiskey. Noel drained it in one swallow and handed back the glass. They gave their orders. The waiter padded away and came back with a wineglass and a bottle of red wine.

"I don't get any?" Mary-Catherine asked.

"I wouldn't want to tempt you into further naughty behavior."

"First, you better not drink a bottle of wine on your own. Particularly when you're on pain meds, and secondly, the Lord Himself was a proponent of the grape. I remember this wedding and water. . . ." She challenged him from beneath lowered brows.

Noel threw back his head and laughed. Too loudly, too long. The waiter left and returned with a second glass. The glasses were filled. He held his up for a toast.

"Here's to the oddest nun I've ever met."

"Had a lot of experience with penguins, have you?"

"Nope. C of E."

"Did you ever attend?"

"Ooh, the lady has teeth. And yes, chapel every Sunday while I was at Cambridge. We mostly go for the music. And to avoid the buggery . . . unlike you lot." She gave him a puzzled look. He sloshed more wine into his glass. "You'll find out."

She took a sip and it seemed like roses blossomed in her mouth. "That's . . . that's wonderful."

Noel picked up the bottle and gave it a critical look. "Château Margaux, '65. I'll have to remember this once I get back—"

He broke off abruptly and she saw the anguish. She changed the subject. "So, Humphrey."

"Won't be easy to get to him. Probably impossible at the convention."

"So, it has to happen at the hotel. Which room were you staying in? Can you get us inside?"

He looked confused. He stared down into his glass and spun the ruby liquid. "I don't think so. I was there, but . . . there were a lot of people. I was . . . Why can I remember things from college but not that night?"

"It's not uncommon. Trauma and injury can affect short-term memory. It will probably come back."

"If I could remember how I got here, maybe. . . ." He shook his head. "As for the hotel. Remember—naked—so no key."

"Well, let me give you what I saw when I went there yesterday. There's security on the front doors. At the elevators—"

"You have the makings of an operative, dear Sister." Food began to arrive. "Let's table this discussion for the moment. I hate to give myself indigestion by planning instead of appreciating."

The food was delicious and as she dug in she realized she couldn't recall when she'd last had a real meal. At last the plates stopped arriving. The waiter brought Noel a snifter of brandy. He rolled the glass between his hands, the long fingers caressing the curve of the glass. Sister Mary-Catherine found herself staring at them.

"You have beautiful hands," she blurted, and felt her cheeks beginning to burn.

"Why, thank you. I would say they are quite my best feature." An awkward silence fell across the table. "So explain to me the purpose of this . . . intervention."

She leaned back, wineglass cupped between her palms. "If Humphrey knows he's going to lose he might be willing to step aside. Throw his support behind McCarthy. Unite the party. If that news got to the protestors all of this"—she gestured at the wider city—"would end."

"Peace, love, and rock 'n' roll," Noel drawled.

"What made you so cynical?"

"Long experience with the world and people who try to make it better."

"I'm sorry for you." She leaned intently in over the table. Laid a hand over his. She realized she was perhaps a bit tipsy, but she didn't pull back from the contact. "Look, upstream, in the future you've left a wife and child. Let's assume you can't get back. What can you do, *here, now,* that would make their lives better?"

His hand twisted until it covered hers and he gripped it hard. "I don't know. Where does McCarthy stand on wild cards? Joker rights in particular? My Niobe is a joker."

"Well, for starters he wants the war in Vietnam to end. Jokers don't get deferments. They get drafted. In my area of expertise he's talked about wanting to increase spending on health care for jokers and funding research on the virus to improve survivability and to reduce the more damaging effects. He understands that civil rights is about all oppressed minorities. He's a good man."

"But can he beat Nixon?"

"Well, according to you Humphrey can't, so the best we can do is hope . . . and reset the board."

"Can one really change history?" Noel murmured. His brow was furrowed again. He pulled out the pills and swallowed two more.

"We won't know until we try."

He set aside the glass. "It's the riots that help ensure Nixon's election." He gave her a thin smile. "The dear cud-chewing citizens of Middle America are horrified by the violence they witness in the streets and turn to Mr. Law and Order. You Americans are a very stupid people."

The patronizing tone had a bubble of anger rising in her breast. She tried to curb her unruly tongue, but to no avail. "Yeah, well, you might recall without our help you'd probably be speaking German now. And by the way, *I'm* from Wisconsin."

Again that smile that held very little humor and made her feel like he was about to bite. "I rest my case."

"You're calling me stupid?"

"Yes." The rudeness rocked her back in the booth. She glared at him. "You have a beautiful face, good legs, and a nice rack. But you chose to become a bride of Christ." The scorn was evident.

"Thank you, I guess, and you're not the first man to notice. Look, the church paid for my education. I couldn't have become a doctor otherwise. And I do more than pray. I've brought aid to people in the Congo, in Guatemala and Bolivia. Saved lives. What's your contribution?"

Judging from his expression, she had hit a nerve. He didn't answer. "If I had my memories I could teleport us into a hallway, but . . ." He shook his head. "Unfortunately there's no Google so I can't get a read on the interior." She opened her mouth and he hurried to add, "I'll explain Google later." He thoughtfully tugged at his upper lip. "I could take ID off a Secret Service agent."

Mary-Catherine's hand went to her throat. She had a sudden disquieting image of Noel choking an agent. Dragging the unconscious (or worse) man into an alley. She cast about for an alternative.

"Or," she said slowly, "we get invited in to see the vice president."

"And how pray tell do we do that?"

The inchoate thoughts began to form into a plan. "We're bringing a message of goodwill from the Holy Father. We just have to get you the proper clothes."

He gave her a droll look. "You want me to mug a priest?"

"No. I want to keep you from mugging anybody."

"You quite suck the joy out of everything. The effect of too much religion, I expect. But it is a very good idea."

She looked around the restaurant. "It's late. These good people would probably like to go home, and you need to get into a bed. Let's find you a hotel."

"Where are you going to sleep?" he asked faintly as she helped him to his feet.

"Not with you. I'm going to go back to the park. The curfew's approaching. The cops will try something so I'll have patients. We'll reconvene in the morning."

Wednesday morning. She had grabbed a few hours of sleep at the convent, bought a paper at a newsstand, and was rapidly reading while she headed to the run-down hotel where they had finally managed to find Noel a room. Today the peace plank was going to be offered into the party's platform. *They'll give the protestors that much of a bone,* she thought. *It will cost them nothing. The only thing damaged by it will be LBJ's pride.*

When Noel answered the door his hair was damp. He had a towel wrapped around his waist. She reached out to touch the bandages over his torn breast and belly and was relieved to find them dry.

"I've been hurt enough times to know not to get the dressings wet," he said.

"Do I even want to know why?"

"Probably not." He limped to his clothes and fished out the bottle of Dilaudid.

It wasn't difficult to locate a Catholic store. The appropriate collar and attire were purchased though the clothing he picked seemed large. When she brought that up he just gave her a mischievous look and didn't answer. A few items of religious jewelry appropriate for a priest to wear, a rosary and a crucifix and a small Latin missal, were added, and they approached the cashier. Noel whispered out of the side of his mouth, "And here I thought all that Latin I had to study at Cambridge was an utter waste of time."

They returned to the hotel room. He shrugged out of the suit jacket and gave a cry of pain. Sweat-darkened rings were beneath his armpits. He looked around the room. "No bloody air-conditioning. Didn't notice last night." Unbuttoning his shirt, he went and opened a window. The rank effluvia from the stockyards came wafting into the room. He gave a mutter of disgust and shut the window again. "I suppose heatstroke is preferable to asphyxiation." He took off the shirt, and fanned himself with a piece of stationery taken from the desk.

"So are we ready?" he asked.

"It would be best if we had a general and bland statement of blessing in these troubled times," she said.

"I'm assuming special stationery?" She nodded. "Anything else distinctive?"

"The papal seal."

"Do you have any examples at your convent?"

"Hardly."

"What time is it?"

She checked her watch. "Ten twenty."

"Still daylight in Rome," he murmured.

"The convention's ending tomorrow. We really don't have time for a European excursion," Mary-Catherine snapped.

He gave her that wolf's smile again. "Going to make another little change here."

He gave a grunt that became a moan. Alarmed, Mary-Catherine watched as the same horrifying rippling and rearranging that occurred when Lilith vanished was taking place beneath his skin. Skin that was shifting from milk white to golden tan. The dark hair became a mane of fiery red gold, and when he raised his lids his eyes were whirling pits of gold. Lilith had been darkness and the silver of starlight. The man who now stood before her was the fire of dawn and sunset. He seemed to blaze in the dimness of the cheap hotel room.

Look away! Look away! a small voice was yammering. It became the aged and cracking voice of Mother Superior. Neither voice had any effect. Mary-Catherine stood drinking in the male perfection that stood before her. The broad shoulders, narrow waist, muscular legs. This entity was taller and broader than Noel. She had thought that Diego, with whom she had shared some heavy petting and passionate kisses in the jungles of Guatemala, had been handsome. He was nothing compared to this man.

"Well. You're . . . he's . . . something." She hated herself for stammering.

The mobile lips twisted into a sneer. "He's a fourteen-year-old's idea of a male ideal. Just like Lilith is that same teenager's sex fantasies about women. Both of them are absurd. Probably to make up for the extremely deficient human that created them."

"I would say you're deficient in terms of your moral compass but otherwise . . ." She shrugged.

She tentatively approached him, and let her eyes range across his body, noting the way the hair on his chest whorled into red-gold patterns, the sheen of sweat on his skin. The scent of him. Perhaps it was just exhaustion, but she swayed and he caught her by the shoulders. Breath caught in the back of her throat and warmth filled her groin. She pulled away.

"Your bandages are too . . . tight . . . now. Let me . . . fix that." She hurried to where she had left her medical bag. She re-dressed the wounds on his chest, belly, and thigh. As a doctor she had touched the bodies of men, but never before had a man bludgeoned her senses in quite this way.

"Do you . . . have you . . . can you . . ." she stammered. She prayed he wouldn't understand, and for an instant that seemed to be the case.

"A name? Yes, several, but recently I've used Etienne." But then his lips curved in a sardonic grin, and that prayer, like all the others she'd been uttering, went unanswered. "But I don't think that's actually what you meant. I think you meant sex, and yes, my equipment is fully functional. As all three entities." Her face was flaming. He seemed to have an uncanny ability to delve into her deepest fantasies. "Though Noel is the least talented in the bedroom. His . . . er . . . equipment is mediocre at best. As you've seen."

As if pulled by a magnet her eyes dropped to his crotch and the reaction only imperfectly covered by the towel. Mary-Catherine's chest felt paralyzed. She wheezed as she tried to breathe. Golden Noel reached out and touched her cheek. "You're a beautiful woman. Why did you make this choice? And what is your real name? I can't believe that any parent would lay that moniker on their daughter."

"It's Jessica," she whispered.

"And that's beautiful too," he said softly. The accent, the gleaming eyes, the curve of his lips, added to the sense she was in a dream far removed from the structured life of Sister Mary-Catherine of the Poor Sisters of St. Francis. He took her hand. With his free hand he touched her cheek. Electricity seemed to pulse through her body.

"You're married," she said faintly. *And I really should mention my vows.*

"And never going to see her again. Jasper. . . ." Tears thickened his voice. He abruptly released her and turned away. "I'm lost, Sister." Grief wailed on every word.

She rushed forward, and gripped his bare shoulders. "But not alone. I'm here."

He spun, buried his head against her chest, and wept. She stroked the luxurious hair, was terribly aware of the powerful hands clutching at her back. His tears wet the front of her blouse. The press of his cheek against her breasts filled her with a heady warmth. He lifted his head. They were a breath apart. She tried to believe it was just him, but it wasn't. She also leaned in and their lips met.

There had been a few fumbling kisses from eager teenage boys back at her high school in Hudson. Hands that immediately tried to reach for her breasts. Diego had been hard and demanding. Maybe that was why she hadn't surrendered completely. This man's hands cupped her back gently, his lips were warm and soft, gentle as they explored her mouth. Breath escaped like a half-whispered prayer. Her lips parted and his tongue briefly touched hers. Fire exploded at the base of her spine, raced up the nerves and vertebrae to fill her head with fireworks. She allowed her tongue to enter his mouth.

He reached up and deftly removed the pins that held the black veil in place over her coif. He held her at arm's length, the golden eyes devouring her face. "Like a hijab," he murmured. "Frames the face so beautifully. What color is your hair?"

Her fingers were trembling as she removed the pins at her temples and at the back of her neck. The white material of her coif slid down her back to puddle on the floor. She reached up self-consciously to her shorn hair.

"Wheat gold. You little Wisconsin beauty," he whispered.

He kissed her again. There was a brief surge of fear and guilt, but the sensations washed them away. She remembered a night of prayer and meditation when she had prepared herself to be a bride of Christ. There had been a moment like this one, a moment of physical ec-stasy, but now her body yearned against a male body and not against the chill air in the chapel. He pulled back enough for her to reach up and unbutton her blouse. A plain bra held her breasts in tight con-finement. His fingers expertly slipped the clasp. Her breasts swung free.

"I . . . I shouldn't," she whispered, but she found herself reaching for the zipper on the back of her skirt.

"Would it help if I . . ." Etienne snatched up the clerical collar from the bag and held it to his throat. It accentuated the gold of his skin, the etched tendons in his neck, the sparkle of stubble along his jawline. She giggled.

"I'm so confused," she whispered as the skirt pooled around her feet, still encased in her sensible black shoes and stockings.

"No you're not. Your body knows. Let your mind follow," he whis-pered as his hands cupped her breasts. His lips nibbled down her neck. He ducked his head and took one breast in his mouth, his tongue teasing at her nipple. Electricity shot through her as the nipple stiff-ened. She moaned and clutched at his hair.

After that it was just a confusing kaleidoscope of hands and lips. Joy, physical ecstasy blended with pain as his penis broke her virginity.

She was a physician. She knew how human reproduction worked, the theory of sex. What she hadn't expected was how he used his body and his penis to bring her to the edge of quivering release, then pulled back and teased her again and again. He was very careful to keep his injuries from hitting her body. She knew he was in pain, but couldn't bring herself to stop him. It all felt too good.

When the release finally came she had a momentary sense of blindness and the feeling the top of her head had come off. Her hands raked at his back, though she remembered to avoid the burns on his shoulder. Spasm after spasm shook her and she cried out. He grinned down at her, sweat trickling through his sideburns. His hips began to thrust again, and then his own release shuddered through him. She felt warmth spreading through her insides and sudden panic hit. Her eyes widened and he once again read her mind.

"No, you aren't going to get pregnant. My sperm has very little motility and that's the case no matter which body I'm wearing. It's why Niobe and I had such trouble conceiving."

"Oh, okay." The sense of relief was enormous. If she was honest she knew she was using this to justify her terrible behavior. He was married. She had taken a vow. None of it mattered.

Her thoughts flitted in a hundred different directions. One stuck. "I thought it would be faster," she blurted. At his expression she hastened to add, "No offense. It was wonderful. I had no idea it could be like that, but when friends in high school talked about it, and I sometimes see—not that I'm spying, but the kids in the park are pretty casual about where they . . . do it—well, it seems like it happens very quickly."

"That's youth and inexperience. This was your first time. It needed to be all about you, not me."

She relaxed back against the sagging mattress. "Aren't you supposed to go to sleep now? That's what all the textbooks say."

"I'm drowsy but my job required I train myself to resist the impulse."

"You used sex in your work?"

He laughed. "Oh yes."

"What about . . . Lilith. Can she . . ."

"No, my ovaries are scarcely developed at all. So I'm the safest fuck anyone can ever have."

He leaned on an elbow next to her and drew a finger down her nose and outlined her lips. "So when is the guilt going to hit?"

She frowned. "I don't know. I should feel guilty. I should be running back to the convent or to the nearest church to confess. . . . Maybe it's all these kids advocating free love." She gave him a shy smile.

"Make love not war," he added as he rolled out of bed. "And that's just what we're going to do. Humphrey out, McCarthy in. War ends. Rainbows and unicorns everywhere," he concluded, and padded to the small bathroom.

After he cleaned up she helped him dress and hooked the clerical collar. The stark black of the shirt made his coloring even more dramatic. "Would you like to come with me?"

"Where?"

"To the Vatican."

She glanced down at her pelvis. "I'm worried I might burst into flames," she drawled. He laughed and it became a groan as he pulled the stitches in his belly. "I'd suggest that you wear dark glasses. There probably aren't all that many ace priests either."

"Good advice. Well, I'm off to work, honey." He vanished. There was a pop as air rushed into the space his body had once inhabited. Mary-Catherine tottered backwards, hit the edge of the bed with the backs of her knees, and sat down abruptly.

This, she reflected as she touched her groin, *was almost too many new experiences for one day.*

When Noel returned he was wearing a pair of wraparound sunglasses and toting a portable typewriter, a plastic pan, a bottle of bleach, a bottle of acetone, and cotton swabs. She raised her eyebrows at the jumble of items.

"It was easier to steal a document that already had the seal rather than steal both stationery and a seal." He handed over the paper. It was on heavy parchment.

She studied it. "It's an Easter greeting. It's August."

"So we're going to rewrite it."

"In Latin?"

"Remember, I went to Cambridge, and if I should make some mistake in declension I doubt anyone on the Humphrey staff or Humphrey himself will catch the error."

"So how do you remove the ink?" she asked.

"Watch and learn."

She hovered as he carefully dipped the paper in bleach then quickly dipped it in acetone, taking care to keep the letterhead and the seal out of the liquid. A gentle blotting with cotton swabs and the ink melted away. Within a few minutes the type was gone, leaving only the seal and the letterhead.

"Now we place it beneath a book." He snatched a copy of the Gideon Bible out of a drawer. "To allow it to dry flat, type in our own message, and voilà!"

"Where did you learn to do this?"

"Spy school." He shot her a grin.

"Yeah, right."

"No, really."

"You're a spy?"

"Was."

In the sweltering room it didn't take long for the paper to dry. Noel ran it into the typewriter and gave her an inquiring look. She dictated a bland message about God giving guidance to the leaders of nations and offering a blessing. Noel turned it into Latin. It was done.

"Now we go to the Hilton." Mary-Catherine swallowed but the lump of fear that blocked her throat didn't ease. "I suppose it wouldn't hurt to know who is the current pope."

That made her laugh. "Yes, it would probably be good if a priest knew that. Pope Paul the Sixth. I'd just refer to him as the Holy Father."

"I don't suppose we'll be lucky and Humphrey is a Catholic."

"No. We've only had one Catholic president and . . ." She couldn't finish. "I was in nursing school when we heard. Classes were canceled. I took the bus home from Minneapolis. Everyone was crying. My parents had a picture of John F. Kennedy right next to our sacred heart and the crucifix and the statue of Mary. I think it helped me make my decision."

"To become a nun." She nodded. "Apparently it inspired Turtle to go public in a time when wild cards were in hiding."

"Really?"

"Yes, it's in his memoirs."

"Memoirs." She shook her head trying to grasp it. "Well, if we succeed we'll have a second Catholic president. McCarthy is Catholic." She looked down at the document they had created.

"I'm trying to decide which is the worst sin I've committed today."

"We'll confess once this is all over," he said glibly.

"You're not Catholic," she accused.

"We have confession in the Anglican Church too."

"Have you ever availed yourself of it?" she snapped.

A bleak expression leached all the animation from his face. "I'd be there for days."

"Bastard! Selfish, shortsighted bastard!" The lamp from the bedside table crashed into the mirror over the dresser. The shards rained down, glass tears as jagged as Etienne's grief.

The sound echoed the breaking of the glass-topped coffee table and the dirty highball glasses on its surface when the Secret Service agents had wrestled Noel to the floor. Mary-Catherine rubbed at her arms, sore and bruised by the agents who had grabbed her as well. Was there anything they could have done differently?—

It had been surprisingly easy to reach Humphrey. The agents at the door of the hotel had waved them in after taking in their clerical garb and explanation. Etienne wore dark glasses, carried a white cane, and gripped her arm, creating the illusion he was a blind man. He did it most convincingly.

At the front desk he fumbled for the letter and allowed her to hand it to the desk clerk. He phoned up to the vice president's suite and a few minutes later an aide had arrived to escort them upstairs. Their escort, a bright-eyed young man whose energy and enthusiasm reminded Sister Mary-Catherine of the young people in the park.

He and Etienne had made conversation while the elevator rose. Mary-Catherine was amazed at the ease with which Etienne conversed . . . and lied. Her throat felt like a tennis ball had been lodged inside. She doubted she could make a sound.

The suite smelled of cigarette smoke, stale food, burnt coffee, and male sweat. Phones were ringing, a Xerox machine was clanking out copies, the rumble of male voices formed the counterpoint to the soprano ring of the phones. There were only a few women present.

They received a few curious glances, a number of suspicious glances from the Secret Service agents in the room, but most of Humphrey's staff ignored them. At one point Etienne blundered into one of the agents and murmured an apology. They continued through to the bedroom, where Humphrey sat with a group of harried-looking men. Mary-Catherine heard the words—delegates, McCarthy, planks—float past. They were discussing the peace plank and their determination to block it. Her hands coiled into fists, and her nails bit into her palms.

The aide leaned down and whispered in Humphrey's ear. His round face was split with a grin and he heaved himself out of his chair.

"Father. Sister. So honored." He pumped Etienne's hand and gave her an oddly courtly little bow.

"Thank you for seeing us, Mr. Vice President. We have a letter from the Holy Father. In these troubled times America is a necessary beacon and he wished to offer his blessing to any of the men who might lead her." Etienne held out the letter, but off to Humphrey's side, nicely continuing the deception.

"Most gracious. Most gracious." Humphrey scanned the page, continuing to smile though it was clear he understood not a word.

"If we might have a brief word in private, Mr. Vice President," Etienne said after a suitable interval. "We have a more personal message from the Holy Father."

Humphrey looked puzzled, but waved out the pols who were present. One of the Secret Service agents hesitated, but Humphrey gave a sharp nod and he left, too. The door closed behind them.

"Really, Father, I find this most unusual. Meaning no offense, but I'm not a Catholic."

"We know." Etienne's intonation had changed. It was now far more clipped and cold. "You're about to become the Democratic nominee—"

"Well, I certainly hope so," Humphrey interrupted, chuckling. His high-pitched voice was one of the things that made the vice president seem so weak.

"—and go on to lose the election to Richard Nixon."

"I beg your pardon?" The genial smile had given way to the angry stubborn look of a frustrated baby.

"I'm an ace. Through a variety of complicated and unimportant reasons I have found myself transported from 2017 into this time period. I don't like it, but I can at least do something to improve on what's to come. Withdraw your nomination, throw your support behind McCarthy. History will thank you for it."

"And I'm supposed to just believe this nonsense? How do I even know you're an ace?"

Etienne removed his glasses. Humphrey took a step back. Fear and anger warred across his round face.

"You're nothing but goddamn fakes! Hippie infiltrators, spinning lies and fairy tales."

"Believe me, I have nothing in common with those unwashed children in the streets," Etienne drawled. "But I'm deadly serious about what happens. You're going to lose. They hate Johnson and they hate you. Dump the Hump!" He stalked toward the older man with a panther's grace and just as much menace.

Humphrey backed away and shouted for security. Etienne lunged for the portly politician, but what Mary-Catherine saw in his face terrified her, and she blocked him, pressing her hands frenziedly against his chest. He gave a hiss of pain at the pressure on the torn breast. The agents boiled into the room and wrestled Etienne to the floor, breaking the coffee table as he fell. An agent grabbed her, his fingers digging into her upper arms. It was shaming as well as painful.

Security began to drag them out of the bedroom. Etienne was struggling and he threw back one last poisonous barb as they were dragged away.

"Johnson was right when he said he had your pecker in his pocket. You're a weak little—"

Humphrey's look of shame and hurt made her cringe. "How . . . how did you know? I never told anyone," the vice president whispered through stiff lips.

"It was on the tapes. He despises you. And I know because I'm from the future, you stupid prat!"

In the outer room of the suite Etienne suddenly twisted and broke free of one of the agents holding him. He roughly yanked Mary-Catherine away from all but one of her captors and pulled her close.

There was a terrifying, disorienting moment of black and cold and a feeling that some rage-filled entity *saw* her and then she was tumbling to the grass in the park. Etienne rolled smoothly to his feet, and kicked the disoriented agent who had accompanied them in the face while at the same time shouting to the gaping crowds.

"Bastard tried to arrest a *nun*. He hurt her!"

There was a growl of rage from the protestors and they began to close on the agent. "No! He didn't—" But Etienne grabbed her before she finished the denial.

There was once more that dizzying sense of being nowhere and everywhere and then they were back in the hotel room—

With glass glittering on the dresser top and Etienne raging around the room. His hands were shaking as he pulled out the bottle of pain pills and gulped down three of them. Blood was wetting the shirt where his stitches had torn.

"Take off your shirt," she ordered.

Both the breast and the belly were bleeding. She grabbed her bag, wiped away the blood, disinfected the area, and reset several stitches.

He groaned and bit his lip as the needle flicked through his skin. "You need to rest."

"I need to act."

"Let's first have a plan, okay?"

Once finished she snapped off her gloves, grabbed her bag, and headed for the door.

"Where are you going?"

"To Grant Park. There's a rally at the bandshell. Dellinger's going to speak and I want to hear it. Also, in this heat I'll have customers."

"I'll come with you."

"You really should rest. And it's going to be really hot."

"And it isn't in here? I can't stay still. I just keep thinking about them."

"Your wife and son."

"Yes. So stupid to think I could make things better for wild cards. Nothing ever works out. Maybe revolution is the only solution. Burn it all down," he raged.

"I've been in revolutions. They're not a good thing. Fires kill and innocents die."

"So have I. Caused a few. And innocents die all the time." His expression was suddenly bleak. "Sometimes it seems like only the innocent die."

"Well, you better not come in this form. There are probably APBs out all over for you after what happened."

"For you too, my dear."

That stopped her for a moment. "Oh, yeah, hadn't thought about that."

"Perhaps a change of dress."

He changed back into Noel, donned Dr. Young's borrowed suit, told her to wait, and left. He returned forty minutes later with jeans, a cute top, and a pair of sandals. She changed, pulled off her coif and veil, and gazed into the bathroom mirror, studying the different woman that now stood before her. She felt like she was taking steps that were inexorably leading her away from her vows, maybe even from the church.

There were thousands of people in the park. On the stage were the leaders of the movement—Rubin, Dellinger, Hayden, and many more. Turtle hovered over the bandshell, revolving slowly as he tried to keep an eye on everything. There were National Guardsmen on the roof of the Field Museum and ringing the protestors was a line of cops. Their expressions sent a shiver down Mary-Catherine's spine.

Noel leaned in and whispered, "They've got shot in their gloves. They're looking to bust heads. Sure you want to stay?"

"All the more reason. I'll probably be needed if this goes sideways."

Mary-Catherine moved through the crowd, tending to a sprained ankle here, a case of heat exhaustion, a bad trip. The speakers took to the bandshell. Noel's mobile upper lip curled with disdain as he listened, but he mercifully made no comment.

The afternoon wore on. At one point a young man ran up onto the bandstand and whispered to the movement leaders assembled there. One of them, the young firebrand Tom Hayden, stepped to the microphone. The amplified voice boomed out across the assembled thousands. People literally swayed as if the words themselves were stones. The peace plank had been voted down. A moan swept through the crowd and morphed into a growl.

A young man ran to the flagpole, climbed up, and began removing the American flag. Noel was looking back over his shoulder. He grabbed Mary-Catherine's arm and she flinched as he hit the bruises.

"Time to go."

She followed his gaze to where the line of blue-helmeted cops was advancing, billy clubs thwacking against gloved palms. At the pole the flag was being replaced with a bloody T-shirt. A line of marshals, organized by the protest leaders with the intent of offering protection to the dissidents and led by Rennie Davis, interposed itself between the scowling cops and the kids. With a roar the cops charged, swinging their billy clubs. Young men collapsed beneath the blows. Turtle flew toward the fighting. On the bandshell people were yelling for calm.

Mary-Catherine saw a knot of young men carrying away Davis. His face was covered with blood and he lolled unconscious in their arms. She ran to help. A blow hard enough to render someone unconscious had a very good chance of cracking that person's skull. Noel, cursing, limped after her.

After a quick exam she said to the young men, "Somebody go get Turtle. He can be our ambulance service again."

"He's holding back the cops," another young man said.

She looked and saw it was true. An invisible barrier was pushing the police back, away from the protestors. Unfortunately officers were figuring out that the telekinetic wall had edges and they were flowing around it.

Noel swept them all with an irritated look. "Oh to hell with this," he said. He clenched his fists and the change began. Within seconds Etienne had returned. "This is going to hurt like a mother," he grunted as he got Davis into a fireman's carry. With his free arm he grasped Mary-Catherine around the waist and teleported them all to the hospital.

A passing nurse dropped a tray. Orderlies shouted in alarm as they appeared. "We need an X-ray," Mary-Catherine shouted. Before she could say or do more Etienne had grabbed her again. They were in the pharmacy. He grabbed several bottles of Dilaudid, and teleported them back to the park.

A knot of kids huddled around a radio. "What's the news from the convention?" she asked.

"They started nominating. Dellinger's got a march line, but the pigs won't let us through. Tom is telling folks to break into small groups and make our way to the Loop. We're not gonna take this anymore."

Sundown. Etienne vanished, but Noel picked up the argument where the golden avatar had left off. She ignored him and joined the crowds filling the area around the Hilton. Camera lenses gazed down on the cops, the paddy wagons, and the protestors, cold emotionless glass eyes. There were chants and shouts. The cops were holding in position, but abruptly everything changed. They charged into the chanting protestors. In their helmets and gas masks they looked like alien invaders. Tear gas canisters were fired into the crowds, billy clubs rose and fell like batons in the hands of conductors of an orchestra of violence. Screams ripped the night. Sirens, shouts from the cops. Weeping, screaming kids rushed past Mary-Catherine and Noel. Overhead Turtle was using his megaphone. Yelling for calm. For everyone to STAND DOWN. No one was listening.

A boy was dragged across the pavement in front of them. His T-shirt was pulled off his body, and his bare back left streaks of blood on the pavement. He was hit several more times before being thrown into the police van.

Noel snatched up the T-shirt and tore it in half. He was coughing, tears running down his face. Mary-Catherine wasn't in any better shape. He ran to a fire hydrant and kicked loose the valve. Water gushed out and ran down the gutters. Noel wet the material in the rushing water and tied it over his face. He offered the other soggy half to Mary-Catherine. She followed suit.

A girl, huddled under the arm of her boyfriend, ran past. "We're their sons and daughters!" Sobs punctuated each word. The boy was bleeding from a cut over his eyes. Mary-Catherine tried to catch them, but they were liked panicked fawns and eluded her.

"The whole world is watching!" Screamed by a thousand voices.

But will they care? Sister Mary-Catherine thought.

"Fuck this," Noel muttered. He moaned and within moments Lilith stood at her side, looking a bit absurd in the suit. She abruptly vanished to reappear standing in the open doors of a police van. She kicked the two cops in the face who were attempting to boost a prisoner inside, grabbed the bleeding boy, and vanished with him.

Mary-Catherine waded in, yelling for anyone hurt to fall back. "I'm a doctor. I can help." As she tried to locate the wounded and pull them away from the riot she searched for Lilith and spotted her appearing and disappearing, taking down cops, removing protestors.

A water cannon truck arrived and was unleashed against the protestors. Kids were knocked to the ground by the force of the water.

Suddenly the streams of water were turned back on the police, sending them tumbling as Turtle unleashed his power. With a screech the water truck and the police vans were pushed down the street by Turtle's telekinesis. At this display of power the police began to gather up their wounded, cops battered and bloodied by Lilith's attacks, and retreat.

Turtle was finally able to get everyone's attention. "BACK TO THE PARK. FALL BACK TO THE PARK."

Limping, crying, cursing, and bleeding, the crowd retreated. The next few hours passed in a blur as Mary-Catherine tended to cuts, bruises, sprains, and concussions. A young girl had been knocked to the ground by a mounted officer, hit her head, hemorrhaged, and died. The death toll now stood at two.

Of Lilith or Noel there was no sign.

At half-past eleven news began to filter through the moaning, defeated mass of people. *"Humphrey's won the nomination."*

"On the first ballot."

"It was all for nothing."

Hours passed. Mary-Catherine labored on broken bodies. Sent the worst to the hospital, patched up those whose injuries weren't as severe. With each cut she bandaged, eyes she wiped clean of tear gas, each dislocated arm, she felt rage rising, choking her. She had seen brutality in the third world, but never expected to see it in her own country.

Near three A.M. the supplies in her bag were depleted and she had reached a state of utter exhaustion. Mary-Catherine made her way toward the edge of the park, past broken guitars and bongo drums, smashed signs. *Make Love Not War.* The rips in the sign and shattered wood handle made a mockery of the sentiment.

She couldn't face the convent. Inside those walls all would be calm, peaceful, quiet, and *useless.* They had closed themselves off to the evils of the world instead of confronting and fighting the evil. She made her way back to the hospital.

Dr. Young reacted when she walked into the emergency room. He grabbed her and pulled her into a curtained alcove.

"Sister, what the hell are you doing here?"

"I had done everything I could in the park." She held up her bag. "And I needed supplies—"

"You're wanted for questioning by the FBI and the Secret Service."

"What? Why?"

"The vice president's been killed. Shot in his bed. One of the agents caught a glimpse of the killer. It was a woman. The woman we treated. Before she . . . uh . . . changed. I've been with the Secret Service. I told them what I knew, that you apparently left with him. Do you know where she . . . he . . . went? Or where she . . . he . . . it is now?"

She stood silent for a moment. Humphrey dead. Could that mean the party would turn to McCarthy? Or would they blame the pro-testors? "Sometimes you have to just burn it all down," she murmured softly.

"What?" She turned away without answering. "You need to go to the authorities," Young called desperately.

She knew enough not to use the main doors or even the doors out of the emergency room. She did take a quick glance toward the emergency room pull-up and spotted the agents lurking. They had obviously been looking for a nun. She was never so glad she had ditched the veil.

She made her way to a basement exit and slipped out. She hoped Noel would be waiting at the hotel. Or would it still be Lilith? Dawn was still several hours away. She had guessed correctly. Lilith was standing in the center of the dingy room, shaking pain pills into her hand.

"Where did you get the gun?" Mary-Catherine asked without pre-amble.

Lilith's throat worked as she tried to swallow the pills. One got stuck. She started coughing. Mary-Catherine brought her a glass of water from the bathroom. Once the obstruction cleared Lilith said, "I'm so glad you don't waste time with obvious questions. I took it when I stumbled into that agent."

"You've made me an accessory."

"Yes, I rather regret that."

"Don't. They declared war on their own citizens," she said. "But you picked the wrong target to kill."

"Now you're a critic?"

"You should have talked to me before you went off half-cocked—"

"So to speak." The Dilaudid was taking effect and Lilith had a manic, almost loopy grin.

"They're not going to turn to McCarthy. They're going to blame his followers and by extension him. They'll probably turn to somebody like Scoop Jackson."

"Who?"

"Thus proving my point about knowing nothing. He's a senator from Washington and a big supporter of the war."

That seemed to penetrate the drug haze. "So who should I have shot?"

"I don't know. Daley? He's probably the one who ordered the police to attack those kids," she said bitterly.

"That can be arranged."

"No, let's not do anything until we see the fallout from this."

"So you're not opposed to me removing a few more impediments?"

"Since you've fired the first shot I don't see how we go back now."

"True. I suggest we decamp. Chicago is no doubt crawling with cops in search of us. It's still dark on the West Coast." Lilith held out a slim hand. "Last chance. You could still go to the authorities. Tell them I forced you. Return to your convent and your prayers."

"No. I'm done with useless gestures."

Despite Lilith's willowy form, the arms that closed around Mary-Catherine were as strong as Etienne's. *Same person different form,* Mary-Catherine reminded herself. Long black hair tangled around her shoulders, and there was that lurch, the sense of implacable hatred, and then they tumbled onto a stone courtyard as Lilith's leg collapsed beneath her. The dome of an observatory bulked against the night sky.

"Where are we?" Her teeth were chattering from the bitter cold of between.

"Los Angeles. Griffith Observatory." Lilith groaned as she climbed to her feet. "Figured that hadn't changed much."

It was a long walk down the hill from the observatory. The lights of the city had a sick yellow hue through the smog that hung over the Los Angeles basin. Mary-Catherine kept an arm around Lilith, acting as a crutch. They came upon some parked cars, and Lilith hot-wired one.

They turned down a street where bums huddled in doorways and shuffled down stained sidewalks. Neon signs glared from bars, promised TOTALLY NAKED GIRLS, adult bookstores, and cheap motels. Mary-Catherine glanced up at a street sign: Hollywood Blvd.

Lilith pulled into the parking lot of a horseshoe-shaped, two-story motel called the Palms. There were three sad examples in the center by an empty, trash-filled swimming pool.

"You take me to the nicest places," Mary-Catherine said.

Lilith's response was a groan. The nun looked over to see the shift occurring. Once it was over Noel started to get out of the car.

"Wait. Your stitches have torn. There's blood on your pants and shirt. I'll go." He didn't argue, just handed over the wallet and slumped back into the car. She went inside and paid for a room. The clerk wore only a wifebeater T-shirt and jeans. A small table fan fluttered his long, greasy hair, and the pages of the girlie magazine he was slowly perusing. He barely looked up as he took the money and shoved over a key.

"You could have gone in. I doubt he would have noticed if you'd been Jetboy himself," she said.

Once in the room he collapsed onto the bed with a groan. The room was a counterpart to the one in Chicago—run-down and dingy—but here neon lights from the strip club across the street glared and flashed through the threadbare curtains. Outside, the fronds on the bedraggled palm trees rattled in the wind. Noel noticed her staring at them.

The cynic twist of the lips was back. "The glamour of Hollywood."

She pulled off his shoes, unhooked the belt, unzipped the pants, and pulled them off. He hissed in pain and chewed at his lower lip. The stitches in his thigh had pulled loose and blood stained his skin. She went into the bathroom for a washcloth and began to wipe away the blood.

They shared the sagging bed. Periodically she would wake to find Noel up, staring out the window and smoking.

"Can't sleep?" she whispered.

He shook his head. "I keep thinking of them. They'll be wondering what happened to me. I should have been home by now."

She joined him at the window. "You said they were both wild cards."

"Yes. Niobe's a joker-ace. Jasper is an ace."

"A live birth, much less an ace birth, is very unusual. You were very lucky."

"No, we had the ultimate superpower. Money. We could afford an expensive fertility technique that could only work because of Niobe's unique power. All sorts of genetic jiggery-pokery and voilà. Jasper."

The very idea that such delicate work was possible made her greedy for that future. "I wish I could see it."

"You're not that old. You probably will." He correctly interpreted her expression. "Ah, yes. Having thrown in with me I suppose a long life isn't necessarily in the cards. I'll do everything in my power to keep you safe."

"At least you're smart enough not to make it a promise," she said tartly. "Now come back to bed."

In the morning she woke to find his butt pressed up against her crotch. There was a sudden warmth in her belly and she reached for him. Only to have him pull away.

"Not like this." He changed into his male avatar.

They made love and she liked it even more this second time. When the golden Etienne left the bed and limped to the bathroom she watched the muscles playing in his back and buttocks and enjoyed the view.

"Why won't you touch me when you're in your real form?" she asked. "Does that feel like you're betraying Niobe? Or are you just ashamed of the Noel body?"

"Good God, woman, we've got more important matters than my psychological issues."

"So a little of both," she said. "Okay."

"I've created a monster," he growled, and disappeared into the bathroom. The water in the shower turned on.

Wrapping a sheet around her, Mary-Catherine snapped on the small black-and-white television on its cheap metal stand. All three networks were carrying only the convention, and from every angle it was chaos. Fistfights were breaking out on the convention floor. Mary-Catherine sank down on the rough carpet and watched in shock as Daley's police roamed the auditorium arresting delegates. Occasionally a nightstick would rise and fall. The voice of the crowd was an animal roar. The news anchors were trying to give some context to the chaos.

Etienne padded out of the bathroom, a small towel imperfectly covering his equipment. Water still beaded the golden skin. Huntley/Brinkley had lost their low, slow delivery and were talking over each other. Cronkite sounded as devastated as he had on the day JFK had died. What became clear was that there had been an attempt to offer up Senator Henry "Scoop" Jackson for the nomination, which had led to an outright revolt by the McCarthy delegates. They had literally rushed the stage to be met by the angry Humphrey delegates blaming them for the vice president's death.

Mary-Catherine took a shower, and went out in search of medical supplies and food. When she returned with sandwiches and fries from McDonald's he was huddled on the bed staring at the television.

She re-dressed his wounds while they watched. Various nominations were offered, speeches were made in support of the various candidates. It was hard to hear them over the boos and cheers and chants. All around the walls of the auditorium Chicago cops stood at the ready. At around nine o'clock Chicago time Lyndon Johnson entered with that distinctive rolling walk. He was barely visible behind the lines of security.

The cameras switched outside, where all activity had ceased. The National Guard stood in lines blocking the route to the convention center. Protestors were in huddles around transistor radios listening to the reports from the convention floor. Turtle was broadcasting the reports over his PA system.

Inside LBJ mounted the steps onto the stage and walked to the podium. His face sagged with fatigue and sorrow. He gripped the edges of the lectern, looked down at the wood surface. When he raised his head grim determination had replaced the earlier emotions.

"First I'd like to ask for a moment of silence for Hubert Horatio Humphrey Jr. Senator, vice president, and my friend." The hall fell silent. The people in the streets outside didn't comply. The chants of "Hey, hey, LBJ, how many kids did you kill today" started up.

After a rather longer than normal silence LBJ resumed. "Our nation is faced with a grave danger. Our union is being torn apart by radicals and secret ace assassins."

"Like that won't start a witch hunt," Etienne grunted.

"Well, you are an ace assassin," Mary-Catherine retorted.

"This is the time for proven leadership and stern resolve. Therefore I am reversing my decision and placing my name into contention for the nomination."

The room erupted in cheers and whistles matched equally by catcalls and loud boos. Mary-Catherine looked over at Etienne. His expression shifted between disbelief and terrifying rage. He leaped to his feet.

"The bastard has just guaranteed Nixon's victory! Son-of-a-bitch." Etienne snatched the television off the stand and threw it against the wall. It shattered, glass flying in all directions. A sliver nicked Mary-Catherine's forehead. A warm trickle ran down her face. She reached up, studied her fingers. They were red with blood.

They fled the hotel. Mary-Catherine made Noel leave money on the bed to replace the broken television. She knew it was incongruous. She had thrown in with the man who had killed the vice president but she was worried about a TV? As they headed down the street Etienne kept glancing at the sun.

"Still fucking daylight here! If I could just change. I've seen the pictures. Teleport in behind him. Double tap. Boom! Problem solved."

In the west the sun sank into the Pacific. Etienne gave a gasp and the body shifted back to Noel. Light still glowed on the horizon. Noel shook out a few more pain pills and gulped them down. "Will they do it? Will they nominate him?"

"Probably. He's the sitting president. Does Johnson ever acknowledge that the war was wrong? Might he end it if he gets a second term?"

"I'm not sure. I believe he had doubts, but his ego wouldn't allow him to admit it," Noel said.

"And on the other side we've got Nixon saying he has a secret plan to end the war. Does he?" Mary-Catherine asked.

"Oh hell no, the war drags on for another four years."

"There's no way to unite the party. Not after all this. Nixon will win unless we can find something awful on him," she said.

"Oh, that will happen, but not until early in the 1970s. A little thing called Watergate."

"What's Watergate?"

He told her as they made their way through the city and down to the beach. A place called Malibu. He also told her of Nixon's disinterest in wild card issues that ultimately led to the Jokertown Riots.

"Maybe we can't change the future. Maybe it's already set," she said. Weariness seemed a crushing weight.

"Nonsense, we already did. Removing a piece off the board definitely changes the future. It just has to be a major piece." He gave her a mad grin. "Like Nixon."

Noel located a bungalow on stilts that stood dark and had a neglected look. He pulled into the carport beneath the house. A quick pick of the lock and they were inside. A few dying flies bumped against a window. Dust coated the surfaces of furniture. Noel opened the windows to allow the flies to escape and to cool the room. The scent of brine and seaweed flowed in along with the boom and hiss of the surf.

He moved panther-like through the house, the pistol in his hand. "No television, but a radio. Guess we best get the news."

He snapped on the radio to discover the die had been cast. Johnson had received the nomination and picked Senator Jackson as his running mate. The news was schizophrenic, jumping between reports of violent protests in major cities. Arrests at the convention. It sounded like a war had broken out in the streets of Chicago.

They looked at each other.

"You want to go back," Noel said.

"Yes. I can help."

"No, you can't. Oh, you can stroke a few fevered brows, and rinse out a few weeping eyes, and splint a few broken bones, but you can't heal this country." His voice was rising. "You can't heal the world. *You can't fix fucking people!*" He was shouting, face twisted with rage and grief and pain.

She grabbed his shoulders and shook him. He gasped in pain as she grabbed the burns and twisted the wounds. "Yeah, you're right. Humans are imperfect. That doesn't mean we don't try! Your family is lost to you. You need to just deal with that fucking reality. Do something *now* that makes you more than just a waste of air."

"Fine." He stepped away and shifted to Lilith. Mary-Catherine grabbed up her medical bag as Lilith grabbed her, and they were abruptly back in Lincoln Park.

"Go get your halo polished, you bloody twonk," Lilith hissed as the billowing tear gas turned the streetlights a sickening shade of yellow. "Be at the restaurant where we had dinner at noon. Etienne will come for you then. Don't be late or I'll bloody well leave you to the tender mercies of the FBI and the Secret Service."

"I'll be there. Thank you." Lilith made a rude noise and vanished.

Mary-Catherine ran toward the screaming.

◆

She couldn't believe what she was seeing. If the riots from Wednesday night were bad they were nothing compared to this. The National Guard formed the first rank with Daley's cops behind them. They looked inhuman in their helmets and gas masks. Ahead of the humans, however, there were *tanks*. Rolling toward the protestors, their treads tearing up the asphalt. The protestors holding bricks and sticks and rocks gaped at the metal monstrosities bearing down on them.

The plink of rocks hitting the armored exteriors was barely audible over the grind and roar of the diesel engines. Tear gas canisters were being constantly fired into the crowd, the billowing gas rising like evil genies to swirl around the young people. Mary-Catherine, choking despite the wet cloth wrapped across her face, wondered how long until some young soldier in the turret of a tank fired his machine gun into the ranks of protestors.

The kids held until the tanks were only feet away, then nerves frayed and snapped and the line of protestors broke and fled. It was a maddened stampede. People were knocked to the ground, trampled by their fellows. Some stopped to try and help them to their feet. Some never got up and the treads of the inexorably advancing tanks ground them up, too.

Mary-Catherine started grabbing people, trying to disrupt the panicked run, to get people off the street, into doorways, anything to avoid the deadly advance. Tom Hayden was doing the same. At one point their streaming eyes met. He gave her a nod and plunged back into the crowd. The problem was that every side street was also blocked by soldiers and cops. They were like the cattle in the nearby stockyards being driven to slaughter.

Turtle was trying to snatch people out of the way with his telekinesis while at the same time pushing back the advancing armor. Mary-Catherine glanced down a side street and saw a soldier settling a bazooka onto his shoulder.

She screamed a warning, but hidden inside his armored shell there was no way for Turtle to hear. The artillery launched and slammed into the hovering ace, exploding and leaving a massive hole in the armor.

The shell careened wildly. A cheer went up from the soldiers and police. People tumbled out of Turtle's telekinetic grip and fell screaming to the street. The shell crashed among the tanks but not before a young soldier sitting in a turret was decapitated by the plunging shell. Blood fountained and the headless body collapsed. Any semblance of order among the protestors vanished.

Mary-Catherine watched as soldiers advanced on the downed shell, the door was forced open, and a somewhat pudgy young man dressed in blue jeans and a *Make Love Not War* T-shirt was pulled out. His face was dark with soot, one arm hung limp, the bone protruding through the skin. He was thrown into the back of a police van.

Realizing that she might also be arrested, she faded back, hurrying to hide herself among the limping, weeping, terrified kids. They ended up penned in the parks with a cordon of cops and Guardsmen tightening the noose. There was no way she was going to be able to reach the restaurant and meet Noel's male avatar. He had been right. She was a twonk—if that meant idiot. To make herself feel less foolish she began to tend to what hurts she could.

There was that familiar *pop* from behind her and Lilith whispered in her ear, "Willing to admit I was right?"

"Well, not now. After you're so smug about it," she shot back, then added, "Get me out of here."

Lilith landed them on the beach in front of the bungalow. Mary-Catherine gazed out at the silver-tipped waves and the vastness of the Pacific stretched out before them. The white foam on the sand as the waves retreated was like lace. "At least this endures," she murmured.

"Oh just wait. You still have climate change to look forward to," Lilith drawled.

Mary-Catherine shivered. The image of the shell, the decapitation, the blood, would not leave her mind. Lilith put an arm around her and hugged her close.

"It was worse than anything I saw in Guatemala or the Congo. Where did my country go?"

"Come to bed. Things will seem clearer in the morning," Lilith said.

The back room of the bungalow contained the single bedroom. It soon became apparent why the house was on stilts. As the tide came in the bedroom was now over the water. With windows on three sides she lay listening to the soft shush of the waves beneath them.

Mary-Catherine buried her face in the pillow and tried to blot out the images. Slender hands were on her shoulders as Lilith sat on Mary-Catherine's hips and began to deliver a massage. At first she tensed wildly, but the strong grip was soon kneading her tight and twisted muscles and it felt so good that she moaned and relaxed despite her psychological discomfort. The massage moved down the length of her back, into her hips. Lilith's hand slipped between her legs and tangled in her bush, and flicked across her clitoris. She gasped, reared up, but felt a rush of warmth and wet into her groin.

"What are you doing? Don't!"

Mary-Catherine squirmed around until she was facing the dark-haired beauty. The waterfall of ebony hair fell over Lilith's shoulders, covering her breasts and the bandage. Her skin was marble white against the dark. Lilith held up her hands in an I-give-up gesture.

"Just trying to make you feel a bit better."

"This isn't the way. I mean, I'm not . . . I mean you're a girl—"

"Am I?"

"Doesn't this bother you?"

"It's just sex. Does the equipment really matter? And I'm rather intimately acquainted with both designs."

"This just feels really . . . wicked and wrong, but . . ."

"Dawn's almost here. Better decide quick. Lilith does have quite the wicked tongue."

"I'd say that goes for all three versions of you," Mary-Catherine snapped. Lilith laughed then groaned. "Besides, you should probably rest too and not indulge in any bedroom gymnastics right now."

Mary-Catherine grabbed the bottle of pills off the nightstand and tossed them to Lilith. She swallowed several. Shook the bottle. "Going to need to replenish these soon."

Dawn came and the shift occurred. Noel fell asleep. She went down to the beach. The retreating tide left a few scattered shells, and long strings of odiferous seaweed. Whatever happened next, she reflected that she probably wasn't going to be donning the veil again. That life had ended when a certain naked ace had crashed into her world. More likely that she would end up in prison or dead.

When she returned Noel was up and had pulled together a breakfast out of what he had found in the cabinets and the fridge. As he set the plate in front of her, he said, "I suppose you're going to make me leave money for these people too."

"Yes. We're supposed to be the heroes." She took a bite. "This is good. I thought you were English."

"Ha, ha. I'll have you know in 2017 we've become well known for our cuisine."

"So what do we do next?" she asked.

"I think we have to take out Nixon. It will create chaos among the Republicans."

"I just saw kids crushed in the streets by tanks. What will Nixon do that's so much worse?"

He stared at her. His eyes seemed clouded and she knew he had taken the last of the pain pills. "You know, you're right. We should take them both out—Nixon and LBJ. And Daley too. He's the one who sent the Guard into Chicago."

Images of bodies crushed beneath tank treads sent rage racing through her again. But then she remembered the young decapitated soldier. He thought he was being a hero. The kids chanting for peace thought they were heroes. Were there no heroes? She had no answer.

Etienne took them back to Chicago. Parts of the city smoldered, for Daley had ordered a huge police presence into Chicago's black neighborhoods. Naturally there were incidents that soon escalated into riots.

What they did learn was that someone—local Republican politi-cians, the party itself—had arranged for Nixon to get a ticker tape parade near where the Democrats' disastrous convention had just ended. As Noel said, it was quite the dickish poke in the eye to the opposing party.

It was easy to determine the route of the parade—the streets were closed off. Etienne made a brief foray into the pharmacy at the hospital to replenish his pain pills. They hid out in an abandoned warehouse waiting for the parade to begin.

Etienne downed three pills. Despite the sleep he'd gotten he was red-eyed and wan. When she touched his cheek he was hot. She started to unbutton his shirt.

"What are you doing?"

"I want to check that belly wound. And take off your pants."

He leered. "Not sure we have time."

She gave him an exasperated look. "Just do it. You're spiking a fever. My guess is one of these injuries is infected."

It was the thigh. The lips of the wound were raw and oozing and red marks were radiating out from the cuts. "Once this is finished I'll need to drain that."

"Fine. But right now I have to get to work." He gave her that mad grin again.

"What is your plan?"

"I'll teleport from rooftop to rooftop. If I'm lucky I'll get a long gun off one of the agents that I'm bound to meet."

"Don't kill them."

"They're going to be trying to kill me," he said.

"They're just men doing their job. Ordinary people. They don't de-serve to die."

"Nobody ever does, my sweet."

"Then take me with you," she said. "I'll guard them while you do . . . what you do."

"Kill. I'm going to kill this man. Say it!"

"Why? What does it matter?"

"Because how can I trust that you're truly committed if you won't?"

"Yes. All right. Fine! You're going to kill Nixon. Happy now?"

The smile he gave her was poisonous. He handed her the pistol. "You know how to use one of these?"

"Yes."

Etienne gathered her in the circle of his arms and they made the jump. The wind for which Chicago was famous covered the sound of their arrival. There were three men on the roof. Etienne took out two of them. Mary-Catherine thrust the gun into the back of the third and he froze before he could move against the ace.

The sun reflecting off the tar roof made the air shimmer. Sweat began to roll down her forehead and down her sides. Some of it was nerves as well as the blistering heat. From the street below she heard faint cheers from the modest crowd that had gathered. Etienne smashed her prisoner against the parapet, knocking him unconscious.

"That wasn't necessary!"

He ignored her. Instead he picked up a rifle that had been leaned against a stanchion. He settled it onto the edge of the parapet and peered through the sight. There was a brief flash of sun on glass.

"Shit! Spotted," he growled. "Get down!"

He teleported behind her and carried her down to the roof as bullets whined past. "Get behind the stanchion." She crawled to it. He was right behind her.

"We need to get out of here!"

"Not until I've done what I came to do."

"You can't shoot him now!"

There was again that feral grin and he pulled a scalpel from his pocket. The thought of it was horrifying to her. It was one thing to shoot the man, but this . . . The pistol was between them. Turn it ever so slightly, pull the trigger, and stop the madness. But she hesitated too long. Etienne leaped to his feet, ran to the parapet, glanced over, and vanished. An instant later bullets slammed into the roof where he had been.

She heard screams and then Etienne was back. The cuff of his shirt and halfway up the sleeve was red and wet with blood. He grabbed her and they teleported away just as agents came boiling onto the roof.

And then they were back in Malibu. She set the pistol on the kitchen counter. The blood from his shirt had stained her T-shirt. It was suddenly horrifying and she tore it off.

"This avatar was once known as the Sword of Allah." He walked the scalpel across his knuckles and through his fingers. "Not quite a sword, but quite adequate to the task."

I should have stopped him, she thought.

"I . . . I have to get alcohol. Some bandages. There was a little store. I'll be right back."

She donned a clean shirt, left the bungalow, and walked up to the market. There were people romping with dogs along the beach. A few mothers with small children who were digging in the wet sand. Cars whizzed past. Many of them convertibles with pretty girls in gaily colored scarves craning their faces into the sun while handsome men in sunglasses drove.

No one looked around as her entrance sent the bell over the door ringing. A clot of young people carrying skateboards, and the market clerks were huddled around a television that sat on the counter next to the register. Walter Cronkite was on the screen. He looked haggard, and at one point he pulled off his glasses to rub his eyes.

"As if this country has not endured enough," he said, his voice hoarse and somber. "If you have children in the room I urge you to remove them. The images we're about to show you are . . . disturbing."

After a moment he nodded and the picture changed to a view of the parade. Nixon standing up in the back of a convertible, beaming arms outstretched giving the V for victory sign. Suddenly Etienne appeared behind him, grabbed his hair, and quickly slit Nixon's throat. He vanished before the security walking next to the car even had time to react.

Vomit rose in the back of her throat. Mary-Catherine clapped a hand over her mouth and tottered backwards. She lost the battle with nausea and emptied the contents of her stomach into the gutter. A kindly girl, her hair in braids and adorned with flowers and ribbons, ran over and offered her a sip from her bottle of Coke. Mary-Catherine gratefully accepted.

"Everything's spoiled now," the girl said. "The revolution's gone toxic."

Mary-Catherine didn't trust herself to answer. She nodded her thanks, and went back inside the store so she could hear more clearly. Reports were coming from the White House that the president had declared martial law, and that he had requested a bill from Congress to authorize a roundup of wild cards in an effort to locate the assassin.

She stood frozen with indecision. Go to the police? She could lead them right to Noel, but he would just teleport away, or worse, kill them and then teleport away. Even if he was arrested how would they hold him? She had begun this cascade of horrors. She had to end it.

She started back toward the bungalow only to realize that if she returned without the supplies Noel would be suspicious. She returned to the store, and mechanically bought the alcohol, bandages, Epsom salts, and antiseptic.

The red-gold hair was wet from the shower and the blood washed away. Except it would never actually be gone. It stained the soul whatever form he might wear.

He noted her pallor. "You okay?"

"Yes." She forced a smile. "You're exhausted. You should get some sleep. Get off that leg. I'll keep watch. Later I'll work on . . ." She gestured at his bare leg exposed beneath the towel he had wrapped around his waist.

He glanced at the bed. "All right."

He limped to the bed, pulled back the covers, and collapsed. Within minutes he was snoring. She went out to the small kitchen, pulled her father's rosary out of her pocket, and studied the suffering figure that hung on the silver cross. She kissed it and hung it around her neck. She then picked up the pistol, walked back to the bedroom, and looked down at him. That body had brought her joy. The mind behind it had damned her.

"You're the devil," she whispered, placed the muzzle against his temple, and pulled the trigger.

It left a surprisingly neat hole. All the skull, blood, and brains were absorbed by the pillow. Death erased the wild card power that had created his avatars. Once that iron will was gone only the core man remained.

She walked to the phone and dialed the newly established emergency number.

"Nine one one. What is your emergency?"

"I've just killed the assassin who killed Vice President Humphrey and Mr. Nixon. Please come and arrest me."

She gave them the address, hung up the phone, returned to the bed, and sat down. In death Noel seemed younger, the lines smoothed away, the bitterness and rage erased. She gently closed his eyes.

A Long Night at
the Palmer House

Part 7

NIGHTHAWK'S FIRST THOUGHT WAS, *At least it's warm this time around*. He'd been getting tired of popping up naked in the snow. His second thought was, *Oh shit, now what?*

They were still on the grounds of Fortune Films. After sending John Fortune and Mr. Nobody back to the future, they'd gone into Fortune's washroom in his office to use the mirror there to punt themselves up to 1968, where he'd detected yet another schism in the time line.

The studio seemed as good a place as any to appear in '68. But they didn't expect it to be a devastated wreck, a virtual shell of itself, like a burned-out sector in a war zone.

A war zone, in fact, that was still inhabited by one of the competing forces that was camping out in the ruins and cooking over a fire built in a cut-down metal drum.

There were maybe thirty of them, most young, most all clearly touched by the wild card. Jokers all, in ways minor and major. Their clothing was tattered and tended to the military. Fatigues and black boots, torn, stained, and some bloodied. They were all dirty and many were bandaged in some place or another. Some of their wounds looked quite recent, some were scarring over. They were almost equally divided between men and women, and all were armed or had arms near at hand. They looked up from their campfire, as surprised to see the two naked men appear in their midst as Nighthawk and Croyd were to see them.

And then they all went for the weapons.

"Hold it!" a harsh voice called out, thankfully before any guns went off, and all obeyed the command.

A huge figure appeared from the shadows cast by a half-blown-down wall. He was about six feet tall, but twice as broad as a normal man. He wore tattered and much patched U.S. Army fatigues that had sergeant stripes on their sleeves. His skin was hairless, glabrous, and dead gray in color, his eyes round and protruding and covered by nictating membranes that were constantly blinking. He had no nose, but a small cluster of tentacles that were constantly twitching. His hands, cradling an old-style automatic rifle, had long, attenuated fingers that looked more like tentacles than normal digits. He smelled faintly of the sea as he came up to Nighthawk and Croyd and looked them over carefully.

Croyd stared at him. "Father Squid?" he finally said in an incredulous voice.

"I ain't your goddamn father," the joker replied in a hard voice.

"But," Croyd rejoined, "you're Father Squid, of the Church of Jesus Christ, Joker. You must be—"

"I ain't no goddamned priest, neither. What the fuck you saying, boy? I'm Squidface. Used to be a sergeant in the Joker Brigade, but I deserted to join the Joker Resistance when the Wild Card Powers Act was passed."

"Something's gone wrong," Nighthawk said, "badly wrong."

"I know you," a young woman said to Nighthawk. She wore a tattered and stained camo T-shirt tucked into holey fatigues, and scuffed work boots. The T-shirt exposed slimly muscular arms, the left one with a fairly clean bandage tied around the biceps. Her dark hair was cut short. Her only eye, set in the classic cyclopean position above her nose, was bright blue. The single eye was the only obvious sign of her jokerhood. "I know you," she repeated. "You're John Nighthawk. I thought you were in the Camp—or dead."

"Camp?" Nighthawk asked.

It was obviously the wrong question. Her hand fell to the butt of the automatic holstered around her slim hip. "What the fuck you talking about?" she said. "Everyone knows about Camp Nixon— the place where President Agnew sent all the aces they could round up—and the lucky jokers. The ones they didn't kill out of hand."

Nighthawk and Croyd looked at each other. "We didn't know," the Sleeper said. "We're not from around here."

"Where the fuck you from?" Squidface asked suspiciously.

Croyd smiled as best he could manage. "We're from the future. We've come to help."

"This is 1968, right?" Nighthawk asked. "What the hell happened?"

Squidface frowned, causing his facial tentacles to wiggle like a nest of disturbed baby snakes. "If you're time travelers," the joker drawled, "you've taken a wrong turn. It's 1975."

Nighthawk looked at Croyd, who shrugged helplessly. "What can I say? This part of the time line seemed pretty turbulent, and I guess I overshot our target by a bit."

"By a bit," Nighthawk muttered.

Squidface and the young woman looked at each other.

"What do you think, Angel Eye?" Squidface asked.

"Maybe they're telling the truth," she said. "Maybe they're spies for the Purity Police. They'd have to be dumb as shit to teleport naked right into the middle of us, though."

"I don't know. Maybe they're aces working for that Agnew bastard," Squidface said in a voice heavy with suspicion. "This is all above my pay grade. Better send a messenger to the Lady. See what she wants to do about them."

Angel Eye nodded. "I'll go myself."

"Hurry back," Squidface said. "I'll keep an eye on our new pals."

Nighthawk didn't like the heavy emphasis he put on the word "pals," nor the flat, hard expression the joker leveled in their direction. He felt particularly vulnerable and exposed standing naked before Squidface and the other members of the Joker Resistance, who were all watching them like deadly carnivores just praying for an excuse to attack.

"You, uh, have any spare pants?" he asked the joker.

It didn't help Nighthawk's mood any when they told him that the clothes he and Croyd were donning had belonged to two members of the Resistance who'd been killed earlier in the day in a skirmish with the Purity Police. Dressing in dead men's clothes was never a good option, but it was marginally better than running around naked. At least the shoes fit.

Angel Eye returned soon after Nighthawk and Croyd had gotten dressed. She nodded to Squidface. "She said to bring them in."

Squidface left the rest of the Resistance fighters to their meager dinner of potatoes on sticks roasted over the steel drums and led them deeper into the complex of buildings that had once been Fortune Films. As they entered what appeared to be the most blown-out area of the old studio, Squidface issued a gruff warning. "Stick close and step exactly where I step. This section is booby-trapped with IEDs."

Nighthawk and Croyd exchanged wordless glances, and stuck very closely to the joker's heels as he took a circuitous route through piles of garbage that had once been buildings. They finally reached what looked to be an old Quonset that squatted discreetly amid the destruction and was also protected by a covering of camouflage netting.

Two large, well-armed, mean-looking jokers appeared seemingly out of nowhere, then melted back into hiding when they recognized Squidface, who breezily waved them off. He knocked at the door of the hut, then entered immediately. The interior was lit by a string of naked bulbs hanging from a cord in the ceiling. It was furnished as living quarters as well as a working office with an old battered desk covered with papers and piles of files with an uncomfortable-looking high-backed wooden chair occupied by a striking joker who gazed narrowly at them as they entered her domain.

"What have you brought me?" she asked in a drawl.

"Damned if I know, Lady," Squidface admitted.

Nighthawk glanced at Croyd, who was openly staring. And who wouldn't? The Lady's skin and flesh were completely transparent, revealing ghostly layers of muscle and the network of veins and arteries pulsing through and among her bones. Her internal organs were hidden by the camo T-shirt she wore. She had no hair and her eyes were a clear, startling blue.

"Chrysalis," Croyd blurted.

Squidface frowned. "This is the Crystal Lady," he said. "She's the leader of the Joker Resistance in the Midwest."

Of course. Nighthawk had never met Chrysalis in the flesh, but he'd read and seen pictures of the joker who'd been a major figure on the New York scene until her murder back in 1988.

"She was called Chrysalis in Manhattan, back in our time line," Croyd said.

"Was I?" she drawled.

"Yeah," Croyd explained. "You ran the best bar in Jokertown. What happened to your British accent?"

Something passed across the Crystal Lady's face. It might have been a sense of loss, a fleeting stab of regret. "I had a dream, once," she said, her muscles gliding smoothly as she shrugged. "I wanted to escape my life and go to New York City and be someone else. But reality intervened, and I ended up here."

"We can change this reality," Nighthawk said. "And give you that dream back." He hesitated, then decided not to say that it would end in her premature death. Like everyone else, she deserved not to know her ultimate fate.

"Can you?" Her voice was flat and unbelieving.

"Yes," Nighthawk said. "I'm John Nighthawk, and this is Croyd Crenson."

She looked at them with what might have been more respect on her face. "Nighthawk and the Sleeper? You two might be the last two aces loose in the Midwest."

"What happened to everyone else?" Croyd asked. "The Turtle?"

The Crystal Lady looked down, almost pensively. "He was shot down trying to defend the students during the riots back in '68 when it was all turning to crap. A couple of National Guardsmen were killed when his shell crashed on them. He was arrested for murder, tried, and eventually executed."

"What?" Croyd blazed with anger. "He was my friend! My god-damned friend!"

The Crystal Lady continued to look sad. "Golden Boy fled the country. He's supposed to be somewhere in South America. Dr. Tachyon was forced to close his clinic and return to Europe."

"There's that new dude out in California," Squidface chimed in. "He's a real badass."

"Yes," the Crystal Lady said. "Calls himself the Radical. He's leading a resistance force out in the Sierras somewhere . . . if we could only reach him, somehow. . . ."

"How did all this begin?" Nighthawk asked in a low voice.

"No one knows for sure," the Crystal Lady said, "but we can pretty well pinpoint the time from information that came out during the show trial they had of the nun."

"Nun?" Croyd said.

"Supposedly she was the lover of these two assassin aces, a man and a woman. The woman killed Hubert Humphrey, who was going to be the Democratic nominee, probably. Shot him dead during the convention here in Chicago in '68. The man killed Richard Nixon, right on television during a ticker tape parade—teleported right behind him and cut his throat with a knife. Near took his head off." The Crystal Lady shook her head. "Later, something happened, some kind of love triangle thing, and the nun shot the guy in the head. The female assassin, this woman with silver eyes, was never found, despite a massive manhunt. Spiro Agnew, Nixon's vice-presidential candidate, was elected president. He rammed through the Wild Card Containment Laws. Which led to all this."

Nighthawk and Croyd looked at each other. "*Lilith,*" they said together.

"You know her?" Crystal Lady asked.

"We do," Croyd said.

"She's one of the people we're tracking through time," Nighthawk explained. "We're collecting people from our time who've been lost in the past. All we have to do is stop them before they cause the time line to change, and send them home."

"When did Lilith make the scene?" Croyd asked.

"That's the strange part," the Crystal Lady said. "Supposedly she just appeared one night in Lincoln Park, bloody and wounded. The nun found her and took her to the hospital. She was also . . ." The Crystal Lady paused for a moment. "Naked. Like you two."

"No doubt about it," Nighthawk said. "She's one of the ones we're after."

"So you *can* change all this?" the Crystal Lady asked.

"All we need is the date Lilith showed up at the park," Croyd said, "and a reflective surface of some kind." There was a hard look in the Sleeper's eyes that Nighthawk didn't like. He hadn't been speeding long enough to turn psychotic yet, but the news they'd heard about the Turtle and the fate of other aces and jokers certainly wasn't helping his mood. "Got a mirror?"

"There's one in the bathroom in the rear of the hut," the Crystal Lady said, but before Nighthawk and Croyd could take more than a step toward it there was a sudden whooshing sound and as a small shoulder-launched rocket blew through the wall of the hut and destroyed the rear half of it in an explosive blast that hurled them all to the floor.

"We're under attack!" Squidface shouted the obvious. He was the first to regain his feet and he lumbered to the front door, which, remarkably, was still latched shut. The moment he burst outside he started firing.

Croyd pulled himself to his knees. "You okay?" he asked Nighthawk, who could hardly hear him through the ringing pulsating in his ears.

"Yeah," Nighthawk said, pulling himself upright and shaking his head to stop the buzzing sound throbbing through it. "Go—I'll catch up."

"Right." Croyd stood, looked around, and chose to exit through the hole punched in the metallic side of the Quonset hut by the rocket that'd taken out the building's rear.

Nighthawk went to follow him, then stopped, shaking his head again to try to clear it. The Crystal Lady was draped over her desk, unmoving. He went to her side, and pulled her up. His right hand came away sticky, coated with blood. He looked at her side and saw a large chunk of jagged metal protruding from it. She groaned. Her eyes fluttered open, blue as the afternoon sky, and looked into his.

Nighthawk pulled her to him. There was little else he could do but hold her.

"Sorry," he said. "There's nothing I can do."

She nodded. Her lips moved. He bent lower to hear her. "Get away," she managed to whisper. "Fix it. Stop . . . it . . ."

Nighthawk nodded. "We will. There is one thing. If you want. I can take away your pain."

She couldn't move, but her eyes told him what she wanted. Nighthawk unwrapped the rag he'd twisted around his left hand, and reached out, caressing her cheek in merciful benediction. She sighed, and her eyes closed.

After a moment he looked up and saw that he was surrounded by men with guns, all pointed right at him. "Get up," one of them said in a hard voice. "You're under arrest on the charge of having impure genes."

◆

The Chicago House of Corrections, Nighthawk knew, had been built in 1871. It looked every moment of its hundred-plus years of age. It loomed like a rambling, gray Gothic monster in the middle of a ninety-six-acre plot at Twenty-sixth Street and California, right next to the Cook County Jail, which had been built in the relatively modern date of 1929, but was clearly out of the neo-penal school of architecture rather than any that aspired to a sense of grace or dignity.

Nighthawk soon learned that Camp Nixon, as the Joker Resistance referred to it, was the colloquial name for the facility in which those deemed to have impure genes were confined. Further information gleaned from conversation with his fellow prisoners filled in the horrific history of this alternate reality. President Spiro Agnew had transferred J. Edgar Hoover from his position as head of the FBI to become the first superintendent of Camp Nixon when it initially opened, with agents from the bureau acting as the shock troops that eventually evolved into the Purity Police. They removed all the felons—the murders, the rapists, the embezzlers, the drug dealers, the assault artists—from the two jails, either placing them in other state prisons or simply freeing them when they'd run out of room, and replaced them with obvious and not so obvious jokers, deuces, and a few aces with minimal powers.

Hoover ran the place like a concentration camp until he dropped dead of a heart attack early in 1972, some saying while he was personally interrogating some poor joker. Others say he wasn't interrogating the joker, but was indulging in some other heated physical activity that proved too much for his overworked heart. In any case, George G. Battle, a special assistant to President Agnew, was then appointed superintendent of the camp and, Nighthawk was told, conditions immediately became even worse.

They were still terrible. When Nighthawk was captured he was booked and fingerprinted. He gave his name as "James Brown," which aroused no trace of suspicion or even interest from the obviously bored guard taking the information. He then had blood drawn, which would be tested for the wild card virus. The test would be his trial, the analysis of his blood his jury, the Wild Card Containment Laws his judge, with a positive result a life sentence of confinement in either Camp Nixon or one of the other detention centers being constructed around the United States.

Then, in the company of a score of other new internees—men, women, and children included—he was ordered to strip naked, his clothes and possessions were taken away, and he was subjected to delousing delivered by a high-pressure water hose. Grim-faced, he dried himself off with the two oversized but inadequate paper towels he was issued, and dressed in a scratchy, much too large jumpsuit. A pair of too small shoes completed his uniform.

Nighthawk was then assigned a place in an eight-by-ten-foot cell meant to house four inmates. There were already eight living in it, males ranging in age from eight to eighty. Since his blood hadn't been analyzed yet, it was considered a holding cell.

"How long have you been waiting?" Nighthawk asked the oldest-looking inmate, an emaciated old man who was stick thin and, although Caucasian, had an unhealthy gray pallor that indicated ill health.

"About six months," the old man said. "Funny thing is, I ain't a joker. I'd know if I was. I'm just skinny." He shook his head. "My brother was a joker, though. They took me along when they grabbed him up."

"How's your brother?" Nighthawk asked quietly.

"Dead," the old man said flatly.

The hours in the cell passed like centuries. As one of the newcomers, Nighthawk didn't have mattress privileges, just an old blanket of dubious cleanliness left behind by a previous inmate who'd unfortunately just been found guilty and been removed to the "hard house," where, the inmates told him, you really had a tough time. Nighthawk couldn't imagine it.

For one of the few times in his long life, Nighthawk fell into true despair. He'd failed, he thought. There was no way out of this and with the mission resting alone on Croyd, there was little chance for success. The weight of his failure was crushing, but the worst thing was not his personal suffering, but the pain he saw all around him, on the hopeless faces of the men he was jailed with, on the utter despair in the face of the young boy who sat alone pressed into the corner, his arms wrapped around his knees.

The cell block marched out for dinner at five o'clock, back in at six. The food was about as bad as you'd expect, though Nighthawk saved some of it for the old man, who was too ill to rise from his iron slab of a bed to attend the meal. The oldster managed to choke down some of the square of desiccated cake. He thanked Nighthawk wanly. Nighthawk sat with his back against the wall without the doubtlessly vermin-ridden blanket. He closed his eyes. His brain raced fruitlessly, circling back always to an overpowering sense of hopelessness. He felt like a wolf caught in a steel net from which there was no escape.

Sometime after they turned off the lights he fell asleep, and after a while he dreamed. Either that or he was having a vision. A vision of a tall, thin black man. He was perhaps of mixed race because his skin was a dark golden color and his eyes were almond shaped. He flew through the night sky unsupported by artificial means and his face had an expression of vengeful wrath. He was following a trail of light and was approaching quickly through the dark sky.

Nighthawk's eyes flew open and he knew that he was awake. *Of course,* he thought, and for the first time since his arrival in this gray fortress of concrete and iron he felt hope.

With his mind's eye he watched the man approach the House of Corrections, flying over the wire-topped fence that surrounded it. He hovered before a window, gestured, and blobs of pure energy the size of softballs crashed into the casement, shattering glass and iron bars alike. The window exploded inward and he entered the structure, landing in a darkened hallway.

John Nighthawk! he heard the man call out in his mind and knew, then, that he was coming for him.

Here! he shouted silently.

I can track your aura, the voice replied calmly in his head. *I'll be with you in a moment.*

Nighthawk got up and went to the locked cell door. He grabbed the bars and looked down the dark corridor. He could hear shouts and shots ringing in the distance, but could see nothing. He felt strange, as if enveloped in amber. Everything stopped, even his brain, and when he blinked a man was standing before the bars to his cell. It was the one he'd seen in his vision, heard in his head. "Step back," he ordered. His voice was rich and deep.

Power blasted from his fingertips and the cell's lock just shattered.

"John Nighthawk, I presume," he said. "Come on, we have to go." He whirled as armed guards entered the corridor, running toward them, guns firing. He gestured. You could feel more than see it, but a protective barrier sprang up and the bullets ricocheted away, screaming through the corridor. He pushed outward and the barrier itself shot down the corridor, slamming into the armed guards, knocking them about like tenpins.

Nighthawk joined him in the corridor and glanced back over his shoulder to the men staring at them from the cell, a mixture of hope and awe on their faces.

"We have to leave them," his rescuer said. "It's the only way they'll be safe. But—I'll be back," he added in a voice full of promise, "and next time I won't come alone."

He looked up at the ceiling and blobs of solidified energy shot from his hands, punching a hole right through it, exposing the night sky. "Come on!"

He threw an arm around Nighthawk's shoulder. Nighthawk responded, and together they rose into the air, exited through the hole he'd blasted through the ceiling, and flew off quick and low, zagging like bats pursuing unseen moths.

"Thanks, Fortunato," Nighthawk said, the air whipping across his face and snatching his words away as he said them.

Fortunato glanced at him momentarily, but renewed his concentration on threading their flight through tall buildings, sticking to the shadows as much as possible. "You know me?"

"We've met under different circumstances," Nighthawk said. He didn't mention that it was at Fortunato's death. "In another time line."

"Uh-huh," Fortunato said. "Squidface called me. I wouldn't believe it from someone else, but he's a solid dude. Knew him well when he first got back from 'Nam. I trust what he has to say, and he said you and the Sleeper can fix this shit. So I got in touch with this guy I know goes by the name of the Mechanic. He flew us here in a small plane below the radar, barely above the treetops." Fortunato shook his head. "Best job of flying by the seat of the pants I ever saw. Almost like he was part of the plane. Anyway—he wanted to come along on this visit to Camp Nixon, but I figured speed and stealth was our best chance so he's waiting on me at this little field he landed us in out of town. We'll wait for nightfall again, then take off back for New York."

"Thanks," Nighthawk said, "and luck. We'll get this done."

"I know you're straight," Fortunato replied, "because my Crenson is asleep right now back at New York, crashed out at my pad. And your Crenson—I know he's the Sleeper, too, because I looked into his mind. Two Sleepers. Alternate time lines. Motherfucker."

"This one's got to be stopped," said Nighthawk. "Snuffed out before it happens."

"And the other one—the one you're from—is better?" Fortunato asked.

"It's not perfect," Nighthawk said, "but it'd be hard to be worse."

Fortunato nodded. They flew on in silence for a bit. Then he said, "Things are tough here, and with the Crystal Lady dead . . . it'll only get tougher. . . ."

"We'll fix it, I promise."

"I'm holding you to it, brother," he said. He angled to the ground and they landed lightly, in familiar territory.

"Jesus Christ, John," Croyd said, coming out of the darkness cast by the standing wall of a shattered building. "He did it! He got you out!"

"Of course," Fortunato said. "But it damn near burned me out. I better go rejuvenate my powers before I head back to the city. Got my own war to fight there."

"Take care, and thanks again," Nighthawk said. "I owe you more than I can say."

Fortunato smiled, and vanished into the darkness.

Nighthawk turned to Croyd. "Let's go get that bitch Lilith," he said.

The Fortune Films lot looked different in 1968 from the version they'd left behind in 1975.

It had a tranquil air, a restful sense of a place where much had been done and now all was slumbering, but ready to awaken if anyone would care to put it to use. The buildings were shuttered and quiet, but they weren't burned out and shot up. The streets and alleys within the warren of buildings, from the great soundstages to the offices and warehouses, were devoid of trash and, thankfully, bullet holes.

Nighthawk took a deep breath and there was a scent of a warm summer morning freshness in the air, almost as if he could sense a promise of future possibilities. It would be terrible, he thought, to lose all this to the wanton destruction of the possible future that lurked just a few years ahead.

"John—" Croyd was kneeling before a large cardboard box that was sitting against the aluminum wall of the storage shed they'd use to reflect his time-traveling energy upon themselves. "John, look at this."

Nighthawk stood above the box, peering down.

"I'm freaking out here, John," Croyd said. "Someone's still trailing us."

It was, Nighthawk admitted, kind of spooky.

"Do you think it's another time traveler?" Croyd asked, his voice rising a little. "Who could it be? What do they want?"

"I have no idea," Nighthawk said, "but apparently they want to help us."

"So far," Croyd said darkly, and emptied out the contents of the box.

It contained, like the anonymous care packages they'd received earlier, two complete outfits, pants, shirts, shoes, and all accoutrements, that perfectly fit the two of them. Both pairs of pants had folding cash stashed in a front pocket. Among his clothes, Croyd found a Baggie of pills along with an unopened pint bottle of tequila to help wash them down.

"Come to poppa!" he exclaimed, shaking a handful of pills onto his palm and reaching for the bottle. He broke the seal, tossed the pills down his throat, and took a healthy swig.

Nighthawk thought that watching someone who looked like Donald Meek popping amphetamines and guzzling tequila was more than a little disturbing. "Careful with that," he warned.

"Hey, man, you're talking to a pro from Dover." Croyd offered the bottle to Nighthawk, who shook his head.

"Not on an empty stomach."

"Hell, man," Croyd said, his earlier anxiety entirely forgotten, "then let's get dressed and go grab some breakfast." He took another swipe from the bottle. "Is there anywhere to get decent huevos rancheros in this town?"

Lincoln Park was a madhouse.

Bands of roving students were everywhere, along with roving bands of armed cops all too ready to confront them. Skirmishes were breaking out every now and again, but nothing serious had gone down. Yet.

Nighthawk inhaled a deep lungful of the Lincoln Park air. Pot, patchouli, and the scent of unwashed bodies. Yes. He was back in the sixties.

As if to confirm this, as he and Croyd strolled through the park they turned a corner and suddenly came upon the Turtle—or rather, his shell. It hovered a foot or two above the ground, and hippie chicks were crawling all over it, painting peace symbols on it and decking it with flowers. "Ah, man," Croyd said.

Nighthawk knew what he meant. Although he had mixed feelings about the sixties—and really, you could say that about any decade—it had been a heady time. There was something in the air, and it wasn't just pot smoke and patchouli. Mainly it was a feeling of possibilities, of things that could be. Perhaps some of those dreams eventually were shattered or simply never came to fruition, but at least people generally gave a damn. Some of them, anyway.

And the Turtle epitomized those days. Nighthawk had never sought out the spotlight. He was more comfortable in the shadows. But the Turtle was a symbol of the shining hope of the sixties. It made him sick to his stomach to think that if they failed in their mission he'd be executed by the government within the next three years.

Nighthawk suddenly remembered something that the Crystal Lady had told them about the events that'd happened in Lincoln Park that night. "The Turtle's the key." He jabbed Croyd in the side with his elbow, to pry his attention away from the hippie chicks swarming the Turtle's shell, some of whom had decided to go shirtless in the warmth of the summer day. "Remember, Chrysalis—the Crystal Lady—told us that the Turtle had airlifted that wounded ace to the hospital. So, we stick with the Turtle . . ."

". . . and we find Lilith," Croyd finished. "That's fine with me."

The day eventually turned tedious as even the thrill of the occasional topless hippie chick soon faded. But the tedium was punctuated by the occasional thrust and counterthrust of demonstrator-police confrontations. As the day slowly turned to evening, the confrontations became more frequent and more violent.

When the sun set and darkness arrived, the police tried to clear the park to enforce a nighttime curfew, but they were thwarted by the actions of the Turtle, much to the cheers and amusement of the gathered demonstrators. In a way, it became almost easier to keep track of the Turtle despite his quick and sometimes erratic movements above the park, because his spotlights shone like beacons as he tirelessly patrolled the skies.

The time finally came when they heard boom across the darkness the words, "WHAT DO YOU NEED, SISTER?"

"That's our cue," Nighthawk said, and they went through the crowd, drawn to the Turtle's spotlight like moths.

The conversation continued as they shoved their way through a knot of demonstrators to see the fallen figure of Lilith sprawled unconscious on the ground. She was naked, of course, her awful wounds desecrating her magnificent body. It was almost as if she wore a sheet of blood.

Her left breast had been nearly severed and she had deep, long claw marks over her right thigh and abdomen. She also had scorch marks on her shoulders from Cyn's flames. Someone had bound her wounds as best they could using what were now blood-soaked T-shirts, but Nighhawk could still see the awful extent of them.

An attractive woman, maybe thirty, made her way through the onlookers, followed by the Turtle hovering seven or eight feet above the scene. She had to be the nun from the Crystal Lady's story, though she wasn't dressed like one.

"THIS MIGHT BE A LITTLE SCARY," the Turtle's booming voice warned, and Nighthawk nudged Croyd as the Turtle's mind reached out and started to lift both the nun and Lilith.

Croyd made a casual yet careful gesture, unnoticed by the onlookers, who were focused on the two women now floating a foot or two above the ground, and Lilith, much to everyone's amazement, vanished.

The Turtle was so startled that he dropped the nun, but she fell only a foot or so before landing on the soft sward.

"WHAT THE HELL HAPPENED TO HER?" the Turtle boomed.

"I—I don't know," the nun said shakily. "I guess she just vanished—like she'd appeared."

Nighthawk and Croyd made their way through the amazed and astonished crowd.

"That'll give them something to tell their grandkids," Croyd said smugly.

A Beautiful Façade

by Mary Anne Mohanraj

NATYA NEVER SLEPT NAKED anymore. Not since the day when she'd packed her things and left her home. She could have stayed and fought for her life, with Minal and Michael, who loved her and wanted to marry her. With their toddler daughter, Isai. But she had made choices, made decisions that seemed right at the time, but which put cops in danger. Michael was too much a cop himself to forgive her for that. If he had, it would have broken him, so Natya had packed and left, to keep him from having to throw her out. To be honest, she hadn't forgiven herself yet either. She'd fucked up, badly.

Minal wanted her to stay, begged her to stay, tears streaming down her face. Swore the three of them could work it out, somehow. But sometimes good intentions, goodwill, weren't enough. Sometimes you broke things beyond repair, and in return, the world broke you. Natya had been living alone since then, wearing the black slacks and white button-down shirts that had practically become her SCARE uniform since joining the agency, and sleeping in pajamas. Naked would have been too much a reminder of everything she'd lost.

So why the fuck was she naked now?

The last she remembered, she'd been watching a poker game. Well, not actually watching the *game*—in theory, Natya was supposed to be bodyguarding Fortune, but she was there to investigate John Nighthawk. Frightening little man, frightening abilities, though he hadn't done nearly as much damage with them as he could have. If the world knew that an immortal walked among them, with a hand of death that could drain the life from anyone he touched, it would've caused utter panic.

But Nighthawk wasn't doing anything that night, just attending on Dutton, quiet and unassuming. She'd had trouble believing the small, dark-skinned man could possibly be as dangerous as her bosses believed. No, it was the waiter who started the trouble. The waiter, the girl spilling the drink, Galante slapping the girl.

Natya had started tapping her foot, building power for a shield, in case she needed to throw it up in defense. But everything happened very fast—the waiter changed shape, grew huge, one of the women started throwing flames, and the stench of scorched flesh filled the air. Natya spun into a pirouette, but she must have been too slow, must have been hit by something that knocked her out, because the screams and chaos disappeared, the room full of people—she'd woken up here, head aching in the sudden silence.

Natya was on the floor, and her elbow hurt, too, as if she'd landed on it, falling. She was naked on the floor of what looked like the hotel room she'd been in a minute before, but no one else was there, and her clothes were gone. Natya couldn't keep from thinking of assault, rape—but it had been months since she'd had sex of any kind, and her body would surely be telling her now if something had happened. She felt fine, normal. A little dizzy still, but even that was improving.

First priority, covering herself. Natya staggered to her feet, the room spinning around her. Steadied herself on the bed and reached for the covers—but then heard a clicking metal sound from the door to the room. A key? Hadn't they used keycards? The door was opening, though, and she had no time for getting to the sheets; instead she spun into her standard pirouette, slightly off-balance, her body not quite responding right. But it lent her wild card enough energy to generate a small forcefield, a little ball of force—the man shouted in surprise, "Hey!" And then Natya threw it at him, hitting him hard, so that he went staggering back, hitting his head on the doorframe. He fell to the floor.

Dammit. She hadn't meant to do that. Natya quickly went over to check—breathing, thankfully. Just knocked out, though with a small trickle of blood on his head. *Sorry, sorry!* She dragged him inside, just far enough so she could close the door, retrieving the heavy metal key from his hand. And then she stood there, key in hand, not sure what to do next. Clothes. She needed clothes. Dressing herself in illusory forcefields was possible, but wouldn't be sustainable for long. Plus, she'd look ridiculous, dancing down the hall, even if she seemed dressed. And she'd *feel* naked.

An open suitcase sat at the far end of the room, and it was a moment's work to rifle through it and pull out dark slacks and a button-down white shirt. The stranger was thankfully close to her height, enough that she could cuff up the pants legs, but he was at least twice as big around as she was. Socks were fine; shoes were impossible. Natya knew she looked like a child playing dress-up. But it felt like her heartbeat finally slowed down to normal once her breasts and butt weren't hanging out anymore, for any stranger to see. She might have a dancer's build, and not much in the way of either breasts or butt, but still, it'd been unnerving to have them completely exposed.

Natya needed to know where she was. Same room? Same view, anyway, the lake beyond, unchanging. But it was daytime now, the sun beating down on the restless waters of Lake Michigan. It had been night before. Had she slept the night away?

The lamps. No outlets for plugging in your devices, and more—the lamps were gas, not electric. She'd been a little girl the last time she saw a real gas lamp; her parents had taken her on a tour of historic Mystic, Connecticut, a seaside town. They'd walked a clipper ship, climbed down into the hold, talked to actors in costume and character from an era long gone. They'd used gas lamps in the old days, now sold them in the gift shop. Her mother had bought one, and lit it on occasion, throwing out a smoky scent that made Natya think of long skirts, billowing sails, and sea air.

What other clues—oh, there! A newspaper on the desk. Gods, yes. First recorded college basketball game, between the Geneva College Covenanters and the New Brighton YMCA. A Belgian general strike, and a massive riot; Belgian parliament approves universal suffrage. Salt Lake Temple finally completed and dedicated, after forty years

of construction. World's Columbian Exposition, opening to the public tomorrow! April 30, 1893. What the hell?

The man on the floor groaned. Natya couldn't be here when he
woke up. She needed money. Knelt down, swiftly removed his wallet,
took all the cash inside, and stuffed it in her pocket. His eyes blinked
open, still dazed, and on impulse Natya bent down, giving him a
swift kiss. *Sorry!* Let him believe for a little while that this was all a
dream—some dreams had bad bits along with the good. She left the
man his key, slipped out the door, closing it behind her.

She needed better clothes, women's clothes. Where might she find
them? The laundry. In the basement? Best bet. Next step, an elevator.
No. If this was really 1893—how was that possible?—the elevator
would be a problem. Her skin was dark enough that people might take
her for black. Were black people even allowed in fancy hotel elevators in this era, if they weren't the ones operating them? Maybe,
maybe if you were rich enough. But not dressed the way she was—too
big a risk that someone would make a fuss, call the cops. Natya didn't
know what they'd make of her, but it wasn't likely to be good. She
had to stay low, under the radar. Stairs. There.

The laundry was easy enough to find, but busy, women coming in
and out. Natya crouched in a dark corner of the hall, waiting for her
chance. Finally, there was only one woman in the room—the best
chance she was likely to get. Natya rose to her feet, pushed herself
into a spin—one, two, three, building energy. Then, pas de bourrée,
jeté, a leap down the hallway, and this was good; Natya felt better,
more herself and more confident as she danced. The energy building
inside her, pouring out in a concealing shimmer of air.

If the woman looked the wrong way, she might blink, wondering
what she was seeing, if she was seeing anything at all. But the gas
lamps were set high, the air smoky and concealing. She would doubt
herself. Long enough for Natya to reach the bin she wanted, the one
full of maids' uniforms, grab a few, and dance away again. Until
finally, in that same dark corner of the hall, she could sort through
them, choose the one that came closest to fitting her, and change.
Black dress, white collar and cuffs, white pinafore. Loose in bodice
and waist, but close enough. Black socks. Shoes were still a problem.

She'd have to buy them. But maybe people wouldn't notice right away. As a maid, she was almost invisible.

Survival was taken care of, for the moment. The man had had forty dollars in his wallet—enough, surely, in 1893, to buy shoes and rent a room and eat for a few days? But what happened after a few days? Croyd must have somehow sent her back in time—but why? Would he come for her? Would anyone? Natya had no way home, and no idea if anyone would come for her. If she'd actually had any-one back home waiting for her, it would have been heartbreaking. As it was . . . well. Maybe this was her punishment, the gods sending her so far away, she could never hurt anyone she loved, ever again. It would be just.

"I hear the Wooded Isle is bee-yoo-ti-ful. Charles says he's gonna get us a gondola, and we're going to take it all around the White City." The woman working the mangle had muscled arms, damp clothes (as they all did), and a pair of long black braids that were frizzing up dramatically.

The second brunette, this one with hair pulled back in a tight bun, said, "Charles promises you a lot of things, girl, but does he ever actually deliver?"

Braid-woman snapped back, "Oh, like your Joe is any better. Still living with his mother, isn't he?"

A third girl, a bouncy blonde, cut in, "Oh, don't fight, girls. We should all go together. I've got enough saved up for tickets. I want to see those girls in Egypt Street." She reminded Natya of Minal—the curvy shape of her, those generous hips and ass. And the way she smiled, bright enough to light the room.

"You go see those girls, your eyes are going to melt out of your head! What would your momma say, Betsy?"

Betsy laughed. "My momma ain't here, is she? I left her behind on the farm! And besides, I want to be a dancer someday, just like them."

The woman with the bun laughed. "Well, maybe wearing a *few* more scarves."

Betsy raised an eyebrow. "A few, maybe. But not too many!"

It had proven easier than Natya had feared to find shoes in the end—they were given out for polishing, so she'd simply stolen a pair in the right size. With her hair braided and pinned up, she fit right in, and when Natya told the laundry supervisor, who went by Aunt Molly, that she was new, the woman hadn't asked any questions—just put her to the worst job, scrubbing out stubborn stains in the sheets. Natya tried not to think about where those stains had likely come from.

She kept her head down and listened to the chatter of the other women, hoping to find information she could use, about a paid job, a place to stay. But all they were talking about was the Columbian Exposition, Chicago's World's Fair, due to open tomorrow, May 1— the city was apparently going mad for it, wondering if it'd actually be finished in time, if it would be the fabulous moneymaker the organizers had promised, or if the city would go broke trying to pull it off. Either way, these women planned to get their fair share of fun.

She dared a question, almost the first words she'd said since starting work: "Do you know if they're hiring dancers?"

Betsy tilted her head, considering. "You dance, honey? You sure look like it. Pretty as a picture, too. Well, I don't know, but it can't hurt to go down and ask. Just don't let Aunt Molly know that you're already looking for another gig; she won't like it. She likes to hold on to her girls."

"Thanks. Really."

"No problem, sugar. Try a little more bleach on that—it'll come out easier."

Braid-woman said, "I didn't catch your name?"

"It's Natya."

"That's a pretty name; I haven't heard it before. I'm Candace, Candy for short. You from around here?"

Natya shook her head. "No—no, I'm from pretty far away. Just moved to Chicago. I'm from out west." West and west, past the setting sun and keep on going. Eventually you'd make it to Sri Lanka, the country she'd been born in, although right now, that'd mean living under British rule. She could try to find her great-great-grandparents, but even if that wouldn't mess up the time line and erase her from existence, she was likely safer here. Although maybe Natya would have a better chance at a dance job if they thought she was from Egypt. . . . "My momma was Egyptian, actually. My daddy was from California; that's where I grew up." She'd spent a year there once, living in Oakland after college.

Candy said, "Whoee! That's so exciting—you've been all over! I'd love to travel someday, maybe Charlie will take me to California. He says there's still gold out there, for anyone with the wit and strength to find it."

Bun-woman shook her head. "Charlie's a fool, Candy."

"You're just jealous. Joe's so cheap, he won't even tip his hat." Candy turned back to Natya. "Listen, we're going to go to the fair Saturday, after work. You want to come with us? Since you're new in town?"

"That'd be great; I'm not working, but I could meet you here? At five?"

"Sounds perfect. Hey, where you staying?"

"Nowhere yet." They all turned to look at her, clearly startled. Natya hurried with her prepared explanation. "I just arrived this morning, on the overnight train. I thought I'd find a place after work; I needed the money. Bad."

Betsy exclaimed, "Oh, sweetheart. Sounds like you're running from something. A man, I bet. Men are the worst—I'm glad I don't have one to fret about."

Natya bit her lip and nodded—might as well let them think that, if it'd make them more sympathetic, more likely to help her. She needed all the help she could get. Was she still running from Michael and Minal? Better not to think about it—they were lost to her now, one way or another.

"I'm Betsy. You can bunk with me tonight, if you want. And we can see if Mrs. O'Brien has any more rooms available. It's not a fancy place, but it's clean, and close to work."

One more problem solved. "Thanks, Betsy. Seriously, thanks."

Betsy gave her a sympathetic smile. "No problem, sweetie. Us girls have to stick together. Chicago's an exciting place to be, but it sure ain't easy."

They took the train down, arriving late afternoon on Saturday at the huge southwest railroad terminus. Immediately, Natya, Candy, and Charlie were assaulted by an overwhelming cacophony of voices, music, and crowds. Inside the grounds, the first sight was the immense Administration Building, a great domed structure, beautifully white to Natya's eyes, after the grime that covered much of Chicago.

"Let's go to the Court of Honor! It's so romantic, Charlie!" Natya obediently trailed behind them as they visited a large reflecting pool containing an elaborate fountain and tremendous gilded statue of the Republic. Orchestral music drifted in from the lakefront, following them as they entered Machinery Hall. Exhibits were crammed into every corner of a vast building that felt like an airplane hangar—Whitney's cotton gin, sewing machines, the world's largest conveyer belt, and the power plant, providing electricity for the entire fair.

Natya soon lost Charlie and Candy in the crowd, but she was more relieved than not—Candy's incessant chattering was annoying. And she wanted to take this in—this was history that she could reach out and touch. Natya would have liked to spend the rest of the day wandering from building to building, but she really needed to find the promised dancers. She did reach out to touch the cotton gin, just for a moment; she had read about it as a little girl in school.

"Keep your hands to yourself, blackie!" a security guard snapped at her, and she jumped back, startled, jostling someone in the process. A white man who glared at her, and a white woman on his arm who said, sneering, "*Some* people just don't know how to behave in a civilized place."

Natya bit her lip—wanting to respond, but feeling the crowd's hostility around her. What would happen to her if they thought she was offering an insult to a white woman? She had known that her skin marked her here, but she hadn't understood, in her bones, just how much she was at risk.

It hadn't been hard to find the dancers in the end—the sound of tambourines, German bands, foreign languages, and screams from passengers on the Ice Railway could be heard in the distance on the Midway Plaisance. Natya just had to follow her ears, passing models of the Eiffel Tower and St. Peter's Basilica, a volcano diorama, a "world's congress of 40 beauties," a German and Javanese village, Old Vienna, and finally her destination, a street in Cairo, Egypt.

"Give me your best hootchy-kootchy moves," the man said, looking her over with dead eyes. Arousal seemed the furthest thing from his mind.

It had been years since she'd tried to dance overtly sexy, but Natya had done a brief stint at a strip club in her college years, and her body fell easily into those moves. No pole to work with here, but scarves were almost as useful; she trailed them across her body, teasing the manager with views that appeared and disappeared. Her hips knew the motions he wanted, and his eyes followed them intently. The hardest part was resisting the urge to use her power, too—she had spent a decade integrating it into her dance, so that she didn't have to think about it climbing her spine, spilling out her fingertips. Now, Natya worked to hold it back—the last thing she needed right now was some dramatic display that would send this man running for the street, screaming.

The man nodded, turning away. "Good. You're lucky; two of my girls are sick with the flu; don't know if they're coming back. For now, you're hired—you can start in the morning. Go talk to Cami out front; she'll fill you in on the routine. Call's at seven A.M."

Cami, it turned out, was actually Kamilah, a soft-spoken Egyptian woman a few years younger than Natya.

"This isn't the sort of thing I usually do, but my husband passed." She stumbled on the word "husband," making Natya wonder if they'd actually been married—not that she cared, but she imagined most people in this era would. "And I have a little girl—do you want to meet her?"

"I'd be happy to."

"Rania! Come here, *habibi*."

The little girl ran up and oh—it hurt, not in the heart, but in the gut. Bad enough to make her want to bend over, but instead, Natya stiffened her spine and stood up straight. The girl was only a little older than Isai, skin a little lighter, eyes a bit more oval. Beautiful, in the way all children were at that age, especially the ones who moved so freely, knowing nothing of how the world was waiting to beat them down. Did Isai cry for her mother at night? Minal had always been the motherly one. . . .

"She's a lovely child," Natya said sincerely.

"I know this isn't the best environment for her," Kamilah said, her brow furrowed in worry, "but the other girls help keep an eye on her."

"I'd be happy to help too."

"Oh, thank you. I didn't mean to imply—" Kamilah flushed. "I'm seeing a gentleman—a *doctor*—and we've only been seeing each other a few weeks, but he's already starting to hint at marriage. It's too soon, of course, but maybe someday . . ."

"Well, you're very lucky." It seemed odd, a doctor wanting to marry a nautch girl from a traveling fair exhibit. But maybe Natya didn't understand this era as well as she thought; perhaps class issues weren't as rigid as she'd expected. And Kamilah *was* very pretty. "I'd love to meet him sometime."

"Oh, of course. He usually brings us some sandwiches for lunch. So you can meet him tomorrow. He's so charming, such a gentleman. I just wish my mother could have met him. She passed a few years ago. So now it's just me and Rania." She bent down and hugged the little girl, who squawked in protest and then ran off.

"You're lucky to have her," Natya said, softly.

"Oh, I know. She's my everything." Kamilah sighed. "But life's hard sometimes."

Natya could only nod in agreement.

The White City, they called it. Natya had seen pictures of the Columbian Exposition, the great World's Fair—old black-and-whites that
completely failed to convey the grandeur, the scale, of what had been
accomplished here. Considering the limited machinery they had to
work with, the time and money constraints, it was astonishing. She
grew used to the train ride, to arriving in the early hours when fog
often still hung over the tall neoclassical buildings on the Midway
Plaisance, the haze softening all the edges, making the illusion complete. Natya was transported back in time—ironically—to the ancient
world, Venice or Greece, away from the dirt and grime of the modern industrial age.

She had been here only three weeks, but Natya was coming un-
moored in time and space, and only the stench of the air grounded
her here, her body telling her, emphatically, that this was real. The
stockyards were nearby, and as the fairgrounds filled, the great
mass of unwashed souls joined their scent to the already thick air
with a pungency unmatched by anything in Natya's life thus far. At
home, she was an ace, but her wild card was a thing of light and
force—it had no power over scent. So Natya suffered, and she danced.
If anything had the power to help her escape, it was the sweat that
dripped off of her, the rising heat of late May in Chicago, with nary
an air conditioner in sight.

Then she'd be brought back to herself, slammed into her body
again, by the cries of the men who crowded the stage, who saw Natya
and the others as playthings, strange, half-animal creatures. The
dancers grew adept at dodging, and still, there were too many days
when some man managed to tear away a bit of sheer fabric, grope a
handful of breast. They were expected to take it in stride; they were
paid for this, after all. Not much, but enough to live on. Natya took
note of the worst ones, and if a little forcefield slipped out, causing
one to slip in the muck and land on his ass, well, she felt she was
still being kind. She could have done much worse.

Once, Natya forgot herself, and danced a little too well. The men loved it, of course. But Fahreda Mazar Spyropoulos, golden coins jingling on her hips, cornered her behind the tent and brandished a wicked little knife in her face. "Little Egypt," as she was called, reminded Natya, "I am the star of this show, and no half-breed girl is going to take my place. Understand, mongrel?" The girl looked rabid, spittle flying from her mouth with her fury, and for a moment, Natya's own frustration rose to meet her. That pathetic little knife—with the tiniest burst of her power, Natya could send it spinning back at its owner. If she wanted, she could take over as queen of Egypt, queen of the fair.

The fantasy lasted only a moment—the fair would end in October, so what would be the point? Better to keep her head down, save her money, so she'd have some real options when winter came. Natya bowed her head, and swallowing bile, apologized. "Little Egypt" stomped off, mollified.

The nights helped. As it turned out, Betsy had had ulterior motives for inviting her to share her bed. Betsy didn't like men at all, but she did like Natya.

"Go on, sweetheart." Betsy's small hands on Natya's shoulders, urging her down, her soft curves rolling under her. Only two breasts, two nipples—nothing like Minal's wealth of flesh—but two seemed sufficient. Natya buried her face between those luscious mounds, slid her body down, slick and eager. Betsy parted her legs for Natya, then wrapped her legs around her back, holding her down. Tangled fingers in Natya's hair and convulsed beneath her, muffling her cries with a pillow, so the thin walls of the boardinghouse didn't give them away.

Mrs. O'Brien ran a good house, she did, didn't let men inside the walls. She took care of her girls, and she didn't want any trouble. Natya was grateful for the solid, if uninspired, meals Mrs. O'Brien provided, for the safety of four walls and doors that you could lock.

She didn't want to risk losing that, but when Betsy rolled her over and started licking her way down Natya's body, the pleasure had to come out somehow. If it couldn't be allowed out in whimpers and moans, then it was stars and fireworks, bright illusions up above, and it was a good thing that Betsy's eyes and attention were so firmly focused down. Natya wouldn't have been able to explain it.

The nights made the days bearable, and even justified the commute. The White City wouldn't last forever, after all; if Natya was truly stuck here in the past, then eventually, the exhibition would close, and she would have to find another job, probably in the city. She didn't want to think about that yet, about whether she and Betsy might set up house together someday, whether she could find work dancing in a show.

That future was too frightening to consider. For now, Natya lived in the moment, exhausting herself with dancing by day, and bed games at night. If she worked hard enough, she could manage to avoid thinking at all.

She had made something of a life for herself, or thought she had—but it all started falling apart in late May. "What's the matter, honey?" Betsy rolled over after their latest bout, the pink slowly fading from her skin, her breath slowing.

Natya shook her head and leaned back against the headboard. "Nothing. I'm fine."

Betsy frowned. "Come on. You're not fine. I wish you'd talk to me. All we do is make love."

Natya raised an eyebrow. "I thought that was what you wanted."

The other woman sniffed. "As if you'd know what I wanted. As if you'd ever bother to ask."

Gods—what did the woman *want*? She'd had a dozen orgasms tonight, and Natya's arm was sore. "You seem happy enough with what I'm giving you."

Betsy grabbed the sheet, pulled it up to cover herself. "What? You're doing this out of charity now? Screwing me out of the kindness of your heart?"

Shit. That hadn't come out so great. "I didn't mean that. I'm sorry, Betsy."

"Sure you are. You always act like you're so special, like you're too good to be with me, to be here with us, down in the muck."

Was that really how Betsy saw her, how Natya came across? Like some perfect statue?

"I know, Betsy, I know," Natya offered, but to no avail.

The little blonde was still ranting, the anger pent up, spilling out. "You came here with *nothing,* princess. You didn't have a pillow to lay your head on, and if I hadn't taken pity on you, there's a good chance you would've ended up sleeping in the street that first night, and who knows if you'd have survived it!"

"I know, I owe you so much. . . ."

Betsy punched her then, in the arm—hard enough to sting. "There you go again, talking like it's some kind of quid pro quo. Are you in my bed because you think you owe me something? I thought you *liked* me. Do you even know what a risk I'm taking, being with you? It's bad enough being friends with someone like you—the other girls don't really like it. If they knew what we were doing . . ."

Someone like her. Brown-skinned, she meant. Betsy was crying now, and Natya awkwardly tried to pull her into a hug, but the other woman pulled away. "Just get out. Go—go walk it off or something. Walk the mean out of you. Don't come back here unless you're ready to be with me, really with me."

"I'm truly sorry, Betsy," Natya said, slowly getting to her feet. "I never meant to hurt you. I wish—"

"If wishes were horses, beggars would ride. That's what my momma used to say, and I guess she knew something after all. Now. Get. Out." She threw a pillow at Natya. A few weeks ago, Natya had watched Betsy working on that pillowcase after dinner, embroidering little pink hearts all along the edge; that should have told her something. Ridiculous as it all was, Natya felt her heart breaking a little, all over again, for Betsy, for herself, for everything. She slipped out the door, letting it close quietly behind her.

Now she was really alone.

"It's very kind of you to let me stay here," Natya said, as Holmes unlocked her room.

"Nonsense. I could hardly let a friend of Kamilah's sleep in the street! When she told me of your desperate situation, I was very glad that I would be able to be of assistance."

She had met Kamilah's gentleman caller, Henry Holmes, a few weeks previously. He was well dressed and handsome, and spoke in fine language; clearly an educated man, as you'd expect from a doctor. Holmes had the most intense blue eyes—not his fault, of course, but they were oddly disconcerting. More of a problem was the way he behaved when Kamilah wasn't there—if she left the area, and he was alone with Natya, those eyes fixed on her.

"You have the most exotic beauty, my dear. I would have liked to meet your mother; she must have been astonishing. I'm sure your father was completely bewitched." Was he implying that it would have taken sorcery for a white man to marry a brown woman? Probably, given this era, but surely not polite to say so out loud. "That hair, so long and thick—it flows like a Nubian river."

Natya had immediately wanted to braid it and tie it up, even tuck it under a scarf, out of sight, but of course, the manager preferred it down. She'd been grateful when Kamilah walked up, her eyes brightening at the sight of the doctor, giving Natya an excuse to duck away. But now here she was, alone with the man, throwing herself on his mercy.

"But the discounted rent . . ." He wouldn't let Natya pay full price, no matter how she protested. And of course, she could use the money.

"It's nothing, my dear. I'm just glad we had a room available. The hotel does get quite full."

The room he showed her into was of decent size, and well kept, although there was something odd about it. Natya couldn't place it at first, and turned slowly, trying to settle the itch in her brain. What was the problem here? Bed, dresser, even a little desk. Washbasin and pitcher. It wasn't until she stepped out of the room and then back in that it all clicked together.

"Something wrong?"

"No, no." The room was narrower than it should be, that was all, based on the door placement to either side. And there was an odd jog at one corner. Perhaps there were some mechanicals in the wall that necessitated the awkward construction. But it didn't matter; it would make no difference to her. "You really have been so kind, and this room is lovely. Thank you."

"My pleasure." Holmes took her hand then, bending over it to drop a kiss. Brief and entirely proper for the era, and yet she shivered, and had to resist the urge to pull her hand away. "I'll leave you to get settled then." He pressed the key into her hand, and walked away.

Natya forced herself to wait until he was safely down the hall before closing the door and locking it firmly. Then she lay down on the bed, still fully clothed, staring up at the ceiling, where the corners seemed to meet in not quite a right angle. Everything in her life had gone askew; it was only appropriate that her new bedroom did as well.

After moving to Holmes's hotel, Natya met more than a few of the people who worked and lived there. She mostly avoided the men; it seemed safer, and some of them, like the carpenter, Pitezel, struck her as more than a little unsavory. But Holmes employed several women—Minnie Williams, for example, had been his personal stenographer, and Natya heard rumors from the other residents that she was actually a railroad heiress, who had come to Chicago for love of the handsome and charming Dr. Holmes. If that was true, what would he want with poor Kamilah?

Of course, Minnie wasn't a threat anymore—apparently her sister Annie had come to visit last April, and soon after, both women disappeared. Some of the residents said Minnie and Holmes had been engaged, that she had "vanished," leaving him brokenhearted. But he didn't act like a man who'd been engaged, or one who was brokenhearted. Probably the women had just gotten homesick and gone home to Texas.

But it was odd, and Natya found herself prowling the hotel late at night, looking, listening, for anything strange. The building was eccentric—she found doors that opened to brick walls, oddly angled hallways, stairways leading to nowhere, and doors that could only be opened from the outside. The residents put it down to construction issues, a series of workers who had misread the plans, creating problems that were too expensive to fix. It was possible, wasn't it? Natya didn't really know anything about building in the 1800s, but she had the impression that Victorian homes had been known for their quirky layouts. Still, it worried her.

Through most of June, Natya joined Kamilah and Rania for lunch on the Wooded Isle. Tucked away between the Japanese architectural compound and the Hunter's Cabin, a monument to Davy Crockett and Daniel Boone, they could usually find an empty park bench to share a shady escape from the press of the crowd. They shared cheese sandwiches today, and crisp apples. Under the trees, Natya could almost forget that she wasn't in a park at home.

The little girl finished eating, and ran off to play a game of pretend, dancing through the trees. "Stay where we can see you, *habibi*!" Kamilah frowned after her, looking simultaneously proud and worried. "Sometimes, I think I should take Rania back to Egypt. She has never seen her homeland; she is growing up entirely American."

"Like me, you mean?" Natya said, her tone lightly ironic.

Kamilah put an apologetic hand on Natya's arm. "Oh, I didn't mean to offend you. It does seem sad, though, losing your mother tongue."

Natya shrugged. "I suppose my mother thought it more important that I learn English. It was hard enough, being a stranger in a strange land."

"Were people very cruel to you?" Her eyes were full of sympathy for Natya's imagined past.

Not really, in truth, though there had been a few incidents, here and there. A hundred years later, less had changed than one might hope. Once, Natya had applied for a job over the phone, and they'd all but promised it to her, but when she showed up at the final interview and they'd seen her brown skin, the job had mysteriously disappeared. Another time, a cashier at the grocery store had mocked her mother's thick Sri Lankan accent, and Natya had been forced to translate for her. Small things, but they burned.

"It wasn't so bad," she said to Kamilah.

"It has been very hard for us, very hard. Sometimes I think I should find some way to take Rania back home, try to find an Egyptian husband. But Dr. Holmes says that no one would dare give offense if we were under his protection, and I'm sure he is right."

"Mama, Mama, I need to use the toilet."

"All right." Kamilah stood up. "Will you come back with us?"

"I'll be back in a little bit. It's just so pleasant here."

"We'll see you at the tent."

Natya watched the pair of them walk away—and then frowned. Was that Holmes walking behind them? She got up quickly and began to follow them, but the crowds grew more pressing as they headed toward the edge of the Isle. By the time she caught up, they were all out of sight—Kamilah, Rania, and Holmes, if he'd been there at all. Had he been watching them, following them? Unnerving thought—and why would he? He could see Kamilah openly enough. Unless he derived some secret pleasure from knowing she couldn't see him, a strange intimacy she hadn't actually granted.

Natya resolved to keep a closer eye on them.

But June slipped to July, and Holmes seemed to behave well enough. For a time Natya stayed close to them, a third wheel, but Kamilah started urging her to go, enjoy the fair, and finally it grew too awkward not to take the hint. There was certainly plenty to see, from the splendid to the ridiculous. Pennsylvania had brought the actual Liberty Bell, and California presented a statue of a medieval knight made entirely of prunes. Natya heard Woodrow Wilson lecture, and was lucky enough to be present when Buffalo Bill, in his gleaming silver-and-white costume, bowed his horse to Susan B. Anthony. She stood up, and the crowd went wild; for a brief, shining moment, Natya was caught up in their excitement.

The Horticultural Building held eight astonishing greenhouses and a massive dome, an explosion of color and scent. But in the end, Natya's favorite part of the fair was the colossal Ferris Wheel, which had finally opened to the public in late June. At first, even she was a bit too nervous to ride it—she had ridden others before, of course, but this one had been the first of its kind. Perhaps all the kinks hadn't quite been worked out? But Natya didn't remember ever hearing anything about Ferris Wheel tragedies at the fair, so in the end, she decided to take her chances.

The cars were large, holding sixty passengers and an attendant, and designed with forty revolving chairs. At night, it was lit, and looked quite splendid, but Natya preferred riding by day, when the White City spread out below her, and Lake Michigan and Chicago beyond. She could stare out at the clouds and imagine herself in her own time and place, as if at any moment, a plane might fly by, on its way to touch down safely at O'Hare.

Riding the Ferris Wheel quickly became one of her great pleasures, and she tried to do so daily, even though it meant waiting in long lines. For the most part, people were patient about the wait, and relatively calm once aboard the car.

But not always. On one of her rides, a man entered with his wife, and seemed to be enjoying himself until the wheel started its upper revolution. Then he started to complain, loudly. "I feel ill. I am most unwell. You must stop this contrivance, and allow me to depart!"

The attendant endeavored to explain that there was no way to stop the wheel, but the man paid no attention. The rest of the car joined in, to no avail, as he grew more and more agitated. He began to pace excitedly up and down the car, shouting, in the process unnerving many of the women, driving them before him, back and forth. Then he began to jump on the sides of the car repeatedly, and actually managed to bend the safety bars. Natya was tempted to knock him out at that—he was risking everyone in the car. But the attendant began to grapple with him, and for a moment, it looked like he'd regain control. A few other men helped, attempting to hold the wild man, but he threw them off easily and made for the locked door. He shook it violently, and succeeded in breaking some of the glass, but couldn't force it open.

Luckily the car had now finished its descent, and the man began to calm; the men let go of him. Natya bit her lip, knowing what was coming. The wheel always made two full revolutions before it stopped, and sure enough, once it began to rise again, the man's frenzy returned. He begged the attendants, "Please, please—for God's sake, hold me down!"

Enough was enough. Natya would use her powers if she must, no matter what the consequences to herself. But she remembered when her daughter, Isai, would work herself into a hysterical toddler fit. Taking the child into a dark room and holding her close would usually calm her. There was no way to make the car dark, of course, not without using her powers—but she could darken the world for one man alone.

Natya unbuckled her skirt at the back, stepped out of it, and threw it over the man's head. He calmed immediately. She wrapped her arms around him and the skirt, holding it down, while they finished going up, and slowly, so slowly, came down. Finally, they were reaching the low point where they would disembark; she pulled back her skirt and buckled it back on. A low, grateful chorus of "well dones" and "good jobs" followed her out—along with, of course, quite a lot of scandalized muttering and shocked stares.

It was Natya's favorite day on the Ferris Wheel.

In late July, Natya met a man, as she jiggled to the end of her set. Re-met him? It was hard to know, with time travel, what the right verbs should be. When she first saw the small man at the forefront of the crowd, very dark-skinned, with wrinkles at the corners of his eyes, she felt a shock of recognition rush through her. She'd studied his file along with the others when given this assignment; she'd last seen him months ago, in that room at the Palmer House where all this began. John Nighthawk—come to take her home? She should be thrilled, shouldn't she?

He said nothing to her—turned and started making his way out of the tent. Natya made quick excuses and slipped out as well, feeling panic claw at her throat when she thought she'd lost him—but then the crowds parted, and through the gap, she saw him, walking away.

She ran up to him, still in her skimpy dance outfit, so inappropriate for these public streets, but who gave a damn? Not her. Natya put her hand on his shoulder, saying in a voice gone high and sharp, "John?"

He turned, blinking up at her. "Excuse me, miss. Do I know you?"

Natya wanted to say yes, but he so clearly didn't. For a moment, nothing made sense—was she losing her mind? The people, the sights and sounds of the fair, spun dizzily around her. Then the details of his file snapped into memory. John Nighthawk, born in 1852—he'd lived through this time, would be forty-one years old now. Eventually his ace would make him practically immortal, letting him suck the life and years from others. But the virus wouldn't be released till 1946—there were no aces in the world right now, none but her.

John was just an ordinary man, but for a moment, she wanted to spill her secrets to him anyway. Natya could tell him everything, and John would believe none of it. Would he want his fearsome power? Would he love it, the way she had once loved hers? Together they could warn the world, so that when the Takisians came, everything might be different. Spare all those thousands who died when their card turned. Was that the right thing to do?

Too much responsibility for her; she'd just fuck it up if she tried. Natya shook her head. "No, no. We've never met, I'm sorry. I thought you were someone I knew."

"Well, my name is John. You got that part right." He smiled at her, a low, sweet smile that made something catch, low in her body. "And I would like to know you better, miss. Can I buy you a drink?"

And maybe it was the smile, or maybe it was the way his dark skin reminded her of Michael's, though otherwise the two men looked nothing alike. Whatever the reason, Natya took him back to her crooked room that night, and for a few brief, feverish hours, lost herself in him.

John Nighthawk worked as a Pullman porter, as it turned out. He left on an early morning train, leaving her with a kiss, taking a little bit of hope with him.

♥

The second week of August—summer was running away, and the end of the fair was fast approaching. The dancers wearily removed their costumes at close of shift, wiping themselves down with thin towels and changing into street clothes. Kamilah gathered Rania into her arms. "Ah, such a good girl, waiting so patiently for Mommy. Yes, that is a beautiful picture, and that one too, and that one. Well done! We'll have an extra-special treat tonight, shall we? A wonderful dinner to celebrate all your lovely art."

"Something special?" Natya asked, as she peeled herself out of the skimpy costume. It itched; that was the worst thing about it. Beaded fringe, translucent hose, embellished blouse that was really closer to a bra. And the white-heeled shoes they had to wear—ugh.

"Dr. Holmes—Henry—has invited us to the hotel for dinner." She hesitated. "He has invited us before, many times, but I did not think it was appropriate, especially with Rania. But we have been seeing each other for four months now, and he is having a small dinner party, and wanted us to meet his friends. If we are to be engaged, I think it is fine. And it's a hotel, after all—it's not as if we were going to a private home."

"Are you engaged?" Natya said, one eyebrow raising as if of its own volition. She didn't *mean* to sound skeptical.

Kamilah blushed. "Not yet, not officially. He is getting a ring made; Henry wants to wait until it's ready. But I have already told him that I will say yes. With the fair ending in two months, I do not want to look for work again; it is time for me to settle down and be a wife."

Well, that seemed definite enough. "Congratulations, Kamilah. I'm very happy for you."

She smiled widely. "This will be good for all of us, Natya. Henry has many fine friends; once I am married, perhaps we can help all of you find other work when the fair closes. Or better yet, husbands!" Kamilah laughed, giving Natya a quick hug, and then turned to usher Rania out of the tent.

Natya watched her go, frowning. There was no good reason to be worried—Kamilah had been seeing Holmes for months, after all, and he'd always treated her well, from what Natya could see. Her friend was very happy. And yet—something about the whole situation still felt off.

Natya slipped out the tent flap and followed them, staying to the shadows and using illusion for concealment when she needed to. That wasn't very often—Kamilah wasn't worried about being followed, after all, and didn't tend to look behind her, except when Rania lagged a bit. It wasn't long before they had left the fairground, and then they made their way westward from Jackson Park.

The walk was long enough that the little girl started to complain, and Kamilah slung her up on her shoulders for the last mile. Finally they were at Holmes's World's Fair Hotel, a handsome three-story corner building. Kamilah entered with an air of ownership, as if she were already thinking about how she might redo the carpet and change the drapes.

Natya hesitated for a moment, not sure how best to proceed. She couldn't exactly barge in on Holmes and Kamilah. But she couldn't just go to her room and go to sleep either, not with worry gnawing at her stomach.

In the end, she waited in the shadows, outside, for two hours, getting colder and hungrier by the minute. Finally, Kamilah and Rania came out, with Holmes beside them, calling a hansom cab to take them home. Everything looked entirely normal, and Natya felt like a tired fool.

What did she think she was doing here, anyway? Playing detective? That was Michael's job, not hers. After leaving home, she'd trained for a few months to work with SCARE, but it wasn't as if she were some kind of super-agent ace, either. Natya had power they wanted, but she didn't even trust what they wanted it for. Working for them had seemed the best thing on offer, once she'd blown up her life in New York. But that didn't mean she was any good at it.

Isai was five now, had started kindergarten and would be in first grade soon. Although what was soon, now that Natya was here in 1893? Her family was stuck in the future forever, frozen in the moment when she'd betrayed them.

Natya had been so young during the riots. Five years old in '83, when the Black July riots swallowed Colombo, and thugs went door-to-door armed with government voter rolls, dragging Tamils out, putting tires around their necks, and setting them on fire. She'd stayed with her parents and younger siblings in a neighbor's house, hidden in a stinking toilet, and prayed for Ariyasiri, the big brother she'd adored. Ari had been at a friend's home that night, and before the night was over, they would learn that he, and his friend, and his friend's parents were all gone. She couldn't help him, couldn't do anything for him, and that had haunted her for almost three decades.

So when Natya's *little* brother got into trouble, got in with the wrong crowd and did terrible things, when Sandip came to her, broken and bleeding and begging for help, what was she supposed to do? Turn her back on him? Fail yet another brother? And of course, Michael was right, she should have trusted her boyfriend, trusted that he would do everything he could to protect her brother from the consequences of his actions. But instead, she had helped Sandip hide, even knowing that he had information Michael needed, information that might save lives.

A mistake, a terrible mistake. Natya had chosen family over integrity, and over her true loves as well. Michael, who went out into a dangerous city every day, risking his life to keep the rest of them safe. Minal, who had dragged herself out of a bad situation, taken the card the disease had dealt, and turned her life around. They loved her, they made mad, passionate love to her, they wanted to marry her. They had loved Kavitha Kandiah, but that woman was gone. Only Natya the ace was left.

Natya walked. Walked and walked, past homeless men and drunks, using the shadows and her power to conceal her, until finally she reached the lake. She was freezing, but the shore was deserted, so there was no one to see her, no one to care when she started to dance.

Women's clothes in this era were too binding. She stripped them off, layer after layer, until she wore only a long one-piece undergarment. Finally, she could move freely, and under cover of night, Natya began to dance. She danced all day, of course, at the fair, but that was work. This was art, this was what she was built for. There was nowhere she could perform here; her art, even without the wild card power, would bewilder the locals. *Don't frighten the horses!*

Or worse, what if they liked it, loved her melding of classic Indian *bharata natyam* and European ballet? What if that style became all the rage, and she changed the history of dance forever? Ruining not just the lives of her family, but possibly the entire world, not knowing what the consequences would be. Every step Natya took seemed a step on the road to disaster, and as the power spilled out of her, she found herself shaping it into a staircase. Step by step, leading out into the lake, climbing up, into the stars. But oh, she was tired. She had danced all day, walked miles to get here, and now, the energy that had once seemed inexhaustible was finally running out.

It would be easy to stop. Natya knew what would happen then— without her movement to fuel the power, the staircase would last only a few moments before dissolving, sending her deep into the cold waters of Lake Michigan. August wasn't icy, certainly, but cold enough. Natya climbed, and counted the steps of her lost loves, spelling out their names in the hardened air. Sixteen letters and sixteen steps, and then she stopped and spun, around and around and around, building a tower that climbed up . . .

. . . and then, because she was not *quite* ready to die, Natya started down again. Step after weary step, back toward the lakeshore and the empty, futile life she had, stuck here in the past, afraid to make a move that might change anything that mattered. But in her exhaustion and misery, she had misjudged her strength. The staircase winked out, yards from the shore, and Natya plunged through the air, into the chilly depths.

As it turned out, there was strength left in Natya after all. Dancing was impossible, under the waves, but frantic thrashing served as well, drawing power from her burning core. The water wanted her to give in, to surrender and sink, but instead she fought for every inch and every breath. The battle couldn't have taken more than a few minutes, but it felt endless, air bubbling out of her lips as she flew upward, power sending Natya shooting out of the water, to land gasping on the rocky shore. Time enough to reconsider everything she'd thought she knew. She had gotten everything, *everything,* wrong.

Natya found a corner of a park to curl up in, behind some sheltering bushes, and fell into the deepest sleep she'd experienced in months. She woke a few hours after dawn. There was just time to go back to the hotel—Natya cleaned up, dressed, went down to the fair to work her shift. A conviction burned within her that she had to investigate Holmes properly, but she also had to keep eating, which meant keeping her job as long as it lasted. Just two more months until the end of the fair; Natya had a few months' worth of living expenses saved up, but soon she'd have to seriously think about what she would do if she was stuck in this century for good.

Dance, if possible, dance for real. If it changed the course of history—so be it. Maybe she *would* warn the world about the Takisians, too, when the time came. Natya couldn't keep living her life this way, afraid of taking any steps for fear of taking the wrong ones; that wasn't really living. If she'd learned anything last night in the cold waters of Lake Michigan, it was that she desperately wanted to live.

"Are you seeing Henry today?" Natya asked the question casually, as the women applied their day's makeup, carefully drawing dramatic eyes with thick kohl.

"Yes," Kamilah said, "we're going there for dinner tonight, just the two of us."

"That sounds nice," Natya said. It sounded terrible; it meant she needed to move fast.

♥

The day's work seemed to fly by, and when it ended, all the wonders of the fair couldn't have kept her from H. H. Holmes's hotel. Just a few miles west, and Natya practically ran it, arriving a little before dinnertime, when the street was bustling.

Her stomach growled fiercely—she'd expended masses of energy, and would need more. Natya stuffed down a cheese sandwich from a horse-drawn wagon, the food tasting like sawdust in her mouth. As soon as it was all down, she headed inside, spinning a forcefield to shield herself from view. If Natya were seen, people might want to talk to her, might remember her later. Tonight, she needed to be invisible.

The ground floor held Holmes's drugstore and various shops, all shuttered for the night. Holmes's office was on the second floor—that was what Natya wanted. Hopefully there she'd find some clue as to whether there really was something wrong with the man, as all her instincts were shrieking, or if her suspicion was just an airy confabulation, born of misery and grief. It would be better if Kamilah were headed toward a happy wedding—but somehow, Natya doubted it.

It was easy enough to climb the stairs to the second floor, staying in the shadows or creating them, as needed. But which door was his office? She tried one door after another, sending a sharp little forcefield to snap open locks as needed. Her investigation was interrupted by the man himself—Holmes came hurrying down the hallway, and Natya barely managed to spin herself a concealing cloak of forcefields before being discovered.

The doctor checked the same doors she had just been at—he must have some sort of alarm system in place to alert him when people were walking around here. That was going to make things harder. But having him here did mean that Natya could follow him around—or at least she did until Holmes went to a hidden trapdoor, opening it to climb down, presumably into a room. Why was it there? When he emerged a few minutes later, Natya had to choose—keep following him, or investigate the room? Holmes headed down the main stairs, and her decision was made when she heard Kamilah's voice.

"Henry, are you sure it's a good idea?"

"My dear, it's for your own benefit. I will pay the premiums, of course, but a personal insurance policy is the best way to ensure Rania's future. I have already adjusted mine to note the pair of you as my beneficiaries, but if you get a policy as well, then she will be assured of a comfortable life, no matter what may befall. This life is so uncertain; you never know when tragedy is lurking around the corner, no matter how carefully you plan."

Oh, he was smooth. Natya hadn't thought money would be involved in this, but why not? Had Holmes ever cared for her friend at all? Was she the first woman he'd done this to? Was she even the only woman he was involved with right now? They were climbing the stairs now, and Natya hid deeper in the shadows, spinning silently to build an impenetrable shield. Pirouette, pirouette, pirouette. No steps, no sound that might give her away.

Kamilah was passing now, her voice low and trusting. "That's so true. If Rania's father could have been here, to take care of her, he would have. Instead, I'm left to struggle alone, as best I could. Well, if you're sure it's the best route; I trust in your judgment, Henry."

"Me too, Uncle Henry!" Rania's little voice added.

"I hope that you may trust me in all things, my dear Kamilah, and you as well, child. Now come—the papers are in my office; you can sign them, Kamilah, and then forget about them entirely. Hopefully, we'll never need to look at them again. We can concentrate, I hope, on wedding plans? Perhaps over dinner, we might discuss your favorite flavor of cake?"

"Cake!"

"Oh, Henry. I don't suppose it's possible to get a rosewater cake here, with a vanilla frosting?"

"For the right price, my dear, I'm sure it's possible. And no expense will be spared for our wedding; I mean it to be a grand affair!"

They headed into his office and closed the door behind them, freeing Natya to come to stillness. Not that she wanted to be still—she wanted to storm in and drag her friend out—but Kamilah wouldn't believe anything was wrong, not without irrefutable proof. Natya couldn't set off more alarms up here—the last thing she needed was Holmes finding her, poisoning her relationship with her friend.

If walking around upstairs was a problem, how about down? The first floor seemed normal enough, but did this building have a basement? Most did in Chicago. Natya went looking, found stairs heading down. Her power made a small glowing light, just enough to see by as she headed into the darkness, fueled by her steps. When she finally arrived, she found—strangeness. A room, with a chute leading to it. A large table covered in some kind of metal—zinc, she thought. No other furniture in the room, but an array of tools, meticulously arranged, as one might need for butchering meat. The hotel didn't have a restaurant. Did they lease the space to one that did prep down here? It seemed barely possible, and yet, deeply unlikely.

Whatever she had been afraid of—that Holmes might be a rapist, or even a killer, she hadn't expected all of *this*. The locals called this hotel the Castle, but if Natya was reading these clues correctly, this place was far more than a simple grandiose gesture on the part of an arrogant man. She needed to warn her friend, needed to get her out of here, even if she had to use force, even if meant Kamilah never spoke to her again. Natya turned, and hurried up the stairs.

Natya stepped out into the hallway—only to feel an arm wrap around her, pinning her against a man's body. A smothering cloth pressed against her face, a sweet, chemical scent overwhelming her senses. She wanted to fight, but her limbs wouldn't obey her; she had been fighting for her life not even twenty-four hours ago, had danced all day, and she was still drained. Natya felt consciousness slipping away, and blackness descending.

Natya woke, groggy and with her head aching, lying on a hard surface. The floor? A table? How much time had passed? She couldn't tell, and the room was pitch-black, not a fragment of light. Her first instinct was to dance, to generate light—but her first attempt at movement revealed that she'd been tightly bound—hog-tied, in fact, wrists to ankles and the coarse rope wrapped around her body as well, pinning her arms to her back. She could barely move at all, and for a moment, Natya despaired. Her heart was racing, and with every moment that passed, it felt harder to take a proper breath.

But the lake hadn't defeated her, and neither would this man. She had always used large movements to fuel her powers, but she had studied dance for more than a decade—she could isolate every muscle in her body, make it tense and release. Tiny motions, but enough—she worked with her legs, and quickly built power, feeling it coiling within her, wanting release. She let a little bit out, to light the space—not a room at all, but a metal box, a vault extending only a few feet around her own body, and no sign of airholes. Holmes had undoubtedly intended it for her coffin, but he hadn't reckoned with the wild card.

Power building. Light was insufficient—what she needed was heat and force. A ball of energy that burned between her bound hands. Oh, it was getting hot, and her hands wanted to flinch away from it, but Natya held on—just a little more, and then she hurled it as hard as she could behind her, at the top of the box. The metal groaned, but held. She did it again, and again, struggling against the dizziness that threatened to overwhelm her, until finally, the metal gave at a seam, ripping open, letting in fresh air.

Once Natya could breathe again, it didn't take long before she fashioned a slender field to slice through the rope that bound her, and then slammed open the metal, bending it back enough to release her from the box. Natya stood free, in yet another room of the Castle, but it was the work of moments to blast the locked door open, and step out. Second floor, which meant Holmes's office was just down the hall. Were Kamilah and Rania still there? Were they still alive?

Natya ran to the office door, tried to turn the knob. Locked, and when she snapped a forcefield to crack open the lock, the door still resisted her. Bolted too? How many locks would Holmes have on his private office? Natya took a deep breath, spun into a routine, a quick sequence of steps that oh, it had been a lifetime since she'd last performed. Six months and a hundred years, but her body remembered, the bend, the twist, and step-step, leap. Power built until she snapped it out, a massive forcefield smashing the door open. And on the other side of it, Rania, fallen on the floor, and Kamilah, unconscious in Holmes's arms, a white cloth pressed to her face.

She could have killed him in that moment. It would have been understandable, justified.

Holmes dropped Kamilah, her head hitting the floor with a nasty thunk. He leaped toward Natya, and was almost fast enough. Fast enough to grab her, to hurl her backwards, to slam her own head into the doorjamb. *Fuck,* that hurt. But that was his one shot, his only chance to knock her out, and the bastard hadn't pulled it off. She wanted to dazzle him, to spin him a nightmare of forcefields and illusion, terrify him so that he'd never dare attack a woman again.

Instead, she spun a cocoon. A smothering field that swallowed him whole, pressing in and taking his air, as he had tried to take hers, so that within minutes, Holmes had gone completely limp within it. Natya had planned this move, had practiced it, ever since that fight years ago, when her little girl had been kidnapped and she'd had no idea how to keep her safe—she'd wanted a way to incapacitate people quickly, should she need it. This worked.

Once Holmes was safely unconscious, she released the fields—if she'd left them around him, he would have suffocated to death. Natya wasn't sure that wasn't the right choice. She knew what Michael would say—that this was a matter for the police, not for vigilante justice. Holmes needed to be investigated—charges should be pressed, and a full team sent out to discover what he'd been hiding. Kamilah and Rania were still breathing. If they hadn't been, Natya wasn't sure even the thought of Michael would have been enough to restrain her.

Tomorrow. She could set the wheels of justice in motion tomorrow. For today, she would take her friend and the little girl to a doctor, make sure they recovered safely. As soon as they were safe, she'd be back for Holmes. She danced again, one more time, arms outstretched in the silent room. Natya raised power to lift her friends, carry them away, out of this hideous place. She would get them to safety, and then she'd be back. For the first time in months, Natya wanted to cry. She had saved them; she had destroyed her own family, but she had saved them. Maybe that meant she was worth saving, too.

It took less than an hour to get them to a hospital, into the care of doctors. Natya had carried them almost to the doorstep, shielding all the way, then dropped the shields and cried out for help. "There's a woman here, and a little girl! They need help!" Then she'd faded away, watched while the medical staff took her friends inside. She hoped they would be all right, but there was nothing else she could do for them now. Then she turned, and ran back, power lending speed to her feet, so that she was almost skating along. She'd never done this before, didn't even know she could, but she was moving at least twice as fast as she normally could run, and for a moment, it was exhilarating. Even here, trapped in the past, there were things worth learning, things worth doing!

All of that excitement drained away when she came back to the hotel to find Holmes had disappeared.

She asked around the next morning, of course—apparently, Holmes had left town for a few days. In addition, she learned that he was engaged to someone else altogether, someone he might actually plan to marry. Natya was determined to let that poor woman know what was going on—she would go confront her the next day. Kamilah and Rania were going to be all right, although they would need a few days to recover, and they had no real memory of what had occurred. Kamilah was bewildered when Natya came to visit her in the hospital: "I was with Henry, and then it almost felt as if he attacked me—but that can't be, can't it? That doesn't make any sense."

"Just stay away from him, for a little while."

"Oh, but we're engaged. I have to talk to him, find out what's going on."

"Please, Kamilah. He's not a good man—he's engaged to someone else."

"What?"

"It was all an insurance scam—I'm so sorry."

That convinced her, when perhaps nothing else would have, and Kamilah, weeping, promised that she would avoid Henry Holmes from now on.

She dashed tears from her eyes to protest, "You can't just sit here by my bedside all day. We're going to be fine," she said, bravely, "and you'll miss the ball."

Natya had forgotten entirely, in the midst of everything. It was Wednesday, August 16, the night of the great Midway Ball. The *Tribune* had called it "The Ball of the Midway Freaks."

"I don't care about that." In fact, she'd been a bit irritated by the *Tribune* article, in which they claimed that the Board of Lady Managers of the fair were upset by the belly dancers, herself included: ". . . what is not considered very much out of the way on the banks of the Nile or in the market places of Syria is entirely improper on the Midway between Jackson and Washington Parks." Those words had burned into her brain. *They* were the barbarians, and didn't know a damned thing about real, serious dance.

"Oh, you *must* go. It's going to be splendid—go for us, so you can tell us everything. Please. And maybe you might dance with Director General Davis, or even Mayor Harrison. He might fall in love with you, want to marry you, and it would solve all of your problems."

"Kamilah, I think you have had more than enough of engagements for the both of us." Still, she might as well go. The manager would expect it of her, especially with Kamilah out of commission. One more evening wouldn't hurt anything, with Holmes out of town. She would take care of him the moment he returned.

The ball took place in the Natatorium, a large building dedicated to swimming and bathing. The ballroom galleries were hung with golden triangles of embroidered silk, incredibly lush. Natya took her place in the procession of Midway performers, dressed not in her belly dance costume, thankfully, but in a more demure robe, topped with a turban. It was tremendously hot, and sweat dripped down her face and body, under the concealing fabric. The maharajah of Kapurthala, visiting that week from India, sat on a throne on the ballroom stage fanned by three servants; Natya wondered if he could tell, looking at her, that she was South Asian rather than Egyptian. The other Egyptians knew she wasn't truly one of them, but no one else seemed to question it.

She danced—danced with a score of men in black dress suits, all ready to be charmed by her. Natya didn't have it in her to be charming, but she did hope to dance with Mayor Harrison. It might be helpful, having him on her side, when she moved to take down Holmes. That man was going to pay for each and every one of his crimes. So she danced, and drank, and ate—a wild exuberance possessed her, born of the lights and the crowd and the overall air of extravagance. The food was astonishing—stuffed ostrich, boiled camel humps, monkey stew, fricassee of reindeer, fried snowballs—a far cry from the cheese sandwiches she'd mostly been subsisting on the last few months. Natya ate, and then went back to dancing, and if there were a few more sparkling lights in the ballroom, everyone assumed it was yet another lavish special effect.

Natya was swinging to the end of a wild reel, hours past midnight, when someone grabbed her arm, stopping her cold. A balding white man, not dressed for the occasion, with eyes dilated wide and sweating profusely. "Come on!" he hissed. "Hurry!" Mr. Meek. That's when she saw the other man, standing just inches away. Well-dressed, in a dark suit. *John Nighthawk,* but not as she had seen him last, young for all his forty-one years, kissing her goodbye. This man looked younger in body, but his eyes—his eyes bore the weight of centuries.

"Oh, no," she said, softly. Time to go home.

A Long Night at
the Palmer House

Part 8

NIGHTHAWK AND CROYD CHECKED into the Palmer
House and enjoyed a lavish dinner in one of the hotel's
fine restaurants. They figured that they owed it to themselves
after aborting that terrible time line they'd just experienced firsthand.
Then they went up to their room, ready to check out of 1968.

Their list of the missing, Nighthawk reflected, was getting
shorter, with only four names left. Kavitha, Cyn, and Meathooks, all
bodyguards, and of course Giovanni Galante, their genial host. Four
more lost chrononauts, and, as best as Croyd could detect, three more
jumps. Nighthawk was getting worried. He was hanging in there, but
Croyd was getting increasingly erratic.

Croyd was jittery when they stood side by side looking into the
mirror.

"Wait a second," he said, and reached into his pocket, pulling out
the Baggie of pills from the last care package. He took a handful and
tossed them into his mouth, dry-swallowing them. He looked at
Nighthawk, his eyes a bit too bright. "Just in case," he said, looked
again into the mirror, and they were gone—

—finding themselves naked as always, in a hotel room that was dark
and quiet, its decor and decorations those of the century past.

"Made it!" Croyd said. Nighthawk didn't like the tinge of surprise in his voice.

At least the room was quiet and empty—although, they soon discovered, not quite.

The first thing that Nighthawk saw was a newspaper on the nightstand by the bed—a copy of the *Tribune,* dated August 11, 1894, open to a page with an article titled "The Ball of the Midway Freaks."

Nighthawk picked it up and scanned it. It was somewhat sarcastically critical of a dance scheduled for that evening at the Columbian Exposition, specifically at the Natatorium.

He looked up as Croyd called to him, "Hey, John, check this out." He was holding two suits hanging in the wardrobe at the foot of the bed.

"And here, we have what might be called a clue," Nighthawk said, holding the newspaper out to Croyd.

Croyd took the paper. He looked up after quickly reading the article. "Everyone loves a World's Fair. Or whatever they actually call it."

"Yes," Nighthawk agreed. "I liked this one just fine the first time I saw it."

The memories came back, fleeting and shady, when he saw her dancing. *Again,* he realized. *Dancing.*

It was several hours past midnight, and the ball was still going full force. There were a lot of people still crowding the huge building that was called the Natatorium, people of all sorts, from the Midway workers themselves to ordinary fairgoers to dignitaries as prominent as the mayor of Chicago and his entourage. The mayor had been introduced to the crowd and been hailed with polite clapping and a smattering of boos, based, Nighthawk figured, on the political affiliations of the onlookers.

There was more to the ball than dancing. Exotic food of all types was spread out on buffet tables along the walls. Croyd came up to him at one point, saying, "Try the monkey stew," which Nighthawk politely declined.

"Focus," Nighthawk said. "We're trying to find our target—"

"It's Natya," Croyd said, polishing off the stew with some relish. "I'm sure of it. I can feel her in my mind—a bright shower of sparkles. Only there's so many goddamn people—"

Nighthawk wasn't sure if it was Natya he was feeling, or the drugs. "Keep looking."

"I am, I am," Croyd said. "But first I want to try some of that stuffed ostrich—"

Nighthawk sighed and turned back to scan the crowd, and then he saw her, dancing with a bald man with a small mustache. She moved gracefully, much more so than her partner, as they whirled about the floor in a wild reel. As he watched them he consulted the memory palace he'd constructed in his mind to preserve a century and a half of memories. It was an old technique that was invented way back in the Middle Ages, but Nighthawk had come to it only in the last twenty years or so, after discovering an article about it on Wikipedia.

You built a literal structure in your mind—in Nighthawk's case a rambling old Victorian wood-frame house with several stories and many rooms. It was an architectural form he admired and he'd lived in several during his time in Chicago. Each room in Nighthawk's memory palace was unique. Each room contained storage furniture or devices—closets with drawers, wooden card catalogs, one even had a computer in it with a comfortable chair set before it. Each was imagined in fine detail, each held a decade of memories.

His earlier memories weren't as sharp as the ones after he'd become an ace, as some details had already slipped away over the years, but they were there, fairly complete, ready to be accessed. Nighthawk stood still on the fringe of the dance floor and closed his eyes and in his mind went to the room that contained the 1890s. It was furnished in the style of the period. He sat down on the swivel chair in front of the card catalog and pulled out the drawer for the year 1894 and accessed his memories of the Columbian Exposition, which had lain unchecked for a long time. And there it was.

Late July on the Midway. A woman's voice calling his name, a light touch on his shoulder, and he'd looked back into a hopeful, beautiful face he'd never seen before. Her stopping him was apparently a case of mistaken identity, but it led to a night of passion that he now recalled in its full intensity. *When you make love to a dancer,* Nighthawk thought, *you never can really forget it.*

She swirled closer with her partner, and the song was over, their dance was ended. She smiled, said something to him, and looked up and their eyes met. There was recognition, initial shock, then a flooding of relief, with a touch of, what, sorrow or regret? She watched him as he threaded past half a dozen couples to reach her side.

"May I have this dance?" he asked, as the band began to play again. Fortunately, it was a much more sedate tune, more suited to conversation than the previous one.

"Oh, no," she said. "You've come to take me home."

"Do you mind?"

She shook her head. "You're older," was the first thing she said.

"Does it show that much?"

"Only in your eyes," Natya said. "They're like they were back at the card game."

Nighthawk nodded. "I'd wanted to see you again," he told her. "You know I was a Pullman porter then. Worked the *City of New Orleans* run. But when we reached New Orleans that time, they switched me to the L.A. route. It took me almost a month to get back to Chicago. And you were gone."

"I understand," Natya said. "But how do we get home?"

"Croyd's the one with the temporal powers," Nighthawk said. "I'm just his Chicago tour guide and keeper."

"Where is he?"

Nighthawk gestured over his shoulder toward the buffet table. "Checking out the stuffed ostrich."

Natya laughed lightly. She suddenly seemed happy, almost carefree.

"So," Nighthawk said, "tell me about your adventures in Chicago."

Nighthawk pulled Croyd out of the buffet line.

"We have to talk," he said, and hustled him over to a corner of the room that was relatively free of onlookers.

"Did you find Natya?" Croyd asked around a mouthful of stuffed ostrich.

"Yes—and listen."

He told Croyd about her adventures with Holmes and her saving the mother and daughter from his murderous clutches.

"Well, good for her—"

"*Good for her?*" Nighthawk repeated. "Look—we're here to repair the time line. That woman was supposed to die. And there were more . . . she was not Holmes's last victim, I am almost sure of that. The unintended consequences—we have to go back, again—as much as I don't want to—and extract Natya before she saves those people."

"John, John, John," Croyd said with forced patience. "We're talking about a mother and a daughter, here, victims of a fucking serial killer, not the fucking North Side mob that you made Khan take out back in '29. Or would that be ahead in '29?"

"Who cares?" Nighthawk said impatiently. "Mother, daughter, fine. What about the daughter's kids? And their kids? And their—"

"What about them?" Croyd said. "What if one of them finds a cure for cancer?"

"We don't know what if—we can't know."

"What if we do change history? A little bit, anyway?" Croyd was getting into it. His eyes were intense, his voice louder than it should be. "History is *fucked*. It's full of massacres, murders, genocides. What's one more or less? Look, here's an idea. While we're doing this, why don't we just go back and help Jetboy and make sure the virus is never released? *That* will solve all our problems."

Nighthawk groaned. "Think, man! First of all, *we're in Chicago, not New York*. Second, I can't even imagine the paradoxes doing something as radical as that would set up. For all we know, the world might implode!"

"I find that possibility very unlikely," Croyd said stiffly.

"You—"

Suddenly Croyd's face took on a more pleasant expression as Natya approached them, smiling. "Natya!" he said, welcomingly. "Great to see you again! Goodbye!"

With that, he pointed, and she was gone.

"Croyd!" Nighthawk gasped in a choked whisper.

"What?" Croyd set his empty plate on the seat of a nearby folding chair.

Nighthawk was about to ask him if he was out of his mind, but he shut his mouth. He couldn't risk pushing him any more in such a public place.

"Nobody saw."

As Nighthawk glanced around he saw expressions on at least three different faces that indicated that, yes, indeed, some saw what happened. Fortunately, it was late, people were tired, the lighting wasn't the best, and many had been imbibing all night. *Let it lie,* Nighthawk told himself.

"Now let's go find a mirror," Croyd said, then paused thoughtfully. "There's probably one in the bathroom. I have to pee anyway."

Meathooks on Ice

by Saladin Ahmed

ALI "MEATHOOKS" HUSSEINI WOKE slowly from dreams of his childhood. Of fourth grade, years before he drew the wild card. A class trip to a state park. He could hear the birds and the insects. He could smell the earth and feel the brisk air on his face.

Inch by inch, Ali's mind climbed into consciousness. He came to and realized he was no longer dreaming. The smell was real. He'd had to hide out in the country a couple of times in his life, and the smell was like that but richer. Thicker. Full of pine. He blinked his eyes open and squinted at the sunlight filtering through the trees above him. A forest. He was in a forest somewhere. And he was on his back, lying cold and naked in a patch of ice and mud.

"What the fuck is this?" He sat up slowly.

Something stung his forearm, just above the point where the thick invulnerable raw meat that formed his huge fist began. A mosquito, the biggest Ali had ever seen, sat there feasting on his blood. He squashed it absent-mindedly

Memories started to return. *The card game. The card game went to shit.* He'd been working a legit job, his best gig since getting out of prison, serving as bodyguard to Charlie fucking Flowers of all people. He was accompanying Mr. Flowers to a high-stakes poker game. A cigar-smoky room full of VIPs and human weapons. Ali couldn't remember how it had started, but there was shouting, a scuffle, and a flash of rainbow light. And then . . . what? *Someone clocked me? Gassed me? Some ace shit?* He remembered everything around him bending and warping and Ali saw some sort of rainbow light. He remembered feeling sick to his stomach. Then blacking out.

It wasn't the first time in his life some motherfucker had knocked Ali out and dragged him somewhere else. Knowing his luck it probably wouldn't be the last.

So now he was in the boonies somewhere. Whatever happened, Ali had apparently been out like a light for some time. He *must* have been out a long time for them to have thrown him in a trunk or whatever and driven him all the way out from downtown Chicago to . . . here. Wherever here was. Had they just dumped him? Were they watching him? You usually didn't drive a guy way the fuck out to the woods and lay him down in the mud unless you planned to kill him.

So who wants to kill me, and why? It was a question he'd had to ask himself countless times in the past, and it almost felt good to be asking it again.

He got to his feet and the forest exploded.

Something leapt at him from behind and cut him. Lines of blood burned down his back and Ali screamed in pain. His feet scrabbled on ice and dead leaves. He fell onto his back.

A tangle of fur and teeth and claws pounced on his prone body. Out of reflex more than anything, Ali threw up his raw red slab-hands. They'd stopped bullets and knives before, and now they saved his ass again. The thing sank its massive fangs into Ali's fist. It didn't hurt, but the creature was stuck and he got his first good look at it.

Ali had done a lot of B&Es in his day and had come across pit bulls, rottweilers, and Dobermans. This was bigger than any of them. But it was . . . *A cat?*

What the fuck is this? The tiger or puma or whatever the fuck it was raked out its claws and tore gouges in Ali's arm and chest. They hurt like hell, and he screamed again. As the pain and anger filled him, the meat spread across his body. Up his arm in sinews and patches. Here and there, fishhooks sprouted from his skin. He felt filled with strength.

Ali brought his other fist down and crushed the giant cat's skull. Blood gushed over his arm and sprayed his face. The thing stopped moving. Ali yanked its fangs out of his fist with a wince, and shoved its body off of him. He got to his feet.

He looked down at the big cat's corpse. It was even bigger than he'd realized. *And those fangs.* He'd seen onc of these things before, he realized. On another class trip. To the natural history museum. It was a fucking saber-toothed tiger.

"*Mash'Allah,*" Ali said out of habit. But he knew he didn't deserve God's protection.

His stomach rumbled. He didn't know where the fuck he was. He didn't know who the fuck had brought him here. He didn't know how the fuck to get home. But he was bleeding and he needed to eat.

Bugs buzzed around the gore on his fists and the wet red slashes on his chest. Ali swatted at them, angry. The mosquitoes were as long as a man's finger. Well, a *normal* man's finger. "Motherfucker. Motherfucker. Motherfucker," he muttered. *What is this? The Amazon? But it's cold.*

"I was trying, God. I was trying to do right. But I'm gonna kill whoever did this." In prison, Ali had learned to talk to God when he was alone. Sometimes it kept shit at bay. Sometimes.

His stomach rumbled again. Ali set out to find food.

His earliest memories were of the smell of bread. *Khubz arabi,* what white people called pita bread. His father had been a baker, making cheese and meat pies for the neighborhood back in Beirut. Ali remembered only flashes of his parents' bakery and the flat above it—flour everywhere, jostling crowds of customers, Arabic singers on the radio, cinder-block walls hung with sepia photos of thick-mustached men. But war drove his parents from Lebanon, with six-year-old Ali and his older sister in tow. When the family came to Detroit, Ali's father had to take a job working for another baker, the brother of a man he couldn't stand in the old country.

School had been hard at first. The white kids, the black kids, and even the kids who'd been in America only a couple years, all teased the new FOB boy. But Ali was big and savvy. When kids pushed, he pushed back. And he learned to make others targets.

He remembered throwing trash at a joker boy they called Stinky who didn't actually stink, but was covered in thick black fur with a white stripe, like a skunk. The boy—Steve was his real name—hadn't stayed in Ali's class for very long. The kids said he had been sent to a special school for jokers. When Ali's own card had turned, the first thing that had come to his mind was Stinky's skunk-like face, crying and covered in old food that Ali had thrown at him.

Though almost all of the trees around him were evergreens, near sunset Ali finally managed to find a tree with leaves, full of fruit that sort of looked like apples. A light jab from his big fist brought down a rain of the big green things. They were sour as hell, but they were food. He sat with his back against the biggest tree he'd ever seen and ate five of them, washing them down with a hunk of ice.

As Ali sat there the sunlight, already dimmed by the thick canopy of pine branches, slowly began to fail completely. He wouldn't starve, at least, or die of thirst. It could be worse. But where the hell *was* he? For one thing, it was freezing cold, which made no sense, since it was summer.

Sleep began to overtake him, and he let it, despite his lack of shelter. For a normal person, sleeping naked in an icy forest would probably be a death sentence. Unlike most normal people, though, Ali had once been locked in a walk-in freezer for three days by a gangster named Crazy-Face Carlos. Ali had been as surprised as anyone to learn that the meat within him had somehow kept his insides from freezing. He felt a brief flash of joy remembering Carlos's extra-crazy face upon seeing Meathooks alive, then he slid into sleep.

The next morning he woke suddenly from a dream of prison. He was cold, hungry, and confused. The wounds on his chest and back no longer hurt, but they were raw and itched like hell. He heard a loud sound, like a dump truck or a bulldozer, and Ali realized that it had been this that had woken him. He sat still and focused. A minute later, there were more big, crashing machine sounds. *Machines means people.* Ali stood and scanned the woods around him, but he didn't see anything but birds and weird-looking squirrels.

He heard the noise again and followed it. About fifty yards ahead of him the land dropped off into a ravine. The noise was coming from down there. Ali got down and crawled to the edge as if he were on a rooftop downtown. He peered over.

The ravine looked like a giant rock had been sheared in two and split apart. There was a steep drop of maybe fifty feet and the bottom was green with vegetation. Huge brown shapes moved back and forth, crushing branches and bushes beneath their feet.

Are those fucking elephants?

Ali gazed a bit longer. Some of the creatures turned and looked up at him lazily, but only for a moment. He could smell their musky fur from where he was. *Fur.*

Not elephants. Mammoths.

"*Ya Allah.* What the fuck is this Flintstones shit?" he spoke aloud, and it felt weird.

It dawned on Ali that it might be not a question of *where* he was, but a question of *when* he was. It was crazy. But maybe no crazier than a guy who could turn into meat-and-metal because he caught an alien disease that allowed other people to fly.

Whatever the fuck had happened, however the fuck it had happened, now he had to find a way back.

Ali's parents had managed to escape the bombs and bullets of Beirut, but the country they'd brought their children to held its own dangers. By the time he was in junior high, Ali had shed his accent and ascended to the top of the junior high food chain. He was too big and too restless to not be dangerous. *Smart enough to get myself into trouble, too dumb to get myself out,* was the way he'd always thought about it.

His parents were quiet, pious people, and Ali had hated them for it. Their rules, their sayings, their expectations. The only person he'd given a shit about was Wafa. His sister had understood him and loved him, even if she didn't approve of his behavior. She had thought him a good person, and Ali could count on one big meaty hand the number of people he could say that about.

In junior high he started doing little bullshit B&Es and nickel-bag hustles under the tutelage of the high school dropouts he thought of as the Older Guys.

In 1988, when Ali was fourteen, the Detroit Tigers were in the World Series and all sorts of people came to Detroit. "All that money out there," as Fadi had put it. Fadi was an older delinquent who drove Ali and his buddies to jobs. They'd gone up and down Trumbull, breaking windows and grabbing car radios while listening to the game announcers express utter bafflement at the poor decisions being made by the Tigers' new manager, Charlie Flowers. Years later Ali would learn, along with the rest of the country, that Charlie Flowers had bet an enormous sum of money against his own team.

By the time he was seventeen, Ali had dropped out of school himself and he was the one giving the lessons. He started working as muscle for southwest Detroit's low-rent hoods. He got his own place and visited home only to see Wafa.

And that's when his whole family drew the wild card.

Ali had come home one night, a week before his eighteenth birthday, coerced by Wafa to sit at a dinner table he wasn't wanted at. He found them all lying on the living room floor, thick blood dribbling from their eyes and mouths and noses. Ali had barely looked at his parents. He knelt by Wafa's side and took her hand. *What happened?* was the last thing he remembered thinking before the convulsions started.

He'd heard that some of those who drew the card were born different. That others went to sleep one night and woke up changed. Ali? Ali had seen it happen to his own body before his eyes, like watching a horror movie while he lived it. His hands had stretched and warped until they looked like slabs of raw meat the size of car batteries. Patches of pink sinew spread on his chest. Fishhooks popped in and out of his skin as he breathed.

And then the meat covered his left hand completely, and a ten-inch iron hook had burst out of the raw red mass.

He'd raged and screamed and torn his parents' living room to shreds in his anger. The police came to his house, as they had more than once before. But this time men with stretchers took his parents and his sister away. When Ali saw the cops' looks of pity, it took all of his strength not to throttle them.

Days passed and nights passed and Ali had no idea how to get home, or even start looking for a way home. He tried to retrace his steps and find the exact spot where he'd first woken up, but it was no use. Most of his time was spent trying to feed himself. With practice he found he could catch fish from the streams in his big hands, but eating them raw nearly made him vomit, and they were mostly bones anyway. Ali tried to start a fire a hundred times by rubbing sticks and striking rocks, but he wasn't a goddamned Boy Scout. He discovered that the biggest pinecones—the ones the size of a normal man's fist—had edible nuts in them, and this saved his life. There was an endless supply of them, and their taste reminded him of Lebanese food, and of home.

He had counted eight or nine nights of sleep when the smell came to him.

The smell brought him back to childhood barbecues, his father surrounded by other Arab men laughing and arguing as shish kebab sizzled on the grill.

Cooking meat. Ali had been hungry before. Days holed up in some room watching a mark. Times in prison where the vindictive guards decided for whatever bullshit reason that he didn't get to eat that day. But he'd never felt hunger like this. And when the smell of meat on a fire hit Ali's nostrils, he growled like an animal. Almost without thinking, he stood up and scrambled toward the scent.

Cooking means people, he realized. What sort of people? Whoever dumped him here? Big white cavemen with clubs? Ali was so hungry and, if he was being honest with himself, so lonely, that it almost didn't matter.

Following his nose in a forest proved harder than Ali thought. The smell of food was so overwhelming that it seemed to be everywhere, and it was intertwined with the omnipresent plant and animal scents that he had grown used to over the past few days. Then Ali saw the smoke.

He followed the smoke to a clearing at the foot of a hill. Ali stayed in the trees and watched. A hundred yards or so across the clearing, a cave of sorts, a little makeshift shelter, was carved out of the side of the hill. Near this entrance was a big pit with a crackling fire. Some sort of animal was cooking on a spit, but what interested Ali were the figures milling around the fire, talking.

People. They were actual people. And not hulking white men with gorilla foreheads and clubs, either, but human fucking beings. There were eight or nine of them, brown-skinned and tough-looking, dressed in furs and armed with long, sharp sticks.

Hungry, lonely, and desperate, Ali burst out of the woods without thinking. He shouted, *"Hey!"* Then all hell broke loose.

As one, the men looked up and started shouting. They exchanged a few words and then charged him. Ali threw his hands up defensively—these were the first people he'd seen in this place, maybe the only people he'd ever see here. He didn't want to kill them if he could help it.

One spear flew at him and he batted it away. Another two came flying and he blocked them with his hands, the points sinking into the meat. He yanked them out and tossed them to the ground and then the hunters surrounded him. Nine of them, all with stone-tipped spears. Ali could see now that some of them were young, barely old enough to have hair on their balls. Ali tried, with word and gesture, to make clear that he wasn't a threat, but it didn't work. He understood. How many times had he himself beat the shit out of some poor chump, only to learn later that it had been the wrong guy?

The smallest boy—he couldn't have been more than thirteen—

lunged and tried to stab Ali. Ali grabbed the spear by its sharp end, the point digging painlessly into his meaty palm. He yanked his hand back and the kid, still holding the spear, was thrown to the ground. "You can try to kill me, you little shit," he said, "but you're not gonna like how that ends up." It felt damn good to talk to another person, even if that person was a teenager who was trying to kill him and couldn't understand a fucking word he said. He pulled the spear out and snapped it in two.

This, apparently, was all the hunters could take. The circle broke, the men and boys fleeing screaming into the woods. Ali tried to calm them, tried to follow them, but it was no use. They were fast and they knew the woods well. Before long Ali was alone again.

He felt his soul sink as he walked. "Why are you doing this to me?" he asked God aloud. God didn't answer.

Ali looked back to the cook-fire and the hunters' shelter. Well, at least he now had a roof to sleep under at night. And some real food to eat.

About as much—or as little—as he had back home, truth be told.

Some people said everything changed after your card turned. And yeah, things were different for Ali after that night. His cronies avoided him. People on the street made faces. He moved into a flophouse for jokers on the east side of Detroit. He had to learn to use his hands all over again. But mostly Ali felt like he'd become on the outside what he was on the inside. Stronger than the rest. Scarier. Uglier.

Before too long, Ali came to see the advantages of having his card turn. He was strong enough to flip a car with one hand now, and he could take a hell of a lot more punches than he could before. The hamhocks he now called hands felt no pain, which was handy for breaking windows and faces. When Ali got angry, the patches of raw meat spread across his body and sprouted metal hooks of all sizes— from the fishing barbs that coated his chest like a sort of mail to the huge meathook that burst forth from his left hand. When he was *really* mad the meat-and-metal grew thick enough to stop bullets, and Ali could lift a bus and tear a car in half with a swing of his hook-fist.

But Wafa was gone and his buddies had abandoned him, even if they were too chickenshit to say why to his face. When a local drug dealer who'd seen Ali handle a gang of four guys at once offered Ali a job doing "security" in Toledo, Ali jumped on the chance to get out of town.

He spent the next dozen years moving from city to city finding work as Meathooks, a tough-as-nails enforcer smart enough to make a plan go right but dumb enough to take his measly pay without asking for more. Meathooks worked as a bodyguard, collector, street soldier, and beat-down man in Chicago, Indianapolis, and half a dozen other rust belt cities.

He killed some people, too. And though he never went to prison for it, when he finally did go to prison—for a crime he didn't commit—he thought often about the men he had murdered.

The hunters' shelter was not, as Ali had first thought, simply a hole dug in the side of the hill. Inside, animal skins covered much of the packed earth and tools of stone and bone and fire-hardened wood lay strewn about, though Ali had no idea what most of them were for. There was also a store of nuts and little raisin-like things and wooden bowls for drawing water from the nearby stream. *"Al'Hamd'Allah,"* he said out loud. *Thank God.*

It was only then, as he stood staring, that Ali realized the dirt walls of the little cave were carved—intricately, and all over. Mostly it was patterns and borders and strange symbols that he didn't recognize. But here and there were little pictures—trees, rivers, birds, animals.

He ate his fill of the huge deer that was still cooking on the spit outside and warmed himself by the fire. Ali realized he should try to keep the fire going, but he had no idea how in the hell to do that. So he went back into his new temporary home, wrapped himself in animal skins that smelled horrible, and, fairly certain that the hunters were too frightened to return, fell asleep staring at tiny earthen images of eagles and stars.

For a few days—three? four?—Ali spent his daylight hours scouting the area around the shelter. He walked along the stream and explored the woods, always careful not to go far enough to get lost. The dead deer began to stink, so Ali dragged it away from the shelter and, with a loud heave, threw it into the woods. The fire died and he couldn't bring it back.

He managed to rip and tie enough fur together to fashion himself a sort of skirt that at least kept his dick and buttcheeks from hanging out. And he began familiarizing himself with the various tools in the shelter, or trying to. There was a long stone knife, remarkably sharp for a rock. That could come in handy. But what was the wooden paddle for? Or the lidded stone bowl with holes in the top?

He'd figure it out. Ali had learned how to use a smartphone with hamhock hands. He'd learned how to sail a boat for that Lake Michigan job back in the day. He'd taught himself Spanish. He'd figure it out. Then he'd figure out how to get the fuck out of here and back home. Or at least back to his own time. He didn't have anything that counted as a home these days.

A number of days—nine? ten?—after he had seen the hunters, Ali awoke to the smell of cooking meat. He lay there for a moment, his stomach rumbling, before he was awake enough to wonder what was going on. Then he leapt to his feet and ran outside.

The firepit was going again, and another deer was roasting on a spit. In the clearing, a hundred yards from the shelter entrance, a dozen men and women stood in a line. Their spears were at their feet and their arms were extended, palms up. They all chanted softly.

As Ali emerged from the shelter, they stopped their chanting and pointed at him, speaking excitedly. Ali, not wanting to frighten them again, raised his huge hands in as non-threatening a manner as he could. A stout old woman, her long black-and-gray hair threaded with beads and shells, strode forward alone. She stopped halfway toward Ali, as if waiting for something. Ali took a chance and walked slowly toward the woman, smiling at her reassuringly, his hands still out and open before him. Unlike the others, this woman didn't look afraid. Ali stopped a few feet in front of her and they stood there for a long moment, sizing each other up. Ali saw that she had three small vertical scars on her forehead, a mark he'd seen on some of the hunters as well.

"Uh, hi," Ali began. As soon as he spoke the woman's people started chattering, agitated. "Look, lady, I didn't mean—"

The woman held up her hand, and Ali fell silent. She took a deep breath, then started speaking words Ali couldn't understand in a loud, deep voice. She gestured toward the deer on the fire, and at bowls of berries and nuts and beads and shells that Ali hadn't seen before. She was speaking but she wasn't talking to him, Ali realized. It sounded more like a formal speech. *Or a prayer.*

When she finished, she pulled out the small pouch tied around her neck and stuck her thumb into it. She pulled her thumb out, and it was covered in some sort of purple dye. She stepped close to Ali and, before he knew what she was doing, pressed her wet thumb hard against his bare chest. When she pulled it away a small indigo oval stained his skin.

"What the fuck?" Ali had no idea what this all meant, but he figured it was good. Most times, someone giving you food was better than someone trying to kill you. The old woman backed away slowly for a dozen paces, then turned and ran. Only then did Ali realize just how afraid she'd actually been.

Before he thought to stop them, the people melted back into the woods, leaving Ali alone again.

As Meathooks, Ali had done dark things that he could never make right. Punched a hole in a man who owed another man money. Threw a police van full of informants off of a cliff. There were screams he would hear his whole life, and perhaps in the world that comes after this one. But for some reason he couldn't name, Ali's mind returned most often to the shakedown job where he'd met a wild card called the Dope Man.

Once a white junkie from the suburbs, the Dope Man was now a shambling mound of drugs, a half man sprouting weed and crack rocks from his skin, with heroin seeping from his open sores. The Dope Man wasn't going to make anyone rich—he grew the stuff like a sheep grows wool, and once he'd been sheared it took time to grow more—but he was a figure of legend among Detroit's drug fiends and small-time users.

Ali learned the Dope Man was real when he found the poor son-of-a-bitch chained up in some meth heads' basement. He looked as if he'd been shaved in some places and flayed in others. The man had looked at Ali in terror. They were around the same age.

"Hehl," the Dope Man had croaked.

"Huh?"

"Are . . . are you here to help me?"

Ali had unshackled the man from the radiator. "No. You're coming with me." The meth heads he'd just killed had had a dog. Ali hadn't wanted to shoot it, but it just. Kept. Yapping. Anyway, a dog meant a leash.

He could remember the sound of the Dope Man pleading as Ali led him out of there like an animal. Ali had sold the man for five thousand dollars. About what a good used car cost at the time.

In prison, when Ali would kneel to his prayers, the look in the man's eyes would return to haunt him.

The old woman didn't visit Ali again. But every few days new offerings would appear. No more deer—Ali supposed meat was pretty rare for these people—but bowls of nuts and fruits and shiny stones. Ali never saw those who left the gifts, if that's what they were. They seemed to visit only when he was away from the shelter. Or sleeping.

Ali decided to wait for them, and to follow them the next time they came.

For a week he lay down before sunset, pretending to fall quickly asleep. Each night no one came. He thought the waiting might make him crazy. Finally, one early evening, from the recesses of the shelter where he feigned sleep, he could see two big young men approaching with baskets brimming with little corn ears. They were clearly scared shitless but trying to look tough for each other. They left the baskets near the cook-fire, then started trotting back toward the woods.

Ali followed.

He gave them as much of a lead as he dared, then got moving. Ali was big and stuck out like a sore thumb. Even so, in a city he knew, he could follow a man like a motherfucking shadow. Here in the woods, not so much. Branches and leaves snapped underfoot as he plodded along, and birds and animals chittered and squawked at him. The hunters had to know they were being followed, but they very pointedly did not look behind them, instead clutching the bone necklaces they wore and mumbling words Ali couldn't hear. They reminded him of his mother muttering Arabic prayers, trying to ward off the evil eye.

They walked for a long time, and he followed. A part of Ali worried that he would lose his way and be unable to return to his shelter. But they were following the course of the stream here almost exactly. And it was worth the risk.

The hunters finally stopped at a cluster of pine trees that stood hard against the stream. Ali stopped farther back into the trees and watched as a mixed group of women, men, and children met the hunters. They had baskets full of the large pine nuts that had sustained Ali when he'd first arrived in this place.

Ali found himself staring at the women's lips and breasts and asses. Over the decades, between his deformity, his line of work, and prison, he'd learned to live without love. Without being touched. He'd gone years at a time without getting laid. But his body was calling to him now. He shook it off and tried to think. He had to talk to these people. But how in the fuck was he supposed to? He didn't know their language, they didn't know his. . . .

The hunters kept stealing nervous glances over their shoulders. They knew Ali was there, even if they couldn't see him. He had to at least try to make himself understood. He took a deep breath and stepped forward.

As soon as he moved, something came charging out of the woods at the group. A bear, bigger than Ali thought bears could be, a fucking mountain of fur and claws growling loud enough to make a grown man shit his pants. And it was pissed about something. The people screamed and scattered. A few of the hunters fumbled for their spears. One of the smaller children was directly in the bear's path.

With a bloodcurdling shout of his own, the meat-and-metal spreading across his skin, Ali charged the beast. It slammed a claw into him and tried to grab him in a crushing hug, but yelped and whined like a dog as the barbs and hooks that had sprouted all over Ali dug into its skin.

Ali punched the bear once, his fist sinking halfway into the animal. It thrashed and fell still. He pulled his bloody meathook from its body, sending a spray of blood and guts everywhere. Only then did Ali realize that the hunters and the others hadn't fled. They were standing there, watching him with awe.

I just saved a kid's life, Ali realized. Then, to his utter shock, he noticed that some of the people were actually *smiling* at him now.

It had been a long, long time since another human being had smiled at him, and it felt so fucking good that Ali thought he might cry.

◆

Ali's criminal career had ended with the death of an eight-year-old boy. It happened when he was back in Detroit, on a job with a local old-school mobster's twerpy little grandson named Jason. A hospital complex. Ali had been in one building, Jason in another. The job went wrong on the twerp's end. It wasn't Ali's fault the job went wrong, but he paid the price.

Ali had done some shit things in his years in the business, but he'd never hurt kids. He could say that at least when God judged him.

Jason the Twerp had panicked and shot an eight-year-old kid. Ali wasn't even in the same building, but the next day dirty cops picked him up, claiming the boy had been found bludgeoned and hacked to death with meathooks.

Set up for the fall, Ali got life in prison.

♥

Weeks passed. The moon grew full and died and grew full again. The People—Ali came to learn that that was what they called themselves—came every so often and left Ali food and little gifts. Eventually they came whether Ali was there or not. Each time they left, Ali followed them a bit farther.

All the while, Ali watched them. He watched how they ate, watched how they fished, watched how they used their tools. He learned their method of making fire with wood and stone.

But mostly Ali listened, trying to learn their words. What they called fire, what they called meat, what they called snow. The words one of them used to let the others know he was going to take a shit. The words one used when she looked tired. He learned the most from listening to the children. It wasn't so different from teaching himself Spanish, really.

Ali finally decided to try to talk to a group of his visitors. Two lanky young men that might have been brothers and a gruff-looking young woman. They'd caught several animals that looked like giant gophers and were cooking them when Ali approached.

"H-hello," Ali tried to say in their language.

The three of them stood stock-still, staring at Ali. One of the brothers dropped his utensil and spit out what sounded like a curse.

"Hello," the young woman said back. Her voice was gravelly, like an old woman's.

"You . . . hunt?" Ali thought he said.

One of the young men screamed. The trio turned and ran.

"Wait!" Ali shouted in English but it was no use. And if he chased them he would only frighten them more.

It was three days before he had another visitor. Ali counted them.

This time, though, his visitor was different. It was the squat old woman who had marked him all those weeks ago. The beads and shells in her hair clicked as she approached him, and she smelled strongly of some sort of flower or herb. A young hunter accompanied her, clearly there to protect her and carry her things. She waved him off to the cook-fire and shuffled confidently into the shelter, gesturing for Ali to follow. For a moment she didn't look at him, just traced her big hard finger along the carvings on the cave wall. They'd started to fade, and Ali had realized that the People probably tended to them somehow. He felt vaguely embarrassed.

"You talk!" the old woman said, turning toward him suddenly. Then she looked him in the eye and talked on and on, her gaze locked on him. Ali understood only a few of her words. "Meat." "Shelter." "The People." He thought she might be reciting something.

Ali noticed that over and over again in her monologue she repeated the word "sleep." Except it wasn't "sleep," exactly. More like "talking sleep." *Dreams? Is she talking about dreams?*

The old woman—Red Herb Woman, as he learned her name was— spent weeks with him, teaching him the language of the People. Ali tried in exchange to teach her English or Arabic but, convinced that Ali was some sort of spirit, she refused. "Spirit words are for spirits," she insisted.

Day in and day out she taught him the words and ways of the People. Numbers and animals and colors and moods. Actions and plants and sizes. For a full month, she taught him. Ali had mostly hated school as a kid, but this was about as different as different got. Red Herb Woman showed no sign of pleasure or displeasure at Ali's progress or lack of it, responding to success and failure alike by sitting there smoking something sour-smelling from a little clay pipe.

One day, without warning, as the smoke plumed and writhed around her, Red Herb Woman pulled out her little pouch of purple dye and put another thumbprint on Ali's chest.

"Yeah," she said. "You ready."

"Ready for what?"

"To see the People's Camp. To meet Biggest Woman."

In prison, Ali found God. Or God found him. Prison gives you a lot of time to think. Sometimes it gives you nothing to do but think. And Ali thought. A tiny child—the boy's name was Christopher, Ali later learned—had been murdered. And while Ali hadn't killed the boy, neither were his monstrous hands clean. He was shaken. Shunned as a babykiller by everyone except the Muslim brothers who believed his story, Ali began really reading the Qur'an for the first time in his life, and attending Friday prayers with other prisoners.

Friday was the only day of the week that Ali had been allowed in gen pop. As one of the prison's half-dozen wild card inmates, he had spent most of his time in EnhanceMax. It took him two run-ins with the power-armored guards and their shock cannons there for Ali to figure out that he couldn't punch his way out of this one.

In the camp—a bustling collection of lean-tos and hill caves built among three hillocks—the People, perhaps a hundred of them, surrounded Ali, chanting. He'd learned a lot of their language over the past few months, but he had no idea what they were saying now.

The ring of people parted and a huge figure wearing beaded suede and carrying a massive spear strode forth. She was taller than the tallest man there, well over six feet. Her long, matted black hair was tied back with a series of leather bands. No one he knew would've called that rough, scarred face pretty, but her eyes were like dark lightning and she smelled like a river and fresh sweat, and Ali was hypnotized.

Good enforcers develop an intuitive sense of pecking order. Knowing who can be fucked with and who can't be fucked with had been an important part of Ali's trade. In all of his dealings with the People so far, Ali knew he was being deferred to, whether out of fear or respect. He could practically smell it in the air when he walked among the People.

With this woman there wasn't even a hint of that.

Biggest Woman looked him in the eye, then she looked him up and down and snorted a half laugh to herself, though Ali had no idea why.

"What word for you?" she asked.

It took Ali a moment to understand. *She wants to know my name.* "Ali," he said. The word felt weird in his mouth, as if he'd never introduced himself to another person before.

"Ah-lee," she repeated. She pronounced it just as he had, the Arabic way. The right way. His pulse raced faster. "What you, Ah-lee?"

"Huh?"

"You spirit?" Biggest Woman looked skeptical.

"No! No spirit. Me no spirit." It had taken Red Herb Woman days to teach Ali this word, but it had been an important one to her.

"You man?"

"Yes. Man. Me man. Me *a* man."

Biggest Woman nodded to herself, as if confirming something. "You help the People? Kill bear? Break wood? Move big stones?"

Over the past few months, Ali had, sometimes quietly, sometimes not so quietly, done these things for the People. "Yes. Bear. Trees. Big stone," he said.

This time Biggest Woman smiled, and Ali felt like a schoolkid who'd never kissed a girl. "Ah-lee," she said again. "You good. We talk."

He never returned to the hunters' shelter after that. The People fashioned him a new shelter, dug out of a hillock that sat a few hundred yards from the edge of their camp. Ali learned that they had several of these semi-permanent camps that they migrated between, depending on the season and the movements of the deer.

Over time he learned more and more of the People. Their ways, their rules, their foods, their songs. The seasons changed and the tasks he did for the People changed. He was hired muscle again. But everything Ali did here brought life, not death. That was something, he figured. Maybe something big.

And then one night he was called to join the People.

Red Herb Woman spoke at the ceremony, and Ali could actually make out most of her words now. "He came when rainbow light shone in sky. He was sent by the People Who Were Here Before to help us. He is Strong Scarred One, who was seen in the Dream. My father gave me the Dream, and his mother gave him the Dream, and her father gave her the Dream. The Dream has been told to the People. The People know the Dream."

"The People know the Dream," everyone but Ali said.

Rainbow light. Ali's mind went back to the card game in Chicago. It had been more than a year ago, he realized with a shock. When everything went to shit at the game, reality seeming to warp around him, he had seen a flash of rainbow light before blacking out. *She's talking about whatever weird shit brought me here,* Ali realized. *They saw the rainbow light when it happened.*

Then Red Herb Woman stepped aside and Biggest Woman stepped into the circle. She gestured to Ali and it took him a moment to realize she wanted him to kneel.

He knelt, and she produced a pale stone knife. Its blade was caked with dried blood. Ali had stayed alive for years only by reacting very quickly when anyone pointed a weapon at him, and he had to smother his instincts as Biggest Woman brought the knife-tip to his forehead. Slowly, deliberately, she cut three short vertical lines in his skin. As she did so, she chanted. "You are not a child," she intoned, "and you are not an enemy. We name you Meat-Man. We name you the Strongest of the People."

Wait. What? They . . . they want me to lead them? Ali had to stop this before it started. "Me not good for Chieftain . . ." he started to say.

Biggest Woman lost her ceremoniousness and looked at him as if he'd lost his mind. Then she cut him off with a loud, derisive laugh. Ali thought the sound was beautiful. "Chieftain? *Chieftain?* You not be Chieftain!" She laughed again "Me Chieftain. You *Strongest,* not Chieftain. Stronger than a man. Know less than a child." She laughed again, and the People laughed with her.

For a moment Ali felt his old, easy anger. He looked at the faces around him and saw mirth, not mockery. He began to laugh louder than any of them.

"Yeah," he said in English, "fair enough." As a kid he'd seen some movie where this brainy white guy woke in the ancient past and taught the people about all sorts of modern inventions. Ali wished he could do that. He didn't know how to make gunpowder or penicillin. But he knew how to pick up heavy shit and how to hit things. Hard. And these people needed that.

The People needed him.

Ali spent six long years in prison. He got an hour of yard time every day unless some shithead CO arbitrarily decided to deny it. He prayed five times a day and paced his cell and read year-old magazines with holes cut in them. More than once Ali listened to one man cry while being raped by another man. Prison nearly killed him.

Then a federal organized crime case brought to light the fact that Ali hadn't killed that little boy. He was cleared of the murder. His remaining charges were chalked up to time served.

When Ali got out of prison, they put him on a bus and dumped him onto Michigan Avenue like an unwanted dog left in the woods. He avoided his old crowd, using his meat-and-metal to work construction or security or whatever he could find. Since getting out of prison he'd been a bouncer, a builder, even a motherfucking stock boy. None of it had stuck. Ali stopped praying regularly. Turned out it was a lot harder to talk to God on the outside than it was in prison.

Warm water flowed down Ali's back, and he felt himself relax. The Bathing Place was a few hours' walk from the main camp, a huge pool of melting snow heated by some sort of underground . . . hot spring? Geyser? Ali didn't know what to call the Bathing Place. Even after a few years here among the People, he was still a city boy.

The People had taught him to wash himself off every day as they did—water from a jug, big flat leaves, rough yarn cloth. But this was different. At the Bathing Place you got *clean*. Ali stood waist-deep in the warm, frothy water and focused on his breathing. He felt long-knotted muscles unkink.

The place was normally more crowded, a handful of the People there at any given time. But Ali found himself alone now, as the sun began to sink in the sky. He dunked his head and felt the warm water run through his shaggy hair and his beard.

Then someone burst through the reeds and made their way to the edge of the water. It was Biggest Woman. All of Ali's tension returned.

Ali had grown used to being naked more often among the People, who didn't always wear a lot of clothes. But that didn't stop him from being mortifyingly aware that his dick was hanging out in the water.

"I sorry. I *am* sorry," Ali said. "I not know you be coming here." Ali had gotten better at the language, but he still had a ways to go. "I not know you be coming here," he said again. "I go." He had learned enough of the People's ways and their pecking order to know that this was what he was supposed to do. *I think.*

"You didn't know I would be here," Biggest Woman said, "but I knew you would be here." She set her spear by the edge of the pool, took off her suedes and woven things, and joined him in the water.

Even in this warm water, Ali felt his face flush with heat. He hoped to God that the frothy water hid the fact that he had a boner. He'd been bad at talking to women even as a teenager. Then his card had turned and . . . well, he'd spent a lot of years alone.

"Did you have children in your Other Land, Ah-lee?" The others all called him Meat-Man or Strongest. Biggest Woman was the only one who called him by his old name. It seemed to amuse her.

"I . . . ah. Other Land," he stammered. He stopped listening to his body and focused on her words. More than once, he'd tried to explain to the People how he'd gotten there, when and where he came from. But though he blamed *someone* at the card game he'd been working, he himself didn't know exactly how he'd ended up there. He'd settled on saying he came from a faraway Other Land, and gave up on trying to describe it. "No small people," he said at last. "Er, no *children.*"

She looked surprised. "You are strong and you are good," Biggest Woman said, striding closer to him in the water. "Not so smart, but not all of the People can be smart."

"I—"

"You should make children, Ah-lee Meat-Man."

"I—" Ratcatcher and Basket Weaver and some of the other men had been teasing Ali for weeks that Biggest Woman, whose son had died last year, had her eye on him to father her next child. But Ali hadn't believed it for a second. Until now.

"You should make children with me, Ah-lee," she said matter-of-factly. Biggest Woman stared at him with those black, electric eyes and Ali felt like someone had thrown a switch within him. She drew herself up and now her tone was almost ceremonial. "I am Biggest Woman, Chieftain. Do you choose to make children with me, Meat-Man Strongest Man?"

Ali looked at his big meat-block hands, then looked up at her. "Yes." The word hung in the damp, florid air, the answer to a question Ali felt had been asked years before this day.

He started to say more, but then Biggest Woman kissed him. She nuzzled her face into his neck and he felt her scars and pockmarks scratch his skin. She took hold of his dick beneath the warm water and they both laughed happily. He smelled her sweat and he put his mouth on her. They pressed their bodies together. Birds screamed in the trees and the setting sun painted the sky with fire.

After months of drifting broke and half-broken through the minefield of ex-con life, Ali got a job offer through an old crony. The guy was shady, turned straight only because he could make more money off casinos than he could off running numbers, but the money was good. A high-stakes card game was in the works and one of the players wanted a big guy to stand behind him and look ugly. And holy shit it turned out the player was none other than "Hustlin'" Charlie Flowers.

Ali could admit to himself, if he wouldn't to anyone else, that he had been excited. *Charlie Fucking Flowers!* But the guy had turned out to be exactly as sleazy and pathetic as the TV jokes made him out to be. And once again Ali found himself standing there using his big, scary-looking fists to make money for a boss who didn't deserve it.

Such tiny hands. It should be impossible.

It was a warm evening but blissfully few insects were out. The air was sweet and the moon shone above like the radiant face of God. Ali looked down at his daughter, only an hour old, nestled in the thick warm meat of his massive palm.

They'd tried. For three cycles of seasons he and Biggest Woman had tried to make a baby. Fucking when Red Herb Woman told them the time was right. Fucking in the positions she dictated. Eating fish livers. Drinking bark teas. But no baby had come. Biggest Woman had told him that she'd had another child years ago, a boy who'd died before he'd learned to walk. So Ali figured the problem had to be with his own junk. Was it just bad luck? Was his wild card to blame? Had time travel fried his sperm?

He began praying again.

And then, a few months ago, Biggest Woman had told him that she was pregnant. With, according to Red Herb Woman, a girl. Ali wasn't stupid enough to think his prayers had done this, but he thanked God all the same. Ali had wanted to name the child Wafa, after his sister. But Biggest Woman, scandalized, had informed him that Biggest Woman's Second was the only acceptable name for her second child. Ali hadn't argued.

Now Ali was holding her—holding Second—in his hands, and looking down into her tiny eyes he could feel God's presence for the first time in years.

Behind him, someone was approaching. Ali's neck muscles tensed the way they had back when he was an enforcer and something was about to pop off.

He smelled the smoke from Red Herb Woman's pipe before he heard her reedy voice.

"Strongest!"

Ali turned slowly, still cradling Biggest Woman's Second.

"Biggest Woman—she is well?" he asked. "Can I speak to her?"

Red Herb Woman's face was grim. "The child didn't come into the world easily. Biggest Woman lost much blood. She can barely speak right now. In time she will heal. But the People have a bigger problem. Come."

An hour later Ali was on the hunters' path a few miles outside the camp, standing over the bloody bodies of Basket Weaver and five more of the People. Each of them had had his right hand chopped off. Messily.

It wasn't the worst hit job Ali had ever seen. But it was a scene from a life he'd thought was over. A life he'd thanked God was over. *I shoulda fucking known better.*

"The Screamers did this," Red Herb Woman said. Ali had heard the People speak in fearful tones of this other tribe before—their brutality, their skill in battle, the war cry that gave them their name. Red Herb Woman picked something out of her teeth and spat. "This is a message. If we don't leave these lands they will kill us all."

"Fuck that," Ali said in English. Basket Weaver had been so kind to him from the beginning. "Let them come and fucking try it."

Red Herb Woman looked at him as if she got the gist. "You could kill them all. But if they come in numbers to the camp they will kill many of the People first." She puffed and shrugged and exhaled a huge cloud of sour-smelling smoke. "You can still catch their killing-party. The ones who were sent to do this. They came to send a message. Send them back to the Screamers' camp with a message."

Ali found them hours later, a dozen men with painted faces and severed hands on leather cords around their necks. They were making camp beside the river.

It was a slaughter.

He announced his presence by screaming and throwing a boulder into the camp. Then he burst into full view of the warriors, forcing the meat-and-metal to pop out all over his body. A few of them fled right away, shouting, "Spirit! Spirit!" To their credit, the rest of them stood firm. The Screamers were a bold people. Most of these men, Ali thought sadly, would die for it.

He seized one man by the face and hurled him fifty yards away, where he hit the ground with a crunch. He hoisted two others, smashing them together like cymbals until they were pulp. He ripped up a tree and beat another man to jelly.

These were things Ali had done before. Things he never thought he would have to do again. Bile burned in his throat but he kept himself from vomiting.

He left two living men standing there among the bloody wreckage of human bodies. "Tell the Screamers!" Ali shouted, pointing at the dead and dying around him. "Tell them their spears and knives can't cut me. Tell them I protect the People. Tell them to stay away from the People's Camp!"

The two men fled. One of them was crying.

Ali wiped the blood and brains from his hands, turned his back on the dead, and went home to hold his daughter.

They'd ridden in a limo to the card game. Mr. Flowers, Ali, and Mr. Flowers's weirdo kid nephew Timmy, a junior high geek who had what Ali suspected was birdshit on his shoulders. *Part of the freaks and losers crowd as usual,* Ali remembered thinking.

When they arrived at the card game, it was hard for Ali not to stand there staring like an asshole. He'd been around huge piles of street money before, but the Palmer House was on a whole other level. The wood. The marble. The silverware. This was real money. Rich-people money. Even the air smelled different. And while he'd been hyped at the thought of working for B-list disgraced celeb Charlie Flowers, the room at that poker game was filled with *real* names.

Golden Boy! Motherfucking *Golden Boy* was there. Ali *had* stared like an asshole at that, until Mr. Flowers nudged him to keep moving.

Giovanni Galante, whose family name still rang out loud on the streets of Chicago and beyond, was there, flanked by ace muscle. There was an Arab guy there, too, some Prince Bigshit Something or Other from the Gulf who spoke a form of Arabic Ali barely understood. He had nodded at Ali and smiled, then proceeded to ignore him.

After a few hours, at Mr. Flowers's insistence, Ali allowed himself to sit. Then everything went to shit.

"Fucking ants. They're going to get into the food." Ali smashed another, then another, then another. It was no use.

"I know you're mad, Poppa, because you're talking your Other Land talk." Ali looked up from his fruitless task to see his daughter approaching.

My daughter. How many years had it been now? Yet sometimes it still stunned him to say it to himself.

Second came up and took his wrist, pulling him out of the shelter. "Poppa, look! Look, I said! I've been working on something."

Several little six-inch-deep pits the size of saucers formed a sort of semicircle perimeter around the entrance to the cave. Each was writhing with ants.

"See, I put a bit of fruit in each pit and the ants swarm to it. Instead of coming and taking our food, they stay out here and fight over this. It only takes a few pieces."

Ali looked down at the child, and he felt something inside. *Pride,* he supposed. *I guess this is what it feels like to be proud of the life you've made.*

Biggest Woman approached, peered into the ant-pits, and nodded. "This is a good thing you've made, Second," she said. "Good enough, I think, to earn your name."

Second let out a happy yelp. Biggest Woman came to stand beside Ali. She kissed his shoulder, then put her arms around him.

Ali thought that this might be what it felt like to be happy.

The game at the Palmer had been going for hours when all hell broke loose.

Giovanni Galante had proven himself to be a miserable little shit unworthy of his family's name. He reminded Ali of Jason, the dipshit gangster's grandson who'd murdered a kid and got Ali sent to prison for it. Even his facial expressions were the same. The resemblance was so strong that Ali had to restrain himself from throttling the fool. The tiger-faced motherfucker flanking Galante had seemed to sense this, and tensed.

But the real trouble had come when Giovanni slapped the teen girl working the bar. All of a sudden the bellhop had leapt at Galante. The girl next to Galante started shooting out flames. Ali had shoved Timmy and Mr. Flowers behind him, throwing up his fists as a shield.

Then there was a burst of rainbow light. And Ali had ended up here. And once he had thought it important to get back. *But who the fuck wants to go back? I'm home now.*

Ali was sitting scraping hides with Biggest Woman when Ratcatcher, the People's most keen-eyed scout, hurried over to them. He looked worried. Ratcatcher nodded a greeting to Ali, then turned to report to Biggest Woman. "You need to see this," he said. "Meat-Man should come, too. Right now, Chieftain of the People."

Minutes later they were halfway up the glacier that loomed over the Bowl, the People's springtime camp. Ratcatcher pointed at a huge shelf of ice, fifty yards long, full of cracks and fissures.

Biggest Woman grunted. "The ice is melting. Falling. There's going to be a landslide. We've got to leave the Bowl." She turned to Ratcatcher. "Tell the People to prepare. Step carefully." She didn't look worried. She never looked worried. Always their Chieftain.

Ratcatcher picked his way carefully back down the slope, and Ali was alone with his wife. "Should we—" he started to say, and then the ground below them rumbled.

There was a noise like thundercrack and a bomb smashed together, and Ali jumped in spite of himself. Biggest Woman didn't. She grabbed his arm and gestured for him to be still. As one, they turned their heads and looked farther up the hill. The massive shelf of ice, crusted with rock and dirt and branches, had broken loose from the glacier. It was half a football field long and it was sliding, an inch at a time, toward them.

Toward the camp.

The Bowl—fertile, hidden from view, cave-riddled—had been a good choice for the camp this season. The ice hadn't looked threatening. Ali had seen a dozen melting seasons with the People, but ice was melting now faster than it had before. Something was changing.

No time to think about that now. If the ice-shelf kept moving like this it would crush the camp and all within it like a mortar smashing herbs in a pestle. Even if all of the People got out, they'd starve without the tools and food.

"Warn the People!" Ali said. "Get everyone out of here!"

Biggest Woman didn't object that *she* was Chieftain, and somehow that frightened Ali. She brought her hard mouth to Ali's and kissed him. She stared at him for a moment and then scrambled swiftly but carefully down into the Bowl.

There was another deafening crack, and the ice-shelf began to slide faster.

"Run!" Ali shouted, and he turned to stop an avalanche.

He trotted up to the ice-shelf, braced himself, and shoved. It pushed him hard, and he began to slide backwards, but he kept from being bowled over.

No. No no no no no. Fuck this. You don't get to do this to me, God. You don't get to take this from me. Not this time. Ali risked a glance behind and below him and saw Biggest Woman and Second and the rest of the People scurrying for safety. The shelf of ice shoved him back and he turned back to it. He slid backwards, a foot every second.

Ali got mad. Madder than he'd ever been. Mad at God. The hook burst out, the meat covered him thicker than it ever had before. He felt new strength fill him. He heaved and shoved and scrabbled his feet forward and the ice-shelf almost stopped shifting. But it wasn't enough.

The sheet of ice groaned and shifted again. Stinging bits of snow and dirt flew loose and got into Ali's eyes. Ali screamed and raged and the meat covered his eyes and he was nothing but meat-and-metal and fury.

He heaved, putting the last of his life into it. *"MOTHERFUCK-ERRRRR!"* he screamed. Then the snow covered him.

When Ali woke, the first thing he saw as he blinked his eyes open was Second's small round face hovering over his. "S-Second." He coughed, his lungs burning with cold.

She threw her arms around his neck and hugged him before correcting him. "*Ant Trapper,* Poppa!"

"Yes, Ant T—" He coughed again, loudly enough to frighten Second.

And then, suddenly, Biggest Woman was there. Tears shone in her eyes. "You're alive," she said. Second—*Ant Trapper*—ran to her mother.

"What happened?"

Biggest Woman took his big meaty hand in hers. "You saved the People, that's what happened. You held it long enough. We dug you out. I . . . I thought you were dead."

A few hours later, after some broth and a nap, Ali felt strong enough to stagger out and greet the People.

All of the People—all ten-tens-and-twenty of them—stopped what they were doing. As one, they rushed over and began chanting. It took Ali a moment to realize what they were chanting.

"*MOTHERFUCKER!*" they shouted, hoisting spears and tools and firebrands. "*MOTHERFUCKER! MOTHERFUCKER! MOTHER-FUCKER! MOTHERFUCKER!*"

Ali laughed and laughed and knew he was home.

The next night, Ali sat at the High Place with Biggest Woman and Ant Trapper. They chewed sweetroot and stared out over the land at the sinking sun. Ali thought that he could die in this place and time and be happy.

Then far away, across the forest, he saw a bright shimmer of rainbow light.

A Long Night at
the Palmer House

Part 9

NIGHTHAWK TOOK A DEEP breath and looked around. They were in a small clearing in a forest that consisted almost entirely of pine trees set on a sloping mountainside. The sun was a big red ball, clear and sharp-edged, sitting on the lip of the horizon. The air was cool on their naked skin, but pleasantly so.

"I grew up in the country," he told Croyd. "It never smelled like this."

Croyd nodded. "I know what you mean. It's so . . . fresh. The air's so crisp that everything has an edge to it. Even the sunset seems cleaner. I mean, back when we were with the dinosaurs it was so muggy that I could barely breathe. But now I feel like we're in an air-freshener commercial. It's like we're the only people in the world."

"That's not quite correct," Nighthawk said, gesturing downslope to the rolling flatland. It was more open than the forest that surrounded them, though there were scattered copses of trees as well as a meandering line of them following a stream or small river.

Croyd looked to where Nighthawk was pointing. Near a bend in the stream a plume of smoke was slowly ascending into the darkening sky.

"Fire," Croyd said.

"And where there's fire . . ."

Croyd sighed. "You know what I miss the most when we time jump?"

"What?"

"Shoes."

"You got that right," Nighthawk said, and they began slowly picking their way downhill.

Things went a little easier on their feet once they reached the flood-plain, but both were limping on bruised soles by then. Croyd was muttering a stream of steady curses and Nighthawk's mood wasn't much better.

"At least," Nighthawk said at one point when they were resting on a grassy bank as dawn was breaking over the fresh and unspoiled land, "our list is getting short."

Croyd grunted. "Cynder, Galante, and that Meathooks guy," he said. "None of them exactly softies."

Nighthawk looked around. "Beautiful scenery, but not much else." He stood up. "Though we should be prepared for the possibility that they might not be alone."

"I'm more worried about hypothermia than cavemen," said Croyd. "If we find Alley Oop, I want that fur dress of his."

"I don't think you'll need it." Nighthawk sat down again on the grassy bank. "Looks like the locals are coming to meet us."

Croyd shaded his eyes, looking across the plain where Nighthawk had noticed distant figures approaching, rippling the waist-high grass through which they walked. There were maybe a dozen altogether. As they approached, Nighthawk and Croyd could see that they were a small, brown-skinned people. They carried long sticks. *Probably spears.* Except for the two walking side by side in the lead. One, they gradually realized, was a tall woman. The other figure, even bigger, was Meathooks himself, Charlie Flowers's bodyguard.

Once they got close enough Nighthawk could see that the woman had an expression that seemed mainly curious on her scarred face, while Ali's showed something between wariness and concern.

The men accompanying them fanned out on either side, content to let those two take the lead. Croyd leaped to his feet, smiling. "Hello, Meathooks," he said. "Remember us?"

The pair approached to within half a dozen feet. The woman carried a spear, holding it casually at ease. Meathooks was empty-handed, but Nighthawk knew he had no need of a weapon. His body grew them at will. The two seemed comfortable with each other. Nighthawk wondered if they were a couple.

For a moment the bodyguard was silent, then he shook his head. "It's been years since I've heard English," he said. His tongue almost seemed to stumble over some of the words, hesitant of their pronunciation.

"Sorry about that," Croyd said. "We got to you as soon as possible. The fact that you ended up so far back in time made our jump a little less precise than I'd like."

That, Nighthawk thought, *and the whole speeding thing.* Though that, he allowed, was better than the alternative. If Croyd ever fell asleep, they'd be totally screwed. The odds of him having time-travel powers when he awoke months later were slim indeed. Croyd was perhaps an imperfect tool, but he was the only one Nighthawk had to work with.

"What do you want?" Meathooks asked.

Nighthawk had a sudden sinking feeling at the bodyguard's words. "Why, we're your ticket home," Croyd said.

There was a sudden, awkward silence. The woman spoke a few words in a surprisingly mellifluous language.

Meathooks listened, his face unchanging. "This is Biggest Woman," he said when she was done. "She's . . ." He paused a moment, as if uncertain how to go on. "My wife. She wants to know if all the other men from my land are as small and skinny as you two."

"Hey, man," Croyd said, "those specimens who came along with you aren't all exactly Golden Boy either."

Meathooks held up his strange-looking hands almost placatingly. "I know. She just expected that the men from my land would be like me."

Croyd's eyes crinkled as he frowned. Nighthawk could see the danger in them. "We're all aces here," the Sleeper said softly.

Of course Biggest Woman couldn't understand his words, but she could hear their intent. She shifted her stance and held her spear in a ready manner.

Nighthawk said, "Easy," in as soothing a tone as he could manage. "We came a long way to find you. To help you and take you home."

Ali's eyes shifted to him. "This is my home. I—we have a child. These people need me. I've found"—he paused a moment, thinking— "my purpose here. My peace."

Croyd sighed. "Well, damn, John."

"It's not that simple," Nighthawk said tightly. "We have the time line to consider—"

"We're thousands of years in the past," Croyd said. He gestured at Meathooks. "This guy is like a pebble tossed into the ocean." He looked at the bodyguard. "No offense."

Meathooks grunted.

"He's introducing the wild card into the human gene pool thousands of years before the Takisians unleashed it on earth," Nighthawk said.

Croyd was unmoved. "Maybe so. Big deal. There have always been stories. You know, myths and legends of shit that happened in the past. Heroes and monsters. Maybe a couple of times his genes met and crossed and produced, I don't know, Hercules, or Leonardo da Vinci, or something. What if that's what happened?"

Nighthawk shut his mouth. Croyd had a point, he thought, but the Sleeper was getting sloppy and impatient to be done. Maybe he just didn't give a damn anymore. He eyed Meathooks dubiously. If the bodyguard didn't want to come along, was he going to force him?

Nighthawk wasn't a praying man, but it almost seemed that that was what the situation called for. *Please, God,* he thought to himself. *Help us get this right.*

"Christ, John, the man's found something here. We already fucked up Julie Cotton's life. You made Khan shoot all those mob motherfuckers. What's the big deal if we leave him? Are we going to return and find mammoths on Michigan Avenue?"

"The butterfly effect—"

"Yeah, yeah, I know. Asimov, Heinlein, who gives a damn? I read the story. Guy steps on a butterfly and when he returns to the present there's a new president. A terrible president. Well, we've already *got* a terrible president."

Nighthawk looked at Meathooks, whose expression was as stoic as ever. He looked at Biggest Woman and their eyes met. God knew she wasn't his idea of heaven, but he'd found his once, and lost it. How could he take that away from another man? "You'd better be right," he finally said in a low voice. "If not—"

"If things are still fucked up after we round up everyone else," Croyd promised, "we can always come back again."

Nighthawk wasn't sure if Meathooks was following everything they were saying—hell, he wasn't sure if he was, himself—but he looked at him, and nodded. For the first time Ali's features relaxed, and he nodded back.

"Great, that's settled," Croyd said. He looked around. "Now, I don't suppose you've invented the mirror since you've been back here."

"No," said Meathooks.

"Any reflective surface will do," said Nighthawk.

Ali snorted. "We have ponds."

A Long Night at
the Palmer House

Part 10

"I DON'T LIKE FLYING BLIND," Croyd said hesitantly.

"Not much we can do about it," Nighthawk replied. It was the best he could come up with to bolster Croyd's flagging spirits. There'd been a definite lack of amphetamines in the Ice Age and while that calmed Croyd down a little, his energy levels were sinking fast. Thankfully they were at the end of their list, with only two names to go. Croyd could feel only one blip on the radar screen of his mind, so that probably meant that both were in a single location, unless one had died and their corpse had been punted somewhere into the time stream.

They had a long way to travel to come back. Nothing like their jaunt across millions of years to the time of the dinosaurs, but Croyd had been fresh for that jump, in complete control of his powers. Nighthawk could see that he was now badly in need of sleep and/or artificial stimuli, neither of which was possible.

"One thing for sure," Nighthawk added in an attempt to cheer him up. "Unless we arrive in the dead of winter, it's gotta be warmer there than here."

The spasms unleashed by Croyd's temporal powers took hold— Nighthawk would never get used to that—and seemed to go on for an uncountably long time. He was on the verge of useless panic when he felt warm, soft grass on the soles of his naked feet, a warm breeze caressing his naked body. *Christ,* Nighthawk thought, *that feels good.*

He opened his eyes and looked around the open landscape. It was early evening, just past sundown, and by the look of the trees whose leaves were just beginning to turn color, early fall. He turned, looking carefully over the vicinity, hoping to find another care package left for them by their unknown benefactor, but it seemed that this time they were on their own.

Croyd slumped down to the ground on his knees, close to exhaustion. Nighthawk bent over him, as always habitually careful to not use his ungloved left hand. "You all right?" he asked, his right hand on his companion's shoulder.

The Sleeper looked up. "That was a tough one. I don't know how much I have left."

"One more jump, Croyd. That's all, just one more jump."

"Christ," he whispered, shutting his eyes. "I can barely stand. We gotta get some clothes somewhere. We gotta find Galante and Cynder—"

"Well, what do we have here?" a voice suddenly drawled from behind him.

Nighthawk turned. Without his support Croyd fell flat on his face. Nighthawk swore to himself. He was getting tired, too. Tired and careless. He should have heard them coming up behind them.

Five of them, in their teens, roughly dressed in worn and dirty clothing. Nighthawk knew their kind. He'd run into them before in every decade of his long life. *Punks.* The breed didn't change much from one era to the next.

They stood in an arc before them. Most were small and weaselly looking. The one who'd spoken was a big brute, though, with an oft broken nose and really bad teeth that were exposed in an openmouthed grin. They seemed unarmed, but the presence of hidden weapons, knives or clubs of some sort, was more than possible.

"I think we found us some nancys," said the big one.

"Dirty sods, they is," replied the runt on his left.

"Real dirty, with a nigger and all," said the one on his right.

Croyd pulled himself to his knees, groaning. "I knew this would eventually happen."

"I'll take care of it," Nighthawk said.

"Ooooh," the big one said. "Take care of this, nancy." He reached behind his back for a long-bladed knife.

"Fuck this," Croyd said, and suddenly there were four piles of clothes. The last punk on the left gaped and gasped. "I left one for you," the Sleeper said.

"Thanks."

He couldn't be much more than his mid-teens. He was shaking with fright. Though his lips were working, no sound came out. Night-hawk reached out and gripped his right forearm. He could feel tremors of fear ripple through his flesh. He gave him his best hard look, used the deepest tones he could muster when he spoke. "Let this be a lesson to you," he said. "Repent!"

And he sucked a day out of his life.

The kid sagged, would have fallen if Nighthawk wasn't holding his arm. He moaned as a sensation of awful loss swept over him. Tears ran down his cheeks. Nighthawk released his arm and he staggered away, sobbing. After a few steps his pace turned into a ragged run. He never looked back.

"Goddamn," Croyd said, standing and sniffing the air. "First time I've seen the shit scared out of someone, literally."

"Lesson learned, I hope." Nighthawk closed his eyes, feeling strength flow back into him. It was better than a good meal and a long night's sleep. It was a feeling that was all too easy to give in to, a temptation he always had to fight.

The worst thing about their stolen clothes this time around was not their poor fit. It was their smell. The only good thing about sending them off into time—and Croyd in his current state wasn't ex-actly sure when he'd sent them—was that it also took their fleas, lice, and other verminous hangers-on with them. The punks had lost their knives as well as their long johns when Croyd dispatched them, but none of them had left any money behind.

As they strode through the early evening, Nighthawk realized where they were.

"We're in Lincoln Park," he told Croyd. Fortunately, their encounter with the nineteenth-century delinquents had taken place in an isolated corner of the preserve, probably where they frequently prowled for privacy, seeking couples whom they could prey on.

"What, again?" Croyd looked around. "Less crowded than last time."

"Yeah." It was still warm, with a hot wind blowing. They passed a bench, with a folded newspaper stuck between the wooden slats of its seat.

"Hang on a minute." Nighthawk went over to the bench, Croyd following him. He picked up the paper, turned it back to the front page.

"What's the matter?" Croyd asked at the sudden look on Nighthawk's face.

"Find out what the time is," Nighthawk said presumptively.

Croyd muttered to himself as he approached a strolling couple. "Excuse me, sir," he asked politely. "Can you tell me the time?"

The man seemed suspicious of Croyd's appearance, but nevertheless he stopped and warily consulted his big, silver-cased pocket watch. "A quarter after seven."

Croyd tipped an imaginary hat. "Thank you, sir."

"God," Nighthawk said. "We've got less than two hours."

"Two hours for what?"

"The date," he said, pointing to the typeface.

"October 8, 1871," Croyd read. "So?"

"We've cut it real close this time. Maybe too close." Memories he'd intentionally buried almost a hundred and fifty years ago raced to the surface of his mind. He had no need to consult his memory palace. These recollections were too raw, too painful, to fade away. *What to do?* he frantically asked himself. *What can I do?*

"John?"

Nighthawk looked at Croyd, and said tonelessly, "The Great Chicago

Fire will start at about nine o'clock tonight. Less than two hours from now."

"Holy crap!"

"It'll destroy almost four square miles of the city and leave a hundred thousand people homeless." *And,* Nighthawk thought, *destroy my life. Unless I change things.*

"And—we can't stop it, can we?" Croyd asked. "I mean, that would alter almost everything."

Nighthawk wanted to tell him, *Yes, let's stop it*—but that would make him the worst type of hypocrite. He said, "And there's Galante and Cynder to consider. How can we find them?" *Before my entire world burns.*

"I don't know," Croyd said. "I can feel a presence, maybe a strong one. It may be both of them, somewhere south of here. But you know I can't focus too finely. Someone out of time is out there and it's got to be them. But exactly where?"

Nighthawk closed his mind and concentrated fiercely. If he ever needed one of his visions, this was the time. He thought so fiercely that he could feel his pulse throb, he could feel his muscles tense like cords of steel throughout his body.

Think, he told himself fiercely, *goddamnit, think!*

But that was not the way it worked. He couldn't try to force his visions to come to him. He had to open himself to them. He had to be ready to accept them. He took a deep breath, forcing himself to relax. He felt the night air on his face, the scratchy material of his rough clothes against his skin, the very pressure of the Earth binding him to its surface. He opened his eyes and he could see nothing. He heard Croyd make vague sounds, as if he were speaking, but they meant nothing to him. Nighthawk let his mind loose, seeking, and somewhere he found it.

Heat. It was hot. Sweat sprang up on his forehead and ran in rivulets down his face as he felt the flames all around him, burning, burning everything in sight. An incendiary Armageddon was sweeping across the world, destroying everything in its path, leaping across rivers and enfolding everything in its greedily hungry grip.

"The Fire," he said suddenly. "It's all got to do with the Fire."

"You sure, John?" Croyd asked dubiously.

"You said they were south of here?"

"As best as I can tell, but—"

"The Fire started south of here and leaped across the Chicago River and roared north through the city, burning all night." Nighthawk nodded. "It's all got to be connected, somehow."

Croyd was doubtful. "I don't know. Seems kind of flimsy to me."

Nighthawk felt sudden, unaccountable anger. "Do you have anything better to go on?"

"Well . . . no."

"We should take a cab," Nighthawk said. "But we don't have any damn money and we can't take the chance of trying to hijack one and getting stopped by the law. Come on."

He started to jog, and after a moment Croyd followed him.

They headed south, exiting the park at Fullerton, found a major cross street heading south, and ran down it, ignoring the glances of curious strollers moving at a more sedate pace. They came to where the Chicago River forked east and north. "You know where you're going," a huffing Croyd said as they crossed the east fork in the pedestrian lane of the nearest bridge.

"Everyone knows where the Chicago Fire started. Mrs. O'Leary's barn."

"I thought . . . thought that was . . . a myth," Croyd rasped.

Nighthawk just shook his head, saving his breath.

No one really knew what caused the Great Chicago Fire, but they sure as hell figured out where it began to burn. He turned west at the first street corner they came to.

The city was becoming sparser, much less densely built, particularly after they crossed the Chicago River again at its main fork, taking the first rickety wooden bridge they came upon. They were on the west side now, though still within city boundaries. The landscape took on a more countrified look. There were no imposing buildings, no paved streets. It was almost like a suburb, if suburbs consisted of rickety wooden houses with accompanying barns, hog pens, and sprawling vegetable gardens.

"Hold up," Croyd wheezed. "I've got a stitch."

Nighthawk eased his pace, and they slowly got their breath back. Croyd, especially, was shaky. He staggered forward a few steps, his legs gone rubbery.

"Good thing we're almost there." Nighthawk indicated a minor street that was more path than thoroughfare. It was unpaved and a sluggish, shallow stream meandered in a slight depression adjacent to it. As they made their way cautiously along the dirt street, on intermittent sidewalks of wooden slats, they passed small, shabby wooden houses of two or three rooms that looked as if they'd been thrown together with little planning, let alone style or grace.

The houses were interspersed between empty patches of land, some fenced with wooden poles and barbed wire into pasturage, others planted as truck gardens. Outbuildings, privies, barns, storage sheds, chicken coops were all scattered almost randomly across the sprawling landscape. "Welcome to urban living, 1871 style," Croyd said.

"Better than crowded tenements," Nighthawk said.

"Not much. It also smells like cowshit. Or horseshit. Or some kind of shit." Croyd suddenly stopped and clutched Nighthawk's arm. "Hold it," he said.

They paused before a haphazardly built two- or three-room structure that had a section of wooden sidewalk before it, bordering the margin of the meandering, garbage-choked stream.

"This it?" Nighthawk asked tensely.

"Close."

They picked their way carefully to the backyard, where a barn almost the same size as the house stood, along with a smaller structure, a single-room cottage that was so close to the barn that its rear wall almost touched one of the barn's sides.

"The legend about the cause of the Great Chicago Fire," Nighthawk said, "it supposedly started in a barn when Mrs. O'Leary's cow kicked over a lantern."

"So . . ." Croyd's voice dwindled into silence.

"The part about the cow was bullshit," Nighthawk said. "Invented by a newspaper reporter who thought it would make a good story. But the Fire did start in or near Mrs. O'Leary's barn."

"Let's just be careful," Croyd suggested.

Carefully they went into the backyard, carefully they approached the cottage, carefully they opened the door a crack, and crowded close together to peer inside.

The single room was more mean than comfortable. It had four items of furniture. A bed without a headboard. A wooden chair. A small vanity table with a mirror, which strangely for such a lower-class dwelling was filled with small containers of perfumes, powders, makeup, and other female accoutrements. Finally, the table had a low, rickety stool before it.

The stool was empty. The bed had a man sleeping in it. The chair was occupied by a young-looking, athletic man who was securely tied to it and gagged.

The cottage had only a single window that let in little light, so the two could discern few details, but it was clear that the young man tied to the chair was terrified. His eyes were nearly bugging out of his skull, his face was strained.

Nighthawk and Croyd exchanged glances, then each pulled out the knife acquired with their clothing. They advanced cautiously into the room. Croyd put a finger to his lips, and the young man nodded vigorously. Nighthawk had the sudden feeling that the fellow looked vaguely familiar. Perhaps he had seen his picture somewhere, as unlikely as that seemed.

Nighthawk stopped at the chair, Croyd went on to the man in the bed.

Up close the youngster seemed scarcely out of his teens. Nighthawk gestured in what he hoped was a soothing manner, clearly showing him the knife, and touching it to the strands of rope that crossed his chest. He started sawing through them as Croyd reached the bed.

The sleeping man was breathing heavily, snoring irregularly but loudly, and was cradling a jug in his arms. Croyd leaned over him and placed the knife gently against his throat. He snorted loudly in his sleep. "Giovanni," Croyd said in a mild, singsong voice. "Giovanni Galante. Wakey, wakey."

Galante snorted loudly again and brushed at his face as if chasing flies away.

"Hey!" Croyd barked. He plucked the jug from Galante's arms and plunked him hard on the forehead with it. "Wake the fuck up!"

Galante snorted even more loudly. Then his eyes flew open, and his whole body twitched as if he meant to jump up out of the bed, but he somehow stopped himself as he felt the pressure on his throat increase.

"Jesus, Galante," Croyd said, "you look terrible."

He did. He was unshaven, his eyes were bloodshot, his tousled hair was greasy. The clothes that he wore were filthier than theirs and he stank of bad tobacco, vile drink, and his own body odor. Nighthawk sawed through some of the ropes binding the young man to the chair and removed his gag.

"Thank God, you saved me, thank God!" he babbled. "They kidnapped me—were going to kill me if the ransom they wanted wasn't paid. They took me right out of my hotel room. I was in town playing with a barnstorming team when they took me—"

"Wait," Nighthawk said. "You're a ballplayer?"

"That's right. I'm Anson. Cap Anson, they call me."

Nighthawk felt the time currents rush over him like a frigid stream. It was impossible.

Cap Anson, nineteen years old at the beginning of his career, went on to become one of the greatest baseball players of the nineteenth century. The first man to accumulate more than three thousand hits in his career, he played for the Chicago White Stockings for two decades and was one of the most important and powerful figures in baseball.

He was also, unfortunately, a virulent racist who was implacably opposed to playing against black players and was a staunch advocate of the color line.

And I'm rescuing him, Nighthawk thought.

Seemingly, in this time line, he'd fallen victim to Galante. Maybe, probably, he was killed. And Anson's absence, along with who knew what other factors, led to the breaking of the color line much earlier than in theirs. *But we're rescuing him—*

Nighthawk kept cutting his bonds. The ballplayer stood shakily, and almost fell. Nighthawk reached out automatically to support him, and as his right hand touched Anson, he could see, even now, the disgust flash across Anson's face.

He had no time to react to it. Suddenly behind him, the cottage door banged open and Nighthawk heard an angry voice call, "They didn't leave the cash, Gio. Kill the bastard. We'll teach them to fear the Black Hand—"

It was Cynder, furious beyond measure. She was better dressed, better groomed, than Galante, but the anger twisting her face turned her countenance demonic. She stood at the cottage threshold, staring, and screamed, *"You!"*

She cocked her arm and Nighthawk dove aside, grabbing Cap Anson and throwing him to the floor a second before the fireball swept over them, close enough for Nighthawk to feel its heat. Behind him, somebody screamed. He hoped it wasn't Croyd. Nighthawk rolled, reached, and grabbed the stool, throwing it in one motion. Cyn, in the process of hurling another fireball, ducked, spoiling her aim. It hit the wall above the vanity and the dry wood burst into flame as the stool smacked Cyn in the side of the head, sending her tumbling to the floor.

Anson was already on his feet. Choosing discretion over valor, he was out the door as flames danced over the cottage walls. Nighthawk hurled himself on Cynder as she tried to get to her feet. They fell to the floor together, rolling. She was cursing and spitting at him. He grabbed her wrists and pinned them to the floor. She bucked like a madwoman, but he held her down and began to drink.

He drained her like a bottle of fine wine and her life felt good coursing through his body. He felt stronger, younger. She looked at him, terror in her eyes.

"What are you doing to me?" she asked in a small voice, but he said nothing, just drank deep.

As she weakened, Nighthawk risked a backwards glance. The bed was ablaze, with Galante on it. He screamed terrifyingly, and leaped to his feet like a flaming torch. He danced between Nighthawk and Croyd, waving his arms like a scarecrow ablaze.

"John!" Croyd reached out, but a wall of flame already separated them. Croyd was trapped in the rear of the cottage. Nighthawk knew that he had to act quickly. He suddenly knew what he had to do. The heat was overpowering as the cottage burned. Croyd made a last gesture in Nighthawk's direction, then he bounced a flash of temporal energy off the mirror, and was gone.

Galante had stopped screaming and collapsed to the floor. He was blazing like a witch tied to a stake. Cyn had also stopped struggling. Her eyes were open, but unseeing as Nighthawk stood over her wrinkled and shrunken body. He had one chance and he took it. He covered his face with his arms, leaped, and crashed through the one window in the cottage wall, diving through a wall of flame headfirst. He felt it licking at his skin and clothes, then hit the ground and rolled, beating at the sparks dancing on his shirt.

He got up from the ground. The fire had already spread to the barn. It would jump the river and rage throughout the city. But maybe he could outrun it.

He ran back to the street, such as it was, through an open field and the first house that neighbored the O'Learys'. He was young again and he ran like he never had. Like he was running for something even more precious than his life. He passed another field and a house. People were already reacting to the fire, appearing in ones and twos outside their homes, staring with gaping mouths. Nighthawk ran. He ran until his gut was busting and his lungs felt as if they themselves were on fire. It wasn't far, he told himself.

He skidded to a stop before a pasture fenced off by wooden stakes and a couple of strands of barbed wire and unlooped the latch from around the gate, pulling it open. He left it open behind him, giving the livestock inside a chance to run for it before the fire reached them, and picked out a likely-looking horse. He'd been in the cavalry once and fought in Cuba next to Teddy Roosevelt and he knew how to ride. He didn't need a saddle or bridle or reins. He grabbed a handful of mane and vaulted lightly onto the horse's back, he kicked his heels into the horse's side and shouted, rousing the other animals to flee in a stampede before him.

He raced up the street. When they hit paved ground he was able to go faster, across the bridge and into the more urban part of the city. He pushed the horse unmercifully, but then, he reflected, he was saving the animal's life. Not many near the source of the fire had survived; none, for example, of Mrs. Leary's fabled cows. At least this animal would have a chance. People who were still out on this hot autumn evening looked at him as if he were mad. They shouted and waved at him, laughing and encouraging him on his way. But he needed no encouragement. He rode, the ride of a long strange lifetime.

He was a hypocrite now, taking Croyd's side in their argument about the butterfly effect. But who could blame him?

He fled east and then north, outrunning the conflagration that pursued him. He pondered briefly the role that the Palmer House had played in all this, from beginning to end. Was it fate, or was it all just random?

Nighthawk reined in the horse at the entrance to the Palmer, as this earlier iteration of the Palmer House had been called. He patted his mount on the neck, hugging it briefly. "Good horse," he whispered. "You're free. Run!" Ignoring all the stares of those around him, he ran into the lobby shouting, *"Fire! Fire! Coming up from the south! Evacuate the hotel!"*

He didn't stop to see if his words had any effect. He kept running until he hit the kitchen and swept into it, almost breathless. *"Fire!"* he shouted. *"Go now! Just go!"*

He went through the kitchen, hurriedly, searching. People here knew him. He worked at the hotel as a porter. He was well liked and his word was trusted, so they believed. He knew that most had escaped the fire. Only a few, a very few, had died when the hotel was set ablaze. He'd been off that night, and no one knew why the ones who were trapped had been trapped. He kept looking, searching . . .

In the end, he finally found her coming out of the ice room. *"Louella!"* he called, and crushed her to him.

She was young, younger than Nighthawk and taller than him, slim and pliant as a willow.

"John? What are you doing—"

She was a cook and waitress at the hotel and he loved her, still loved her after all this time, more than anyone or anything in the world. "No time to talk—we have to move. There's a big fire coming.

It'll sweep the hotel—" *And kill you,* he thought, almost choking, *and I'll never know why you died.*

"You crazy?" she asked him. "I've got to take an order up to the top floor—"

"Louella, please. If you love me, come with me, now."

"But—our things, what about—"

"No time for that. We've got to get out of the burn zone. Please."

"But—we'll lose everything!"

"We'll have each other," Nighthawk said. "And that's all we'll need."

A Long Night at
the Palmer House

Epilogue

NO ONE NOTICED NIGHTHAWK when he quietly entered the room. He was a man of silence and shadows, anyway, and he never sought the spotlight.

Croyd Crenson was sprawled on one of the sofas, sound asleep. Charles Dutton stood over him, tucking a pillow under his head. Half a dozen of the others were there as well, some looking on with concern, others with no more than mild interest. Not all of them, not by any means. Croyd's power moved people through time, not space. Only some had returned to the Palmer House. Some had been there long enough to dress. Others were wrapped in blankets, or still naked.

It was Khan who first sensed Nighthawk's presence. He looked up, right into his eyes, and for a moment even the tiger man was startled. Finally, he grunted, and smiled.

Nighthawk smiled back and walked into the sitting room.

Some of them actually jumped, others looked like they were seeing a ghost.

Nighthawk took off his hat, smiled back. He was dressed in one of his dark pin-striped suits, natty and out of time, as always.

Dutton was the last to catch on. "Mr. Nighthawk. This is a surprise."

"Nice to see you, too."

"You look older," Dutton said.

Nighthawk straightened one of the overturned chairs and took a seat at the poker table. "It has been a long night. A hundred and forty-six years?"

"How did you return to the present without Croyd's powers?" asked John Fortune.

"Day by day," Nighthawk said. "I just lived through it all."

"*Lived?*" That was Mr. Nobody, wearing the face of Rod Taylor.

"That would make me"—Nighthawk smiled—"three hundred and five years old now."

"What happened?" Dutton asked him.

"Well," Nighthawk said, "that's a long story. But I can hit the highlights. You see, I lost the love of my life to the Great Chicago Fire. You all"—he gestured at those before them—"gave me a second chance to save her. For that, I'll always be grateful. We had fifty years together before I lost her again."

"You changed history," Dutton pointed out. "Your children . . ."

Nighthawk shook his head. "We had none of our own. Louella couldn't have any. But we took care of others. We surely did. You see, I did a bit of real estate speculating. Right after the Fire, every bit of money we had we put into this swampland north of the city. People laughed at us, said we were fools. We bought it for pennies an acre, hundreds of acres. Then, in the 1880s Harry Palmer—funny how he keeps coming up in this story—bought some of our land and filled in the swamp. We sold it to him on the condition he fill in our other acreage, which he was glad to do. He built a mansion on the land and all his rich friends followed and built nearby. The area's now known as Chicago's Gold Coast." Nighthawk shrugged. "They wanted land. We had it. We made a fortune."

Dutton studied him "You changed many lives."

"Stepped on a lot of butterflies," said Khan.

Nighthawk shrugged. "Maybe. Or maybe Croyd was right all along. Maybe time is a river, and we're just throwing stones in the water, making little ripples. They're there momentarily, then they're gone."

"Like my movies." John Fortune laughed. "Gone and forgotten."

"Of course, some stones are pebbles, and some are boulders," Nighthawk said. "That's why I did what I could to help Croyd and myself along the way. I left care packages, clues, clothing, in all the places where I knew we'd be turning up."

"You left Meathooks," said Fortune. "And Irina, the bar girl."

"Pebbles," said Nighthawk.

"That makes things easier in a way," said Charles Dutton. "Gentlemen, we have seven million dollars in the wall safe. Shall we divide it between all those who returned?"

"That's a very generous idea," John Fortune said. "As it happens, Jerry and I have a nice inheritance coming from our grandfather Tor."

Jerry smiled. "I got plenty out of the deal."

Dutton looked at Nighthawk, who shook his head. "My bank account is fine."

Dutton looked at Jack Braun, who shrugged. "What the hell, I lost it all, anyway. I guess I can find a way to take it off my taxes. Sure, I'll take a cut."

"I'll take mine too," said Khan. "I damn well earned it."

"Splendid," Dutton said. "We will have to hunt down the others. They will be popping up naked all over Chicago by now, the ones who haven't arrived already. I am sure most of them will be glad of the money." Death smiled at them all and somehow managed to not seem too sinister as he did so. "Now my best advice to you," he said, "is don't lose it."

Everyone had left the suite, except Nighthawk and Dutton . . . and Croyd, snoring on the sofa. He still looked like Donald Meek. The changes hadn't started to come over him yet.

"Are you angry at him," Dutton asked, "for leaving you behind?"

Nighthawk pursed his lips. "Can't say I was happy when it happened, but it did help me make up my mind. Louella was always in my head, but I was afraid of changing history. Croyd's leaving kind of forced my hand. I made up my mind to save her, and I'm glad I did."

"You didn't tell the whole story, did you?" Dutton asked.

Nighthawk looked into that Grim Reaper face, those dark, unblinking eyes. "You figured that out, did you?" He sighed. "Well, I didn't lie. Everything I said was true. Only . . ." He paused. "After the Fire, they never found Louella's body. Among the half dozen or so of those trapped in the hotel . . . well, there wasn't enough left of any of them to identify them positively. But I always thought that she was one of them. Everybody did. Now . . . I'm not so sure. When I warned her about the Fire and took her away from the hotel, I realized that the next day my earlier self would look for her. I was afraid of a possible time paradox, so I convinced her to leave the city immediately. In the face of all that chaos it wasn't difficult to disappear."

"In essence," Dutton said, "you think that you may have stolen her from yourself?"

"Yes," Nighthawk said. "But I had to do it. If I'd done the noble thing and faded away after saving her and my younger self had found her the next day, my life would have been irrevocably changed. I would not be the same John Nighthawk who wound up dying of old age in that charity ward in a New York City hospital on September 15, 1946. I would have never caught the wild card virus. I would never have gone back in time to save her."

"A paradox, indeed," Dutton murmured.

"But in doing so, I condemned myself to a life without her. It was a hard and lonely life. I never married. I drifted from job to job, place to place, always looking for something that I knew I'd lost and could never find." Nighthawk fell silent.

"Well," Dutton said. "In the end, was it worth it?"

"Those fifty years with her? Yes. Yes it was."

"Then you did do the right thing."

Nighthawk nodded. He looked down at Croyd, who was muttering something about monkey stew under his breath. "What are you going to do with him?" he asked.

Dutton sighed. "I'll take him back to New York City," he said. "I have a place in the back of the Dime Museum he uses from time to time."

Nighthawk smiled. "When he does wake up, will you give him a message from me?"

"Gladly."

"Tell him it was Bradbury."